'My grandfather on my father's side bought me *The Ruby Knight* by David Eddings when I was nine or ten. It was the first modern fantasy I ever read, and I remember being utterly captivated by Mr Eddings' story of knights and magic and monsters, and thinking, "I like this!" I liked it so much, in fact, that I raced to our local library and, over the course of several months, devoured every novel Mr Eddings had published. I even went so far as to purchase all five books of the series you now hold. *The Belgariad* is a wonderful introduction to fantasy. A classic coming-of-age epic, it features a young farm boy with a mysterious past; a mad, twisted god for a villain; true love; thrilling duels and battles; a unique land; and some of the most interesting characters in the genre. Mr Eddings influenced how I approach fantasy, both as a reader and as an author. *The Belgariad* will always have a place of honor on my bookshelves'

Christopher Paolini, author of *Eragon*

'I read the five books of *The Belgariad* more times then I can recall when I was a teenager. I was a big fantasy fan, and these were some of the best fantasy books I'd ever read. The story of a young, seemingly ordinary boy, who gets swept away from his village, and involved in the world of wizards and kings, it lacks the imaginative scope of Tolkien, but it's fun, exciting, intriguing fantasy in which the characters are as important as the quest and magical elements. Easy to read and great to share, this was one of the most popular series of books at my school, appealing even to those who didn't read fantasy. Immerse yourself and enjoy!'

Darren Shan, author of *The Saga of Darren Shan*

'Fabulous . . . Eddings has a marvellous storyteller style'

Anne McCaffrey, author of the *Pern* series

By
DAVID EDDINGS

THE BELGARIAD

Book One:
PAWN OF PROPHECY
Book Two:
QUEEN OF SORCERY
Book Three:
MAGICIAN'S GAMBIT
Book Four:
CASTLE OF WIZARDRY
Book Five:
ENCHANTERS' END GAME

THE MALLOREON

Book One:
GUARDIANS OF THE WEST
Book Two:
KING OF THE MURGOS
Book Three:
DEMON LORD OF KARANDA
Book Four:
SORCERESS OF DARSHIVA
Book Five:
SEERESS OF KELL

and published by Corgi Books

DAVID
EDDINGS

Book Five of
THE MALLOREON

SEERESS
OF KELL

CORGI BOOKS

TRANSWORLD PUBLISHERS
61–63 Uxbridge Road, London W5 5SA
A Random House Group Company
www.transworldbooks.co.uk

**SEERESS OF KELL
A CORGI BOOK: 9780552168601**

First published in Great Britain in 1991 by Bantam Press,
a division of Transworld Publishers
Corgi edition published 1992
Corgi edition reissued 2013

Addresses for Random House Group Ltd companies outside the UK
can be found at: www.randomhouse.co.uk
The Random House Group Ltd Reg. No. 954009

The Random House Group Limited supports the Forest Stewardship
Council (FSC®), the leading international forest-certification
organization. Our books carrying the FSC label are printed on
FSC®-certified paper. FSC is the only forest-certification scheme endorsed
by the leading environmental organizations, including Greenpeace.
Our paper-procurement policy can be found
at www.randomhouse.co.uk/environment.

Typeset in Sabon by
Falcon Oast Graphic Art.
Printed and bound by
Clays Ltd, St Ives PLC

2 4 6 8 10 9 7 5 3 1

For Lester,

We've been at this for a decade now. About all either of us could have reasonably expected from that was to come out of it ten years older, but it appears that we did just a bit more. Between us, I think we raised a fairly good boy. I hope it was as much fun for you as it was for me, and I think we can both take a certain pride in the fact that we didn't kill each other in the process, a tribute more to the inhuman patience of a pair of special ladies than to any particular virtue of ours, I expect.

All my best,
David Eddings

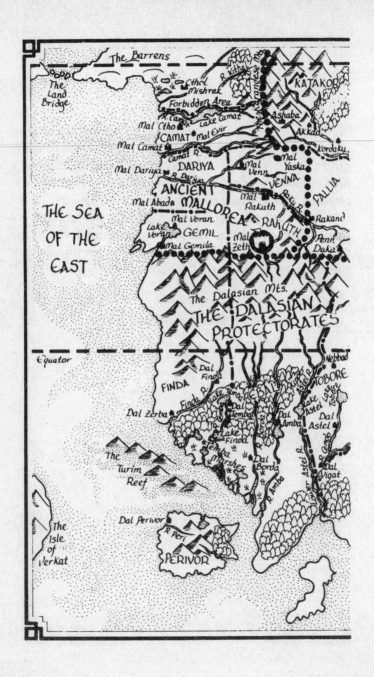

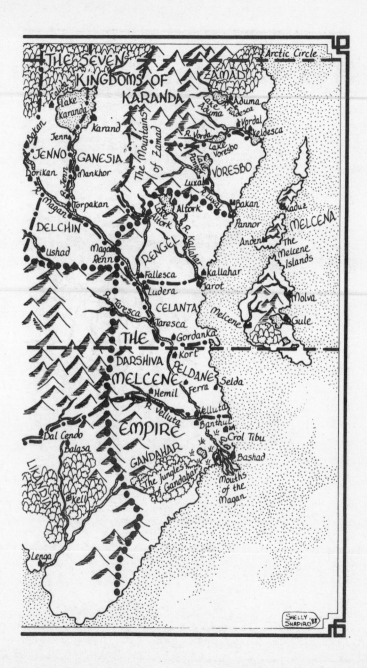

PROLOGUE

Excerpts from *The Book of Ages*, Book One of *THE MALLOREAN GOSPELS*

Now These are the Ages of Man:

In the First Age was man created, and he awoke in puzzlement and wonder as he beheld the world about him. And Those that had made him considered him and selected from his number those that pleased Them, and the rest were cast out and driven away. And some went in search of the Spirit known as UL, and they left us and passed into the west, and we saw them no more. And some denied the Gods, and they went into the far north to wrestle with demons. And some turned to worldly matters, and they went away into the east and built mighty cities there.

But we despaired, and we sat us down upon the earth in the shadow of the mountains of Korim, and in bitterness we bewailed our fate that we had been made and then cast out.

And it came to pass that in the midst of our grief a woman of our people was seized by a rapture, and it was as if she had been shaken by a mighty hand. And she arose from the earth upon which she sat, and she bound her eyes with a cloth, signifying that she had seen that which no mortal had seen before, for lo, she was the first seeress in all the world. And with the touch of her vision still upon her, she spake unto us, saying:

'Behold! A feast hath been set before Those who made us, and this feast shall ye call the Feast of Life. And Those who made us have chosen that which pleased Them, and that which pleased Them not was not chosen. Now *we*

9

are the Feast of Life, and ye sorrow that no Guest at the feast hath chosen ye. Despair not, however, for one Guest hath not yet arrived at the feast. The other Guests have taken their fill, but this great Feast of Life awaiteth still the Beloved Guest who cometh late, and I say unto all the people that it is *He* who will choose us. Abide therefore against his coming, for it is certain. Put aside thy grief and turn thy face to the sky and to the earth that thou mayest read the signs written there, for this I say unto all the people. It is upon *ye* that His coming rests. For behold, He may not choose *ye* unless ye choose *Him*. And this is the Fate for which we were made. Rise up, therefore, and sit no more upon the earth in vain and foolish lamentation. Take up the task which lies before ye and prepare the way for Him who will surely come.'

Much we marveled at these words, and we considered them most carefully. We questioned the seeress, but her answers were dark and obscure. And so it was that we turned our faces to the sky and bent our ears to the whispers which came from the earth that we might see and hear and learn. And as we learned to read the book of the skies and to hear the whispers within the rocks, we found myriad warnings that *two* spirits would come to us and that the one was good and the other evil. Long we labored, but still were sorely troubled, for we could not determine which spirit was the true one and which the false. For truly, evil is disguised as good in the book of the heavens and in the speech of the earth, and no man is wise enough to choose between them.

Pondering this, we went out from beneath the shadow of the mountains of Korim and into the lands beyond, where we abode. And we put aside the concerns of man and bent all our efforts to the task which lay before us. Our witches and our seers sought the aid of the spirit world, our necromancers took counsel with the dead, and our diviners sought advice from the earth. But lo, none of these knew more than we.

Then gathered we at last upon a fertile plain to bring

together all that we had learned. And these are the truths which we have learned from the stars, from the rocks, from the hearts of men and from the minds of the spirits:

Know ye that all adown the endless avenues of time hath division marred all that is – for there is division at the very heart of creation. And some have said that this is natural and will persist until the end of days, but it is not so. Were the division destined to be eternal, then the purpose of creation would be to contain it. But the stars and the spirits and the voices within the rocks speak of the day when the division will end and all will be made one again, for creation itself knows that the day *will* come.

Know ye further that two spirits contend with each other at the very center of time, and these spirits are the two sides of that which hath divided creation. And in a certain time shall those spirits meet upon *this* world, and then will come the time of the Choice. And if the Choice be *not* made, then shall this world vanish, and the Beloved Guest of whom the seeress spoke will never come. For it is this which she meant when she said to us: 'Behold, He may not choose *ye* unless ye choose *Him*.' And the Choice we must make is the choice between good and evil, and the division between good and evil, and the reality that will exist after we have made the Choice will be a reality of good or a reality of evil, and it will prevail so until the end of days.

Behold also this truth: The rocks of this world and of all other worlds murmur continually of the two stones which lie at the center of the division. Once these stones were one, and they stood at the very center of all of creation, but, like all else, they were divided, and in the instant of division they were rent apart with a force that destroyed whole suns. And where these stones come into the presence of each other again, there surely will be the last confrontation between the two spirits. Now the day will come when all will be made one again, *except* that the division between the two stones is so great that they can never be rejoined. And in the day when the division ends

11

shall one of the stones cease forever to exist, and in that day also shall one of the spirits forever vanish.

These then were the truths which we had gathered, and it was our discovery of these truths which marked the end of the First Age.

Now the Second Age of man began in thunder and earthquake, for lo, the earth herself split apart, and the sea rushed in to divide the lands of men even as creation itself is divided. And the mountains of Korim shuddered and groaned and heaved as the sea swallowed them. And we knew that this would come to pass, for our seers had warned us that it would be so. We went our way, therefore, and found safety before the world was cracked and the sea first rushed away and then rushed back and never departed more.

And in the days which followed the rushing in of the sea, the children of the Dragon God fled from the waters, and they abode to the north of us beyond the mountains. Now our seers told us that the children of the Dragon God would one day come among us as conquerors. And we took counsel with each other and considered how we might least offend the children of the Dragon God when they should come so that they would not interrupt our studies. In the end we concluded that our warlike neighbors would be least apprehensive about simple tillers of the soil living in rude communities on the land, and we so ordered our lives. We pulled down our cities and carried away the stones and we betook ourselves back to the land so that we might not alarm our neighbors nor arouse their envy.

And the years passed and became centuries, and the centuries passed and became eons. And as we had known they would, the children of Angarak came down amongst us and established their overlordship. And they called the lands in which we dwelt 'Dalasia,' and we did what they wished us to do and continued our studies.

Now at about this time it came to pass in the far north that a disciple of the God Aldur came with certain others

12

to reclaim a thing that the Dragon God had stolen from Aldur. And that act was so important that when it was done, the Second Age ended, and the Third Age began.

Now it was in the Third Age that the priests of Angarak, which men call Grolims, came to speak to us of the Dragon God and of His hunger for our love, and we considered what they said even as we considered all things men told us. And we consulted the book of the heavens and confirmed that Torak was the incarnate God-aspect of one of the spirits which contend at the center of time. But where was the other? How might men choose when but one of the spirits came to them? Then it was that we perceived our dreadful responsibility. The spirits would come to us, each in its own time, and each would proclaim that it was good and the other was evil. It was man, however, who would choose. And we took counsel among ourselves, and we concluded that we might accept the *forms* of the worship the Grolims so urgently pressed upon us. This would give us the opportunity to examine the nature of the Dragon God and make us better prepared to choose when the other God appeared.

In time the events of the world intruded upon us. The Angaraks allied themselves by marriage with the great city-builders of the east, who called themselves Melcene, and between them they built an empire which bestrode the continent. Now the Angaraks were doers of deeds, but the Melcenes were performers of tasks. A deed once done is done forever, but a task returns every day, and the Melcenes came among us to seek out those who might aid them in their endless tasks. Now as it chanced to happen, one of our kinsmen who aided the Melcenes had occasion to journey to the north in performance of one of those tasks. And he came to a place called Ashaba and sought shelter there from a storm which had overtaken him. And the Master of the house at Ashaba was neither Grolim nor Angarak nor any other man. Our kinsman had come unaware upon the house of Torak. Now Torak was curious about our people, and He sent for the traveler, and

13

our kinsman went in to behold the Dragon God. And in the instant that he looked upon the face of Torak, the Third Age ended, and the Fourth Age began. For lo, the Dragon God of Angarak was *not* one of the Gods for whom we waited. The signs which were upon Him did not lead beyond Him, and our kinsman saw in an instant that Torak was doomed, and that which He was would die with Him.

And then we perceived our error, and we marveled at what we had not seen – that even a God might be but the tool of destiny. For behold, Torak was *of* one of the two fates, but he was not the *entire* fate.

Now it happened that on the far side of the world a king was slain, and all his family with him – save one. And this king had been the keeper of one of the two stones of power, and when word of this was brought to Torak, He exulted, for He believed that an ancient foe was no more. Then it was that He began His preparations to do war upon the kingdoms of the west. But the signs in the heavens and the whispers in the rocks told us that it was not as Torak believed. The stone was still guarded, and the line of the guardian remained unbroken. Torak's war would bring Him to grief.

The preparations of the Dragon God were long, and the tasks He laid upon his people were the tasks of generations. And even as we, Torak watched the heavens to read there the signs which would tell Him when to move against the west. But Torak watched only for the signs He wished to see and He did not read the *entire* message written in the sky. Reading thus but a small part of the signs, He set His forces in motion on the worst possible day.

And, as we had known it must, disaster befell the armies of Torak on a broad plain lying before the city of Vo Mimbre in the far west. And the Dragon God was bound in sleep to await the coming of His enemy.

And then it was that a whisper began to reach us with yet another name. The whisper of that name became clearer to us, and upon the day of his birth the whisper of his name became a great shout. Belgarion the Godslayer had come at last.

And now the pace of events quickened, and the rush toward the awful meeting became so swift that the pages of the book of the heavens became as a blur. And then upon the day which men celebrate as the day the world was made, the stone of power was delivered up to Belgarion; and in the instant that his hand closed upon it, the book of the heavens filled with a great light, and the sound of Belgarion's name rang from the farthest star.

And then we felt Belgarion moving toward Mallorea bearing the stone of power, and we could feel Torak stirring as his sleep grew fitful. And finally there came that dreadful night. As we watched helplessly, the vast pages of the book of the heavens moved so rapidly that we could not read them. And then the book stopped, and we read the one terrible line, 'Torak is slain,' and the book shuddered, and all the light in all of creation went out. And in that awful instant of darkness and silence, the Fourth Age ended, and the Fifth Age began.

And as the Fifth Age began, we found a mystery in the book of the heavens. Before, all had moved toward the meeting between Belgarion and Torak, but now events moved toward a different meeting. There were signs among the stars which told us that the fates had selected yet other aspects for their final encounter, and we could feel the movements of those presences, but we knew not who or what they might be, for the pages of the great book were dark and obscure. Yet we felt a presence shrouded and veiled in darkness, and it moved through the affairs of men, and the moon spoke most clearly, advising us that this dark presence was a woman.

One thing we saw in all the vast confusion which now clouded the book of the heavens. The Ages of man grew shorter as each one passed, and the Events which were the meetings between the two fates were growing closer and closer together. The time for leisurely contemplation had

15

passed, and now we must hasten lest the last Event come upon us all unaware.

We decided that we must goad or deceive the participants in that final Event so that they should both come to the appointed place at the destined time.

And we sent the similitude of She Who Must Make the Choice to the veiled and hooded presence of dark and to Belgarion the Godslayer, and she set them upon the path which would lead them at last to the place of our choosing.

And then we all turned to *our* preparations, for much remained to be done, and we knew that this Event would be the last. The division of creation had endured for too long; and in *this* meeting between the two fates the division would end and all would be made one again.

Part One

KELL

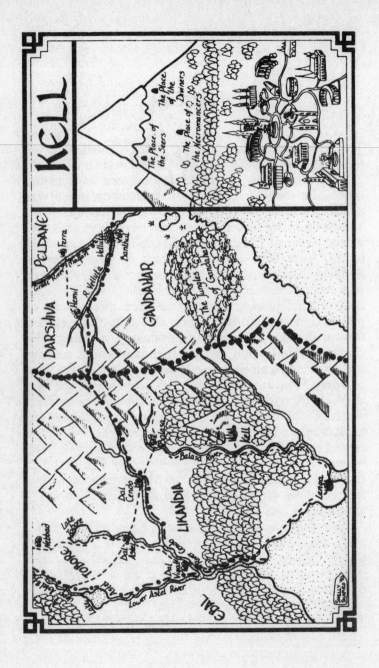

CHAPTER ONE

The air was thin and cool and richly scented with the odor of trees which shed no leaves but stood dark green and resinous from one end of their lives to the other. The sunlight on the snow-fields above them was dazzling, and the sound of tumbling water seething down and down rocky streambeds to feed rivers leagues below on the plains of Darshiva and Gandahar was constantly in their ears. That tumble and roar of waters rushing to their destined meeting with the great River Magan was accompanied by the soft, melancholy sighing of an endless wind passing through the deep green forest of pine and fir and spruce which clad hills that reached toward the sky in a kind of unthinking yearning. The caravan route Garion and his friends followed rose up and up, winding along streambeds and mounting the sides of ridges. From atop each ridge they could see yet another, and looming over all was the spine of the continent where peaks beyond imagining soared upward to touch the very vault of heaven, peaks pure and pristine in their mantle of eternal snow. Garion had spent time in mountains before, but never had he seen such enormous peaks. He knew that those colossal spires were leagues and leagues away, but the mountain air was so clear that it seemed he could almost reach out and touch them.

There was an abiding peace here, a peace that washed away the turmoil and anxiety that had beset them all on the plains below and somehow erased care and even thought. Each turn and each ridge top brought new vistas, each filled with more splendor than the last until they could only ride in silence and wonder. The works of man shrank into insignificance here. Man would never, *could* never, touch these eternal mountains.

It was summer, and the days were long and filled with sunlight. Birds sang from the trees beside the winding track, and the smell of sun-warmed evergreens was touched lightly with the delicate odors of the acre upon acre of wildflowers carpeting the steep meadows. Occasionally, the wild, shrill cry of an eagle echoed from the rocks.

'Have you ever considered moving your capital?' Garion asked the Emperor of Mallorea, who rode beside him. His tone was hushed. To speak in a louder voice would somehow profane what lay around them.

'No, not really, Garion,' Zakath replied. 'My government wouldn't function here. The bureaucracy is largely Melcene. Melcenes appear to be prosaic people, but actually they aren't. I'm afraid my officials would spend about half their time looking at the scenery and the other half writing bad poetry. Nobody would get any work done. Besides, you have no idea what it's like up here in the winter.'

'Snow?'

Zakath nodded. 'People up here don't bother to measure it in inches. They measure it in feet.'

'Are there people up here? I haven't seen any.'

'There are a few — fur-trappers, gold-hunters, that sort of thing.' Zakath smiled faintly. 'I think it's just an excuse, really. Some people prefer solitude.'

'This is a good place for it.'

The Emperor of Mallorea had changed since they had left Atesca's enclave on the banks of the Magan. He was leaner now, and the dead look was gone from his eyes. Like Garion and all the rest, he rode warily, his eyes and ears constantly alert. It was not so much his outward aspect that marked the change in him, however. Zakath had always been a pensive, even melancholy man, given often to periods of black depression, but filled at the same time with a cold ambition. Garion had often felt

20

that the Mallorean's ambition and his apparent hunger for power was not so much a driving need in him as it had been a kind of continual testing of himself, and, at perhaps a deeper level, deriving from an urge toward self-destruction. It had seemed almost that Zakath had hurled himself and all the resources of his empire into impossible struggles in the secret hope that eventually he would encounter someone strong enough to kill him and thereby relieve him of the burden of a life which was barely tolerable to him.

Such was no longer the case. His meeting with Cyradis on the banks of the Magan had forever changed him. A world which had always been flat and stale now seemed to be all new to him. At times, Garion even thought he detected a faint touch of hope in his friend's face, and hope had never been a part of Zakath's make-up.

As they rounded a wide bend in the track, Garion saw the she-wolf he had found in the dead forest back in Darshiva. She sat patiently on her haunches waiting for them. Increasingly, the behavior of the wolf puzzled him. Now that her injured paw was healed, she made sporadic sweeps through the surrounding forests in search of her pack, but always returned, seemingly unconcerned about her failure to locate them. It was as if she were perfectly content to remain with them as a member of their most unusual pack. So long as they were in forests and uninhabited mountains, this peculiarity of hers caused no particular problems, but they would not always be in the wilderness, and the appearance of an untamed and probably nervous wolf on the busy street of a populous city would be likely to attract attention, to say the very least.

'How is it with you, little sister?' he asked her politely in the language of wolves.

'It is well,' she replied.

'Did you find any traces of your pack?'

'There are many other wolves about, but they are not of my kindred. One will remain with you for yet a while longer. Where is the young one?'

Garion glanced back over his shoulder at the little two-wheeled carriage trundling along behind them. 'He sits beside my mate in the thing with round feet.'

The wolf sighed. 'If he sits much longer, he will no longer be able to run or hunt,' she said disapprovingly, 'and if your mate continues to feed him so much, she will stretch his belly, and he will not survive a lean season when there is little food.'

'One will speak with her about it.'

'Will she listen?'

'Probably not, but one will speak with her all the same. She is fond of the young one and takes pleasure in having him near her.'

'Soon one will need to teach him how to hunt.'

'Yes. One knows. One will explain that to one's mate.'

'One is grateful.' She paused, looking about a bit warily. 'Proceed with some caution,' she warned. 'There is a creature who dwells here. One has caught his scent several times, though one has not seen him. He is quite large, however.'

'How large?'

'Larger than the beast upon which you sit.' She looked pointedly at Chretienne. Familiarity had made the big gray stallion less nervous in the presence of the she-wolf, though Garion suspected that he would be much happier if she did not come quite so close.

'One will tell the pack-leader of what you have said,' Garion promised. For some reason, the she-wolf avoided Belgarath. Garion surmised that her behavior might reflect some obscure facet of wolfly etiquette of which he was not aware.

'One will continue one's search then,' she said, rising to her feet. 'It may happen that one will come upon this beast, and then we will know him.' She paused. 'His scent tells one that he is dangerous, however. He feeds on all things – even on things which we would shun.' Then she turned and loped off into the forest, moving swiftly and silently.

'That's really uncanny, you know,' Zakath observed. 'I've heard men talk to animals before, but never in their own language.'

'It's a family peculiarity,' Garion smiled. 'At first I didn't believe it either. Birds used to come and talk to Aunt Pol all the time – usually about their eggs. Birds are awfully fond of talking about their eggs, I understand. They can be very silly at times. Wolves are much more dignified.' He paused a moment. 'You don't necessarily have to tell Aunt Pol I said that,' he added.

'Subterfuge, Garion?' Zakath laughed.

'Prudence,' Garion corrected. 'I have to go talk with Belgarath. Keep your eyes open. The wolf says that there's some kind of animal out there somewhere. She says it's bigger than a horse and very dangerous. She hinted at the fact that it's a man-eater.'

'What does it look like?'

'She hasn't seen it. She's smelled it, though, and seen its tracks.'

'I'll watch for it.'

'Good idea.' Garion turned and rode back to where Belgarath and Aunt Pol were deep in a discussion.

'Durnik needs a tower somewhere in the Vale,' Belgarath was saying.

'I don't see why, father,' Polgara replied.

'All of Aldur's disciples have towers, Pol. It's the custom.'

'Old customs persist – even when there's no longer any need for them.'

'He's going to need to study, Pol. How can he possibly study with you underfoot all the time?'

She gave him a long, chilly stare.

'Maybe I should rephrase that.'

'Take as long as you need, father. I'm willing to wait.'

'Grandfather,' Garion said, reining in. 'I was just talking with the wolf, and she says there's a very large animal out in the forest.'

'A bear maybe?'

'I don't think so. She's caught its scent a few times, and she'd probably recognize the smell of a bear, wouldn't she?'

'I'd think so, yes.'

'She didn't say it exactly, but I got the impression that it's not too selective about what it eats.' He paused. 'Is it my imagination, or is she a very strange wolf?'

'How do you mean, exactly?'

'She stretches the language about as far as it will go, and I get the feeling that she still has more to say.'

'She's intelligent, that's all. It's an uncommon trait in females, but it's not unheard of.'

'What a fascinating turn this conversation has taken,' Polgara observed.

'Oh,' the old man said blandly, 'are you still here, Pol? I thought you'd have found something else to do by now.'

Her gaze was icy, but Belgarath seemed totally unperturbed. 'You'd better warn the others,' he told Garion. 'A wolf would pass an ordinary animal without comment. Whatever this thing is, it's unusual, and unusual usually means dangerous. Tell Ce'Nedra to get up here among the rest of us. She's a bit vulnerable trailing along behind the way she is.' He considered it. 'Don't say anything to alarm her, but have Liselle ride in the carriage with her.'

'Liselle?'

'The blond girl. The one with the dimples.'

'I know who she is, Grandfather. Wouldn't Durnik – or maybe Toth – be a better idea?'

'No. If either of them got in the carriage with Ce'Nedra, she'd know something was wrong, and that might frighten her. An animal who's hunting can smell fear. Let's not expose her to that kind of danger. Liselle's very well-trained, and she's probably got two or three daggers hidden in various places.' He grinned slyly. 'I'd imagine Silk could tell you where they are,' he added.

'Father!' Polgara gasped.

'You mean you didn't know, Pol? My goodness, how unobservant of you.'

24

'One for your side,' Garion noted.

'I'm glad you liked it.' Belgarath smirked at Polgara.

Garion turned Chretienne so that his aunt would not see his smile.

They took a bit more care setting up camp that night, choosing a small grove of aspens backed by a steep cliff and with a deep mountain river at its front. As the sun sank into the eternal snowfields above them and twilight filled the ravines and gorges with azure shadows, Beldin returned from his wide-ranging vigil. 'Isn't it a bit early to be stopping?' he rasped after he had shimmered and changed.

'The horses are tired,' Belgarath replied, casting a side-long glance at Ce'Nedra. 'This is a very steep trail.'

'Wait a bit,' Beldin told him, limping toward the fire. 'It gets steeper on up ahead.'

'What happened to your foot?'

'I had a little disagreement with an eagle – stupid birds, eagles. He couldn't tell the difference between a hawk and a pigeon. I had to educate him. He bit me while I was tearing out a sizeable number of his wing-feathers.'

'Uncle,' Polgara said reproachfully.

'He started it.'

'Are there any soldiers coming up behind us?' Belgarath asked him.

'Some Darshivans. They're two or three days behind, though. Urvon's army is retreating. Now that he and Nahaz are gone, there's not much point in their staying.'

'That gets at least *some* of the troops off our backs,' Silk said.

'Don't be too quick to start gloating,' Beldin told him. 'With the Guardsmen and the Karands gone, the Darshivans are free to concentrate on us.'

'That's true, I suppose. Do you think they know we're here?'

'Zandramas does, and I don't think she'd hide the information from her soldiers. You'll probably hit snow sometime late tomorrow. You might want to be thinking about some way to hide your tracks.' He looked around. 'Where's your wolf?' he asked Garion.

'Hunting. She's been looking for signs of her pack.'

'That brings something up,' Belgarath said quietly, looking around to make sure that Ce'Nedra was out of earshot. 'The wolf told Garion that there's a large animal of some kind in this area. Pol's going to go out and take a look around tonight, but it might not hurt if you nosed around tomorrow as well. I'm not in the mood for any surprises.'

'I'll see what I can find.'

Sadi and Velvet sat on the far side of the fire. They had placed the little earthenware bottle on its side and were trying to coax Zith and her children out with morsels of cheese. 'I wish we had some milk,' Sadi said in his contralto voice. 'Milk is very good for young snakes. It strengthens their teeth.'

'I'll remember that,' Velvet said.

'Were you planning a career as a snakeherdess, Margravine?'

'They're nice little creatures,' she replied. 'They're clean and quiet, and they don't eat very much. Besides, they're very useful in emergencies.'

He smiled at her affectionately. 'We'll make a Nyissan of you yet, Liselle.'

'Not if *I* can help it,' Silk muttered darkly to Garion.

They had broiled trout for supper that evening. After Durnik and Toth had finished setting up their encampment, they had adjourned to the riverbank with their poles and lures. Durnik's recent elevation to disciplehood had changed him in some ways, but had not lessened his appetite for his favorite pastime. It was no longer necessary for him and his mute friend even to discuss these excursions. Anytime they camped in the vicinity of a lake or stream, their reaction was automatic.

After supper, Polgara flew off into the shadowy forest, but when she returned, she reported having seen no sign of the large beast the she-wolf had warned them about.

It was cold the following morning, and there was a trace of frost in the air. The horses' breath steamed in the mountain air as they set out, and Garion and the others rode with their cloaks wrapped tightly about them.

As Beldin had predicted, they reached the snow line late that afternoon. The first windrows of white in the wagon-ruts were thin and crusty, but farther on ahead they could see deeper drifts. They made camp below the snow and set out again early the following morning. Silk had devised a sort of yoke for one of the pack-horses, and trailing on ropes behind the yoke were a dozen or so head-sized round rocks. The little man critically examined the tracks the rocks made in the snow as they started up the track into the world of perpetual white. 'Good enough,' he said in a self-congratulatory tone.

'I don't quite see the purpose of your contrivance, Prince Kheldar,' Sadi confessed.

'The rocks leave trails that look about the same as wagon tracks,' Silk explained. 'Horse tracks by themselves might make the soldiers coming up behind us suspicious. Wagon tracks on a caravan route aren't going to look all that remarkable.'

'Clever,' the eunuch said, 'but why not just cut bushes and drag them behind us?'

Silk shook his head. 'If you brush out all the tracks in the snow, it looks even more suspicious. This is a fairly well-traveled route.'

'You think of everything, don't you?'

'Sneaking was his major field of study at the academy,' Velvet said from the little carriage she shared with Ce'Nedra and the wolf pup. 'Sometimes he sneaks just to keep in practice.'

'I don't know if I'd go *that* far, Liselle,' the little man objected in a pained tone.

'Don't you?'

'Well, yes, I suppose so, but you don't have to come right out and say it — and "sneak" has such an ugly ring to it.'

'Can you think of a better term?'

'Well, "evasion" sounds a bit nicer, doesn't it?'

'Since it means the same thing, why quibble over terminology?' She smiled winsomely at him, her cheeks dimpling.

'It's a question of style, Liselle.'

The caravan track grew steeper, and the snow had piled in deeper and deeper drifts along the sides. Miles-long plumes of snow blew from the mountaintops ahead, and the wind grew stronger with a biting, arid chill to it.

About noon, the peaks ahead were suddenly obscured by an ominous-looking cloudbank rolling in from the west, and the she-wolf came loping down the track to meet them. 'One advises that you seek shelter for the pack and your beasts,' she said with a peculiar kind of urgency.

'Have you found the creature who dwells here?' Garion asked.

'No. This is more dangerous.' She looked meaningfully back over her shoulder at the approaching cloud.

'One will tell the pack leader.'

'That is proper.' She pointed her muzzle at Zakath. 'Have this one follow me. There are trees a short way ahead. He and I will find a suitable place.'

'She wants you to go with her,' Garion told the Mallorean. 'We've got bad weather coming, and she thinks we should take shelter in some trees just ahead. Find a place, and I'll go warn the others.'

'A blizzard?' Zakath asked.

'I'd guess so. It takes something fairly serious in the way of weather to make a wolf nervous.' Garion wheeled Chretienne and rode back down to alert the others. The steep, slippery track made haste difficult, and the chill wind was whipping stinging pellets of snow about them by the time they reached the thicket to which the wolf had led Zakath. The trees were slender pine saplings, and they grew very close together. At some time in the not too distant past an avalanche had cut a swath through the

28

thicket and had piled a jumble of limbs and broken trunks against the face of a steep rock cliff. Durnik and Toth went to work immediately even as the wind picked up and the snow grew thicker. Garion and the others joined in, and before long they had erected a latticed frame for a long lean-to against the cliff face. They covered the frame with tent canvas, tying it securely in place and weighting it down with logs. Then they cleared away the interior and led the horses into the lower end of the rude shelter just as the full force of the storm hit.

The wind shrieked insanely, and the thicket seemed to vanish in the swirling snow.

'Is Beldin going to be all right?' Durnik asked, looking slightly worried.

'You don't have to worry about Beldin,' Belgarath said. 'He's ridden out storms before. He'll either go above it or change back and bury himself in a snowdrift until it passes.'

'He'll freeze to death!' Ce'Nedra exclaimed.

'Not under the snow, he won't,' Belgarath assured her. 'Beldin tends to ignore weather.' He looked at the she-wolf, who sat on her haunches at the opening of the lean-to staring out at the swirling snow. 'One is grateful for your warning, little sister,' he said formally.

'One is a member of your pack now, revered leader,' she replied with equal formality. 'The well-being of all is the responsibility of all.'

'Wisely said, little sister.'

She wagged her tail but said nothing else.

The blizzard continued for the rest of the day and then on into the night while Garion and the others sat around the fire Durnik had built. Then, about midnight, the wind died as quickly as it had come. The snow continued to sift down among the trees until morning, and then it, too, abated. It had done its work, however. The snow outside the lean-to reached above Garion's knees. 'We're going to have to break a trail, I'm afraid,' Durnik said soberly. 'It's a quarter of a mile back up to that caravan track, and there are all sorts of things hidden under this fresh snow. This is not a good time – or place – to start breaking the horses' legs.'

'What about my carriage?' Ce'Nedra asked him.

'I'm afraid we'll have to leave it behind, Ce'Nedra. The snow's just too deep. Even if we could get it back up onto the road, the carriage horse wouldn't be able to drag it through the drifts.'

She sighed. 'It was such a nice carriage, too.' Then she looked at Silk with a perfectly straight face. 'I certainly want to thank you for lending it to me, Prince Kheldar,' she told him. 'I've finished with it now, so you can have it back.'

It was Toth who broke the initial trail up the steep slope to the caravan track. The others followed behind him, trampling the trail wider and searching for hidden logs and branches with their feet. It took nearly two hours to plow out the trail back to the caravan track, and they were all panting from the exertion at this high altitude.

They started back down toward the lean-to where the ladies waited with the horses, but about half-way down, the wolf suddenly laid back her ears and snarled.

'What is it?' Garion said.

'The creature,' she growled. 'He hunts.'

'Get ready!' Garion shouted to the others. 'That animal is out there!' He reached back over his shoulder and drew Iron-grip's sword.

It came out of the thicket on the far side of the avalanche track. Its shaggy coat was clotted with snow, and it shuffled along in a brutish half-crouch. Its face was hideous and chillingly familiar. It had piglike eyes sunk beneath heavy brow ridges. Its lower jaw jutted out, and two massive yellow tusks curved up over its cheeks. It opened its mouth and roared, pounding on its vast chest with its fists and rising to its full height. It was almost eight feet tall.

'That's impossible!' Belgarath exclaimed.

'What is it?' Sadi demanded.

'It's an Eldrak,' Belgarath said, 'and the only place the Eldrakyn live is in Ulgoland.'

'I think you're wrong, Belgarath,' Zakath disagreed. 'That's what's called an ape-bear. There are a few of them in these mountains.'

'Do you gentlemen suppose we could discuss its exact species some other time?' Silk suggested. 'The main question now is whether we fight or run.'

'We can't run in this snow,' Garion said grimly. 'We're going to have to fight it.'

'I was afraid you might say that.'

'The main thing is to keep it away from the ladies,' Durnik said. He looked at the eunuch. 'Sadi, would the poison on your dagger kill it?'

Sadi looked dubiously at the shaggy beast. 'I'm sure it would,' he said, 'but that thing is awfully large. It would take a while for the poison to work.'

'That's it, then,' Belgarath decided. 'The rest of us will keep its attention and give Sadi time to get around behind it. After he stabs it, we'll fall back and give the poison time to take effect. Spread out, and don't take any chances.' He blurred into the form of a wolf.

They moved into a rough half-circle, their weapons at the ready as the monster continued to roar and pound on its chest at the edge of the trees, working itself up into a frenzy. Then it lumbered forward with the snow spraying out from its huge feet. Sadi edged his way uphill, his small dagger held low even as Belgarath and the she-wolf darted in to tear at the beast with their fangs.

Garion's mind was working very clearly as he advanced through the deep snow, swinging his sword threateningly. He saw that this creature was not as quick as Grul the Eldrak had been. It was not able to respond to the sudden, darting attacks of the wolves, and the snow around it was soon spotted with its blood. It roared in frustration and rage and made a desperate rush at Durnik. Toth, however, stepped in and drove the tip of his heavy staff squarely into the beast's face. It howled in pain and spread its huge

31

arms wide to catch the big mute in a crushing embrace, but Garion slashed it across one shoulder with his sword even as Zakath ducked under the other shaggy arm and gashed it across the chest and belly with whiplike sword strokes.

The creature bellowed, and its blood spurted from its wounds.

'Any time now, Sadi,' Silk said urgently, ducking and feinting and trying to get a clean throw with one of his heavy daggers.

The wolves continued their harrying attacks on the animal's flanks and legs as Sadi cautiously advanced on the raging beast's back. Desperately, the creature flailed about with its huge arms, trying to keep its attackers away.

Then, with almost surgical precision, the she-wolf lunged in and ripped the heavy muscle at the back of the beast's left knee with her fangs.

The agonized shriek was dreadful – all the more so because it was strangely human. The shaggy beast toppled backward, clutching at its maimed leg.

Garion reversed his great sword, grasping the cross-piece of the hilt, bestrode the writhing body and raised the weapon, intending to drive the point full into the shaggy chest.

'Please!' it cried, its brutish face twisted in agony and terror. 'Please don't kill me!'

CHAPTER TWO

It was a Grolim. The huge beast lying in the blood-stained snow blurred and changed even as Garion's friends moved in with their weapons ready to deliver the last fatal strokes.

'Wait!' Durnik said sharply. 'It's a man!'

They stopped, staring at the dreadfully wounded priest lying in the snow.

Garion bleakly set the point of his sword under the Grolim's chin. He was terribly angry. 'All right,' he said in a cold voice, 'talk – and I think you'd better be very convincing. Who put you up to this?'

'It was Naradas,' the Grolim groaned, 'arch-priest of the temple at Hemil.'

'The henchman of Zandramas?' Garion demanded. 'The one with white eyes?'

'Yes. I was only doing what he commanded. Please don't kill me.'

'Why did he tell you to attack us?'

'I was supposed to kill one of you.'

'Which one?'

'He didn't care. He just said to make sure that one of you died.'

'They're still playing that tired old game,' Silk noted, sheathing his daggers. 'Grolims are so unimaginative.'

Sadi looked inquiringly at Garion, holding up his slim little knife suggestively.

'No!' Eriond said sharply.

Garion hesitated. 'He's right, Sadi,' he said finally. 'We can't just kill him in cold blood.'

'Alorns,' Sadi sighed, rolling his eyes up toward the clearing sky. 'You do know, of course, that if we leave him here in this condition, he'll die anyway. And if we try to take him along, he'll delay us – not to mention the fact that he's hardly the sort to be trusted.'

'Eriond,' Garion said, 'why don't you go get Aunt Pol? We'd better get those wounds of his tended before he bleeds to death.' He looked at Belgarath, who had changed form again. 'Any objections?' he asked.

'I didn't say anything.'

'I appreciate that.'

'You should have killed him before he changed form on you,' a familiar harsh voice came from the thicket behind them. Beldin was sitting on a log, gnawing at something that was uncooked and still had a few feathers clinging to it.

'I suppose it didn't occur to you to give us a hand?' Belgarath asked acidly.

'You were doing all right.' The dwarf shrugged. He belched and tossed the remains of his breakfast to the she-wolf.

'One is grateful,' she said politely as her jaws crunched into the half-eaten carcass. Garion could not be sure that Beldin understood, though he guessed that the gnarled little man probably did.

'What's an Eldrak doing here in Mallorea?' Belgarath asked.

'It's not exactly an Eldrak, Belgarath,' Beldin replied, spitting out a few soggy feathers.

'All right, but how did a Mallorean Grolim even know what an Eldrak looks like?'

'You weren't listening, old man. There are a few of those things up here in these mountains. They're distantly related to the Eldrakyn, but they're not the same. They're not as big, for one thing, and they're not as smart.'

'I thought all the monsters lived in Ulgoland.'

'Use your head, Belgarath. There are Trolls in Cherek, Algroths range down into Arendia and the Dryads live in southern Tolnedra. Then there's that Dragon. Nobody knows for sure *where* she lives. There are monsters

34

scattered all over. They're just a little more concentrated in Ulgo, that's all.'

'I suppose you're right,' Belgarath conceded. He looked at Zakath. 'What did you call the thing?'

'An ape-bear. It's probably not too accurate, but the people who live up here aren't very sophisticated.'

'Where's Naradas right now?' Silk asked the injured Grolim.

'I saw him at Balasa,' the Grolim replied. 'I don't know where he went from there.'

'Was Zandramas with him?'

'I didn't see her, but that doesn't mean she wasn't there. The Holy Sorceress doesn't show herself very often any more.'

'Because of the lights under her skin?' the weasel-faced little man asked shrewdly.

The Grolim's face grew even more pale. 'We're forbidden to discuss that – even among ourselves,' he replied in a frightened tone of voice.

'That's all right, friend.' Silk smiled at him and drawing one of his daggers. 'You have my permission.'

The Grolim swallowed hard and then nodded.

'Stout fellow.' Silk patted him on the shoulder. 'When did those lights start to appear?'

'I can't say for sure. Zandramas was off in the west with Naradas for a long time. The lights had started to appear when she came back. One of the priests at Hemil used to gossip a great deal. He said it was some kind of plague.'

'Used to?'

'She found out about what he'd said and had his heart cut out.'

'That's the Zandramas we've come to know and love, all right.'

Aunt Pol came up along the path trampled through the snow, followed by Ce'Nedra and Velvet. She tended the Grolim's wounds without comment while Durnik and Toth went back to the lean-to and led out the horses. Then they untied the tent canvas and broke down the frame. When they led the horses up to the place where the wounded Grolim lay, Sadi went to his saddle and opened the red leather case. 'Just to be on the safe side,' he muttered to Garion, taking out a little vial.

Garion raised one eyebrow.

'It won't hurt him,' the eunuch assured him. 'It'll make him tractable, though. Besides, since you're in this humanitarian mood, it should also numb the pain of his wounds.'

'You don't approve, do you?' Garion said. 'That we didn't kill him, I mean?'

'I think it's imprudent, Belgarion,' Sadi said seriously. 'Dead enemies are safe enemies. Live ones can come back to haunt you. It's your decision, though.'

'I'll make a concession,' Garion said. 'Stay close to him. If he starts getting out of hand, do whatever seems appropriate.'

Sadi smiled faintly. 'Much better,' he approved. 'We'll teach you the rudiments of practical politics yet.'

They led the horses up the steep hill to the caravan route and mounted. The howling wind which had accompanied the blizzard had scoured most of the snow from the track, although there were deep drifts in sheltered places where the road curved behind bands of trees and rock outcroppings. They made good time when the road was in the open, but it was slow going when they came to the drifts. Now that the storm had passed, the sunlight on the new snow was dazzling, and even though he squinted his eyes nearly shut, Garion found that after about an hour he was beginning to develop a splitting headache.

Silk reined in. 'I think it's time for a precaution or two,' he announced. He took a light scarf from inside his cloak and bound it across his eyes. Garion was suddenly reminded of Relg and the way the cave-born zealot had always covered his eyes when out in the open.

'A blindfold?' Sadi asked. 'Have you suddenly become a seer, Prince Kheldar?'

'I'm not the sort to have visions, Sadi,' Silk replied. 'The scarf is thin enough so that I can see through it. The idea is to protect the eyes from the glare of sunlight on the snow.'

'It *is* rather bright, isn't it?' Sadi agreed.

'It is indeed, and if you look at it long enough, it can blind you – at least temporarily.' Silk adjusted the covering on his eyes. 'This is a trick the reindeer herders in northern Drasnia came up with. It works fairly well.'

'Let's not take any chances,' Belgarath said, also covering his eyes with a piece of cloth. He smiled. 'Maybe this is how the Dalasian wizards struck the Grolims blind when they tried to go to Kell.'

'I'd be terribly disappointed if it were that simple,' Velvet said, trying a scarf across her eyes. 'I like to have my magic nice and inexplicable. Snow blindness would be such a prosaic thing.'

They plowed on through the drifts, climbing now toward a high pass between two towering peaks. It was midafternoon when they reached the pass. The track wound up between massive boulders, but straightened out when they reached the summit. They stopped to rest the horses and to look out over the vast wilderness which lay beyond the pass.

Toth unbound his eyes and gestured to Durnik. The smith pulled down his protective scarf, and the big mute pointed. Durnik's face was suddenly filled with awe. 'Look!' he said in a half-choked whisper.

The rest of them also uncovered their eyes.

'Belar!' Silk gasped. 'Nothing can be that big!'

The peaks around them that had seemed so enormous shrank into insignificance. Standing quite alone in solitary splendor rose a mountain so huge and high that the mind could not comprehend it. It was perfectly symmetrical, a steep, white cone with sharply sloping sides. Its base was enormous, and its summit soared thousands of feet above nearby peaks. An absolute calm seemed to surround it, as if, having achieved everything that any mountain could, it simply existed.

'It's the highest peak in the world,' Zakath said very

quietly. 'The scholars at the University of Melcene have calculated its height and compared that with the heights of peaks on the western continent. It's thousands of feet higher than any other mountain.'

'Please, Zakath,' Silk said with a pained look, 'don't tell me how high.'

Zakath looked puzzled.

'As you may have noticed, I'm not really a very large person. Immensity depresses me. I'll admit that your mountain is bigger than I am. I just don't want to know how *much* bigger.'

Toth was gesturing to Durnik again.

'He says that Kell lies in the shadow of that mountain,' the smith said.

'That's a little unspecific, Goodman,' Sadi said wryly. 'I'd guess that about half the continent lies in the shadow of that thing.'

Beldin came soaring in again. 'Big, isn't it?' he said, squinting at the huge white peak looming into the sky.

'We noticed,' Belgarath replied. 'What's on up ahead?'

'A fair amount of downhill going – at least until you get to the slopes of that monster there.'

'I can see that from here.'

'Congratulations. I found a place where you can get rid of your Grolim. Several places, actually.'

'Exactly how do you mean "get rid of", uncle?' Polgara asked suspiciously.

'There are quite a few high cliffs alongside this track on the way down,' he replied blandly. 'Accidents do happen, you know.'

'Out of the question. I didn't treat his wounds just to keep him going until you found time to throw him off a cliff.'

'Polgara, you're interfering with the practice of my religion.'

She raised one eyebrow.

'I thought you knew. It's an article of the faith: "Kill every Grolim you come across."'

'I might even consider converting to that religion,' Zakath said.

'Are you absolutely *certain* you're not Arendish?' Garion said to him.

Beldin sighed. 'Since you're going to be such a spoilsport about this, Pol, I found a group of sheepherders below the snowline.'

'Shepherds, uncle,' she corrected.

'It means the same thing. If you really look at it, it's even the same word.'

'Shepherd sounds nicer.'

'Nicer,' he snorted. 'Sheep are stupid, they smell bad, and they taste worse. Anybody who spends his life tending them is either defective or degenerate.'

'You're in rare form this afternoon,' Belgarath congratulated him.

'It's been a great day for flying,' Beldin explained with a broad grin. 'Do you have any idea of how much warm air comes up off new snow when the sun hits it? I flew up so high once that I started getting spots in front of my eyes.'

'That's stupid, uncle,' Polgara snapped. 'You should *never* go up where the air's that thin.'

'We're all entitled to a little stupidity now and then.' He shrugged. 'And the dive from that height is unbelievable. Why don't you join me, and I'll show you.'

'Will you never grow up?'

'I doubt it, and I certainly hope not.' He looked at Belgarath. 'I think you'd better go down a mile or so and make camp.'

'It's early yet.'

'No. Actually it's late. That afternoon sun is quite warm – even up here. All this snow's starting to get soft. I've seen three avalanches already. If you make a wrong guess up here, you might get down a lot quicker than you want to.'

'Interesting point there. We'll get down out of this pass and set up for the night.'

'I'll go on ahead.' Beldin crouched and spread his

39

arms. 'Are you sure you don't want to come along, Pol?'

'Don't be silly.'

He left a ghostly chuckle behind him as he soared away.

They set up for the night on a ridge line. Although it exposed them to the constant wind, it was free from the danger of avalanche. Garion slept poorly that night. The wind which raked the exposed ridge set the taut canvas of the tent he shared with Ce'Nedra to thrumming, and the noise intruded itself upon him as he tried again and again to drift off. He shifted restlessly.

'Can't you sleep either?' Ce'Nedra said in the chill darkness.

'It's the wind,' he replied.

'Try not to think about it.'

'I don't have to think about it. It's like trying to sleep inside a big drum.'

'You were very brave this morning, Garion. I was terrified when I heard about that monster.'

'We've dealt with monsters before. After a while, you get used to it.'

'My, aren't we getting blasé?'

'It's an occupational trait. All of us mighty heroes have it. Fighting a monster or two before breakfast helps to sharpen the appetite.'

'You've changed, Garion.'

'Not really.'

'Yes, you have. When I first met you, you'd never have said anything like that.'

'When you first met me, I took everything very seriously.'

'Don't you take what we're doing seriously?' She said it almost accusingly.

'Of course I do. It's the little incidental things along the way I sort of shrug off. There's not much point in worrying about something after it's already over, is there?'

40

'Well, as long as neither of us can sleep anyway—' And she drew him to her and kissed him rather seriously.

The temperature plunged that night, and when they arose, the snow, which had been dangerously soft the previous afternoon, had frozen, and they were able to proceed with little danger of avalanche. Because this side of the summit had taken the full force of the wind during the blizzard, the caravan track had little snow on it, and they made good time going down. By mid afternoon they passed the last of the snow and rode down into a world of spring. The meadows were steep and lush and speckled with wildflowers bending in the mountain breeze. Brooks, which came directly out of the faces of glaciers, purled and danced over gleaming stones, and soft-eyed deer watched in gentle astonishment as Garion and the others rode by.

A few miles below the snow line, they began to see herds of sheep grazing with witless concentration, consuming grass and wildflowers with indiscriminate appetite. The shepherds who watched them all wore simple white smocks, and they sat on hillocks or rocks in dreamy contemplation while their dogs did all the work.

The she-wolf trotted sedately beside Chretienne. Her ears twitched occasionally, however, and she watched the sheep, her tawny eyes intent.

'One advises against it, little sister,' Garion said to her in the language of wolves.

'One was not really considering it,' she replied. 'One has encountered these beasts before – and the man-things and dog-things which guard them. It is not difficult to take one of them, but the dog-things grow excited when one does, and their barking disturbs one's meal.' Her tongue lolled out in a wolfish sort of grin. 'One could make the beasts run, however. All things should know to whom the forest belongs.'

'The pack-leader would disapprove, one is afraid.'

'Ah,' she agreed. 'Perhaps the pack-leader takes himself too seriously. One has observed that quality in him.'

'What did she say?' Zakath asked curiously.

'She was thinking about chasing the sheep,' Garion replied, 'not necessarily to kill any of them but just to make them run. I think it amuses her.'

'Amuses? That's an odd thing to say about a wolf.'

'Not really. Wolves play a great deal, and they have a very refined sense of humor.'

Zakath's face grew thoughtful. 'You know something, Garion?' he said. 'Man thinks he owns the world, but we share it with all sorts of creatures who are indifferent to our overlordship. They have their own societies, and I suppose even their own cultures. They don't even pay any attention to us, do they?'

'Only when we inconvenience them.'

'That's a crushing blow to the ego of an emperor.' Zakath smiled wryly. 'We're the two most powerful men on earth, and wolves look upon us as no more than a minor inconvenience.'

'It teaches us humility,' Garion agreed. 'Humility is good for the soul.'

'Perhaps.'

It was evening when they reached the shepherds' encampment. Since a sheep-camp is a more or less permanent thing, it is usually more well-organized than the hasty encampments of travelers. The tents were larger, for one thing, and they were stretched over pole frames. The tents lined either side of a street made of logs laid tightly side by side. The corrals for the shepherds' horses were at the lower end of the street, and a log dam had backed up a mountain brook to form a sparkling little pond that provided water for the sheep and horses. The shadows of evening were settling over the little valley where the camp lay, and blue columns of smoke rose straight up from the cookfires into the calm and windless air.

A tall, lean fellow with a deeply tanned face, snowy white hair, and the simple white smock that seemed to be the common garb of these shepherds came out of one of the tents as Garion and Zakath reined in just outside the camp. 'We have been advised of your coming,' he said. His voice was very deep and quiet. 'Will you share our evening meal with us?' Garion looked at him closely, noting his resemblance to Vard, the man whom they had met on the Isle of Verkat, half a world away. There could be no question now that the Dals and the slave race in Cthol Murgos were related.

'We would be honored,' Zakath responded to the invitation. 'We do not wish to impose, however.'

'It is no imposition. I am Burk. I will have some of my men care for your mounts.'

The others rode up and stopped.

'Welcome all,' Burk greeted them. 'Will you step down? The evening meal is almost ready, and we have set aside a tent for your use.' He looked gravely at the she-wolf and inclined his head to her. It was evident that her presence did not alarm him.

'Your courtesy is most becoming,' Polgara said, dismounting, 'and your hospitality is quite unexpected this far from civilization.'

'Man carries his civilization with him, Lady,' Burk replied.

'We have an injured man with us,' Sadi told him, 'a poor traveler we came across on our way over the mountain. We gave him what aid we could, but our business is pressing, and I'm afraid our pace is aggravating his injuries.'

'You may leave him with us, and we will care for him.' Burk looked critically at the drugged priest slumped in his saddle. 'A Grolim,' he noted. 'Is your destination perhaps Kell?'

'We have to stop there,' Belgarath said cautiously.

'This Grolim would not be able to go with you then.'

'We've heard about that,' Silk said, swinging down from his horse. 'Do they really go blind when they try to go to Kell?'

'In a manner of speaking, yes. We have such a one here in our camp with us now. We found him wandering in the forest when we were bringing the sheep up to summer pasture.'

Belgarath's eyes narrowed slightly. 'Do you suppose I might be able to talk with him?' he asked. 'I've made a study of such things, and I'm always eager to get additional information.'

'Of course,' Burk agreed. 'He's in that last tent on the right.'

'Garion, Pol, come along,' the old man said tersely and started along the log street. Oddly, the she-wolf accompanied them.

'Why the sudden curiosity, father?' Polgara asked when they were out of earshot.

'I want to find out just how effective this curse the Dals have laid around Kell really is. If it's something that can be overcome, we might run into Zandramas when we get there after all.'

They found the Grolim sitting on the floor in his tent. The harsh angularity of his face had softened, and his sightless eyes had lost the burning fanaticism common to all Grolims. His face instead was filled with a kind of wonder.

'How is it with you, friend?' Belgarath asked him gently.

'I am content,' the Grolim replied. The word seemed peculiar coming from the mouth of a priest of Torak.

'Why is it that you tried to approach Kell? Didn't you know about the curse?'

'It is not a curse. It is a blessing.'

'A blessing?'

'I was ordered by the Sorceress Zandramas to try to reach the holy city of the Dals,' the Grolim continued. 'She told me that I would be exalted should I be successful.' He smiled gently. 'It was in her mind, I think, to test the strength of the enchantment to determine if it might be safe for her to attempt the journey.'

'I gather that it wouldn't be.'

'That is difficult to say. Great benefit might come to her if she tried.'

'I'd hardly call going blind a benefit.'

44

'But I am not blind.'

'I thought that's what the enchantment was all about.'

'Oh, no. I cannot see the world around me, but that is because I see something else – something that fills my heart with joy.'

'Oh? What's that?'

'I see the face of God, my friend, and will until the end of my days.'

CHAPTER THREE

It was always there. Even when they were in deep, cool forests they could feel it looming over them, still and white and serene. The mountain filled their eyes, their thoughts, and even their dreams. Silk grew increasingly irritable as they rode day after day toward that gleaming white enormity. 'How can anyone possibly get anything done in this part of the world with that thing there filling up half the sky?' he burst out one sunny afternoon.

'Perhaps they ignore it, Kheldar,' Velvet said sweetly.

'How can you ignore something that big?' he retorted. 'I wonder if it knows how ostentatious – and even vulgar – it is.'

'You're being irrational,' she said. 'The mountain doesn't care how we feel about it. It's going to be there long after we're all gone.' She paused. 'Is that what bothers you, Kheldar? Coming across something permanent in the middle of a transient life?'

'The stars are permanent,' he pointed out. 'So's dirt, for that matter, but they don't intrude the way that beast does.' He looked at Zakath. 'Has anybody ever climbed to the top of it?' he asked.

'Why would anybody want to?'

'To beat it. To reduce it.' Silk laughed. 'That's even more irrational, isn't it?'

Zakath, however, was looking speculatively at the looming presence that filled the southern sky. 'I don't know, Kheldar,' he said. 'I've never considered the possibility of fighting a mountain before. It's easy to beat men. To beat a mountain, though – now that's something else.'

'Would it care?' Eriond asked. The young man so seldom spoke that he seemed at times to be as mute

46

as Toth. He had of late, however, seemed even more withdrawn. 'The mountain might even welcome you.' He smiled gently. 'I'd imagine it gets lonesome. It could even want to share what it sees with anyone brave enough to go up there and look.'

Zakath and Silk exchanged a long, almost hungry look. 'You'd need ropes,' Silk said in a neutral sort of tone.

'And probably certain kinds of tools as well,' Zakath added. 'Things that would dig into the ice and hold you while you climbed up higher.'

'Durnik could figure those out for us.'

'Will you two stop that?' Polgara said tartly. 'We have other things to think about right now.'

'Just speculation, Polgara,' Silk said lightly. 'This business of ours won't last forever, and when it's over – well, who knows?'

They were all subtly changed by the mountain. Speech seemed less and less necessary, and they all thought long thoughts, which, during quiet times around the campfire at night, they tried to share with each other. It became somehow a time of cleansing and healing, and they all grew closer together as they approached that solitary immensity.

One night Garion awoke with a light as bright as day in his eyes. He slipped out from under the blankets and turned back the flap of the tent. A full moon had arisen, and it filled the world with a pale luminescence. The mountain stood stark and white against the starry blackness of the night sky, glowing with a cool incandescence that seemed almost alive.

A movement caught his eye. Aunt Pol emerged from the tent she shared with Durnik. She wore a white robe that seemed almost a reflection of the moon-washed mountain. She stood for a moment in silent contemplation, then turned slightly. 'Durnik,' she murmured softly, 'come and look.'

Durnik emerged from the tent. He was bare-chested, and his silver amulet glittered in the moonlight. He put his

47

arm about Polgara's shoulders, and the two of them stood drinking in the beauty of this most perfect of nights.

Garion was about to call out to them, but something stayed his tongue. The moment they were sharing was too private to be intruded upon. After quite some time, Aunt Pol whispered something to her husband, and, smiling, the two of them turned and went hand in hand back into their tent.

Quietly, Garion let the tent flap drop and went back to his blankets.

Slowly, as they continued in a generally southwesterly direction, the forest changed. When they were still in the mountains, the trees had been evergreens interspersed here and there with aspens. As they approached the lowlands at the base of the huge mountain, they increasingly came across groves of beech and elm. And then at last they entered a forest of ancient oaks.

As they rode beneath the spreading branches in sun-dappled shade, Garion was sharply reminded of the Wood of the Dryads in southern Tolnedra. One glance at his little wife's face revealed that the similarity was not lost on her either. A kind of dreamy contentment came over her, and she seemed to be listening to voices only she could hear.

It was about noon on a splendid summer day that they overtook another traveler, a white-bearded man dressed in clothing made from deer-skin. The handles of the tools protruding from the lumpy bundle on the back of his pack mule proclaimed him to be a gold hunter, one of those vagrant hermits who haunt wildernesses the world over. He was riding a shaggy mountain pony so stumpy that its rider's feet nearly touched the ground on either side. 'I thought I heard somebody coming up from behind,' the gold-hunter said as Garion and Zakath, both in their mail shirts and helmets, drew alongside him. 'Don't see many in these woods – what with the curse and all.'

'I thought the curse only worked on Grolims,' Garion said.

'Most believe it doesn't pay to take chances. Where are you bound?'

'To Kell,' Garion replied. There was no real point in making a secret of it.

'I hope you've been invited. The folk at Kell don't welcome strangers who just take it upon themselves to go there.'

'They know we're coming.'

'Oh. It's all right then. Strange place, Kell, and strange people. Of course living right under that mountain the way they do would make anybody strange after a while. If it's all right, I'll ride along with you as far as the turn-off to Balasa a couple miles on up ahead.'

'Feel free,' Zakath told him. 'Aren't you missing a good time to be looking for gold, though?'

'Got myself caught up in the mountains last winter,' the old fellow replied. 'Supplies ran out on me. Besides, I get hungry for talk now and then. The pony and the mule listen pretty good, but they don't answer very well, and the wolves up there move around so much that you can't hardly get a conversation started with them.' He looked at the she-wolf and then astonishingly spoke to her in her own language. 'How is it with you, mother?' he asked. His accent was abominable, and he spoke haltingly, but his speech was undeniably that of a wolf.

'How remarkable,' she said with some surprise. Then she responded to the ritual greeting. 'One is content.'

'One is pleased to hear that. How is it that you go with the man-things?'

'One has joined their pack for a certain time.'

'Ah.'

'How did you manage to learn the language of wolves?' Garion asked in some amazement.

'You recognized it, then.' The old fellow sounded pleased about that for some reason. He leaned back in his saddle. 'Spent most of my life up there where the wolves are,' he explained. 'It's only polite to learn the language of your neighbors.' He grinned. 'To be honest about it,

49

though, at first I couldn't make much out of it, but if you listen hard enough, it starts to come to you. Spent a winter in a den with a pack of them about five years back. That helped quite a bit.'

'They actually let you live with them?' Zakath asked.

'It took them a while to get used to me,' the old man admitted, 'but I made myself useful, so they sort of accepted me.'

'Useful?'

'The den was a little crowded, and I got them there tools.' He jerked his thumb at his pack mule. 'I dug the den out some larger, and they seemed to appreciate it. Then, after a while, I took to watching over the pups while the rest was out hunting. Good pups they was, too. Playful as kittens. Some time later I tried to make up to a bear. Never had much luck with that. Bears are a stand-offish bunch. They keep to theirselves most of the time, and deer are just too skittish to try to make friends with. Give me wolves every time.'

The old gold-hunter's pony did not move very fast, so the others soon caught up with them.

'Any luck?' Silk asked the old gold-hunter, his nose twitching with interest.

'Some,' the white-bearded man answered evasively.

'Sorry,' Silk apologized. 'I didn't mean to pry.'

'That's all right, friend. I can see that you're an honest man.'

Velvet muffled a slightly derisive chuckle.

'It's just a habit I picked up,' the fellow continued. 'It's not really too smart to go around telling everybody how much gold you've managed to pick up.'

'I can certainly understand that.'

'I don't usually carry that much with me when I come down into the low country, though – only enough to pay for what I need. I leave the rest of it hid back up there in the mountains.'

'Why do you do it then?' Durnik asked. 'Spend all your

time looking for gold, I mean? You don't spend it, so why bother?'

'It's something to do.' The fellow shrugged. 'And it gives me an excuse to be up there in the mountains. A man feels sort of frivolous if he does that without no reason.' He grinned again. 'Then, too, there's a certain kind of excitement that comes with finding a pocket of gold in a streambed. Like some say, finding is more fun than spending, and gold's sort of pretty to look at.'

'Oh, it is indeed,' Silk agreed fervently.

The old gold hunter glanced at the she-wolf and then looked at Belgarath. 'I can see by the way she's acting that you're the leader of this group,' he noted.

Belgarath looked a bit startled at that.

'He's learned the language,' Garion explained.

'How remarkable,' Belgarath said, unconsciously echoing the comment of the wolf.

'I was going to pass on some advice to these two young fellows, but you're the one who probably ought to hear it.'

'I'll certainly listen.'

'The Dals are a peculiar sort, friend, and they've got some peculiar superstitions. I won't go so far as to say they think of these woods as sacred, but they do feel pretty strongly about them. I wouldn't advise cutting any trees and don't, whatever you do, kill anything or anybody here.' He pointed at the wolf. 'She knows about that already. You've probably noticed that she won't hunt here. The Dals don't want this forest profaned with blood. I'd respect that, if I were you. The Dals can be helpful, but if you offend their beliefs, they can make things mighty difficult for you.'

'I appreciate the information,' Belgarath told him.

'It never hurts a man to pass on things he's picked up,' the old fellow said. He looked up the track. 'Well,' he said. 'This is as far as I go. That's the road to Balasa just on up ahead. It's been nice talking with you.' He doffed his shabby hat politely to Polgara, then looked at the wolf. 'Be well, mother,' he said, then he thumped his heels against his pony's flanks. The pony broke into an ambling sort of trot and jolted around a bend in the road to Balasa and out of sight.

'What a delightful old man,' Ce'Nedra said.

'Useful, too,' Polgara added. 'You'd better get in touch with Uncle Beldin, father,' she said to Belgarath. 'Tell him to leave the rabbits and pigeons alone while we're in this forest.'

'I'd forgotten about that,' he said. 'I'll take care of it right now.' He lifted his face and closed his eyes.

'Can that old fellow really talk with wolves?' Silk asked Garion.

'He knows the language,' Garion replied. 'He doesn't speak it very well, but he knows it.'

'One is sure he understands better than he speaks,' the she-wolf said.

Garion stared at her, slightly startled that she had understood the conversation.

'The language of the man-things is not difficult to learn,' she said. 'As the man-thing with the white fur on his face said, one can learn rapidly if one takes the trouble to listen. One would not care to speak your language, however,' she added critically. 'The speech of the man-things would place one's tongue in much danger of being bitten.'

A sudden thought came to Garion then, accompanied by an absolute certainty that the thought was entirely accurate. 'Grandfather,' he said.

'Not now, Garion. I'm busy.'

'I'll wait.'

'Is it important?'

'I think so, yes.'

Belgarath opened his eyes curiously. 'What is it?' he asked.

'Do you remember that conversation we had in Tol Honeth — the morning it was snowing?'

'I think so.'

52

'We were talking about the way everything that happened seemed to have happened before.'

'Yes, now I remember.'

'You said that when the two prophecies got separated, things sort of stopped – that the future can't happen until they get back together again. Then you said that until they do, we'd all have to keep going through the same series of events over and over again.'

'Did I really say that?' the old man looked a bit pleased. 'That's sort of profound, isn't it? What's the point of this, though? Why are you bringing it up now?'

'Because I think it just happened again.' Garion looked at Silk. 'Do you remember that old gold hunter we met in Gar og Nadrak when the three of us were on our way to Cthol Mishrak?'

Silk nodded a bit dubiously.

'Wasn't the old fellow we just talked with almost exactly the same?'

'Now that you mention it . . .' Silk's eyes narrowed. 'All right, Belgarath, what does it mean?'

Belgarath squinted up at the leafy branches overhead. 'Let me think about it for a minute,' he said. 'There are some similarities all right,' he admitted. 'The two of them are the same kind of people, and they both warned us about something. I think I'd better get Beldin back here. This might be very important.'

It was no more than a quarter of an hour later when the blue-banded hawk settled out of the sky and blurred into the misshapen sorcerer. 'What's got you so excited?' he demanded crossly.

'We just met somebody,' Belgarath replied.

'Congratulations.'

'I think this is serious, Beldin.' Belgarath quickly explained his theory of recurring events.

'It's a little rudimentary,' Beldin growled, 'but there's nothing remarkable about that. Your hypotheses usually are.' He squinted. 'It's probably fairly accurate though – as far as it goes.'

'Thanks,' Belgarath said drily. Then he went on to describe the two meetings, the one in Gar og Nadrak and the other here. 'The similarities are a little striking, aren't they?'

'Coincidence?'

'Shrugging things off as coincidence is the best way I know of to get in trouble.'

'All right. For the sake of argument, let's say it wasn't coincidence.' The dwarf squatted in the dirt at the roadside, his face twisted in thought. 'Why don't we take this theory of yours a step farther?' he mused. 'Let's look at the notion that these repetitions crop up at significant points in the course of events.'

'Sort of like signposts?' Durnik suggested.

'Exactly. I couldn't have found a better term myself. Let's suppose that these signposts point at really important things that are right on the verge of happening – that they're sort of like warnings.'

'I'm hearing a lot of "notions" and "supposes",' Silk said sceptically. 'I think you're off into the realm of pure speculation.'

'You're a brave man, Kheldar,' Beldin said sardonically. 'Something could be trying to warn you about a potential catastrophe, and you choose to ignore the warning. That's either very brave or very stupid. Of course I'm giving you the benefit of the doubt by using the word "brave" instead of the other one.'

'One for his side,' Velvet murmured.

Silk flushed slightly. 'But how do we know what it is that's going to happen?' he objected.

'We don't,' Belgarath said. 'The circumstances just call for some extra alertness, is all. We've been warned. The rest is up to us.'

They took some special precautions when they set up their encampment that evening. Polgara prepared supper quickly, and the fire was extinguished as soon as they had finished eating. Garion and Silk took the first watch.

They stood atop a knoll behind the camp, peering into the darkness.

'I hate this,' Silk whispered.

'Hate what?'

'Knowing that *something* is going to happen without knowing what it is. I wish those two old men would keep their speculations to themselves.'

'Do you really like surprises?'

'A surprise is better than living with this sense of dread. My nerves aren't what they used to be.'

'You're too high-strung sometimes. Look at all the entertainment you're getting out of anticipation.'

'I'm terribly disappointed in you, Garion. I thought you were a nice, sensible boy.'

'What did I say?'

'Anticipation. In this situation, that's just another word for "worry", and worry isn't good for anybody.'

'It's just a way to get us ready in case something happens.'

'I'm always ready, Garion. That's how I've managed to live so long, but right now I feel almost as tightly wound as a lute string.'

'Try not to think about it.'

'Of course,' Silk retorted sarcastically. 'But doesn't that defeat the purpose of the warning? Aren't we supposed to think about it?'

The sun had not come up yet when Sadi came back to their camp, moving very quietly and going from tent to tent with a whispered warning. 'There's somebody out there,' he warned after he had scratched on the flap of Garion's tent.

Garion rolled out from under his blankets, his hand automatically reaching for his sword. He paused then. The old gold-hunter had warned them against the shedding of blood. Was this the event for which they had been waiting? But were they supposed to obey the prohibition, or to step over it in response to some higher need? There was not time now to stand locked in indecision, however. Sword in hand, Garion rushed from the tent.

The light had that peculiar steely tint that comes from a colorless sky before the sun rises. It cast no shadows and what lay beneath the broad-spread oaks was not so much darkness as it was a fainter light. Garion moved quickly, his feet avoiding almost on their own the windrows of years-old dead leaves and the fallen twigs and branches which littered the floor of this ancient forest.

Zakath stood atop the knoll, holding his sword.

'Where are they?' Garion's voice was not so much a whisper as a breath.

'They were coming up from the south,' Zakath whispered back.

'How many?'

'It's hard to say.'

'Are they trying to sneak up on us?'

'It didn't really look that way. The ones we saw could have hidden back there among the trees, but they just came walking through the forest.'

Garion peered out into the growing light. And then he saw them. They were dressed all in white – robes or long smocks – and they made no attempts at concealment. Their movements were deliberate and seemed to have a placid, unhurried calm about them. They came in single file, each following the one in front at a distance of about ten yards. There was something hauntingly familiar about the way they moved through the forest.

'All they need are the torches,' Silk said from directly behind Garion. The little man made no attempt to keep his voice down.

'Be still!' Zakath hissed.

'Why? They know we're here.' Silk laughed a caustic little laugh. 'Remember that time on the Isle of Verkat?' he said to Garion. 'You and I spent a half hour or so crawling through the wet grass following Vard and his people, and I'm absolutely sure now that they knew we were there all the time. We could have just walked along behind them and saved ourselves all the discomfort.'

'What are you talking about, Kheldar?' Zakath demanded in a hoarse whisper.

'This is another of Belgarath's repetitions,' Silk shrugged. 'Garion and I have been through it before.' He sighed ruefully. 'Life is going to get terribly boring if nothing new ever happens.' Then he raised his voice to a shout. 'We're over here,' he called to the white-robed figures out in the forest.

'Are you mad?' Zakath exclaimed.

'Probably not, but then crazy people never really know, do they? Those people are Dals, and I seriously doubt that any Dal has ever hurt anybody since the beginning of time.'

The leader of the strange column halted at the foot of the knoll and pushed back the cowl of his white robe. 'We have been awaiting you,' he announced. 'The Holy Seeress has sent us to see you safely to Kell.'

CHAPTER FOUR

King Kheva of Drasnia was irritable that morning. He had overheard a conversation the previous evening between his mother and an emissary of King Anheg of Cherek, and his irritation grew out of a sort of moral dilemma. To reveal to his mother that he had been eavesdropping would of course be quite out of the question, and so he could not discuss with her what he had heard until she broached the subject herself. It seemed quite unlikely that she would do so, and so Kheva was at an impasse.

It should be stated here that King Kheva was not really the sort of boy who would normally intrude on his mother's privacy. He was basically a decent lad. But he was also a Drasnian. There is a national trait among Drasnians which, for want of a better term, might be called curiosity. All people were curious to a certain degree, but in Drasnians the trait was quite nearly compulsive. Some contend that it was their innate curiosity which has made spying their national industry. Others maintain with equal vigor that generations of spying had honed the Drasnian's natural curiosity to a fine edge. The debate was much like the endless argument about the chicken and the egg, and almost as pointless. Quite early in life, Kheva had trailed unobtrusively along behind one of the official court spies and thereby discovered the closet hidden behind the east wall of his mother's sitting room. Periodically he would slip into that closet in order to keep track of affairs of state and any other matters of interest. He was the king, after all, and thus he had a perfect right to the information. He reasoned that by spying, he could obtain it while sparing his mother the inconvenience of passing it on to him. Kheva was a considerate boy.

The conversation in question had concerned the mysterious disappearance of the Earl of Trellheim, his ship *Seabird* and a number of other individuals, including Trellheim's son Unrak.

Barak, Earl of Trellheim, was considered in some quarters to be an unreliable sort, and his companions in this vanishing were, if anything, even worse. The Alorn kings were disquieted by the potential for disaster represented by Barak and his cohorts roaming loose in the Gods only knew what ocean.

What concerned young King Kheva, however, was not so much random disasters as it was the fact that his friend Unrak had been invited to participate while he had not. The injustice of that rankled. The fact that he was a king seemed to automatically exclude him from anything that could even remotely be considered hazardous. Everyone went out of his way to keep Kheva safe and secure, but Kheva did not *want* to be kept safe and secure. Safety and security were boring, and Kheva was at an age where he would go to any lengths to avoid boredom.

Clad all in red, he made his way through the marble halls of the palace in Boktor that winter morning. He stopped in front of a large tapestry and made some show of examining it. Then, at least relatively sure that no one was watching – this *was* Drasnia, after all – he slipped behind the tapestry and into the small closet previously mentioned.

His mother was conferring with the Nadrak girl Vella and with Yarblek, Prince Kheldar's shabby partner. Vella always made King Kheva nervous. She aroused certain feelings in him with which he was not yet prepared to cope, and so he customarily avoided her. Yarblek, on the other hand, could be quite amusing. His speech was blunt and often colorful and laced with oaths Kheva was not supposed to know the meaning of.

'They'll turn up, Porenn,' Yarblek was assuring Kheva's mother. 'Barak just got bored, that's all.'

'I wouldn't be so concerned if he'd gotten bored by

himself,' Queen Porenn replied, 'but the fact that this boredom seems to be an epidemic worries me. Barak's companions aren't the most stable men in the world.'

'I've met them,' Yarblek grunted. 'You might just be right.' He paced up and down for a moment. 'I'll have our people keep an eye out for them.'

'Yarblek, I've got the finest intelligence service in the world.'

'Perhaps so, Porenn, but Silk and I have more men than you do, and we've got offices and warehouses in places Javelin hasn't even heard of.' He looked at Vella. 'Do you want to go back to Gar og Nadrak with me?' he asked.

'In the wintertime?' Porenn objected.

'We'll just wear more clothes, that's all,' Yarblek shrugged.

'What are you going to do there?' Vella asked. 'I'm not really very interested in sitting around listening to you talk business.'

'I thought we'd go to Yar Nadrak. Javelin's people don't seem to be having much luck finding out what Drosta's up to.' He broke off and looked speculatively at Queen Porenn. 'Unless they've picked up something lately I haven't heard about yet,' he added.

'Would I keep secrets from you, Yarblek?' she asked with mock innocence.

'Probably, yes. If you've got something, Porenn, share it with me. I don't want to make the trip for nothing, and Yar Nadrak's a miserable place in the winter.'

'Nothing yet,' she replied seriously.

Yarblek grunted. 'I didn't think so. Drasnians look too much like Drasnians to be able to move around in Yar Nadrak without attracting attention.' He glanced at Vella. 'Well?' he asked.

'Why not?' she agreed. 'Don't take this personally, Porenn, but this project of yours – trying to turn me into a lady – is starting to distract me just a little. Would you believe that yesterday I left my room with only one of my daggers? I think I need some fresh air and stale beer to clear my head.'

Kheva's mother sighed. 'Try not to forget everything I've taught you, Vella.'

'I have a very good memory, and I can tell the difference between Boktor and Yar Nadrak. Boktor smells better for one thing.'

'How long will you be gone?' Porenn asked the rangy Yarblek.

'A month or two, I'd imagine. I think we'll want to go to Yar Nadrak by a roundabout route. I don't want to announce to Drosta that I'm coming.'

'All right then,' the queen agreed. Then she thought of something. 'One last thing, Yarblek.'

'Yes?'

'I'm very fond of Vella. Don't make the mistake of selling her while you're in Gar og Nadrak. I'd be very put out if you did that.'

'Who'd buy her?' Yerblek responded. Then he grinned and skipped out of the way as Vella automatically went for one of her daggers.

Eternal Salmissra looked with some distaste at her current Chief Eunuch, Adiss. In addition to being incompetent, Adiss was slovenly. His iridescent robe was food-spotted, and his scalp and face were sparsely stubbled. He had never, she concluded, been more than an opportunist, and now that he had ascended to the position of Chief Eunuch and felt more or less secure there, he had given himself over to the grossest sorts of debauchery. He consumed staggering quantities of some of the most pernicious drugs available in Nyissa and frequently came into her presence with the vacant-eyed shamble of a sleepwalker. He bathed infrequently, and the combination of the climate of Sthiss Tor and the various drugs he used gave his body a rank, almost rancid, odor. Since the Serpent Queen now sampled the air with her flickering tongue, she could not only smell him but also taste him.

He groveled on the marble floor before the dais, delivering a report on some unimportant matter in a whining, nasal voice. Unimportant matters filled the Chief Eunuch's days. He devoted himself to petty things, since significant things were beyond his capabilities. With the mindless concentration of a man with severely limited talents, he expanded the trivial out of all proportion and reported it as if it were of earth-shaking importance. Most of the time, Salmissra suspected, he was blithely ignorant of the things that should really be receiving his full attention.

'That will be all, Adiss,' she told him in her sibilant whisper, her coils moving restlessly on her divanlike throne.

'But, my Queen,' he protested, the half-dozen or so drugs he had taken since breakfast making him brave, 'this matter is of utmost urgency.'

'To you, perhaps. I am indifferent to it. Hire an assassin to cut off the Satrap's head and have done with it.'

Adiss stared at her in consternation. 'B-but, Eternal Salmissra,' he squeaked in horror, 'the Satrap is of vital importance to the security of the nation.'

'The Satrap is a petty time-server who bribes you to keep himself in office. He serves no particular purpose. Remove him and bring me his head as proof of your absolute devotion and obedience.'

'H-his head?'

'That's the part that has eyes in it, Adiss,' she hissed sarcastically. 'Don't make a mistake and bring me a foot instead. Now leave.'

He stumbled backward toward the door, genuflecting every step or two.

'Oh, Adiss,' she added, 'don't ever enter the throne room again unless you've bathed.'

He gaped at her in stupid incomprehension.

'You stink, Adiss. Your stench turns my stomach. Now get out of here.'

He fled.

'Oh, my Sadi,' she sighed half to herself, 'where are you? Why have you deserted me?'

Urgit, High King of Cthol Murgos, was wearing a blue doublet and hose, and he sat up straight on his garish throne in the Drojim Palace. Javelin privately suspected that Urgit's new wife had a great deal to do with the High King's change of dress and demeanor. Urgit was not bearing up too well under the stresses of marriage. His face had a slightly baffled look on it as if something profoundly confusing had entered his life.

'That is our current assessment of the situation, your Majesty,' Javelin concluded his report. 'Kal Zakath has so reduced his forces here in Cthol Murgos that you could quite easily sweep them into the sea.'

'That's easy for you to say, Margrave Khendon,' Urgit replied a bit petulantly, 'but I don't see you Alorns committing any of *your* forces to assist with the sweeping.'

'Your Majesty raises a slightly delicate point,' Javelin said, thinking very fast now. 'Although we have agreed from the start that we have a common enemy in the Emperor of Mallorea, the eons of enmity between the Alorns and the Murgos cannot be erased overnight. Do you *really* want a Cherek fleet off your coast or a sea of Algar horsemen on the plains of Cthan and Hagga? The Alorn kings and Queen Porenn will give instructions, certainly, but commanders in the field have a way of interpreting royal commands to suit their own preconceptions. Your Murgo generals might very well also choose to misunderstand *your* instructions when they see a horde of Alorns bearing down on them.'

'That's true, isn't it?' Urgit conceded. 'What about the Tolnedran legions then? There have always been good relations between Tolnedra and Cthol Murgos.'

Javelin coughed delicately and then looked around with some show of checking for unwanted listeners. Javelin knew that he must move with some care now. Urgit was proving to be far more shrewd than any of them had anticipated. Indeed, he was at times as slippery as an eel and he seemed to know instinctively exactly the way Javelin's fine-tuned Drasnian mind was working. 'I trust this won't go any further, your Majesty?' he said in a half-whisper.

'You have my word on it, Margrave,' Urgit whispered back. 'Although anyone who takes the word of a Murgo – *and* a member of the Urga Dynasty as well – shows very poor judgment. Murgos are notoriously untrustworthy, and all Urgas are quite mad, you know.'

Javelin chewed on a fingernail, strongly suspecting that he was being outmaneuvered. 'We've received some disquieting information from Tol Honeth.'

'Oh?'

'You know how the Tolnedrans are – always alert for the main chance.'

'Oh, my goodness, yes,' Urgit laughed. 'Some of the fondest memories of my childhood come from the times when Taur Urgas, my late, unlamented father, fell to chewing on the furniture when he received the latest proposal from Ran Borune.'

'Now mind you, your Majesty,' Javelin went on, 'I'm not suggesting that Emperor Varana himself is in any way involved in this, but there are some fairly high-ranking Tolnedran nobles who've been in contact with Mal Zeth.'

'That's disturbing, isn't it? But Varana controls the legions. As long as *he's* opposed to Zakath, we're safe.'

'That's true – as long as Varana's alive.'

'Are you suggesting the possibility of a coup?'

'It's not unheard of, your Majesty. Your own kingdom gives evidence of that. The great families in northern Tolnedra are still infuriated about the way the Borunes and Anadiles pulled a march on them and put Varana on the imperial throne. If something happens to Varana and he's succeeded by a Vordue or a Honeth or a Horbite, all assurances go out the window. An alliance between Mal Zeth and Tol Honeth could be an absolute disaster for Murgo and Alorn alike. More than that, though, if such an alliance were kept a secret and you had Tolnedran legions in force here in Cthol Murgos and they received sudden instructions to change sides, you'd be caught between an army of Tolnedrans and an army of Malloreans. That isn't my idea of a pleasant way to spend a summer.'

Urgit shuddered.

'Under the circumstances, your Majesty,' Javelin went on smoothly, 'I'd advise the following course.' He began ticking items off on his fingers. 'One: There's a vastly diminished Mallorean presence here in Cthol Murgos. Two: An Alorn force inside your borders would be neither necessary nor advisable. You have enough troops of your own to drive the Malloreans out, and we'd be ill-advised to risk any accidental confrontations between your people and ours. Three: The rather murky political situation in Tolnedra makes it extremely risky to contemplate bringing the legions down here.'

'Wait a minute, Khendon,' Urgit objected. 'You came here to Rak Urga with all sorts of glowing talk about alliances and commonality of interests, but now when it's time to put troops into the field, you back down. Why have you been wasting my time?'

'The situation has changed since we began our negotiations, your Majesty,' Javelin told him. 'We did not anticipate a Mallorean withdrawal of such magnitude, and we certainly didn't expect instability in Tolnedra.'

'What am *I* going to get out of this then?'

'What is Kal Zakath likely to do the minute he gets word that you're marching on his strongholds?'

'He'll turn around and send his whole stinking army back to Cthol Murgos.'

'Through a Cherek fleet?' Javelin suggested. 'He tried that after Thull Mardu, remember? King Anheg and his berserkers sank most of his ships and drowned his troops by the regiment.'

'That's true, isn't it?' Urgit mused. 'Do you think Anheg might be willing to blockade the east coast to keep Zakath's army from returning?'

'I think he'd be delighted. Chereks take such childlike pleasure in sinking other peoples' boats.'

'He'd need charts in order to make his way around the southern tip of Cthol Murgos, though,' Urgit said thoughtfully.

Javelin coughed. 'Ah – we already have those, your Majesty,' he said deprecatingly.

Urgit slammed his fist down on the arm of his throne. 'Hang it all, Khendon! You're here as an ambassador, not as a spy.'

'Just keeping in practice, your Majesty,' Javelin replied blandly. 'Now,' he went on, 'in addition to a Cherek fleet in the Sea of the East, we're prepared to line the northern and western borders of Goska and the northwestern border of Araga with Algar cavalry and Drasnian pikemen. That would effectively cut off escape routes for the Malloreans trapped in Cthol Murgos, block Kal Zakath's favorite invasion route down through Mishrak ac Thull, *and* seal off the Tolnedran legions in the event of an accommodation between Tol Honeth and Mal Zeth. That way, everybody defends more or less his own territory, and the Chereks keep the Malloreans off the continent so that we can settle it all to our own satisfaction.'

'It also totally isolates Cthol Murgos,' Urgit pointed out the one fact that Javelin had hoped to gloss over. 'I exhaust my kingdom pulling your chestnut out of the fire, and then the Alorns, Tolnedrans, Arends, and Sendars are free to march in and eliminate the Angarak presence on the western continent.'

'You have the Nadraks and Thulls as allies, your Majesty.'

'I'll trade you,' Urgit said drily. 'Give me the Arends and the Rivans, and I'll gladly give you the Thulls and Nadraks.'

'I think it's time for me to contact my government on these matters, your Majesty. I've already over-extended my authority. I'll need further instructions from Boktor.'

'Give Porenn my regards,' Urgit said, 'and tell her that I join with her in wishing a mutual relative well.'

Javelin felt a lot less sure of himself as he left.

The Child of Dark had smashed all the mirrors in her quarters in the Grolim Temple at Balasa that morning. It had begun to touch her face now. Dimly, she had seen the swirling lights beneath the skin of her cheeks and forehead and then had broken the mirror which had revealed the fact to her – and all the others as well. When it was done, she stared in horror at the gash in the palm of her hand. The lights were even in her blood. Bitterly, she recalled the wild joy which had filled her when she had first read the prophetic words, 'Behold; the Child of Dark shall be exalted above all others and shall be glorified by the light of the stars.' But the light of the stars was no halo or glowing nimbus. The light was a creeping disease that encroached upon her inch by inch.

It was not only the swirling lights, however, that had begun to consume her. Increasingly, her thoughts, her memories, and even her dreams were not her own. Again and again she awoke screaming as the same dream came again and again. She seemed to hang bodiless and indifferent in some unimaginable void, watching all unconcerned as a giant star spun and wobbled on its course, swelling and growing redder as it shuddered towards inevitable extinction. The random wobble of the off-center star was of no real concern until it became more and more pronounced. Then the bodiless and sexless awareness drifting in the void felt a prickle of interest and then a growing alarm. This was wrong. This had not been intended. And then it happened. The giant red star exploded in a place where that explosion was not supposed to happen; and, because it was in the wrong place, other stars were caught up in it. A vast, expanding ball of burning energy rippled outward, engulfing sun after sun until an entire galaxy had been consumed.

The awareness in the void felt a dreadful wrench within

itself as the galaxy exploded, and for a moment it seemed to exist in more than one place. And then it was no longer one. 'This must not be,' the awareness said in a soundless voice.

'Truly,' another soundless voice responded.

And that was the horror that brought Zandramas bolt upright and screaming in her bed night after night – the sense of another presence when always before there had been the perfect solitude of eternal oneness.

The Child of Dark tried to put those thoughts – memories, if you will – from her mind. There was a knock at the door of her chamber, and she pulled up the hood of her Grolim robe to hide her face. 'Yes?' she said harshly.

The door opened, and the Archpriest of this temple entered. 'Naradas has departed, Holy Sorceress,' he reported. 'You wanted to be told.'

'All right,' she said in a flat voice.

'A messenger has arrived from the west,' the Arch-priest continued. 'He brings news that a western Grolim, a Hierarch, has landed on the barren west coast of Finda and now moves across Dalasia toward Kell.'

Zandramas felt a faint surge of satisfaction. 'Welcome to Mallorea, Agachak,' she almost purred. 'I've been waiting for you.'

It was foggy that morning along the southern tip of the Isle of Verkat, but Gart was a fisherman and he knew the ways of these waters. He pushed out at first light, steering more by the smell of the land behind him and the feel of the prevailing current than by anything else. From time to time he would stop rowing, pull in his net, and empty the struggling, silver-sided fish into the large box beneath his feet. Then he would cast out his net again and resume his rowing while the fish he had caught thumped and flapped beneath him.

It was a good morning for fishing. Gart did not mind the fog. There were other boats out, he knew, but the fog created the illusion that he had the ocean to himself, and Gart liked that.

It was a slight change in the pull of the current on his boat that warned him. He hastily shipped his oars, leaned forward, and began to clang the bell mounted in the bow of his boat to warn the approaching ship that he was here.

And then he saw it. It was like no other ship Gart had ever seen before. It was long and it was big and it was lean. Its high bowsprit was ornately carved. Dozens of oars propelled it hissing through the water. There could be no mistaking the purpose for which that ship had been built. Gart shivered as the ominous vessel slid past.

Near the stern of the ship, a huge red-bearded man in chain mail stood leaning over the rail. 'Any luck?' he called to Gart.

'Fair,' Gart replied cautiously. He did not wish to encourage a ship with that big a crew to drop anchor and begin hauling in *his* fish.

'Are we off the southern coast of the Isle of Verkat yet?' the red-bearded giant asked.

Gart sniffed at the air and caught the faint scent of the land. 'You're almost past it now,' he told them. 'The coast takes a bend to the northeast about here.'

A man dressed in gleaming armor joined the big red-bearded fellow at the rail. The armored man held his helmet under one arm, and his black hair was curly. 'Thy knowledge of these waters doth seem profound, friend,' he said in an archaic form of address Gart had seldom heard before, 'and thy willingness to share thy knowledge with others doth bespeak a seemly courtesy. Canst thou perchance advise us of the shortest course to Mallorea?'

'That would depend on exactly where you wanted to go in Mallorea,' Gart replied.

'The closest port,' the red-bearded man said.

Gart squinted, trying to recall the details of the map he had tucked on a shelf at home. 'That would be Dal Zerba in southwestern Dalasia,' he said. 'If it were me, I'd go on due east for another ten or twenty leagues and then come about to a northeasterly course.'

'And how long a voyage do we face to reach this port thou hast mentioned?' the armored man asked.

Gart squinted at the long, narrow ship alongside him. 'That depends on how fast your ship goes,' he replied. 'It's three hundred and fifty leagues or so, but you have to swing back out to sea again to get around the Turim reef. It's very dangerous, I'm told, and no one tries to go through it.'

'Peradventure we might be the first, My Lord,' the armored man said gaily to his friend.

The giant sighed and covered his eyes with one huge hand. 'No, Mandorallen,' he said in a mournful voice. 'If we rip out my ship's bottom on a reef, we'll have to swim the rest of the way, and you're not dressed for it.'

The huge ship began to slide off into the fog.

'What kind of a ship is that?' Gart called after the disappearing vessel.

'A Cherek war boat,' the rumbled reply came back with a note of pride. 'She's the largest afloat.'

'What do you call her?' Gart shouted between his cupped hands.

'*Seabird*,' the reply came ghosting back to him.

CHAPTER FIVE

It was not a large city, but its architecture was at a level of sophistication Garion had never seen before. It nestled in a shallow valley near the foot of the vast white peak, looking somehow as if it were resting in the mountain's lap. It was a city of slender white spires and marble colonnades. The low buildings spaced among the spires often had entire walls of glass. There were wide lawns around the buildings and groves of trees with marble benches beneath them. Formal gardens were spaced about the lawns – boxy hedges and beds of flowers lined by low, white walls. Fountains played in the gardens and in the courtyards of the buildings.

Zakath gaped at the city of Kell in stunned amazement. 'I never even knew this was here!' he exclaimed.

'You didn't know about Kell?' Garion asked him.

'I knew about Kell, but I didn't know it was like *this*.' Zakath made a face. 'It makes Mal Zeth look like a collection of hovels, doesn't it?'

'Tol Honeth as well – and even Melcene,' Garion agreed.

'I didn't think the Dals even knew how to build a proper house,' the Mallorean said, 'and now they show me something like this.'

Toth had been gesturing to Durnik.

'He says that it's the oldest city in the world,' the smith supplied. 'It was built this way long before the world was cracked. It hasn't changed in almost ten thousand years.'

Zakath sighed. 'They've probably forgotten how to do it then. I was going to press some of their architects into service. Mal Zeth could use a bit of beautifying.'

71

Toth gestured again, and a frown appeared on Durnik's face. 'I can't have gotten that right,' he muttered.

'What did he say?'

'The way I got it was that nothing the Dals have ever done has ever been forgotten.' Durnik looked at his friend. 'Is that what you meant?' he asked.

Toth nodded and gestured again.

Durnik's eyes went wide. 'He says that every Dal alive today knows everything that every Dal who's ever lived knew.'

'They must have very good schools then,' Garion suggested.

Toth only smiled at that. It was a strange smile, tinged slightly with pity. Then he gestured briefly to Durnik, slid down from his horse, and walked away.

'Where's he going?' Silk asked.

'To see Cyradis,' Durnik replied.

'Shouldn't we go with him?'

Durnik shook his head. 'She'll come to us when she's ready.'

Like all the Dals Garion had ever seen, the inhabitants of Kell wore simple white robes with deep cowls attached to the shoulders. They walked quietly across the lawns or sat in the gardens in groups of two or three engaged in sober discussion. Some carried books or scrolls. Others did not. Garion was somehow reminded of the University of Tol Honeth or the one at Melcene. This community of scholars, he was convinced, however, was engaged in studies far more profound than the often petty research which filled the lives of the professors at those exalted institutions.

The group of Dals who had escorted them to this jewel-like city led them along a gently curving street to a simple house on the far side of one of the formal gardens. An ancient, white-robed man leaned on a long staff in the doorway. His eyes were very blue, and his hair was snowy white. 'We have long awaited your coming,' he said to them in a quavering voice, 'for the *Book of*

Ages has fortold that in the Fifth Age the Child of Light and his company would come to us here at Kell to seek guidance.'

'And the Child of Dark?' Belgarath asked him, dismounting. 'Will she also come here?'

'No, Ancient Belgarath,' the elderly man replied. 'She may not come here, but will find direction elsewhere and in a different manner. I am Dallan, and I am bid to greet you.'

'Do you rule here, Dallan?' Zakath asked, also dismounting.

'No one rules here, Emperor of Mallorea,' Dallan said, 'not even you.'

'You seem to know us,' Belgarath noted.

'We have known you all since the book of the heavens was first opened to us, for your names are written large in the stars. And now I will take you to a place where you may rest and await the pleasure of the Holy Seeress.' He looked at the oddly placid she-wolf at Garion's side and the frolicking puppy behind her. 'How is it with you, little sister?' he asked in formal tones.

'One is content, friend,' she replied in the language of wolves.

'One is pleased that it is so,' he replied in her own tongue.

'Does everyone in the whole world except me speak wolf?' Silk asked with some asperity.

'Would you like lessons?' Garion asked.

'Never mind.'

And then with tottering step the white-haired man led them across the verdant lawn to a large marble building with broad, gleaming steps at the front. 'This house was prepared for you at the beginning of the Third Age, Ancient Belgarath,' the old man said. 'Its first stone was laid on the day when you recovered your Master's Orb from the City of Endless Night.'

'That was quite some time ago,' the sorcerer observed.

'The Ages were long in the beginning,' Dallan agreed.

73

'They grow shorter now. Rest well. We will attend to your mounts.' Then he turned and, leaning on his staff, he went back toward his own house.

'Someday a Dal is going to come right out and say what he means without all the cryptic babble, and the world will come to an end,' Beldin growled. 'Let's go inside. If this house has been here for as long as he said it has, the dust's likely to be knee-deep in there, and it's going to need to be swept out.'

'Tidiness, uncle?' Polgara laughed as they started up the marble steps. 'From you?'

'I don't mind a certain amount of dirt, Pol, but dust makes me sneeze.'

The interior of the house, however, was spotless. Gossamer curtains hung at the windows, billowing in the sweet-scented summer breeze, and the furniture, although oddly constructed and strangely alien-looking, was very comfortable. The interior walls were peculiarly curved, and there were no corners anywhere to be seen.

They wandered about this strange house, trying to adjust themselves to it. Then they gathered in a large, domed central room where a small fountain trickled water down one wall.

'There isn't any back door,' Silk noted critically.

'Were you planning to leave, Kheldar?' Velvet asked him.

'Not necessarily, but I like to have that option open if the need should arise.'

'You can always jump out a window if you have to.'

'That's amateurish, Liselle. Only a first-year student at the academy dives out of windows.'

'I know, but sometimes we have to improvise.'

There was a peculiar murmuring sound in Garion's ears. At first he thought it might be the fountain, but somehow it didn't quite sound like running water. 'Do you think they'd mind if we went out and had a look around?' he asked Belgarath.

'Let's wait a bit before we do that. We were sort of put

here. I don't know yet if that means we're supposed to stay or what. Let's feel things out before we take any chances. The Dals here – and Cyradis in particular – have something we need. Let's not offend them.' He looked at Durnik. 'Did Toth give you any hints about when she'll be coming here?'

'Not really, but I got the impression it wouldn't be too long.'

'That's not really too helpful, brother mine,' Beldin said. 'The Dals have a rather peculiar notion of time. They keep track of it in ages rather than years.'

Zakath had been rather closely examining the wall a few yards from the trickling fountain. 'Do you realize that there's no mortar holding this wall together?'

Durnik joined him, took his knife from its sheath, and probed at the slender fissure between two of the marble slabs. 'Mortise and tenon,' he said thoughtfully, 'and very tightly fit, too. It must have taken years to build this house.'

'And centuries to build the city, if it's all put together that way,' Zakath added. 'Where did they learn how to do all this? And when?'

'Probably during the First Age,' Belgarath told him.

'Stop that, Belgarath,' Beldin snapped irritably. 'You sound just the way they do.'

'I always try to follow local customs.'

'I still don't know any more than I did before,' Zakath complained.

'The First Age covered the period of time from the creation of man until the day when Torak cracked the world,' Belgarath told him. 'The beginning of it is a little vague. Our Master was never very specific about when He and His brothers made the world. I expect that none of Them want to talk about it because Their Father disapproved. The cracking of the world is fairly well pinpointed, though.'

'Were you around when it happened, Lady Polgara?' Sadi asked curiously.

'No,' she replied. 'My sister and I were born a while later.'

'How long a while?'

'Two thousand years or so, wasn't it, Father?'

'About that, yes.'

'It chills my blood, the casual way you people shrug off eons,' Sadi shuddered.

'What makes you think they learned this style of building before the cracking of the world?' Zakath asked Belgarath.

'I've read parts of the *Book of Ages*,' the old man said. 'It fairly well documents the history of the Dals. After the world was cracked and the Sea of the East rushed in, you Angaraks fled to Mallorea. The Dals knew that eventually they'd have to come to terms with your people, so they decided to pose as simple farmers. They dismantled their cities – all except this one.'

'Why would they leave Kell intact?'

'There was no need to take it apart. The Grolims were the ones they were really worried about, and the Grolims can't come here.'

'But other Angaraks can,' Zakath noted shrewdly. 'How is it that none of them has ever reported a city like this to the bureaucracy?'

'They're probably encouraged to forget,' Polgara told him.

He looked at her sharply.

'It's not really that difficult, Zakath. A hint or two can usually erase memories.' An expression of irritation crossed her face. 'What *is* that murmuring sound?' she demanded.

'I don't hear anything,' Silk said, looking slightly baffled.

'You must have your ears stopped up, then, Kheldar.'

About sunset, several young women in soft white robes brought supper to them on covered trays.

'I see that things are the same the world over,' Velvet

said wryly to one of the young women. 'The men sit around and talk, and the women do the work.'

'Oh, we don't mind,' the girl replied earnestly. 'It's an honor to serve.' She had very large dark eyes and lustrous brown hair.

'That's what makes it even worse,' Velvet said. 'First they make us do all the work, and then they persuade us that we like it.'

The girl gave her a startled look, then giggled. Then she looked around guiltily and blushed.

Beldin had seized a crystal flagon almost as soon as the young women had entered. He filled a goblet and drank noisily. Then he began to choke, spraying a purplish liquid over half the room. 'What is this stuff?' he demanded indignantly.

'It's fruit juice, sir,' the young woman with the dark hair assured him earnestly. 'It's very fresh. It was pressed only this morning.'

'Don't you let it set long enough to ferment?'

'You mean when it goes bad? Oh, no. We throw it out when that happens.'

He groaned. 'What about ale? Or beer?'

'What are those?'

'I knew there was going to be something wrong with this place,' the dwarf growled to Belgarath.

Polgara, however, had a beatific smile on her face.

'What was that all about?' Silk asked Velvet after the Dalasian women had left, 'all that chit-chat, I mean?'

'Groundwork,' she replied mysteriously. 'It never hurts to open channels of communication.'

'Women,' he sighed, rolling his eyes toward the ceiling.

Garion and Ce'Nedra exchanged a quick look, both of them remembering how often each of them had said approximately the same thing in the same tone early in their marriage. Then they both laughed.

'What's so funny?' Silk asked suspiciously.

'Nothing, Kheldar,' Ce'Nedra replied. 'Nothing at all.'

Garion slept poorly that night. The murmuring in his

ears was just enough of a distraction to bring him back from the edge of sleep over and over again. He arose the next morning sandy-eyed and out of sorts.

In the large round central room he found Durnik. The smith had his ear pressed against the wall near the fountain.

'What's the trouble?' Garion asked him.

'I'm trying to pinpoint that noise,' Durnik said. 'It might be something in the plumbing. The water in this fountain has to come from somewhere. Probably it's piped in, and then the pipe runs under the floor or up through the walls.'

'Would water running through a pipe make that sort of noise?'

Durnik laughed. 'You never know what sort of sounds are going to come out of the plumbing, Garion. I saw a whole town abandoned once. They all thought the place was haunted. The noise turned out to be coming from the municipal water supply.'

Sadi came into the room once again wearing his iridescent silk robe.

'Colorful,' Garion observed. For the past several months, the eunuch had been wearing a tunic, hose, and Sendarian half-boots.

Sadi shrugged. 'For some reason I feel homesick this morning,' he sighed. 'I think I could live out my life in perfect contentment if I never saw another mountain. What are you doing, Goodman Durnik? Still examining the construction?'

'No. I'm trying to track down the source of that noise.'

'What noise?'

'Surely you can hear it.'

Sadi cocked his head to one side. 'I hear some birds just outside the window,' he said, 'and there's a stream somewhere nearby, but that's about all.'

Garion and Durnik exchanged a long, speculative look. 'Silk couldn't hear it yesterday either,' Durnik recalled.

'Why don't we get everybody up?' Garion suggested.

'That might make some of them a little unhappy, Garion.'

'They'll get over it. I think this might be important.'

There were some surly looks directed at Garion as the others filed in.

'What's this all about, Garion?' Belgarath asked in exasperation.

'It's what you might call an experiment, Grandfather.'

'Do your experiments on your own time.'

'My, aren't *we* cross this morning?' Ce'Nedra said to the old man.

'I didn't sleep very well.'

'That's strange. I slept like a baby.'

'Durnik,' Garion said, 'would you stand over there, please?' He pointed to one side of the room, 'and Sadi, you over there.' He pointed to the other side. 'This will only take a few minutes,' he told them all. 'I'm going to whisper a question to each of you, and I want you to answer yes or no.'

'Aren't you being just a bit exotic?' Belgarath asked sourly.

'I don't want to contaminate the experiment by giving all of you the chance to talk it over.'

'It's a sound scientific principle,' Beldin approved. 'Let's humor him. He's stirred up my curiosity.'

Garion went from person to person, whispering a single question: 'Can you hear that murmuring sound?' Depending on the answer, he asked each of them to join either Sadi or Durnik. It did not take long, and the result confirmed Garion's suspicions. Standing with Durnik were Belgarath, Polgara, Beldin, and – somewhat surprisingly – Eriond. Standing with Sadi were Silk, Velvet, Ce'Nedra, and Zakath.

'Now do you suppose you could explain all this rigamarole?' Belgarath asked.

'I asked everybody the same question, Grandfather. The people standing with you can hear that sound. The people over there can't.'

'Of course they can. It kept me awake half the night.'

'Maybe that's why you're so dense this morning,' Beldin grunted. 'Good experiment, Garion. Now, why don't you explain it to our fuzzy-headed friend?'

'It's not difficult, Grandfather,' Garion said deprecatingly. 'It's probably so simple that you're overlooking it. The only people who can hear the sound are those with what you used to call "talent". Ordinary people can't.'

'I'll be honest, Belgarath,' Silk said. 'I can't hear a sound.'

'And I've been hearing it ever since we first caught sight of Kell,' Durnik added.

'Now isn't that interesting?' Beldin said to Belgarath. 'Shall we take it a few steps further, or did you want to go back to bed?'

'Don't be absurd,' Belgarath replied absently.

'All right then,' Beldin continued, 'we've got a sound that ordinary people can't hear, but that we can. I can think of another right offhand as well, can't you?'

Belgarath nodded. 'The sound of someone using sorcery.'

'This is not a natural sound, then,' Durnik mused. He suddenly laughed. 'I'm glad you worked this out, Garion. I was right on the verge of tearing up the floor.'

'What on earth for?' Polgara asked him.

'I thought the noise was coming from a water pipe somewhere.'

'This isn't sorcery, though,' Belgarath said. 'It doesn't sound the same and it doesn't feel the same.'

Beldin was scratching thoughtfully at his matted beard. 'How does this idea strike you?' he said to Belgarath. 'The people here have enough concentrated power to deal with any Grolim or group of Grolims who might come along, so why go to the trouble of laying down that curse of theirs?'

'I don't quite follow you.'

'A large proportion of Grolims are sorcerers, right? So they'd be able to hear this sound. What if that

80

enchantment is there to keep the Grolims far enough away so that they won't hear it?'

'Aren't you getting a little exotic, Beldin?' Zakath asked sceptically.

'Not really. Actually, I'm simplifying. A curse designed to keep away people you're not really afraid of doesn't make sense. Everybody's always thought that the curse was there to protect Kell itself, and that doesn't make any sense either. Isn't it simpler to assume that there's something more important that has to be protected?'

'What is there about this sound that would make the Dals so concerned about having it overheard?' Velvet asked, sounding perplexed.

'All right,' Beldin said. 'What is a sound?'

'Not *that* again,' Belgarath sighed.

'I'm not talking about the noise in the woods. A sound is just a noise unless it's meaningful. What do we call a meaningful sound?'

'Talk, isn't it?' Silk ventured.

'Exactly.'

'I don't understand,' Ce'Nedra confessed. 'What are the Dals saying that they want to keep secret? Nobody understands what they're saying anyway.'

Beldin spread his hands helplessly, but Durnik was pacing up and down, his face creased with thought. 'Maybe it's not so much *what* they're saying, but *how*.'

'And you accuse *me* of being obscure,' Beldin said to Belgarath. 'What are you getting at, Durnik?'

'I'm groping,' the smith admitted. 'The noise, or sound – whatever you want to call it – isn't a signal that somebody's turning people into frogs.' He stopped. 'Can we really do that?' he asked.

'Yes,' Beldin said, 'but it's not worth the trouble. Frogs multiply at a ferocious rate. I'd rather have one person who irritated me instead of a million or so aggravating frogs.'

'All right, then,' Durnik continued. 'It's not the noise that sorcery makes.'

'Probably not,' Belgarath agreed.

'And I think Ce'Nedra's right. Nobody really understands what the Dals are saying – except for other Dals. Half the time I can't follow what Cyradis is saying from one end of a sentence to the other.'

'What does that leave?' Beldin asked intently, his eyes alight.

'I'm not sure. I've got the feeling though that "How" is more important than "What".' Durnik suddenly looked slightly embarrassed. 'I'm talking too much,' he confessed. 'I'm sure that some of the rest of you have more important things to say about this than I do.'

'I don't really think so,' Beldin told him. 'I think you're right on the edge of it. Don't lose it.'

Durnik was actually sweating now. He covered his eyes with one hand, trying to collect his thoughts. Garion noticed that everyone in the room was almost breathlessly watching his old friend labor with a concept that was probably far beyond the grasp of any of the rest of them.

'There has to be something that the Dals are trying to protect,' the smith went on, 'and it has to be something that's very simple – for them at least – but something they don't want anybody else to understand. I wish Toth were here. He might be able to explain it.' Then his eyes went very wide.

'What is it, dear?' Polgara asked.

'It can't be that!' he exclaimed, suddenly very excited. 'It couldn't be!'

'Durnik!' she said in exasperation.

'Do you remember when Toth and I first began to talk to each other – in gestures, I mean?' Durnik was suddenly talking very fast and he was almost breathless. 'We'd been working together, and a man who works with someone else begins to know exactly what the other one is doing – and even what he's thinking.' He stared at Silk. 'You and Garion and Pol use that finger-language' he said.

'Yes.'

'You've seen the gestures Toth makes. Would the secret

language be able to say all that much with just a few waves of the hand – the way he does it?'

Garion already knew the answer.

Silk's voice was puzzled. 'No,' he said. 'That would be impossible.'

'But I know exactly what he's trying to say,' Durnik told them. 'The gestures don't mean anything at all. He does it just to make me – to give me some rational explanation for what he's really doing.' Durnik's face grew awed. 'He's been putting the words directly into my mind – without even talking. He has to, because he *can't* talk. What if that's what this murmuring we hear is? What if it's the sound of the Dals talking to one another? And what if they can do it over long distances?'

'And over time, too,' Beldin said in a startled voice. 'Do you remember what your big, silent friend said when we first got here? He said that nothing the Dals have ever done has ever been forgotten and that every Dal alive knows everything that every Dal who's ever lived knew.'

'You're suggesting an absurdity, Beldin,' Belgarath scoffed.

'No. Not really. Ants do it. So do bees.'

'We aren't ants – or bees.'

'I can do almost anything a bee can do.' The hunchback shrugged. 'Except make honey – and you could probably build a fairly acceptable ant hill.'

'Will one of you please explain what you're talking about?' Ce'Nedra asked crossly.

'They're hinting at the possibility of a group mind, dear,' Polgara said quite calmly. 'They're not doing it very well, but that's what they're groping toward.' She gave the two old men a condescending sort of smile. 'There are certain creatures – usually insects – that don't have very much intelligence individually, but as a group they're very wise. A single bee isn't too bright, but a bee-hive knows everything that's ever happened to it.'

The she-wolf had come padding in, her toe-nails clicking on the marble floor and with the puppy scampering along behind her. 'Wolves do it as well,' she supplied, indicating that she had been listening at the door.

'What did she say?' Silk asked.

'She said that wolves do the same thing,' Garion translated. Then he remembered something. 'I was talking with Hettar once, and he said that horses are the same way. They don't think of themselves as individuals – only as parts of the herd.'

'Would it really be possible for *people* to do something like that?' Velvet asked incredulously.

'There's one way to find out,' Polgara replied.

'No, Pol,' Belgarath said very firmly. 'It's too dangerous. You could be drawn into it and never be able to get back out.'

'No, Father,' she replied quite calmly. 'The Dals may not let me in, but they won't hurt me or keep me in if I want to leave.'

'How do you know that?'

'I just do.' And she closed her eyes.

CHAPTER SIX

They stood watching her apprehensively as she lifted her flawless face. Eyes closed, she concentrated. Then a strange expression came to her features.

'Well?' Belgarath asked.

'Quiet, Father. I'm listening.'

He stood drumming his fingers impatiently on the back of a chair, and the others watched breathlessly.

At last Polgara opened her eyes with a vaguely regretful sigh. 'It's enormous,' she said very quietly. 'It has every thought these people have ever had – and every memory. It even remembers the beginning, and every one of them shares in it.'

'And so did you?' Belgarath asked her.

'For a moment, father. They let me catch a glimpse of it. There are parts of it that are blocked off, though.'

'We might have guessed that,' Beldin said, scowling. 'They're not going to provide access to anything that would give us the slightest advantage. They've been perched on *that* fence since the beginning of time.'

Polgara sighed again and sat on a low divan.

'Are you all right, Pol?' Durnik asked with some concern.

'I'm fine, Durnik,' she replied. 'It's just that for a moment I saw something I've never experienced before, and then they asked me to leave.'

Silk's eyes narrowed slightly. 'Do you think they'd object if we left this house and had a look around?'

'No. They won't mind.'

'I'd say that's our next step then,' the little man suggested. 'We know that the Dals are the ones who are going to make the final choice – at least Cyradis is

– but this oversoul of theirs is probably going to provide her some direction.'

'That's a very interesting term, Kheldar,' Beldin noted.

'What is?'

'Oversoul. How did you come up with it?'

'I've always had a way with words.'

'There may be some hope for you after all. Someday we'll have to have a long talk.'

'I shall place myself at your disposal, Beldin,' Silk said with a florid bow. 'Anyway,' he continued, 'since the Dals are going to decide things, I think we ought to get to know them better. If they're leaning in the wrong direction, maybe we can sway them back.'

'Typically devious,' Sadi murmured, 'but probably not a bad idea. We should split up, though. We'll be able to cover more ground that way.'

'Right after breakfast,' Belgarath agreed.

'But, Grandfather,' Garion protested, impatient to be off.

'I'm hungry, Garion, and I don't think well when I'm hungry.'

'That might explain a lot,' Beldin noted blandly. 'We should have fed you more often when you were younger.'

'You can be terribly offensive sometimes, do you know that?'

'Why, yes, as a matter of fact I do.'

The same group of young women brought breakfast to them, and Velvet drew aside the large-eyed girl with the glossy brown hair and spoke with her briefly. Then the blond girl returned to the table. 'Her name is Onatel,' she reported, 'and she's invited Ce'Nedra and me to visit the place where she and the other young women work. Young women talk a great deal, so we might pick up something useful.'

'Wasn't Onatel the name of that seeress we met on the Isle of Verkat?' Sadi asked.

'It's a common name among Dalasian women,' Zakath told him. 'Onatel was one of their most honored seeresses.'

'But the Isle of Verkat is in Cthol Murgos,' Sadi pointed out.

'It's not all that strange,' Belgarath said. 'We've had some fairly strong hints that the Dals and the slave-race of Cthol Murgos are closely related and keep in more or less constant contact. This is just some additional confirmation.'

The morning sun was warm and bright as they emerged from the house and strolled off in various directions. Garion and Zakath had removed their armor and left their swords behind, although Garion prudently carried the Orb in a pouch tied to his belt. The two of them walked across a dewy lawn toward a group of larger buildings near the center of the city.

'You're always very careful with that stone, aren't you, Garion?' Zakath asked.

'I'm not sure that careful is the exact word,' Garion replied, 'but then again, maybe it is – in a broader sense. You see, the Orb is very dangerous, and I don't want it hurting people by accident.'

'What does it do?'

'I'm not really sure. I've never seen it do anything to anybody – except possibly Torak – but that might have been the sword.'

'And you're the only one in the world who can touch the Orb?'

'Hardly. Eriond carried it around for a couple of years. He kept trying to give it to people. They were mostly Alorns, so they knew better than to take it.'

'Then you and Eriond are the only people who can touch it?'

'My son can,' Garion said. 'I put his hand on it right after he was born. It was very happy to meet him.'

'A stone? Happy?'

'It's not like other stones.' Garion smiled. 'It can be a little silly now and then. It gets carried away by its own enthusiasm. I have to be very careful about what I think sometimes. If it decides I really want something, it might just take independent action.' He laughed. 'Once I was speculating about the time when Torak cracked the world, and it proceeded to tell me how to patch it.'

'You're not serious!'

'Oh, yes. It has no conception of the word impossible. If I really wanted it to, it could probably spell out my name in stars.' He felt a small twitch in the pouch at his belt. 'Stop that!' he said sharply to the Orb. 'That was just an example, not a request.'

Zakath was staring at him.

'Wouldn't that look grotesque?' Garion said wryly. "Belgarion" running from horizon to horizon across the night sky?'

'You know something, Garion,' Zakath said. 'I've always believed that someday you and I would go to war with each other. Would you be terribly disappointed if I decided not to show up?'

'I think I could bear it,' Garion grinned at him. 'If nothing else, I could always start without you. You could drop by from time to time to see how things were going. Ce'Nedra can fix you supper. Of course, she's not a very good cook, but we all have to make a few sacrifices, don't we?'

They looked at each other for a moment and then burst out laughing. The process which had begun at Rak Urga with the quixotic Urgit was now complete. Garion realized with a certain amount of satisfaction that he had taken the first few steps toward ending five thousand years of unrelenting hatred between Alorn and Angarak.

The Dals paid little attention to them as they strolled along marble streets and past sparkling fountains. The inhabitants of Kell went about their activities quietly and contemplatively, their eyes lost in thought. They spoke but little, since speech among them was largely unnecessary.

88

'It's an eerie sort of place, isn't it?' Zakath observed. 'I'm not used to cities where nobody does anything.'

'Oh, they're doing something, all right.'

'You know what I mean. There aren't any shops, and nobody's even out sweeping the streets.'

'It is a little odd, I suppose.' Garion looked around. 'What's even odder is that we haven't seen a single seer since we got here. I thought this was the place where they lived.'

'Maybe they stay indoors.'

'That's possible, I suppose.'

Their morning stroll gained them little information. They tried occasionally to strike up conversations with the white-robed citizens, and although the Dals were unfailingly polite, they volunteered little in the way of talk. They answered questions which were put to them and that was about all.

'Frustrating, wasn't it?' Silk said when he and Sadi returned to the house which had been assigned to them. 'I've never met a group of people so disinterested in talk. I couldn't even find anybody willing to discuss the weather.'

'Did you happen to see which way Ce'Nedra and Liselle went?' Garion asked him.

'Someplace over on the other side of town, I think. I imagine they'll come back when those young women bring us our lunch.'

Garion looked around at the others. 'Did anybody happen to see any of the seers?' he asked.

'They aren't here,' Polgara told him. She sat by a window mending one of Durnik's tunics. 'One old woman told me they have a special place. It's not in the city.'

'How did you manage to get an answer out of her?' Silk asked.

'I was fairly direct. You have to push the Dals a bit when you want information.'

As Silk had predicted, Velvet and Ce'Nedra returned with the young women who were bringing their meals to them.

89

'You have a brilliant wife, Belgarion,' Velvet said after the Dalasian women had left. 'She sounded for all the world as if there weren't a brain in her head. She spent the morning babbling.'

'Babbling?' Ce'Nedra objected.

'Weren't you?'

'Well, I suppose so, but "babbling" is such an unflattering word.'

'I presume there was a reason for it?' Sadi suggested.

'Of course,' Ce'Nedra said. 'I saw fairly soon that those girls weren't going to be very talkative, so I filled up the spaces. They began to loosen up after a bit. I talked so that Liselle could watch their faces.' She smiled smugly. 'It worked out fairly well, even if I do say it myself.'

'Did you get anything out of them?' Polgara asked.

'A few things,' Velvet replied. 'Nothing all that specific, but a few hints. I think we should be able to get a bit more this afternoon.'

Ce'Nedra looked around. 'Where's Durnik?' she asked, 'and Eriond?'

'Where else?' Polgara sighed.

'Where did they find any water to fish in?'

'Durnik can smell water from several miles away,' Polgara told her in a resigned tone of voice, 'and he can tell you what kind of fish are in it, how many, and probably even what their names are.'

'I've never cared all that much for fish myself,' Beldin said.

'I don't know that Durnik does either, Uncle.'

'Why does he bother them then?'

She spread her hands helplessly. 'How should I know? The motives of fishermen are dreadfully obscure. I can tell you one thing, though.'

'Oh? What's that?'

'You've said a number of times that you want to have some long conversations with him.'

'Yes, I do.'

'You'd better learn how to fish then. Otherwise, he probably won't be around.'

'Has anybody come by to give us any kind of word about Cyridis?' Garion asked.

'Not a soul,' Beldin replied.

'We don't really have time for an extended stay,' Garion fretted.

'I might be able to stir an answer out of somebody,' Zakath offered. 'She commanded me to present myself to her here at Kell.' He winced slightly. 'I can't believe I just said that. Nobody's commanded me to do anything since I was about eight years old. Anyway, you know what I mean. I could insist that somebody take me to her so I can obey her orders.'

'I think you might choke on that one, Zakath,' Silk said lightly. 'Obey is a difficult concept for someone in your position.'

'He's an irritating little fellow, isn't he?' Zakath said to Garion.

'I've noticed.'

'Why, your Majesties,' Velvet said, all wide-eyed innocence, 'what a thing to suggest.'

'Well, isn't he?' Zakath said pointedly.

'Of course, but it's not nice to talk about it.'

Silk looked slightly offended. 'Would you people like for me to go away so you can talk freely?'

'Oh, that won't be necessary, Kheldar,' Velvet said with a dimpled smile.

They gained little more in the way of information that afternoon, and the frustration of the fruitless quest made them all irritable. 'I think perhaps we should follow up that idea of yours,' Garion said to Zakath after supper. 'First thing tomorrow morning, why don't we go see that old man, Dallan? We'll tell him right out that you're supposed to present yourself to Cyradis. I think it's time to start pushing a little.'

'Right,' Zakath agreed.

Dallan, however, proved to be as unresponsive as all

the rest of the citizens of Kell. 'Be patient, Emperor of Mallorea,' he advised. 'The Holy Seeress will come to you at the proper time.'

'And when is that?' Garion asked bluntly.

'Cyradis knows, and that's all that's really important, isn't it?'

'If he weren't so old and feeble, I'd shake some answers out of him,' Garion muttered as he and Zakath walked back to the house.

'If this goes on much longer, I might just ignore his age and infirmity,' Zakath said. 'I'm not in the habit of having my questions evaded this way.'

Velvet and Ce'Nedra were approaching the house from the other direction as Garion and Zakath reached the broad marble steps. The two young women were walking quickly, and Ce'Nedra's expression was triumphant.

'I think we managed to get something useful at last,' Velvet said. 'Let's go inside so we can tell everyone at once.'

They gathered again in the domed room, and the blond girl spoke to them quite seriously. 'This isn't too precise,' she admitted, 'but I think it might be all we're likely to get out of these people. This morning, Ce'Nedra and I went back to that house where those young women work. They were weaving, and that's the sort of thing that tends to make people a little less than alert. Anyway, that girl with the large eyes, Onatel, wasn't there, and Ce'Nedra put on her most empty-headed expression and—'

'I most certainly did not,' Ce'Nedra said indignantly.

'Oh, but you did, dear – and it was absolutely perfect. She stood there all wide-eyed and innocent and asked the young women where we could find our "dear friend", and one of them let something slip that she probably wasn't supposed to have. She said that Onatel had been summoned to serve in "the place of the seers." Ce'Nedra's eyes went – if possible – even more vacant, and she asked where that might be. Nobody answered, but one of them looked at the mountain.'

'How can you avoid looking at that monster?' Silk scoffed. 'I'm a little dubious about this, Liselle.'

'The girl was weaving, Kheldar. I've done that myself a few times, and I know you have to keep your eyes on what you're doing. She looked away in response to Ce'Nedra's question, and then she jerked her eyes back and tried to cover her mistake. I've been to the academy, too, Silk, and I can read people almost as well as you can. That girl might as well have screamed it out loud. The Seers are somewhere up on that mountain.'

Silk made a face. 'She's probably right, you know,' he admitted. 'That's one of the things they stress at the academy. If you know what you're looking for, most people's faces are like open books.' He squared his shoulders. 'Well, Zakath,' he said, 'it looks as if we'll get to climb that mountain a little sooner than we'd expected.'

'I don't think so, Kheldar,' Polgara said firmly. 'You could spend half a lifetime poking around in those glaciers and still not find the seers.'

'Have you got a better idea?'

'Several, actually.' She rose to her feet. 'Come along, Garion,' she said. 'You too, uncle.'

'What are you up to, Pol?' Belgarath asked.

'We're going to go up and have a look.'

'That's what I suggested already,' Silk objected.

'There's one difference, though, Kheldar,' she said sweetly. 'You can't fly.'

'*Well*,' he said in an offended tone, 'if you're going to be *that* way about it.'

'I am, Silk. It's one of the advantages of being a woman. I get to do all sorts of unfair things, and you have to accept them because you're too polite not to.'

'One for her side,' Garion murmured.

'You keep saying that,' Zakath said, puzzled. 'Why?'

'It's an Alorn joke,' Garion told him.

'Why don't you save yourself a bit of time, Pol?'

Belgarath suggested. 'See if you can get some confirmation from that group mind before you go swooping off!'

'That's a very good idea, Father,' she agreed. She closed her eyes and lifted her face. After a moment she shook her head. 'They won't let me back in,' she sighed.

'That's a kind of confirmation in itself,' Beldin chuckled.

'I don't exactly follow that,' Sadi said, rubbing his freshly shaved scalp.

'The Dals may be wise,' the hunchback told him, 'but they're not very shrewd. These two girls of ours have picked up some information. If the information weren't correct, there wouldn't be any reason to keep Pol out. Since they *did* keep her out, it indicates that we're on to something. Let's go outside of town,' he suggested to Polgara, 'so that we don't give away any secrets.'

'I don't really fly all that well, Aunt Pol,' Garion said dubiously. 'Are you sure you need me?'

'Let's not take chances, Garion. If the Dals go out of their way to make this place inaccessible, we might need to use the Orb to break through. We'll save time if you come along with it in the first place.'

'Oh,' he said, 'maybe you're right.'

'Keep in touch,' Belgarath said as the three of them started out the door.

'Naturally,' Beldin grunted.

Once they were out on the lawn, the dwarf squinted around. 'Over there, I think,' he said, pointing. 'That thicket on the edge of town should hide what we're doing.'

'All right, uncle,' Polgara agreed.

'One other thing, Pol,' he added, 'and I'm not trying to be offensive.'

'That's a novelty.'

'You're in good form this morning,' he grinned. 'Anyway, a mountain like that one breeds its own weather — and most particularly, its own winds.'

'Yes, Uncle, I know.'

'I know how fond you are of snowy owls, but the feathers are too soft. If you get into a high wind, you could end up coming back naked.'

She gave him a long, level look.

'Do you *want* all your feathers blown off?'

'No, Uncle, as a matter of fact, I don't.'

'Why don't you do it my way then? You might even find that you like being a hawk.'

'Blue banded, I suppose?'

'Well, that's up to you, but you do look good in blue, Pol.'

'You're impossible.' She laughed. 'All right, uncle, we'll do it your way.'

'I'll change first,' he offered. 'Then you can use me as a model to make sure you get the shape right.'

'I know what a hawk looks like, Uncle.'

'Of course you do, Pol. I'm just trying to be helpful.'

'You're too kind.'

It felt very strange to take a shape other than that of a wolf. Garion looked himself over carefully, making frequent comparisons to Beldin, who perched fierce-eyed and magnificent on a branch overhead.

'Good enough,' Beldin told him, 'but next time make your tail feathers a little fuller. You need them to steer with.'

'All right, gentlemen,' Polgara said from a near-by limb, 'let's get started.'

'I'll lead,' Beldin said. 'I've had more practice at this. If we hit a downdraft, sheer away from the mountain. You don't want to get banged up against those rocks.' He spread his wings, flapped a few times, and flew off.

The only time Garion had been aloft before had been on the long flight from Jarviksholm to Riva after Geran had been abducted. He had flown that time as a speckled falcon. The blue-banded hawk was a much bigger bird, and flying over mountain terrain was much different from flying over the vast open expanse of the Sea of the Winds. The air currents eddied and swirled around the rocks, making them unpredictable and even dangerous.

The three hawks spiraled upward on a rising column of air. It was an effortless way to fly, and Garion began to understand Beldin's intense joy in flight.

He also discovered that his eyes were incredibly sharp. Every detail on the mountainside stood out as if it were directly in front of him. He could see insects and the individual petals of wildflowers. His talons twitched involuntarily when a small mountain rodent scurried across a rockfall.

'Pay attention to what we're here for, Garion,' he heard Aunt Pol's voice in the silences of his mind.

'But—' The yearning to plummet down with his talons spread wide was almost irresistible.

'No buts, Garion. You've already had breakfast. Just leave the poor little creature alone.'

'You're taking all the fun out of it for him, Pol,' Garion heard Beldin protest.

'We're not here to have fun, uncle. Lead on.'

The buffeting was sudden, and it took Garion by surprise. A violent downdraft hurled him toward a rocky slope, and it was only at the last instant that he was able to veer away from certain disaster. The downdraft pushed him this way and that, wrenching at his wings, and it was suddenly accompanied by a pelting rainstorm, huge, icy drops that pounded at him like large wet hammers.

'It isn't natural, Garion!' Aunt Pol's voice came to him sharply. He looked around desperately, but he could not see her.

'Where are you?' he called out.

'Never mind that! Use the Orb! The Dals are trying to keep us away!'

Garion was not entirely positive that the Orb could hear him in that strange place to which it went when he changed form, but he had no choice but to try. The driving rain and howling wind currents made settling to earth and resuming his own shape unthinkable. 'Make it stop!' he called out to the stone, '– the wind, the rain, all of it!'

The surge he felt when the Orb unleashed its power sent him staggering through the air, flapping his wings desperately to hold his balance. The air around him seemed suddenly bright blue.

And then the turbulence and the rain which had accompanied it was gone, and the column of warm air was back, rising undisturbed into the summer air.

He had lost at least a thousand feet in the downdraft, and he saw Aunt Pol and Beldin, each over a mile away in opposite directions. As he began again to spiral upward, he saw that they also were rising and veering through the air toward him. 'Stay on your guard,' Aunt Pol's voice told him. 'Use the Orb to muffle anything else they try to throw at us.'

It took them only a few minutes to regain the height they had lost, and they continued upward over forests and rockslides until they reached that region on the flanks of the mountain above the tree-line and below the eternal snows. It was an area of steep meadows with grass and wildflowers nodding in the mountain breeze.

'There!' Beldin's voice seemed to crackle. 'It's a trail.'

'Are you sure it's not just a game trail, uncle?' Polgara asked him.

'It's too straight, Pol. A deer couldn't walk in a straight line if his life depended on it. That trail is man-made. Let's see where it goes.' He tilted on one wing and swooped down toward the well-traveled track stretching up one of the meadows toward a gap in a rocky ridge. At the upper end of the meadow, he flared his wings. 'Let's go down,' he told them. 'It might be better if we follow the rest of the way on foot.'

Aunt Pol and Garion followed him down, and the three of them blurred back into their own forms. 'It was touch and go there for a while,' Beldin said. 'I came within a few feet of bending my beak on a rockslide.' He looked critically at Polgara. 'Would you like to revise your theory about the Dals not hurting any-body?'

'We'll see.'

'I wish I had my sword,' Garion said. 'If we run into trouble, we're pretty much defenseless.'

'I don't know if your sword would be much use against the kind of trouble we're likely to come up against,' Beldin told him. 'Don't lose contact with the Orb, though. Let's see where this goes.' He started up the steep trail toward the ridge.

The gap in the ridge was a narrow pass between two large boulders. Toth stood in the center of the trail, mutely blocking their way.

Polgara looked him coolly in the face. 'We *will* go to the place of the seers, Toth. It is fore-ordained.'

Toth's eyes grew momentarily distant. Then he nodded and stepped aside for them.

CHAPTER SEVEN

The cavern was vast, and there was a city inside. The city looked much like Kell, thousands of feet below, except, of course, for the absence of lawns and gardens. It was dim, since the blindfolded seers needed no light, and the eyes of their mute guides had, Garion surmised, become adjusted to the faint light.

There were few people abroad in those shadowy streets, and those they saw as Toth led them into the city paid no attention to them. Beldin was muttering to himself as he stumped along.

'What is it, uncle?' Polgara asked him.

'Have you ever noticed how much some people are slaves to convention?' he replied.

'I don't quite see what you're getting at.'

'This town is inside a cave, but they still put roofs on the houses. Isn't that sort of an absurdity? It isn't going to rain in here.'

'But it will get cold – particularly in the winter. If a house has no roof, it's a little hard to keep the heat in, wouldn't you say?'

He frowned. 'I guess I didn't think of that,' he admitted.

The house to which Toth led them was in the very center of this strange subterranean city. Although it was no different from those around it, its location hinted that the inhabitant was of some importance. Toth entered without knocking and led them to the simple room where Cyradis sat waiting for them, her pale young face illuminated by a single candle.

'You have reached us more quickly than we had expected,' she said. In a peculiar way her voice was different from the way it had sounded in their previous meetings.

99

Garion uneasily felt that the seeress was speaking in more than one voice, and the result was startlingly choral.

'You knew that we could come, then?' Polgara asked her.

'Of course. It was but a question of time before you would complete your three-fold task.'

'Task?'

'It was but a simple endeavor for one as powerful as thou art, Polgara, but it was a necessary test.'

'I don't seem to recall—'

'As I told thee, it was so simple that doubtless thou hast forgotten it.'

'Remind us,' Beldin said gruffly.

'Of course, gentle Beldin,' she smiled. 'You have found this place; you have subdued the elements to reach it; and Polgara hath spoken correctly the words which gained you entry.'

'More riddles,' he said sourly.

'A riddle is sometimes the surest way to make the mind receptive.'

He grunted.

'It was necessary for the riddle to be solved and the tasks to be completed 'ere I could reveal to you that which must be revealed.' She rose to her feet. 'Let us depart from this place then, and go down even unto Kell. My guide and dear companion will bear the great book which must be delivered into the hands of Ancient Belgarath.'

The mute giant went to a shelf on the far side of the dimly lit room and took down a large book bound in black leather. He tucked it under his arm, took his mistress by the hand, and led them back out of the house.

'Why the secrecy, Cyradis?' Beldin asked the blind-folded girl. 'Why do the seers hide up here on the mountain instead of staying at Kell?'

'But this *is* Kell, gentle Beldin.'

'What's that city down in the valley, then?'

'Also Kell.' She smiled. 'It hath ever been thus among us. Unlike the cities of others, our communities are wide-spread. This is the place of the seers. There are many other places on this mountain – the place of the wizards, the place of the necromancers, the place of the diviners – and all are a part of Kell.'

'Trust a Dal to come up with an unnecessary complication.'

'The cities of others are built for different purposes, Beldin. Some are for commerce. Some are for defense. Our cities are built for study.'

'How can you study if you have to walk all day in order to talk with your colleagues?'

'There is no need for walking, Beldin. We can speak to each other whenever we choose. Is this not the way in which thou and Ancient Belgarath converse?'

'That's different,' he growled.

'In what way?'

'Our conversations are private.'

'We have no need of privacy. The thoughts of one are the thoughts of all.'

It was shortly before noon when they emerged from the cavern into the warm sunlight again. Gently guiding Cyradis, Toth led them back to the gap in the ridge and down the steep path that crossed the high meadows. After about an hour of descent, they entered a cool green forest where birds caroled from the tree tops and insects whirled like specks of fire in the slanting columns of sunlight.

The trail was still steep, and Garion soon discovered one of the disadvantages of walking downhill for any extended period of time. A large and painful blister was forming atop one of the toes on his left foot, and a few twinges from his right clearly indicated that he would soon have a matched set. He gritted his teeth and limped on.

It was nearly sunset when they reached the gleaming city in the valley. Garion noticed with a certain satisfaction that Beldin was also limping as they walked along the marble street that led to the house Dallan had lodged them in.

101

The others were eating when they entered. As it chanced to happen, Garion was looking at Zakath's face when the Mallorean saw that Cyradis was with them. His olive-skinned face paled slightly, a pallor made more pronounced by the short black beard he had grown to conceal his identity. He rose to his feet and bowed slightly. 'Holy Seeress,' he said respectfully.

'Emperor of Mallorea,' she responded. 'As I promised thee in cloud-dark Darshiva, I surrender myself up to thee as thy hostage.'

'There's no need to talk of hostages, Cyradis,' he replied with a slightly embarrassed flush. 'I spoke in haste in Darshiva, before I clearly understood what it is that I am to do. I am committed now.'

'I am, nonetheless, thy hostage, for it is thus pre-ordained, and I must accompany thee unto the Place Which Is No More to face the task which awaits me.'

'You must all be hungry,' Velvet said. 'Come to the table and eat.'

'I must complete one task first, Huntress,' Cyradis told her. She held out both hands, and Toth placed the heavy book he had carried down from the mountain in them. 'Ancient Belgarath,' she said in that strangely choral voice, 'thus do we commend into thy hands our holy book as the stars have instructed us to do. Read it carefully, for thy destination is revealed in its pages.'

Belgarath rose quickly, crossed to her, and took the book, his hands trembling with eagerness. 'I thank you, Cyradis. I know how precious the book is, and I will care for it while it is in my hands and return it once I've found what I need.' Then he went to a smaller table near the window, sat, and opened the heavy volume.

'Move over,' Beldin told him, stumping to the table and drawing up another chair. The two old men bent their heads over the crackling pages, oblivious to all around them.

'Will you eat now, Cyradis?' Polgara asked the blind-folded girl.

'Thou art kind, Polgara,' the Seeress of Kell replied. 'I have fasted since thine arrival here in preparation for this meeting, and mine hunger weakens me.'

Polgara gently led her to the table and seated her between Ce'Nedra and Velvet.

'Is my baby well, Holy Seeress?' Ce'Nedra asked urgently.

'He is well, Queen of Riva, although he doth yearn to be returned to thee.'

'I'm surprised he even remembers me.' Ce'Nedra said it with some bitterness. 'He was only a baby when Zandramas stole him.' She sighed. 'There's so much I've missed – so many things I'll never see.' Her lower lip began to tremble.

Garion went to her and put his arms comfortingly around her. 'It's going to be all right, Ce'Nedra,' he assured her.

'Will it, Cyradis?' she asked in a voice near to tears. 'Will everything really be all right again?'

'That I cannot say, Ce'Nedra. Two courses stand before us, and not even the stars know upon which we will place our feet.'

'How was the trip?' Silk asked, more, Garion thought, to get past an uncomfortable moment than out of any burning curiosity.

'Nervous,' Garion replied. 'I don't fly very well, and we ran into some bad weather.'

Silk frowned. 'But it's been absolutely clear all day.'

'Not where we were, it wasn't.' Garion glanced at Cyradis and decided not to make an issue of the near-disastrous downdraft. 'Is it all right to tell them about the place where you live?' he asked her.

'Of a certainty, Belgarion,' she smiled. 'They are of thy company, and thou shouldst conceal nothing from them.'

'Do you remember Mount Kahsha in Cthol Murgos?' Garion asked his friend.

'I've been trying to forget.'

'Well, the seers have a city that's sort of like the

one the Dagashi built at Kahsha. It's inside a very large cave.'

'I'm glad I didn't go there, then.'

Cyradis turned her face toward him, a concerned little frown touching her forehead. 'Hast thou not yet mastered this unreasoning fear of thine, Kheldar?'

'Not noticeably, no – and I'd hardly call it unreasoning. Believe me, Cyradis, I have reasons – lots and lots of reasons.' he shuddered.

'Thou must summon up thy courage, Kheldar, for the time will surely come when thou must enter a place such as thou holdest in dread.'

'Not if I can help it, I won't.'

'Thou must, Kheldar. No choice is open to thee.'

His face was bleak, but he said nothing.

'Tell me, Cyradis,' Velvet said then, 'were *you* the one who interrupted the progress of Zith's pregnancy?'

'Thou art shrewd to have perceived the pause in that most natural of events, Liselle,' the Seeress told her, 'but nay, it was not I. The wizard Vard on the Isle of Verkat bade her to wait until her task at Ashaba was completed.'

'Vard is a wizard?' Polgara asked in some surprise. 'I can usually detect them, but in his case, I didn't sense a thing.'

'He is most subtle,' Cyradis agreed. 'Things stand so in Cthol Murgos that great care must be exercized in the practice of our arts. The Grolims in the land of the Murgos are ever alert to the disturbances such acts inevitably cause.'

'We were quite put out with you on Verkat,' Durnik told her. 'That was before we understood the reason for what you did. I'm afraid I treated Toth very badly for a while. He was good enough to forgive me, though.'

The big mute smiled at him and made a few gestures.

Durnik laughed. 'You don't really have to do that any more, Toth,' he told his friend. 'I finally figured out how you were talking to me.'

Toth lowered his hands.

Durnik seemed to listen for a moment. 'Yes,' he agreed. 'It's much easier this way – and faster, too – now that we don't have to wave our hands at each other. Oh, by the way, Eriond and I found a pond a little ways below the city here. It has some very nice trout in it.'

Toth grinned broadly.

'I thought you might feel that way.' Durnik grinned back.

'I'm afraid we've corrupted your guide, Cyradis,' Polgara apologized.

'Nay, Polgara.' The Seeress smiled. 'This passion hath been upon him since boyhood. Oft times in our travels he hath found excuse to linger for a time by some lake or stream. I do not chide him for this, for I am fond of fish, and he doth prepare them exquisitely.'

They finished their meal and sat, talking quietly to avoid disturbing Belgarath and Beldin who still sat pouring over the *Mallorean Gospels*.

'How is Zandramas going to find out where we're all going?' Garion asked the Seeress. 'Since she's a Grolim, she can't come here.'

'That I may not tell thee, Child of Light. She will, however, arrive at the appointed place at the proper time.'

'With my son?'

'As it hath been foretold.'

'I'm looking forward to that meeting.' He said it bleakly. 'There are a great many things Zandramas and I have to settle.'

'Let not thy hatred blind thee to thy tasks,' she told him quite seriously.

'And what *is* my task, Cyradis?'

'That thou wilt know when it doth face thee.'

'But not before?'

'Nay. Thy performance of that task would be marred shouldst thou consider it overlong.'

'And what is *my* task, Holy Seeress?' Zakath asked her. 'You said you would instruct me here at Kell.'

'I must reveal that to thee in private, Emperor of

Mallorea. Know, however, that thy task will begin when thy companions have completed theirs, and it will consume the balance of thy life.'

'As long as we're talking about tasks,' Sadi said, 'perhaps you could explain mine to me.'

'You have already begun it, Sadi.'

'Am I doing it very well?'

She smiled. 'Passing well, yes.'

'I might do a little better if I knew what it is.'

'Nay, Sadi. Even as Belgarion's, thy task would be marred shouldst thou know of it.'

'Is this place we're going to very far?' Durnik asked her.

'Many leagues, and there is yet much to be done.'

'I'll need to talk with Dallan about supplies, then. And I think I'll want to check the horses' hooves before we start. This might be a good time to get them shod again.'

'That's impossible!' Belgarath suddenly burst out.

'What is it, father?' Aunt Pol asked him.

'It's Korim! The meeting is supposed to take place at Korim!'

'Where's that?' Sadi asked in puzzlement.

'It's no place,' Beldin growled. 'It's not there anymore. It was a mountain range that sank into the sea when Torak cracked the world. The *Book of Alorn* mentions it as "The High Places of Korim, which are no more.".'

'There's a certain perverted logic to it,' Silk observed. 'That's what these assorted prophecies have meant all along when they talked about a Place Which Is No More.'

Beldin tugged thoughtfully at one ear. 'There's something else, too,' he noted. 'You remember the story Senji told us back at Melcene? About the scholar who stole the Sardion? His ship was last seen rounding the southern tip of Gandahar, and it never came back. Senji said he thought that it had gone down in a storm off the Dalasian coast. It's beginning to sound as if he was right. We have to go where the Sardion is, and I've got the uncomfortable feeling that it's resting on top of a mountain that sank into the sea over five thousand years ago.'

106

CHAPTER EIGHT

The Queen of Riva was in a pensive mood as they set out from the glowing marble city of Kell. A peculiar kind of languor seemed to come over her as they rode through the forest to the west of Kell, a languor that grew more pronounced with each passing mile. She took no part in the general conversation, but was content merely to listen.

'I don't see how you can be so calm about this, Cyradis,' Belgarath was saying to the blindfolded Seeress as they rode along. 'Your task will fail the same as ours will if the Sardion is lying at the bottom of the sea. And why are we making this side trip to Perivor?'

'It is there that the instruction thou received from the Holy Book will be made clear to thee, Ancient Belgarath.'

'Couldn't you just explain it to me yourself? We're a little pressed for time, you know.'

'That I may not do. I may not give thee any aid which I do not also give to Zandramas. It is thy task – and hers – to unravel this riddle. To aid one of thee and not the other is forbidden.'

'Somehow I thought you might look at it that way,' he said glumly.

'Where's Perivor?' Garion asked Zakath.

'It's an island off the south coast of Dalasia,' the Mallorean replied. 'The inhabitants there are very strange. Their legends say that they're descendants of some people from the west who were aboard a ship that was blown off-course and wrecked on the island about two thousand years ago. The island's of little value, and the people there are fearsome fighters. The general opinion in Mal Zeth has always been that the place wouldn't be worth the trouble it would take to subdue it, and Urvon didn't even bother to send Grolims there.'

107

'If they're so savage, won't it be sort of dangerous for us to go there?'

'No. Actually they're civil and even hospitable – as long as you don't try to land an army there. That's when things start to take a turn for the worse.'

'Have we really got the time to go to this place?' Silk asked the Seeress of Kell.

'Ample time, Prince Kheldar,' she replied. 'The stars have told us for eons that the Place Which Is No More awaits the coming of thee and thy companions, and that thou and thy companions will come there upon the day appointed for the meeting.'

'And so will Zandramas, I suppose?'

She smiled a gentle little smile. 'How can there be a meeting if the Child of Dark be not also present?' she asked him.

'I think I detected a faint glimmer of humor there, Cyradis,' he bantered. 'Isn't that a bit out of character for one of the seers?'

'How little you know us, Prince Kheldar.' She smiled again. 'Oft times we have been convulsed with laughter at some message writ large in the stars and at the absurd lengths to which others go to ignore or avoid that which is pre-ordained. Submit to the instruction of the heavens, Kheldar. Spare thyself the agony and turmoil of trying to evade thy fate.'

'You throw the word fate around awfully lightly, Cyradis,' he said disapprovingly.

'Hast thou not come here in response to a fate laid down for thee at the beginning of days? All thy concern with commerce and espionage have been but a diversion to occupy thee until the appointed day.'

'That's a polite way to tell someone he's been behaving like a child.'

'We are all children, Kheldar.'

Beldin came soaring through the sun-dappled forest, avoiding tree trunks with deft shifts of his wings. He settled to earth and changed form.

'Trouble?' Belgarath asked him.

'Not as much as I'd expected.' The dwarf shrugged. 'And that worries me a bit.'

'Isn't that a little inconsistent?'

'Consistency is the defense of a small mind. Zandramas couldn't go to Kell, right?'

'As far as we know.'

'Then she has to follow *us* to the meeting place, right?'

'Unless she's found some other way to find out where it is.'

'That's what worries me. If she had to follow us, wouldn't it be logical for her to have ringed this forest with troops and Grolims to find out which way we were going?'

'I suppose so, yes.'

'Well, there's no army out there – only a few patrols, and they're just going through the motions.'

Belgarath frowned. 'What's she up to?'

'My point exactly. I'd guess that she's got a surprise in store for us somewhere.'

'Keep your eyes open, then. I don't want her slipping up behind me.'

'It might simplify things if she did.'

'I doubt it. Nothing about this entire affair has been simple, and I don't expect things to change at this stage.'

'I'll go scout ahead.' The dwarf blurred and soared away.

They made their encampment that evening beside a spring that gushed out of an outcropping of moss-covered rock. Belgarath seemed moody and out of sorts, so the rest of them avoided him as they worked at tasks they had repeated so many times that they had become habitual.

'You're very quiet this evening,' Garion said to Ce'Nedra as they sat by the fire after supper. 'What's the matter?'

'I just don't feel like talking.' The peculiar lethargy that had come over the little queen had not diminished as the day wore on, and she had actually found herself dozing in her saddle several times during the late afternoon.

'You look tired,' he observed.

'I am, a bit. We've been traveling for a long time now. I think it might be starting to catch up with me.'

'Why don't you go to bed then? You'll feel better after a good night's sleep.'

She yawned and held out her arms to him. 'Carry me,' she said.

He looked startled. Ce'Nedra enjoyed startling her husband. His face always looked so wide-eyed and boyish. 'Aren't you feeling well?' he asked.

'I'm fine, Garion. I'm just sleepy, and I want to be babied a bit. Carry me to the tent, put me to bed, and tuck me in.'

'Well, if that's what you want . . .' He rose, picked her up easily, and carried her across the encampment to their tent.

'Garion,' she murmured drowsily after he had gently drawn their blankets up around her shoulders.

'Yes, dear?'

'Please don't wear your mail shirt when you come to bed. It makes you smell like an old iron pot.'

Ce'Nedra's sleep that night was disturbed by strange dreams. She seemed to see people and places she had not seen or even thought of in years. She saw legionnaires guarding her father's palace, and Lord Morin, her father's chamberlain, hurrying down a marble corridor. Then she seemed to be at Riva, holding a long, incomprehensible conversation with Brand, the Rivan Warder, while Brand's blond niece sat spinning flax by the window. Arell seemed unconcerned about the dagger hilt protruding from between her shoulder blades. Ce'Nedra stirred, muttering to herself, and immediately began to dream again.

She seemed then to be at Rheon in eastern Drasnia. Casually, she plucked a dagger from the belt of Vella, the Nadrak dancer, and just as casually drove it to the hilt into the belly of black-bearded Ulfgar, the head of the Bear-cult. Ulfgar was speaking sneeringly to Belgarath as Ce'Nedra sank the knife into him, and he did not even pay any attention to her as she slowly twisted the blade in his vitals.

And then she was at Riva again, and she and Garion were sitting naked beside a sparkling forest pool while thousands of butterflies hovered over them.

She traveled in her restless dream to the ancient city of Val Alorn in Cherek, and then went on to Boktor for the funeral of King Rhodar. And once again she saw the battlefield at Thull Mardu, and once more the face of her self-appointed protector, Brand's son, Olban.

There was no coherence to the dream. She seemed to go from place to place without effort, moving through time and space looking for something, although she could not remember what it was she had lost.

When she awoke the next morning, she was as tired as she had been the previous evening. Every movement was an effort, and she kept yawning.

'What's the matter?' Garion asked her as they dressed. 'Didn't you sleep well?'

'Not really,' she replied. 'I kept having the strangest dreams.'

'Do you want to talk about them? Sometimes that's the best way to put them to rest so they don't keep coming back night after night.'

'They didn't make any sense, Garion. They just kept jumping around. It was almost as if someone were moving me from place to place for some reason of her own.'

'Her? Was this someone a woman?'

'Did I say "her"? I can't imagine why. I never saw this person.' Ce'Nedra yawned again. 'I hope whoever it was got finished with it, though. I'd rather not go through another night like that.' Then she gave him a sly, sidelong glance through her eyelashes. 'There were some parts of the dream that were rather nice, though,' she said. 'Once, we were sitting by that pool back at Riva. Do you want to know what we were doing?'

A slow blush crept up Garion's neck. 'Uh, no, Ce'Nedra. I don't really think so.'

111

But she told him anyway – in great detail – until he finally fled from the tent.

Her restless night increased the peculiar lassitude which had lain on her since they had left Kell, and she rode that morning in a half-doze which, try though she might, she could not seem to shake off. Garion spoke with her several times to warn her that she was allowing her horse to stray, and then, apparently seeing that she just couldn't keep her eyes open, he took her reins from her hands and led her horse.

About midmorning, Beldin rejoined them. 'I think you'd better take cover,' he tersely told Belgarath. 'There's a Darshivan patrol coming along this trail.'

'Are they searching for us?'

'Who knows? If they are, they're not being very serious about it. Go back into the woods for a couple hundred yards and let them ride on by. I'll keep an eye on them and let you know when they've passed.'

'All right.' Belgarath turned aside from the trail and led the rest of them back into the concealment of the forest.

They dismounted and waited tensely. Soon they heard the jingling of the soldiers' equipment as they rode along the forest trail at a trot.

Even in this potentially dangerous situation, Ce'Nedra simply could not keep her eyes open. Dimly, she could hear the whispered conversations of the others until she finally dozed off again.

And then she came awake – or at least partially so. She was walking alone through the forest, her mind all bemused. She knew that she should be alarmed at being separated from the others, but oddly, she was not. She walked on, not so much going anywhere in particular as following some sort of subtle summoning.

Then at last she reached a grassy clearing and saw a tall blond girl standing among the wildflowers and holding a blanket-wrapped bundle in her arms. The girl's blond braids were coiled at her temples, and her complexion was like new milk. It was Brand's niece, Arell. 'Good morning, your Majesty,' she greeted the Queen of Riva. 'I've been waiting for you.'

Something deep in Ce'Nedra's mind tried to scream at her that this was wrong – that the tall Rivan girl could not possibly be here. But Ce'Nedra could not remember why, and the moment passed. 'Good morning, Arell,' she said to her dear friend. 'What on earth are you doing here?'

'I came to help you, Ce'Nedra. Look at what I've found.' She turned back the corner of the blanket to reveal a tiny face.

'My baby!' Ce'Nedra exclaimed, almost overcome with joy. She ran forward, her arms extended hungrily, and took the sleeping infant from her friend and held him to her body, her cheek pressed against his soft curls. 'How did you possibly find him?' she asked Arell. 'We've been looking for him for the longest time now.'

'I was traveling alone through this forest,' Arell replied, 'and I thought I smelled the smoke of a campfire. I went to investigate and I found a tent set up beside a little stream. I looked inside the tent, and there was Prince Geran. There was no one else around, so I picked him up and came looking for you.'

Ce'Nedra's mind was still trying to scream at her, but she was too deliriously happy to pay any attention. She held her baby, rocking back and forth and crooning to him.

'Where is King Belgarion?' Arell asked.

'Back there someplace.' Ce'Nedra gestured vaguely.

'You should go to him and let him know that his son is safe.'

'Yes. He'll be very happy.'

'I have something that I really have to attend to, Ce'Nedra,' Arell said. 'Do you think you'd be able to find your way back alone?'

'Oh, I'm sure I could, but couldn't you come along? His Majesty is sure to want to reward you for restoring our son to us.'

Arell smiled. 'The happiness on your face is all the

reward I need, and this matter I must take care of is extremely important. I may be able to join you later, however. Which way will you be traveling?'

'South, I think,' Ce'Nedra replied. 'We have to get to the sea coast.'

'Oh?'

'Yes. We're going to an island – Perivor, I think the name is.'

'There's supposed to be a meeting of some kind very soon, isn't there? Is Perivor the place where it's going to happen?'

'Oh, no,' Ce'Nedra laughed, still cuddling her baby. 'We're just going to Perivor to get some more information about it. We'll be going on from there.'

'I may not be able to join you at Perivor,' Arell said, frowning slightly. 'Perhaps you could tell me where the meeting's supposed to take place. I'm sure I'll be able to meet you there.'

'Let me see,' Ce'Nedra pondered. 'What did they call it? Oh, now I remember. It's some place that's called Korim.'

'*Korim?*' Arell exclaimed in astonishment.

'Yes. Belgarath seemed dreadfully upset when he first found out about it, but Cyradis told him that everything would be all right. That's why we have to go to Perivor. Cyradis says that there's something there that will make everything clear. It seems to me that she said something about a chart or something.' She laughed a bit giddily. 'To be honest with you, Arell, I've been so sleepy for the last few days that I can barely keep track of what the people around me are saying.'

'Of course,' Arell said absently, her face creased in thought. 'Why would Perivor be the key?' she mused to herself. 'What could possibly be there to explain an absurdity? Are you absolutely certain the word was Korim? Perhaps you misunderstood.'

'That was the way I heard it, Arell. I didn't read it for myself, but Belgarath and Beldin kept talking about "the

114

High Places of Korim, Which Are No More," and isn't the meeting supposed to be at the Place Which Is No More? I mean, it does sort of fit together, doesn't it?'

'Yes,' Arell replied, frowning strangely. 'Now that I think about it, it does.' The she straightened, smoothing her gown. 'I'll have to leave you now, Ce'Nedra,' she said. 'Take your baby back to your husband. Give him my regards.' Her eyes seemed to glint in the sunlight. 'Give my best to Polgara as well,' she added. There seemed to be something slightly malicious in the way she said it. She turned then and walked away, crossing the flowery meadow toward the dark edge of the forest.

'Goodbye, Arell,' Ce'Nedra called after her, 'and thank you so much for finding my baby.'

Arell neither turned nor answered.

Garion was frantic. When he first discovered that his wife was missing, he leaped into his saddle and rode Chretienne off into the forest at a gallop. He had gone three hundred yards before Belgarath finally caught up with him. 'Garion! Stop!' the old man shouted.

'But, Grandfather!' Garion shouted back. 'I've got to find Ce'Nedra!'

'Where do you plan to start looking? Or are you just going to ride around in circles trusting to luck?'

'But—'

'Use your head, boy! We have another way that's much faster. You know what she smells like, don't you?'

'Of course, but—'

'Then we have to use our noses. Get down off that horse and send him back. We'll change form and follow her trail. It's faster and a great deal more certain.'

Garion felt suddenly very foolish. 'I wasn't thinking, I guess,' he confessed.

'I didn't think you were. Get rid of that horse.'

Garion slid down and slapped Chretienne sharply on the rump. The big gray bolted back toward where the others were still concealed. 'What on earth was she thinking of?' Garion fumed.

'I'm not sure if she was,' Belgarath grunted. 'She's been acting strangely for the past few days. Let's get on with this. The quicker we find her, the quicker we can get her back to the others. Your aunt can get to the bottom of this.' The old man was already blurring into the shape of the huge silver wolf. 'You lead,' he growled at Garion. 'Her scent is more familiar to you.'

Garion changed and cast back and forth until his nose caught Ce'Nedra's familiar fragrance. 'She went this way,' he cast his thought to Belgarath.

'How fresh is the trail?' the old wolf asked.

'It can't be much more than a half hour old,' Garion replied, bunching himself to run.

'Good. Let's go find her.' And the two of them ran smoothly through the woods, their noses to the ground in the manner of hunting wolves.

They found her after about a quarter of an hour. She was coming happily back through the forest, crooning softly to a bundle she was carrying tenderly in her arms.

'Don't startle her,' Belgarath warned. 'There's something very wrong here. Just go along with anything she tells you.' The two of them shimmered and changed.

Ce'Nedra gave a little cry of delight when she saw them. 'Oh, Garion!' she exclaimed, running toward them. 'Look! Arell found our baby!'

'Arell? But Arell's—'

'Just let it lie!' Belgarath snapped under his breath. 'Don't send her into hysterics!'

'Why – uh – that's wonderful, Ce'Nedra,' Garion said, trying to make it sound natural.

'It's been so long,' Ce'Nedra said, her eyes brimming with tears, 'and he looks just the same as he did before. Look, Garion. Isn't he beautiful?'

She turned back the blanket, and Garion saw that what she was holding so tenderly was not a baby, but a bundle of rags.

116

Part Two

PERIVOR

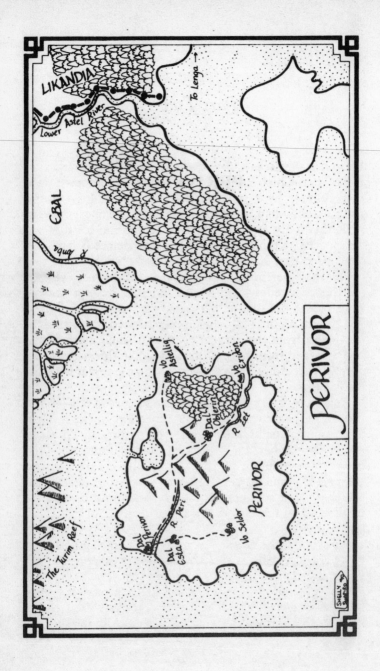

LIKANDIA

To Lenga →

Lower Astel River

CBAL

R. Camba

The Turim Reef

Vo Astellig

Dal Oberrin

Vo Enron

R. Let

Dal Perivor

R. Peri

Dal Esha

Vo Seldor

PERIVOR

PERIVOR

SHELLY SHAPIRO '90

CHAPTER NINE

Eternal Salmissra had dispensed with the services of Adiss, her Chief Eunuch, that morning. Stunned into forgetfulness by a massive dose of one of his favorite drugs, Adiss had shambled into the throne room to make his daily report. When he had come to within a dozen feet of the dais, Salmissra had detected from his rank odor that he had disobeyed her command that he never enter her presence unbathed. Cold-eyed, she had watched the eunuch prostrate himself on the marble floor before the throne to deliver his report in a slurred voice. The report had never been finished. At a sibilant command from the Serpent Queen, a small green snake had emerged from beneath the divanlike throne, purring quietly, and Adiss had received a suitable reward for his disobedience.

And now Eternal Salmissra coiled pensively on her throne, idly contemplating her reflection in the mirror. The troublesome business of selecting a new Chief Eunuch still lay before her, and she was not really in the mood for it. She decided finally to forgo the chore for a time to give the palace eunuchs the opportunity to scramble for the position. That scramble usually resulted in a number of fatalities, and there were really too many eunuchs in the palace anyway.

From under the throne there was an irritated grumbling. Her pet green snake was obviously distressed about something. 'What is it, Ezahh?' she asked him.

'Can't you have them washed before you ask me to bite them, Salmissra?' Ezahh replied plaintively. 'You might have at least warned me what to expect.' Although Ezahh and Salmissra were of different species, their languages were to some degree compatible.

'I'm sorry, Ezahh. It was inconsiderate of me, I suppose.' In rather sharp contrast to her dealings with humans, whom she held more or less in general contempt, the Serpent Queen was unfailingly polite to other reptiles – particularly the venomous ones. This is considered the course of wisdom in the world of snakes.

'It was not entirely your fault, Salmissra.' Ezahh was also a snake, and he was also very polite. 'I just wish there was some way to get the taste out of my mouth.'

'I could send for a saucer of milk. That might help.'

'Thank you, Salmissra, but the taste of him might curdle it. What I'd really like is a nice fat mouse – alive, preferably.'

'I'll see to it at once, Ezahh.' She turned her triangular face around on her slender neck. 'You,' she hissed to one of the chorus of eunuchs kneeling in adoration at one side of the throne, 'go catch a mouse. My little green friend is hungry.'

'At once, Divine Salmissra,' the eunuch replied obsequiously. He jumped to his feet and backed toward the door, genuflecting at every other step.

'Thank you, Salmissra,' Ezahh purred. 'Humans are such trivial things, aren't they?'

'They respond only to fear,' she agreed, 'and to lust.'

'That raises a point,' Ezahh noted. 'Have you had time to consider the request I made the other day?'

'I have some people looking,' she assured him, 'but your species is very rare, you know, and finding a female for you might take some time.'

'I can wait, if necessary, Salmissra,' he purred. 'We are all very patient.' He paused. 'I'm not trying to be offensive, but if you hadn't chased Sadi away, you wouldn't have to take the trouble. His little snake and I were on very good terms.'

'I noticed that on occasion. You might even be a father by now.'

The green snake slid his head out from under the throne and regarded her. Like all snakes of his kind, he had a bright red stripe down his green back. 'What's a father?' he asked in a dull, incurious tone.

'It's a difficult concept,' she replied. 'Humans make much of it for some reason.'

'Does any real creature care about the perverse peculiarities of humans?'

'I certainly don't – at least not any more.'

'You were always a serpent at heart, Salmissra.'

'Why, thank you, Ezahh,' she said in a pleased hiss. She paused, her restless coils rubbing drily against each other. 'I must select a new Chief Eunuch,' she mused. 'It's a bothersome thing.'

'Why trouble yourself? Select one at random. Humans are all alike, after all.'

'Most of them, yes. I've been attempting to locate Sadi, however. I'd like to persuade him to come back to Sthiss Tor.'

'That one is different,' Ezahh agreed. 'One might almost believe that he is somewhat akin to us.'

'He does have certain reptilian qualities, doesn't he? He's a thief and a scoundrel, but he still managed the palace better than anyone else has ever been able to. If I hadn't been moulting when he fell into disgrace, I might have forgiven him.'

'Shedding one's skin is always a trying procedure,' Ezahh agreed. 'If you don't mind a bit of advice, Salmissra, you should probably make the humans stay away from you at those times.'

'I need a few of them around me. If nothing else, it gives me someone to bite.'

'Stick to mice,' he advised. 'They taste better, and at least they can be swallowed.'

'If I can persuade Sadi to return, it may just solve both our problems,' she hissed drily. 'I'll have someone to run the palace without bothering me, and you'll get your little playmate back.'

'Interesting notion, Salmissra.' He looked around. 'Is that human you sent out to fetch my mouse raising it from infancy?' he asked.

Yarblek and Vella slipped into Yar Nadrak late one snowy evening just before the gates were closed for the night. Vella had left her lavender satin gowns at Boktor and had reverted to her traditional tight leather garb. Because it was winter, she wore in addition a sable coat which would have cost a fortune in Tol Honeth. 'Why does this place always smell so bad?' she asked her owner as they rode through snow-clogged streets toward the river front.

'Probably because Drosta let the contract for the sewer system out to one of his cousins,' Yarblek shrugged, pulling the collar of his shabby felt coat up around his neck. 'The citizens paid a great deal in taxes for the system, but Drosta's cousin turned out to be a better embezzler than he was an engineer. I think it runs in the family. Drosta even embezzles from his own treasury.'

'Isn't that sort of absurd?'

'We have an absurd sort of king, Vella.'

'I thought the palace was over that way.' She pointed toward the center of town.

'Drosta won't be in the palace at this time of night,' Yarblek told her. 'He gets lonesome when the sun goes down, and he usually goes out looking for companionship.'

'He could be anywhere, then.'

'I doubt it. There are only a few places in Yar Nadrak where he's welcome after dark. Our king isn't widely loved.' Yarblek pointed up a littered alley. 'Let's go this way. We'll stop by the office of our factor and get you some suitable clothing.'

'What's wrong with what I'm wearing?'

'Sable attracts attention in the part of town we're going to visit, Vella, and we're trying to be inconspicuous.'

The office in Yar Nadrak of Silk and Yarblek's far-flung commercial empire was in a loft over a cavernous warehouse filled with bales of furs and deep-piled Mallorean

122

carpets. The factor was a squinty-eyed Nadrak named Zelmit, who was probably almost as untrustworthy as he looked. Vella had never really liked him and she customarily loosened her daggers in their sheaths whenever she came into his presence, making very sure that he saw her doing so to be certain that there would be no misunderstandings. Technically, of course, Vella was one of Yarblek's possessions, and Zelmit had a reputation for making rather free with things which belonged to his employer.

'How's business?' Yarblek asked as he and Vella entered the cluttered little office.

'We're getting by,' Zelmit said in a rasping voice.

'Specifics, Zelmit,' Yarblek said brusquely. 'Generalities make my teeth itch.'

'We've found a way to bypass Boktor and evade Drasnian customs.'

'That's useful.'

'It takes a bit longer, but we can get our furs to Tol Honeth without paying Drasnian duties. Our profits in the fur market are up by sixty percent.'

Yarblek beamed. 'If Silk ever comes back through here, I don't think you really need to tell him about it,' he cautioned. 'Sometimes he breaks out in a rash of patriotism, and Porenn *is* his aunt, after all.'

'I wasn't really thinking of telling him. We still have to carry the Mallorean carpets through Drasnia, though. The best market for those is still the great fair in central Arendia, and we can't pay anybody enough to get him to freight them across Ulgoland.' He frowned. 'Someone's cutting the prices on us, though. Until we can find out what's going on, it might not be a bad idea to curtail our imports.'

'Did you manage to sell off those gemstones I brought back from Mallorea?'

'Naturally. We smuggled them out and sold them here and there on our way south.'

'Good. It always depresses the market when you show

up in one place with a bushel basket full of them. Do you know if Drosta's in the usual place tonight?'

Zelmit nodded. 'He went there just before sundown.'

'Vella's going to need a sort of nondescript cloak,' Yarblek said then.

Zelmit squinted at the girl.

Vella opened her fur coat and put her hands on the hilts of her daggers. 'Why don't you go ahead and try it now, Zelmit?' she said. 'Let's get it over with.'

'I wasn't really planning anything, Vella,' he said innocently. 'I was just sizing you up, that's all.'

'I noticed,' she said drily. 'Did that cut on your shoulder ever heal?'

'It aches a little in damp weather,' he complained.

'You should have kept your hands to yourself.'

'I think I've got an old cloak that'll fit you. It's a little shabby, though.'

'So much the better,' Yarblek said. 'We're going to the One-Eyed Dog and we'd like to sort of blend in.'

Vella removed her sable and laid it across a chair. 'Don't lose track of this, Zelmit,' she warned. 'I'm fond of it, and I'm sure we'd both hate what would happen if it accidentally wound up on a caravan bound for Tol Honeth.'

'You don't have to threaten him, Vella,' Yarblek said mildly.

'That wasn't a threat, Yarblek,' she retorted. 'I just wanted to be sure that Zelmit and I understood each other.'

'I'll get that cloak,' Zelmit offered.

'Do that,' she said.

The cloak was not so much shabby as it was tattered, and it smelled as if it had never been washed. Vella pulled it on over her shoulders with some reluctance.

'Put the hood up,' Yarblek told her.

'I'll have to wash my hair if I do.'

'So?'

'Do you know how long it takes hair like mine to dry in the wintertime?'

'Just do it, Vella. Why do you always argue with me?'

'It's a matter of principle.'

He sighed mournfully. 'Take care of our horses,' he told Zelmit. 'We'll walk the rest of the way.' And then he led Vella out of the office. When they reached the street, he took a length of clinking chain with a leather collar on one end out of a side pocket of his overcoat. 'Put this on,' he told her.

'I haven't worn a chain or collar in years,' she said.

'It's for your own protection, Vella,' he said wearily. 'We're going into a very rough part of town, and the One-Eyed Dog is the roughest place down there. If you're chained, nobody will bother you – unless he wants to fight with me. If you're loose, some of the men in the tavern might misunderstand.'

'That's what my daggers are for, Yarblek.'

'Please, Vella. Oddly enough, I sort of like you, and I don't want you getting hurt.'

'Affection, Yarblek?' she laughed. 'I thought the only thing you really liked was money.'

'I'm not a *complete* scoundrel, Vella.'

'You'll do until the real thing comes along,' she said, fastening the collar around her neck. 'As a matter of fact, I sort of like you, too.'

His eyes widened, and he grinned.

'Not *that* much, though,' she added.

The One-Eyed Dog was perhaps the foulest tavern Vella had ever entered, and Vella had been in a large number of low dives and shabby taverns in her life. Since the age of twelve, she had always relied on her daggers to ward off unwanted attentions. Although she had seldom been obliged to kill anyone – except for a few enthusiasts – she had nonetheless established a reputation for being a girl no sensible man would attempt. Sometimes that rankled a bit, though, since there were times when Vella might have welcomed an attempt. A nick or two in some unimportant places upon an ardent admirer would sustain her honor, and then – well, who knows?

'Don't drink any of the beer here,' Yarblek cautioned as they entered. 'The vat is open, and there are usually a few drowned rats floating around in it.' He wrapped her chain around his hand.

Vella looked around. 'This is really a revolting place, Yarblek,' she told him.

'You've been spending too much time with Porenn,' he said. 'You're starting to get delicate.'

'How would you like to have me gut you?' she offered.

'That's my girl,' he grinned. 'Let's go upstairs.'

'What's up there?'

'The girls. Drosta doesn't come here for rat-flavored beer.'

'That's disgusting, you know?'

'You've never met Drosta, have you? Disgusting only begins to describe him. He even turns *my* stomach.'

'Are you planning to just walk in on him? Aren't you going to snoop around a bit first?'

'You've been in Drasnia too long,' he replied as they started up the steps. 'Drosta and I know each other. He knows better than to try to lie to me. I'll get to the bottom of this right away, and then we can get out of this stinking town.'

'I think you're starting to get delicate as well.'

There was a door at the end of the hall, and the pair of Nadrak soldiers standing at either side of it proclaimed by their presence that King Drosta lek Thun was inside.

'How many so far?' Yarblek asked them as he and Vella stopped in front of the door.

'Three, isn't it?' one of the soldiers asked the other.

'I lost count,' the other soldier shrugged. 'They all look the same to me. Three or four. I forget.'

'Is he busy right now?' Yarblek asked.

'He's resting.'

'He must be getting old. He never used to have to rest

126

after only three. Do you want to tell him I'm here? I've got a business proposition for him.' Yarblek suggestively shook Vella's chain.

One of the soldiers eyed Vella up and down. 'She might be able to wake him up at that,' he leered.

'And I can put him back to sleep just as fast,' Vella said, opening her shabby cloak to reveal her daggers.

'You're one of those wild women from up in the forest, aren't you?' the other soldier asked. 'We really shouldn't let you in there with him with those daggers.'

'Would you like to try to take them away from me?'

'Not me, girl,' he replied prudently.

'Good. Resharpening a dagger is very tedious, and I've been hitting bone a great deal lately.'

The other soldier opened the door. 'It's that Yarblek fellow again, your Majesty,' he said. 'He's got a girl he wants to sell you.'

'I just bought three,' a shrill voice replied with an obscene giggle.

'Not like *this* one, your Majesty.'

'It's so nice to be appreciated,' Vella murmured.

The solder grinned at her.

'Yarblek, get in here!' King Drosta's high-pitched voice commanded.

'Right away, your Majesty. Come along, Vella.' Yarblek tugged on her chain and led her into the room.

Drosta lek Thun, King of Gar og Nadrak, lay half-dressed on a rumpled bed. He was by far the ugliest man Vella had ever seen. Even the hunchbacked dwarf Beldin was handsome by comparison. He was scrawny and had bulging eyes. His face was pockmarked, and his beard scraggly. 'You idiot!' he snapped at Yarblek. 'Yar Nadrak is overrun with Mallorean agents. They know that you're Prince Kheldar's partner and that you practically live in Porenn's palace.'

'Nobody saw me, Drosta,' Yarblek said, 'and even if they did, I've got a perfectly legitimate reason to be here.' He shook Vella's chain.

'Do you really want to sell her?' Drosta said, eyeing the girl.

'Hardly, but we can tell anybody curious about it that we couldn't agree on a price.'

'Why are you really here, then?'

'Porenn's a little curious about your activities. Javelin's got some spies in your palace, but you're sneaky enough to hide what you're doing from them. I thought I'd save some time and come right to the source.'

'What makes you think I've been up to something?'

'You usually are.'

Drosta laughed shrilly. 'That's true, I suppose, but why should I tell you?'

'Because if you don't, I'll set up camp in the palace, and the Malloreans will think you're crossing them.'

'That's blackmail, Yarblek,' Drosta accused.

'Some people call it that, yes.'

Drosta sighed. 'All right, Yarblek,' he said, 'but this is for Porenn's ears only, and I don't want you and Silk taking advantage of it. I've been trying to mend my fences with Zakath. He was very angry when I switched sides at Thull Mardu. It's only a question of time until he subdues all of Cthol Murgos, and I don't want him to get the idea of coming north looking for me. I've been negotiating with Brador, the chief of his bureau of internal affairs, and we've almost reached an accommodation. I get to keep my skin if I allow Brador's agents to pass through Gar og Nadrak to infiltrate the west. Zakath's pragmatic enough to forgo the pleasure of having me skinned alive if I'm useful to him.'

Yarblek looked at him sceptically. 'All right, Drosta, what else? That's hardly enough to keep Zakath from peeling you like an apple.'

'Sometimes you're too smart for your own good, Yarblek.'

'Give, Drosta. I don't want to have to spend the next month here in Yar Nadrak being conspicuous.'

Drosta gave up. 'I've cut the import duties on Mallorean

carpets. Zakath needs tax revenue to continue the war in Cthol Murgos. If I cut those duties, Mallorean merchants can undersell you and Silk in the market places to the west. The whole plan is to make myself so indispensable to his Imperial Majesty that he'll leave me alone.'

'I was wondering why our profits in carpets have been falling off,' Yarblek mused. 'That's all?' he asked.

'I swear it is, Yarblek.'

'Your oaths tend to be a little worthless, my King.'

Drosta had been looking at Vella appreciatively. 'Are you absolutely positive you don't want to sell this girl?' he asked.

'You couldn't really afford me, Your Majesty,' Vella told him, 'and sooner or later your appetite would get the better of you. I'd have to take steps at that point.'

'You wouldn't actually draw a knife on your own king, would you?'

'Try me.'

'Oh, one other thing, Drosta,' Yarblek added. 'From now on, Silk and I will be paying the same import duties you're charging the Malloreans.'

Drosta's eyes bulged even more. 'That's out of the question!' he almost screamed. 'What if Brador found out about it?'

'We'll just have to make sure he doesn't, then, won't we? That's my price for keeping my mouth shut. If you *don't* cut those fees, I'll just have to let it be known that you *have*. You'll stop being so indispensible to Zakath at that point, won't you?'

'You're robbing me, Yarblek.'

'Business is business, Drosta,' Yarblek said blandly.

King Anheg of Cherek had journeyed to Tol Honeth to confer with Emperor Varana. When he had been admitted to the imperial apartments, he got right to the point. 'We've got a problem, Varana,' he said.

'Oh?'

'You know my cousin, the Earl of Trellheim?'

'Barak? Of course.'

'He hasn't been seen for quite some time. He's off with that oversized ship of his and he's got some friends with him.'

'It's a free ocean, I suppose. Who are these friends?'

'Cho-Hag's son Hettar, that Mimbrate Mandorallen, and Lelldorin the Asturian. He also has his own son Unrak along and the Ulgo fanatic Relg.'

Varana frowned. 'That's a dangerous group,' he noted.

'I couldn't agree more. It's sort of like a natural disaster looking for a place to happen.'

'Any ideas about what they're doing?'

'If I knew which way they're going, I could make a few guesses.'

There was a polite tap on the door. 'There's a Cherek out here, your Imperial Majesty,' one of the guards outside the door announced. 'He's a sailor, I think, and he says he needs to talk with King Anheg.'

'Send him in,' the emperor instructed.

It was Greldrik, and he was slightly drunk. 'I think I've solved your problem, Anheg. After I dropped you off on that pier, I wandered around on the docks for a while to see what kind of information I could pick up.'

'In taverns, I see.'

'You don't find sailors in tea-rooms. Anyway, I came across the captain of a Tolnedran merchantman. He'd picked up a cargo of Mallorean goods, and he was coming south across the Sea of the East toward the southern end of Cthol Murgos.'

'That's very interesting, but I don't quite see the point.'

'He saw a ship, and when I described *Seabird* to him, he agreed that it had been the ship he saw.'

'That's a start, anyway. Where's Barak going?'

'Where else? Mallorea, of course.'

After about a week's voyage, the *Seabird* made port at Dal Zerba on the southwest coast of the Mallorean continent. Barak asked a few questions and then led his friends to the offices of Silk's factor in the port city.

The factor was a very thin man, not so much under-nourished as he was emaciated.

'We're trying to locate Prince Kheldar,' Barak rumbled to him. 'It's a matter of some urgency, and we'd appreciate any information you might be able to give us as to his whereabouts.'

The factor frowned. 'The last I heard was that he was in Melcene on the other side of the continent, but that was over a month ago, and Prince Kheldar moves around a great deal.'

'That's Silk, all right,' Hettar murmured.

'Do you have any guesses about where he might have gone from Melcene?' Barak asked.

'This office is fairly new,' the factor said, 'and I'm sort of at the tail-end of the route of any couriers.' He made a sour face. 'The factor up at Dal Finda was a bit put out when Kheldar and Yarblek set up this office. I guess he felt that I might be in competition with him. Sometimes he forgets to pass things on to me. His office has been well-established for some time, so the couriers always stop there. If anybody in this part of Dalasia knows anything about Kheldar's location, he would.'

'All right. Where's Dal Finda, then?'

'Upriver about forty leagues.'

'Thanks for the help, friend. Do you happen to have a map of this part of Mallorea?'

'I believe I could find one for you, yes.'

'I'd appreciate it. We're not familiar with this part of the world.'

'So we go upriver?' Hettar said when Silk's factor was out of the room looking for the map.

'If it's the only place where we can find out where Garion and the others are, we'll have to,' Barak replied.

The current in the Finda River was sluggish, and the oarsmen made good time as they rowed upstream. They reached the river town late the following day and went immediately to Silk's offices there.

The factor here was almost the reverse of the man in Dal Zerba. He was bulky more than fat and he had huge meaty hands and a florid face. He was not particularly co-operative. 'How do I know you're the prince's friends?' he demanded suspiciously. 'I'm not going to reveal his location to complete strangers.'

'Are you trying to be difficult?' Barak asked.

The factor looked at the big red-bearded man and swallowed hard. 'No, but sometimes the prince wants his whereabouts kept secret.'

'Probably when he's planning to steal something,' Hettar added.

'Steal?' the factor objected in a shocked voice. 'The prince is a respectable business man.'

'He's also a liar, a cheat, a thief, and a spy,' Hettar told him. 'Now, where is he? We'd heard that he'd been in Melcene a while back. Where did he go from there?'

'Can you describe him?' the factor countered.

'Short,' Hettar replied, 'sort of thin. He's got a face like a rat and a long, pointed nose. He's got a clever mouth and he thinks he's funny.'

'That's a fair description of Prince Kheldar,' the factor conceded.

'We have heard that our friend standeth in a certain amount of danger,' Mandorallen said. 'We have sailed many leagues to offer our assistance.'

'I was sort of wondering why most of you were wearing armor. Oh, all right. The last I heard was that he was bound for a place called Kell.'

'Show me,' Barak said, unfolding his map.

'It's over here,' the factor said.

'Is that river navigable?'

'As far north as Balasa.'

'Good. We can sail around the southern end of the continent and go up that river. How far back from the main channel is this Kell place?'

132

'A league or so from the east bank. It's at the foot of a very big mountain. I'd be careful, though. Kell's got a very peculiar reputation. The seers live there, and they don't particularly welcome strangers.'

'We'll have to chance it,' Barak said. 'Thanks for your help, friend. We'll give Kheldar your regards when we catch up with him.'

They set out downriver the following morning. There was enough of a breeze so that the sails were able to aid the oarsmen, and they made excellent time. It was shortly before noon when they heard a number of cracking detonations coming from somewhere just ahead.

'Methinks we will encounter a storm 'ere long.' Mandorallen said.

Barak frowned. 'The sky's perfectly clear, Mandorallen,' he disagreed, 'and that doesn't sound exactly right for thunder.' He raised his voice. 'Ship oars and lower the sail,' he commanded his sailors, swinging his tiller over sharply so that *Seabird* coasted to the bank.

Hettar, Relg, and Lelldorin came up from below. 'Why are we stopping?' Hettar asked.

'There's something peculiar going on just up ahead,' Barak replied. 'I think we'd better go have a look before we blunder into anything.'

'You want me to get the horses?'

'I don't think so. It's not very far, and men on horseback are kind of conspicuous.'

'You're starting to sound like Silk.'

'We've been together for quite a while. Unrak!' he shouted to his son, who had been riding in the bow. 'We're going to go see what that noise is all about. You're in charge here until we get back.'

'But, father!' the red-haired boy protested.

'That's an order, Unrak!' Barak thundered.

'Yes, sir.' Unrak sounded slightly sullen.

The *Seabird* swung slowly around in the current and bumped gently against the brush-covered river bank.

Barak and the others jumped from the rail to the bank and started cautiously inland.

There were more of those strange detonations that did not sound exactly like thunder.

'Whatever it is, it's coming from just up ahead,' Hettar said quietly.

'Let's stay out of sight until we find out what's going on,' Barak said. 'We've heard that kind of sound before – at Rak Cthol when Belgarath and Ctuchik were fighting.'

'Sorcerers, thinkest thou?' Mandorallen suggested.

'I'm not positive, but I'm beginning to have some strong suspicions in that direction. I think we'd better stay under cover until we can see just who or what is out there.'

They crept to the edge of a clump of scrubby trees and looked out at an open field.

A number of black-robed figures lay smoking on the turf. Others huddled fearfully near the edge of the field.

'Murgos?' Hettar sounded startled.

'Methinks not, my Lord,' Mandorallen said. 'If thou wilt look closely, thou wilt see that the hoods of their cloaks are lined in diverse colors. Those colors do indicate rank among the Grolims. Thou wert wise, my Lord of Trellheim, to advise caution.'

'What's making them smoke like that?' Lelldorin whispered, nervously fingering his bow.

As if in answer to his question, a black-robed and hooded figure rose at the top of a knoll and gestured almost contemptuously. A bell of incandescent fire seemed to leap from the figure's hand, sizzled across the open field, and struck one of the frightened Grolims full in the chest with another of those cracking detonations. The Grolim shrieked and, clutching at his chest, fell to the earth.

'I guess that explains the noise,' Relg observed.

'Barak,' Hettar said quietly, 'that one on top of the knoll is a woman.'

'Are you sure?'

'I've got very good eyes, Barak, and I can tell the difference between a man and a woman.'

'So can I, but not when they're all wrapped up in cloaks like that.'

'Look at her elbows the next time she raises her arms. Women's elbows are hinged differently from ours. Adara says it has to do with carrying babies.'

'Did you fear to come alone, Agachak?' the woman atop the little hill demanded with contempt. Then she flicked another fireball, and another Grolim crumpled to the ground.

'I fear nothing, Zandramas,' a hollow voice came from the trees at the edge of the field.

'Now we know who they are,' Hettar said. 'But why are they fighting?'

'Zandramas is a woman?' Lelldorin asked in amazement.

Hettar nodded. 'Queen Porenn found out about it some time back. She sent word to the Alorn kings, and Cho-Hag told me.'

Zandramas almost casually felled the three remaining Grolims. 'Well, Agachak,' she said then, 'will you come out of hiding now? Or must I come and find you?'

A tall, cadaverous-looking Grolim stepped out of the trees. 'Your fire will have no effect on me, Zandramas,' he said, advancing toward the hooded woman.

'I wasn't thinking of fire, Agachak,' she almost purred. '*This* will be your fate.' She suddenly seemed to blur and shimmer, and then standing in the place she had occupied was an enormous, hideous beast. It had a long, snake like neck and huge bat wings.

'Belar!' Barak swore. 'She just turned into a dragon!'

The dragon spread her wings and flapped into the air. The cadaverous Grolim shrank back, then raised both arms. There was a shocking sound, and the dragon was suddenly encased in a sheet of green fire. The voice that came thundering from the dragon's mouth was still the voice of Zandramas. 'You should have paid more attention to your studies, Agachak. If you had, you'd know that Torak made dragons immune to sorcery.' The dragon hovered over the now-terrified Grolim. 'Incidentally, Agachak,' she said, 'you'll be happy to know that Urvon is dead. Give him my regards when you see him.' And then she struck, sinking her talons into Agachak's chest. He shrieked once before a sudden billow of sooty fire burst from the dragon's mouth and engulfed his face. And then the dragon bit his head off.

Lelldorin made a retching sound. 'Great Chamdar!' he gasped in a revolted voice. 'She's eating him!'

There was a horrid crunching sound as the dragon continued her ghastly feast. Then at last with a shrill scream of triumph, she spread her huge wings and flew off to the east.

'Is it safe to come out now?' a shaking voice asked from nearby.

'You'd better,' Barak said ominously, drawing his sword.

It was a Thull. He was young, with muddy-colored hair and a slack-lipped mouth.

'What's a Thull doing in Mallorea?' Lelldorin asked the stranger.

'Agachak brought me,' the Thull replied, trembling violently.

'What's your name?' Relg asked him.

'I'm Nathel, King of Mishrak ac Thull. Agachak said he'd make me Overking of Angarak if I'd help him with something he had to do here. Please, don't leave me alone.' Tears were streaming down his face.

Barak looked at his companions. They all had expressions of pity on their faces. 'Oh, all right,' he said grudgingly. 'Come along, I guess.'

CHAPTER TEN

'What's the matter with her, Aunt Pol?' Garion was looking at Ce'Nedra, who sat crooning over her blanket-wrapped bundle of rags.

'That's what I need to find out,' Polgara said. 'Sadi, I need some Oret.'

'Is that really wise, Lady Polgara?' the eunuch asked. 'In her present condition—' He spread his thin-fingered hands suggestively.

'If there's any danger, Aunt Pol—' Garion began.

'Oret is relatively harmless,' she cut him off. 'It stimulates the heart a bit, but Ce'Nedra's heart is strong. I can hear it beating half a continent away. We need to know what happened right now, and Oret is the fastest way.'

Sadi had opened his red leather case and he handed Polgara one of his little vials. She judiciously tapped three drops of the yellow liquid into a cup and then filled the cup with water. 'Ce'Nedra, dear,' she said to the little queen, 'you must be thirsty. This might help.' She handed the cup to the red-haired girl.

'Why, thank you, Lady Polgara.' Ce'Nedra drank deeply. 'As a matter of fact, I was just about to ask someone for a drink of water.'

'Very smooth, Pol,' Beldin whispered.

'Rudimentary, uncle.'

'Do you have any idea of what they're talking about?' Zakath asked Garion.

'Aunt Pol implanted the notion of thirst into Ce 'Nedra's mind.'

'You people can actually do that?'

'As she said, it's rudimentary.'

'Can *you* do it?'

137

'I don't know. I've never tried.' Garion's attention was, however, firmly fixed on his blissfully smiling little wife.

Polgara calmly waited.

'I think you can begin now, Lady Polgara,' Sadi said after a few minutes.

'Sadi,' she said absently, 'we know each other well enough by now to skip the formalities. I'm not going to choke over "your Excellency," so why should you strangle on "my Lady"?'

'Why, thank you, Polgara.'

'Now, Ce 'Nedra,' Polgara said.

'Yes, Aunt Pol?' the tiny queen said, her eyes slightly unfocused.

'There's a first,' Silk said to Beldin.

'She's been living with Garion for quite a while now,' the dwarf replied. 'Things do rub off after a bit.'

'I wonder what Polgara'd do if *I* called her by that name?'

'I don't recommend experimentation,' Beldin told him. 'It's up to you, though, and you'd make a very interesting-looking radish.'

'Ce'Nedra,' Polgara said, 'why don't you tell me exactly how you got you baby back?'

'Arell found him for me,' Ce'Nedra smiled. 'Now I have even more reason to love Arell.'

'We all love Arell.'

'Isn't he beautiful?' Ce'Nedra turned back the blanket to reveal her rags.

'He's lovely, dear. Did you and Arell have a chance to talk at all?'

'Oh, yes, Aunt Pol. She's doing something that's very important. That's why she couldn't join us just now. She said she might be able to catch up with us at Perivor – or maybe later at Korim.'

'Then she knew where we're going?'

'Oh, no, Aunt Pol,' Ce'Nedra laughed. 'I had to tell her. She does *so* want to be with us, but she has this important thing to do. She asked me where we were going, and I told her about Perivor and Korim. She seemed a little surprised about Korim, though.'

Aunt Pol's eyes narrowed. 'I see,' she said. 'Durnik, why don't you set up a tent? I think Ce'Nedra and her baby should get a little rest.'

'Right away, Pol,' her husband agreed after a quick look at her.

'Now that you mention it, Aunt Pol,' Ce'Nedra said happily, 'I *do* feel a little tired, and I'm sure Geran needs a nap. Babies sleep so much, you know. I'll nurse him, and then he'll sleep. He always sleeps after he nurses.'

'Steady,' Zakath said quietly to Garion as the Rivan King's eyes filled with tears. The Mallorean Emperor put his hand firmly on his friend's shoulder.

'What's going to happen when she wakes up, though?'

'Polgara can fix it.'

After Durnik had set up the tent, Polgara led the bemused girl inside. After a moment, Garion felt a slight surge and heard a whisper of sound. Then his aunt came out of the tent carrying Ce'Nedra's bundle. 'Get rid of this,' she said, pushing it into Garion's hands.

'Is she going to be all right?' he asked her.

'She's asleep now. She'll wake up in about an hour and, when she does, she won't remember that any of this happened. None of us will mention it to her, and that will be the end of it.'

Garion took the bundle back into the woods and hid it under a bush. When he returned, he approached Cyradis. 'It was Zandramas, wasn't it?' he demanded.

'Yes,' Cyradis replied simply.

'And you knew it was going to happen, didn't you?'

'Yes.'

'Why didn't you warn us?'

'To have done so would have been an interference in an event which had to occur.'

'That was cruel, Cyradis.'

'Necessary events sometimes are. I tell thee, Belgarion, Zandramas could not go to Kell as thou didst. Therefore, she had to find the location of the meeting from one of thy companions, else she would not be at the Place Which Is No More at the proper time.'

'Why Ce'Nedra?'

'Zandramas, thou wilt recall, hath imposed her will upon thy queen in times past. It is not difficult for her to reimpose that bond.'

'I'm not going to forgive this, Cyradis.'

'Garion,' Zakath said, 'let it go. Ce'Nedra hasn't been hurt, and Cyradis was only doing what she had to do.' The Mallorean seemed peculiarly defensive.

Garion turned and stalked away, his face livid with anger.

When Ce'Nedra awoke, she appeared to have no memory of the meeting in the woods and seemed to have returned to normal. Durnik struck the tent, and they rode on.

They reached the edge of the forest about sunset and set up for the night there. Garion rather studiously avoided Zakath, not trusting himself to be civil to his friend after he had jumped to the defense of the blindfolded Seeress. Zakath and Cyradis had engaged in a lengthy conversation before they had all left Kell, and now the emperor seemed wholly committed to her cause. His eyes were sometimes troubled, though, and he frequently turned in his saddle to look at her.

That night, however, when they were both on watch, it was no longer possible for Garion to avoid his friend.

'Are you still angry with me, Garion?' Zakath asked.

Garion sighed. 'No, I guess not,' he said. 'I don't think I was really angry – just a little irritated, is all. Most of all, I'm angry with Zandramas, not with you and Cyradis. I don't like people who play tricks on my wife.'

'It really had to happen, you know. Zandramas had to find out where the meeting's going to take place. She has to be there, too.'

'You're probably right. Did Cyradis give you any details about your task?'

'A few. I'm not supposed to talk about it, though. About all I can tell you is that somebody very important is coming, and I'm supposed to help him.'

'And that's going to take you the rest of your life?'

'And probably the lives of a lot of others, as well.'

'Mine, too?'

'I don't think so. I think your task will be over after the meeting. Cyradis sort of implied that you've done enough already.'

They set out early that morning and rode out onto a rolling plain along the west side of the Balasa River. There were farm villages here and there, villages which looked rude, but in which the houses were really very well-constructed. The Dalasian villagers labored in the fields with the simplest of tools.

'And it's all subterfuge,' Zakath said wryly. 'These people are probably far more sophisticated than even the Melcenes, and they've gone to a great deal of trouble to hide the fact.'

'Would thy people or the priests of Torak have left them unmolested had the truth been known?' Cyradis asked him.

'Probably not,' he admitted. 'The Melcenes in particular would likely have pressed most of the Dals into service in the bureaucracy.'

'That would not have been compatible with our tasks.'

'I understand that now. When I get back to Mal Zeth, I think I'll make some changes in imperial policy toward the Dalasian Protectorates. Your people are doing something much, much more important than raising beets and turnips for the rest of Mallorea.'

'If all goes well, our work will be done once the meeting hath taken place, Emperor Zakath.'

'But your studies will continue, won't they?'

She smiled. 'Inevitably. The habits of eons die very hard.'

Belgarath pulled his horse in beside Cyradis. 'Could you be a bit more specific about what we're supposed to be looking for when we get to Perivor?' he asked her.

'It is as I told thee at Kell, Ancient Belgarath. At Perivor thou must seek out the map which will guide thee to the Place Which Is No More.'

'How is it that the people of Perivor know more about it than the rest of the world?'

She did not reply.

'I gather that this is another one of those things you're not going to tell me.'

'I may not at this time, Belgarath.'

Beldin came soaring in. 'You'd better get ready,' he said. 'There's a patrol of Darshivan soldiers just ahead.'

'How many?' Garion asked quickly.

'A dozen or so. They've got a Grolim with them. I didn't want to get too close, but I think it's white-eyes. They're hiding in ambush in a grove of trees in the next valley.'

'How would he know we're coming this way?' Velvet asked in perplexity.

'Zandramas knows that we're going to Perivor,' Polgara replied. 'This is the shortest route.'

'A dozen Darshivans don't really pose much of a threat,' Zakath said confidently. 'What's the purpose of this, then?'

'Delay,' Belgarath told him. 'Zandramas wants to hold us up so that she can get to Perivor before we do. She can communicate with Naradas over long distances. We can probably expect him to set traps for us every few miles all the way to Lengha.'

Zakath scratched at his short beard, frowning in concentration. Then he opened one of his saddle bags, took out a map, and consulted it. 'We're still about fifteen leagues from Lengha,' he said. He squinted at Beldin. 'How fast could you cover that distance?'

'A couple hours. Why?'

'There's an imperial garrison there. I'll give you a message to the garrison commander with my seal on it. He'll move out with troops and spring those traps from behind. As soon as we join those forces, Naradas won't be bothering us any more.' Then he remembered something. 'Holy Seeress,' he said to Cyradis, 'back in Darshiva, you told me to leave my troops behind when I came to Kell. Is that prohibition still in effect?'

'Nay, Kal Zakath.'

'Good. I'll write that message.'

'What about the patrol hiding just ahead?' Silk asked Garion. 'Or are we just going to wait here until Zakath's troops arrive?'

'I don't think so. What's your feeling about a little exercise?'

Silk's answering grin was vicious.

'There's still a problem, though,' Velvet said. 'With Beldin on his way to Lengha, we won't have anyone to scout out any other ambushes.'

'Tell the she with yellow hair not to be concerned,' the wolf said to Garion. 'One is able to move without being seen, or if one is seen, the man-things will pay no heed.'

'It's all right, Liselle,' Garion said. 'The wolf will scout for us.'

'She's a very useful person to have along,' Velvet smiled.

'Person?' Silk said.

'Well, isn't she?'

He frowned. 'You know, you might be right at that. She has a definite personality, doesn't she?'

The wolf wagged her tail at him and then loped off.

'All right, gentlemen,' Garion said, loosening Iron-grip's sword in its sheath, 'let's go pay these lurking Darshivans a visit.'

'Won't Naradas cause some problems?' Zakath asked, handing his note to Beldin.

'I certainly hope he *tries*,' Garion replied.

Naradas, however, proved to no longer be among the Darshivan soldiers hidden in the grove of trees. The skirmish was short, since most of the ambushers seemed to be much better at running than at fighting.

143

'Amateurs,' Zakath said scornfully, wiping his sword blade on the cloak of one of the fallen.

'You're getting fairly competent with that, you know?' Garion complimented him.

'The training I was given when I was young seems to be coming back,' Zakath replied modestly.

'He handles that sword almost the same way Hettar handles his saber, doesn't he?' Silk noted, pulling one of his daggers out of a Darshivan's chest.

'Much the same,' Garion agreed, 'and Hettar got his training from Cho-Hag, the finest swordsman in Algaria.'

'Which Taur Urgas discovered the hard way,' Silk added.

'I'd have given a great deal to watch that fight,' Zakath said wistfully.

'So would I,' Garion said, 'but I was busy somewhere else at the time.'

'Sneaking up on Torak?' Zakath suggested.

'I don't think "sneaking" is the right word. He knew I was coming.'

'I'll go get the ladies and Belgarath,' Durnik said.

'Beldin spoke with me,' Belgarath told them when he rode up. 'Naradas flew out of this grove before you got here. Beldin considered killing him, but he had that parchment in his talons.'

'What form did he take?' Silk asked, 'Naradas, I mean?'

'A raven,' Belgarath said with distaste. 'Grolims are always fond of ravens for some reason.'

Silk suddenly laughed. 'Remember the time when Asharak the Murgo changed into a raven on the plain of Arendia, and Polgara called that eagle down to deal with him? It rained black feathers for almost an hour.'

'Who's Asharak the Murgo?' Zakath asked.

'He was one of Ctuchik's underlings,' Belgarath replied.

'Did the eagle kill him?'

'No,' Silk said. 'Garion did that later.'

'With his sword?'

144

'No. With his hand.'

'That must have been a mighty blow. Murgos are bulky people.'

'Actually it was only a slap,' Garion said. 'I set fire to him.' He hadn't thought of Asharak in years. Surprisingly, he found that the memory no longer bothered him.

Zakath was staring at him in horror.

'He was the one who killed my parents,' Garion told him. 'The action seemed appropriate. He burned them to death, so I did the same thing to him. Shall we ride on?'

The tireless she-wolf ranged out ahead of them, and located two more groups of ambushers before the sun went down. The survivors of the first, failed ambush had spread the word, however, and as soon as these other two groups of Darshivans saw Garion and his companions bearing down upon them, they fled in panic.

'Disappointing,' Sadi said after they had flushed out the second group. He slipped his small, poisoned dagger back into its sheath.

'I expect that Naradas is going to speak quite firmly with those fellows when he finds out that he's gone to all this trouble for nothing,' Silk added gaily. 'He'll probably sacrifice a goodly number of them just as soon as he can find an altar.'

They met the men of Zakath's imperial garrison from Lengha about noon the following day. The commander of the garrison rode forward and stared at Zakath in some amazement. 'Your Imperial Majesty,' he said, 'is that really you?'

Zakath rubbed at his black beard. 'Oh, you mean this, Colonel?' he laughed. 'It was the suggestion of that old man over there.' He pointed at Belgarath. 'We didn't want people to recognize me, and my face is stamped on every coin in Mallorea. Did you have any trouble on your way north?'

'Nothing worth mentioning, your Majesty. We encountered a dozen or so groups of Darshivan soldiers – usually hiding in clumps of trees. We encircled each clump, and they all surrendered immediately. They're very good at surrendering.'

'They run quite well, too, we've noticed,' Zakath smiled.

The colonel looked at his emperor a bit hesitantly. 'I hope you won't be offended at my saying this, your Majesty, but you seem to have changed since the last time I was in Mal Zeth.'

'Oh?'

'I've never seen you under arms, for one thing.'

'Troubled times, Colonel. Troubled times.'

'And if you'll forgive my saying so, your Majesty, I've never heard you laugh before – or even seen you smile.'

'I've had little reason before, Colonel. Shall we go on to Lengha?'

When they arrived in Lengha, Cyradis, with Toth's assistance, led them directly to the harbor, where a strangely configured ship awaited them.

'Thank you, Colonel,' Zakath said to the garrison commander. 'Providing this ship was most considerate of you.'

'Excuse me, your Majesty,' the colonel replied, 'but I had nothing to do with the ship.'

Zakath gave Toth a startled look, and the big mute smiled briefly at Durnik.

Durnik frowned slightly. 'Brace yourself, Kal Zakath,' he said. 'The arrangements for the ship were made several thousand years ago.'

Belgarath's face was suddenly creased by a broad smile. 'It would seem that we're right on schedule then. I do so hate to be late for an appointment.'

'Really?' Beldin said. 'I remember one time when you showed up five years after you were supposed to.'

'Something came up.'

'Something usually does. Wasn't that during the period when you were spending your time with the girls in Maragor?'

Belgarath coughed and cast a slightly guilty look at his daughter.

Polgara raised one eyebrow but didn't say anything.

The ship was manned by the same sort of mute crew as had conveyed them from the coast of Gorut in Cthol Murgos to the Isle of Verkat. Once again Garion was struck by that haunting sense of repetition. As soon as they were on board, the crew cast off all lines and made sail.

'Peculiar,' Silk observed. 'The breeze is coming in off the sea, and we're sailing directly into it.'

'I noticed that,' Durnik agreed.

'I thought you might have. It appears that normal rules don't apply to the Dals.'

'Wilt thou, Belgarion, and thy friend Zakath accompany me to the aft cabin?' Cyradis said as they cleared the harbor.

'Of course, Holy Seeress,' Garion replied. He noticed that as the three of them moved aft, Zakath took the blindfolded girl's hand to lead her, almost unconsciously duplicating Toth's solicitude. A peculiar notion crossed the mind of the Rivan King at that point. He looked rather closely at his friend. Zakath's face was strangely gentle, and his eyes had an odd look in them. The notion was absurd, of course, but as clearly as if he had seen directly into the Mallorean Emperor's heart, Garion knew that it was absolutely true. He rather carefully concealed a smile.

In the aft cabin stood two gleaming suits of armor, looking for all the world like those of the knights at Vo Mimbre.

'These must garb you at Perivor,' Cyradis told them.

'There's a reason, I assume,' Garion said.

'Indeed. And when we approach that coast, thou must each lower thy visor and under no circumstances raise it whilst we are on the isle unless I give thee leave.'

'And you're not going to tell us what the reason is, are you?'

She smiled gently and laid one hand on his arm. 'Know only that it is needful.'

'I sort of thought she might take that position,' Garion said to Zakath. He went to the door of the cabin. 'Durnik,' he called, 'we're going to need some help down here.'

'We don't have to put it on yet, do we?' Zakath asked him.

'Have you ever worn full armor before?'

'No. I can't say that I have.'

'It takes a bit of getting used to. Even Mandorallen grunted a bit when he first put his on.'

'Mandorallen? That Mimbrate friend of yours?'

Garion nodded. 'He's Ce'Nedra's champion.'

'I thought you were.'

'I'm her husband. Different rules apply.' He looked critically at Zakath's sword, a rather light and slim-bladed weapon. 'He's going to need a bigger sword, Cyradis,' he told the Seeress.

'In that cabinet, Belgarion.'

'She thinks of everything,' Garion said wryly. He opened the cabinet. Inside, standing almost to shoulder height was a massive broadsword. He lifted it out with both hands. 'Your sword, your Majesty,' he said, extending the hilt to Zakath.

'Thank you, your Majesty,' Zakath grinned. As he took the sword, his eyes suddenly went wide. 'Torak's teeth!' he swore, almost dropping the huge weapon. 'Do people actually use these things on each other?'

'Frequently. It's a major form of entertainment in Arendia. If you think that one's heavy, you should try mine.' Then Garion remembered something. 'Wake up,' he said rather peremptorily to the Orb.

The murmur of the stone was slightly offended.

'Don't overdo this,' Garion instructed, 'but my friend's sword is just a bit heavy for him. Let's make it lighter — a little at a time.' He watched as Zakath strained to raise the sword. 'A little more,' he instructed the Orb.

The sword point came up — slowly.

148

'How's that?' Garion asked.

'A bit more, maybe,' Zakath grunted.

'Do it,' Garion said to the Orb.

'That's better,' Zakath sighed, 'but is it really safe to talk to that stone that way?'

'You have to be firm. It's like a dog or a horse sometimes – or even a woman.'

'I will not forget thy remark, King Belgarion,' Cyradis said in a crisp tone.

He grinned at her. 'I didn't expect you to, Holy Seeress,' he said mildly.

'One for your side,' Zakath said.

'You see how useful that is?' Garion laughed. 'I'll make an Alorn of you yet.'

CHAPTER ELEVEN

The ship continued to move against the wind, and when they were perhaps three leagues out from the harbor, the albatross appeared, ghosting along on motionless, seraph-like wings. It made one solitary cry, and Polgara inclined her head in response. Then it took a position just in advance of the bowsprit as if it were leading the vessel.

'Isn't that peculiar?' Velvet said. 'It's just like the one we saw on the way to the Isle of Verkat.'

'No, dear,' Polgara told her. 'He's the same one.'

'That's impossible, Lady Polgara. That was half a world away.'

'Distance has no meaning to a bird with wings like that.'

'What's he doing here?'

'He has a task of his own.'

'Oh? What's that?'

'He did not choose to tell me, and it would have been impolite of me to ask.'

Zakath had been walking up and down the deck trying to set his armor into place. 'This always *looks* so splendid, but it's really very uncomfortable, isn't it?'

'Not nearly as uncomfortable as not having it on when you really need it,' Garion told him.

'You get used to it in time, though, don't you?'

'Not appreciably, no.'

Although it was some distance to the island of Perivor, the strange ship with its silent crew made good time and landed them on a wooded coast about noon the following day.

'To be perfectly honest with you,' Silk said to Garion as they unloaded the horses, 'I'm just as happy to be off that vessel. A ship that sails against the wind and sailors who don't swear make me nervous somehow.'

'There are a great many things about this entire business that are making *me* nervous,' Garion replied.

'The only difference is that I'm just an ordinary man. You're a hero.'

'What's that got to do with it?'

'Heroes aren't allowed to be nervous.'

'Who made up that rule?'

'It's a known fact. What happened to that albatross?'

'He flew off as soon as we came in sight of land.' Garion put his visor down.

'I don't care what Polgara says about them,' Silk said with a shudder. 'I've known a lot of sailors, and I've never heard one of them with anything good to say about those birds.'

'Sailors are superstitious.'

'Garion, there's some basis in fact for all superstitions.' The little man squinted at the dark woods lining the upper end of the beach. 'Not a very inviting coast, is it? I wonder why the ship didn't put us down in some seaport?'

'I don't think anybody really knows why the Dals do anything.'

After the horses had been unloaded from the ship, Garion and the others mounted and rode up the beach into the woods. 'I think I'd better cut you and Zakath some lances,' Durnik said to Garion. 'Cyradis had some reason for putting you two in armor, and I've noticed that an armored man usually looks a little undressed without a lance.' He dismounted, took his axe, and went back among the trees. He returned a few moments later with two stout poles. 'I'll put points on them when we stop for the evening,' he promised.

'This is going to be awkward,' Zakath said, fumbling with his lance and shield.

'You do it like this,' Garion said, demonstrating. 'Buckle the shield on your left arm and hold the reins in your left hand. Then set the butt of the lance in the stirrup beside your right foot and hold it in place with your free hand.'

'Have you ever fought with a lance?'

'A few times, yes. It's fairly effective against another man wearing armor. Once you knock him off his horse, it takes him quite a while to get back on his feet again.'

Beldin, as usual, had been scouting ahead. He came drifting back, ghosting among the trees on almost motionless wings. 'You're not going to believe this,' he said to Belgarath after he had changed back into his own form.

'What's that?'

'There's a castle up ahead.'

'A what?'

'A large building. They usually have walls, moats, and drawbridges.'

'I know what a castle is, Beldin.'

'Why did you ask then? Anyway, the one ahead looks almost as if it had been transplanted directly from Arendia.'

'Do you suppose you could clarify this for us, Cyradis?' Belgarath asked the Seeress.

'It is really no mystery, Ancient Belgarath,' she replied. 'Some two thousand years ago, a group of adventurers from the west were shipwrecked on the coast of this island. Seeing that there was no way to make their ship whole again, they settled here and took wives from among the local populace. They have retained the customs and manners and even the speech of their homeland.'

'Lots of thee's and thou's?' Silk asked her.

She nodded.

'And castles?'

She nodded again.

'And the men all wear armor? The same as Garion and Zakath are wearing?'

'It is even as thou hast said, Prince Kheldar.'

He groaned.

'What's the problem, Kheldar?' Zakath asked him.

152

'We've traveled thousands of leagues only to find Mimbrates again.'

'The reports I received from the battlefield at Thull Mardu all said that they're very brave. That might explain the reputation of this island.'

'Oh, it does indeed, Zakath,' the little man told him. 'Mimbrates are the bravest people in the world – probably because they don't have brains enough to be afraid of anything. Garion's friend Mandorallen is totally convinced that he's invincible.'

'He is,' Ce'Nedra said in automatic defense of her knight. 'I saw him kill a lion once with his bare hands.'

'I've heard of his reputation,' Zakath said. 'I thought it was exaggerated.'

'Not by very much,' Garion said. 'I heard him suggest to Barak and Hettar once that the three of them attack an entire Tolnedran legion.'

'Perhaps he was joking.'

'Mimbrate knights don't know *how* to joke,' Silk told him.

'I will not sit here and listen to you people insult my knight,' Ce'Nedra said hotly.

'We're not insulting him, Ce'Nedra,' Silk told her. 'We're describing him. He's so noble he makes my hair hurt.'

'Nobility is an alien concept to a Drasnian, I suppose,' she noted.

'Not alien, Ce'Nedra. Incomprehensible.'

'Perhaps in two thousand years they've changed,' Durnik said hopefully.

'I wouldn't count on it,' Beldin grunted. 'In my experience, people who live in isolation tend to petrify.'

'I needs must warn ye all of one thing, however,' Cyradis said. 'The people of this island are a peculiar mixture. In many ways they are even as ye have described them, but their heritage is also Dal, and they are conversant with the arts of our people.'

'Oh, fine,' Silk said sardonically, 'Mimbrates who use

sorcery. That's assuming they can figure out which way to point it.'

'Cyradis,' Garion said, 'is this why Zakath and I are wearing armor?'

She nodded.

'Why didn't you just say so?'

'It was necessary for ye to find that out for yourselves.'

'Well, let's go have a look,' Belgarath said. 'We've dealt with Mimbrates before, and we've usually managed to stay out of trouble.'

They rode on through the forest in golden afternoon sunshine and, when they reached the edge of the trees, they saw the structure Beldin had reported. It stood atop a high promentory, and it had the usual battlements and fortifications.

'Formidable,' Zakath murmured.

'There's no real point in lurking here in the trees,' Belgarath told them. 'We can't get across all that open ground without being seen. Garion, you and Zakath take the lead. Men in armor are usually greeted with some courtesy.'

'Are we just going to ride up to the castle?' Silk asked.

'We might as well,' Belgarath said. 'If they still think like Mimbrates, they'll almost be obliged to offer hospitality for the night, and we need a certain amount of information anyway.'

They rode out onto an open meadow and proceeded at a walk toward the grim-looking castle. 'You'd better let me do most of the talking when we get there,' Garion said to Zakath. 'I sort of know the dialect.'

'Good idea,' Zakath agreed. 'I'd probably choke on all the thee's and thou's.'

From inside the castle a horn blew a brazen note, announcing that they had been seen, and a few minutes later a dozen gleaming knights rode out across the draw-bridge at a rolling trot. Garion moved Chretienne slightly to the front.

'Prithee, abate thy pace, Sir Knight,' the man who

appeared to be the leader of the strangers said. 'I am Sir Astellig, Baron of this place. May I ask of thee thy name and what it is that brings thee and thy companions to the gates of my keep?'

'My name I may not reveal, Sir Knight,' Garion replied. 'There are certain reasons which I will disclose unto thee in due course. My fellow knight and I are embarked with these diverse companions on a quest of gravest urgency, and we have come here in search of shelter for the night, which shall descend upon us, methinks, within the next few hours.' Garion was rather proud of the speech.

'Thou needst but ask, Sir Knight,' the baron said, 'for all true knights are compelled by honor, if not by courtesy, to offer aid and shelter to any fellow knight engaged in a quest.'

'I cannot sufficiently express our gratitude to thee, Sir Astellig. We have, as thou canst see, ladies of quality with us whom the rigors of our journey have sorely fatigued.'

'Let us proceed straightway to my keep then, Sir Knights. Attending to the well-being of ladies is the paramount duty of all men of gentle birth.' He wheeled his horse with a grand flourish and led the way up the long hill to his castle with his men close behind him.

'Elegant,' Zakath commented admiringly.

'I spent some time at Vo Mimbre,' Garion told him. 'You can pick up their speech after a while. About the only problem with it is that the sentences are so involved that you sometimes lose track of what you're saying before you get to the bottom end of it.'

Baron Astellig led the way across the drawbridge, and they all dismounted in a flagstoned courtyard. 'My servants will see thee and thy companions to suitable quarters, Sir Knight,' he said, 'where ye may all refresh yourselves. Then, an it please you, join me in the great hall and disclose unto me how I may aid thee in thy noble quest.'

'Thy courtesy is most seemly, my Lord,' Garion said. 'Be assured that my brother knight and I will join you straightaway, as soon as we have seen to the comfort of the ladies.'

They followed one of the baron's servants to comfortable quarters on the second floor of the main keep.

'I'm truly amazed at you, Garion,' Polgara said. 'I didn't think you had the faintest idea of how to speak a civilized language.'

'Thank you,' he said, 'I think.'

'Maybe you and Zakath should speak with the baron alone,' Belgarath told Garion. 'You've covered your own need for anonymity fairly well, but if the rest of us are around, he might start asking for introductions. Feel him out rather carefully. Inquire about local customs, that sort of thing, and ask him about any incidental wars going on.' He looked at Zakath. 'What's the capital of the island?'

'Dal Perivor, I think.'

'That's where we'll want to go then. Where is it?'

'On the other side of the island.'

'Naturally,' Silk sighed.

'You'd better get started,' Belgarath told the two armored men. 'Don't keep our host waiting.'

'When this is all over, would you consider hiring him out to me?' Zakath asked Garion as the two of them clanked down the hall. 'You could make a tidy profit, you know, and I'd have the most efficient government in the world.'

'Do you really want a man who's likely to live forever running your government?' Garion asked in an amused tone, 'not to mention the fact that he's probably more corrupt than Silk and Sadi put together? That is a very bad old man, Kal Zakath. He's wiser than whole generations, and he's got a large number of disgusting habits.'

'He's your grandfather, Garion,' Zakath protested. 'How can you talk about him like that?'

'Truth is truth, your Majesty.'

'You Alorns are a very strange people, my friend.'

'We've never tried to hide that, my friend.'

There was a clicking of toenails from behind, and the

she-wolf slipped up between them. 'One wonders where you are bound,' she said to Garion.

'One and one's friend go to speak with the master of this house, little sister,' he replied.

'One will accompany you and your friend,' she said. 'If needful, one may help to prevent missteps.'

'What did she say?' Zakath asked.

'She's coming along to keep us from making any serious mistakes,' Garion said.

'A wolf?'

'This is no ordinary wolf, Zakath. I'm beginning to have some suspicions about her.'

'One is gratified that even a puppy may show some semblance of perception,' the wolf sniffed.

'Thank you,' he said. 'One is happy to gain approval from one so dearly loved.'

She wagged her tail at him. 'One requests, however, that you keep your discovery to yourself.'

'Of course,' he promised.

'What was that all about?' Zakath asked.

'It's a wolfy sort of thing,' Garion said. 'It doesn't really translate.'

Baron Astellig had removed his armor and sat in a massive chair before a crackling hearth. 'It is ever thus, Sir Knights,' he said. 'Stone doth provide protection from foes, but it is forever cold, and the chill of winter is slow to seep away from its obdurate surface. Perforce we are required to maintain our fires even when summer doth bathe our isle with its gentle warmth.'

'It is, my Lord, as thou sayest,' Garion replied. 'E'en the massive walls of Vo Mimbre do harbor this oppressive chill.'

'And thou, Sir Knight, hath seen Vo Mimbre?' the baron asked in wonder. 'I would give all that I own or ever will to behold that fabled city. What is it truly like?'

'Large, my Lord,' Garion said, 'and its golden stones do flash back the light of the sun as if to shame the heavens by its magnificence.'

The baron's eyes filled with tears. 'Blessèd am I, Sir Knight,' he said in a voice choked with emotion. 'This unexpected encounter with a knight of noble purpose and passing fair eloquence hath been the crown of my life, for the memory of Vo Mimbre, echoing down through the endless progression of years hath sustained those of us in lonely exile here, though its echoes grow more remote with each passing season e'en as dearly loved faces of those gone before us are remembered only in a dream that fades and dies as cruel eld creepeth upon us.'

'My Lord,' Zakath said a bit haltingly, 'thy speech hath touched my heart. If I have power – and I do – I will convey thee at some future date even unto Vo Mimbre and present thee before the throne in the palace there, that we may re-unite thee with thy kindred.'

'You see,' Garion murmured to his friend, 'it gets to be habit-forming.'

The baron wiped his eyes unashamed. 'I note this hound of thine, Sir Knight,' he said to Garion to ease them past an embarrassing moment, 'a bitch, I perceive—'

'Steady,' Garion said firmly to the she-wolf.

'That is a *very* offensive term,' she growled.

'He didn't invent it. It's not his fault.'

'She is of a lean and lithesome configuration,' the baron continued, 'and her golden eyes do bespeak intelligence far beyond that of the poor mongrels which do infest this kingdom. Canst thou perhaps, Sir Knight, identify her breed?'

'She is a wolf, my Lord,' Garion told him.

'A wolf!' the baron exclaimed, leaping to his feet. 'We must flee ere the fearsome beast fall upon us and devour us.'

It was a bit ostentatious, but sometimes things like that impress people. Garion reached down and scratched the wolf's ears.

'Thou art brave beyond belief, Sir Knight,' the baron said almost in wonder.

'She is my friend, my Lord,' Garion replied. 'We are linked by ties beyond thine imagining.'

'One advises that you stop that,' the wolf told him, 'unless you have a paw to spare.'

'You *wouldn't!*' he exclaimed, snatching his hand back.

'But you're not entirely sure, are you?' She bared her teeth almost in a grin.

'Thou speakest the language of beasts?' the baron gasped.

'Of a few, my Lord,' Garion said. 'They each have their own, thou knowest. I have not yet mastered the speech of the serpent. I think it has to do with the shape of my tongue.'

The baron suddenly laughed. 'Thou art a droll man, Sir Knight. Thou hast presented me here with much to ponder and much at which to marvel. Now, to the main point. What canst thou reveal to me of thy quest?'

'Be very careful here,' the wolf warned Garion.

Garion considered. 'As thou mayest know, my Lord,' he began, 'there is a great evil abroad in the world now.' That was fairly safe. There was *always* a great evil abroad in the world.

'Truly,' the baron agreed fervently.

'It is the sworn task of my steadfast companion here and myself to confront this evil. Know thou, however, that rumor, like a barking dog, would run before us, announcing – should they be known – our identities to the foul miscreant upon whom we mean to do war. Should, all forewarned, this vicious enemy learn of our approach, its minions would waylay us. Thus it is that we must conceal ourselves behind our visors and refrain from declaring before all the world our names – which have some smirch of honor upon them in diverse parts of the world.' Garion was beginning to enjoy this. 'We, neither one, fear any living thing.' Mandorallen himself could not have said it more confidently. 'We have, however, dear companions in this quest, whose lives we dare not endanger. Moreover, our quest is fraught with perilous enchantments which may even vaunt our prowess. Thus, though it is distasteful, we must, with thieflike stealth, approach this despised miscreant that we may administer suitable chastisement.' He said the last word with something as close to the crack of doom as he could manage.

The baron got the point immediately. 'My sword, and those of my knights, are at thine immediate disposal, my Lord. Let us eradicate this evil for good and all.' The baron was a Mimbrate to the bone, all right.

Garion raised one regretful hand. 'Nay, my Lord of Astellig,' he said. 'It may not be so, though I would welcome thee and thy brave companions with all my heart. This task hath been lain upon me and upon my dear companions. To accept thine aid in this endeavor would be to anger the minions of the spirit-world, which, no less than we, do contend in this matter. We – all of us – are but mortal, and the spirit world is a world of immortals. To defy the commands of the spirits might well confound the purpose of those friendly spirits which take our part in this ultimate battle.'

'Though it wounds my heart, Sir Knight,' the baron said sadly, 'I must agree that thine argument hath cogency. Know, moreover, that a kinsman of mine hath but recently arrived from the capital at Dal Perivor and hath advised me privately of a disturbing turn of events at court. No more than a few days ago, a wizard appeared at the king's palace. Doubtless using enchantments such as thou hast mentioned, he beguiled our king within the space of a few hours and gained the king's ear and is now his closest advisor. He now doth wield almost absolute authority in the kingdom. Guard yourselves well, Sir Knights. Should, perchance, this wizard be one of the minions of your foe, he now hath power to do thee gravest injury.' The baron made a wry face. 'Methinks the beguiling of the king was no serious task for him. It is improper of me to say it, perhaps, but his Majesty is not a man of profound intellectual gifts.' This from a *Mimbrate?* 'This wizard,' the baron continued, 'is a wicked man, and I must advise thee in the spirit of true comradeship to avoid him.'

'I thank thee, my Lord,' Garion said, 'but our destiny, and that of our quest, compels us to Dal Perivor. If needs be, we will confront this wizard and rid the kingdom of his influence.'

'May the Gods and the spirits guide thy hand,' the baron said fervently. Then he grinned. 'Mayhap, an it please thee, I might watch as thou and thy valiant, laconic companion administer such chastisement as thou seest fit.'

'We would be honored, my Lord,' Zakath assured him.

'With that end in view then, my Lords,' the baron said, 'be advised that I and diverse nobles journey on the morrow toward the king's palace at Dal Perivor, there to participate in the grand tourney which our Lord King hath ordained to select champions of the kingdom to deal with a certain recurrent problem which hath confronted us. Know, moreover, that by centuries-old tradition, misunderstandings and frictions are held in the abeyance of general truce during this period and we may expect general tranquility on our journey to the west. An it please you, my Lords, may I entreat you to accompany me to the capital?'

'My Lord,' Garion said, bowing with a slight creaking of armor, 'your suggestion and gracious invitation could not suit our purposes more. And now, if we may, we will retire to make our preparations.'

As Garion and Zakath strode down the long hall, the wolf's toenails had an almost metallic ring to them. 'One is pleased,' she said. 'You didn't do all that badly – for a couple of puppies.'

CHAPTER TWELVE

Perivor proved to be a pleasant island with rolling, emerald-green hills where sheep grazed and with dark plowed fields where meticulously straight rows of crops flourished. Baron Astellig looked about with some pride. 'It is a fair land,' he observed, 'though doubtless not so fair as far-off Arendia.'

'Methinks thou wouldst be somewhat disappointed by Arendia, my Lord,' Garion told him. 'Though the land be fair, the kingdom is much marred by civil turmoil and by the misery of the serfs.'

'Doth that sad institution still prevail there? It was abolished here many centuries ago.'

Garion was a bit surprised at that.

'The folk who inhabited this isle 'ere we came are a gentle people, and our forebears sought wives from among them. At first these common folk were bound in serfdom, as had always been the practice in Arendia, but our ancestors soon perceived that this was the grossest injustice, since the serfs were kinsmen by marriage.' The baron frowned slightly. 'Doth this civil discord thou spake of truly mar our ancestral homeland to any great extent?'

Garion sighed. 'We have some small expectation that it may abate, my Lord. Three great duchies warred with each other for centuries until one – Mimbre – finally achieved nominal mastery. Rebellion lurked ever beneath the surface, however. Moreover, the barons of southern Arendia make bloody war upon each other for the most trivial of reasons.'

'War? Truly? Such affairs arise here on Perivor as well, but we have attempted to formalize the conflict to such degree that few are ever slain.'

162

'How meanst thou "formalize", My Lord?'

'Such disputes as arise are – except in cases of outrage or gravest insult – customarily settled by tourneys.' The baron smiled. 'Indeed, I have known of a number of disputes which were counterfeited by the mutual contrivance of the principals merely as an excuse to hold such tourneys – which do entertain nobles and commons alike.'

'How very civilized, my Lord,' Zakath said.

The strain of phrasing such involuted sentences was beginning to wear on Garion. He asked the baron to excuse him, pleading the need to confer with his companions, and rode back to talk with Belgarath and the others.

'How are you and the baron getting along?' Silk asked him.

'Quite well, actually. The intermarriage with the Dals has altered certain of the more irritating Arendish tendencies.'

'Such as?'

'Gross stupidity for one thing. They've abolished serfdom, and they usually settle disputes with tournaments rather than open war.' Garion looked at the dozing Belgarath. 'Grandfather.'

Belgarath opened his eyes.

'Do you think we've managed to get here ahead of Zandramas?'

'There's no way to know for sure.'

'I could use the Orb again.'

'It's probably better if you don't just yet. If she's on the island, there's no way to know where she landed. She may not have come this way, so the Orb wouldn't react to her trail. I'm sure she can feel it, though, and about all we'd succeed in doing would be to let her know we're here. Besides, the Sardion is in this part of the world. Let's not wake it up just yet.'

'You might ask your friend the baron,' Silk suggested. 'If she's here, he might have heard something about her.'

'I doubt it,' Belgarath said. 'In the past she's usually gone to a great deal of trouble to remain unobserved.'

'That's true,' Silk conceded, 'and I think she'll go to even more trouble now. She might have some difficulty trying to explain those lights under her skin.'

'Let's wait until we get to Dal Perivor,' Belgarath decided. 'I want to sort things out there before we do anything irrevocable.'

'Do you suppose it would do any good to ask Cyradis?' Garion asked quietly, glancing back at the Seeress, who rode in the splendid carriage the baron had provided for the ladies.

'No,' Belgarath said. 'She won't be permitted to answer us.'

'I think we might have a certain advantage in all this,' Silk observed. 'Cyradis is the one who's going to make the choice, and the fact that she's traveling with us instead of with Zandramas bodes rather well, wouldn't you say?'

'I don't think so,' Garion disagreed. 'I don't think she's traveling with *us* so much as she's here to keep an eye on Zakath. He has something very important to do, and she doesn't want him to stray.'

Silk grunted. 'Where do you propose to start looking for this map you're supposed to find?' he asked Belgarath.

'A library probably,' the old man replied. 'This map is another one of those "mysteries", and I've had a fair degree of luck finding the others in libraries. Garion, see if you can persuade the baron to take us to the king's court in Dal Perivor. Palace libraries are usually the most complete.'

'Of course,' Garion agreed.

'I want to take a look at this wizard anyway. Silk, do you have an office in Dal Perivor?'

'I'm afraid not, Belgarath. There's nothing here worth trading in.'

'Well, no matter. You're a businessman, and there'll be others in the city. Go talk business with them. Tell them you want to check over shipping routes. Look at every map you can lay your hands on. You know what we're looking for.'

'You're cheating, Belgarath,' Beldin growled.

'How do you mean?'

'Cyradis told you that *you* were supposed to find the map.'

'I'm only delegating responsibility, Beldin. It's perfectly legitimate.'

'I don't think she'd see it that way.'

'You can explain it to her. You're much more persuasive than I am.'

They traveled in easy stages, more to spare the horses, Garion felt, than for any other reason. The horses of Perivor were not large, and they labored under the weight of men in full armor. So it was that it was several days before they crested a hill and looked down at the seaport city which was the capital of Perivor.

'Behold Dal Perivor,' the baron proclaimed, 'the crown and the heart of the isle.'

Garion saw immediately that the shipwrecked Arends who had arrived on this shore two thousand years ago had made a conscious effort to duplicate Vo Mimbre. The city walls were high and thick and yellow, and brightly colored pennons flew from spires within those walls.

'Where did they find the yellow stone, my Lord?' Zakath asked the baron. 'I have seen no such rock on our journey here.'

The baron coughed a bit apologetically. 'The walls are painted, Sir Knight,' he explained.

'Whatever for?'

'To serve as a remembrance of Vo Mimbre,' the baron said a bit sadly. 'Our ancestors were homesick for Arendia. Vo Mimbre is the jewel of our ancestral home, and its golden walls speak to our blood even across the endless miles.'

'Ah,' Zakath said.

'As I have promised thee, Sir Knight,' the baron said to Garion, 'gladly will I convey thee and thy companions forthwith to the king's palace where he will doubtless honor ye and offer ye his hospitality.'

'Once more we are in thy debt, my Lord,' Garion replied.

The baron smiled a bit slyly. 'I confess it to thee, Sir Knight, that my motives are not altogether magnanimous. I will accrue much credit by presenting at court stranger knights bent on a noble quest.'

'That's quite all right, my friend,' Garion laughed. 'This way there's something for everybody.'

The palace was almost identical to that in Vo Mimbre, a fortress within a fortress with high walls and a stout gate.

'At least this time I don't think my grandfather will have to grow a tree,' Garion murmured to Zakath.

'Do what?'

'When we first went to Vo Mimbre, the knight in charge of the palace gate didn't believe Mandorallen when he introduced Grandfather as Belgarath the Sorcerer, so Grandfather took a twig from his horse's tail and made an apple tree grow right there in the square in front of the palace. Then he ordered the sceptical knight to spend the rest of his life taking care of it.'

'Did the knight actually do it?'

'I assume so. Mimbrates take those kinds of commands very seriously.'

'Strange people.'

'Oh yes, indeed. I had to force Mandorallen to marry a girl he'd loved since childhood, and I had to stop a war in the process.'

'How do you stop a war?'

'I made some threats. I think they took me seriously.' He thought about it. 'The thunderstorm I created may have helped, though,' he added. 'Anyway, Mandorallen and Nerina had loved each other for years, but they'd been suffering in silence beautiful for all that time. I finally got tired of it, so I made them get on with it. I made some more threats. I've got this big knife back here.' He poked his thumb over his shoulder. 'It attracts a lot of attention sometimes.'

'Garion!' Zakath laughed. 'You're a peasant.

'Yes. Probably,' Garion admitted. 'But it got them married, after all. They're both deliriously happy now, and if anything goes wrong, they can always blame me, can't they?'

'You're not like other men, my friend,' Zakath said very seriously.

'No.' Garion sighed, 'Probably not. I'd like to be, though. The world lies very heavily on you and me, Zakath, and it doesn't leave us any time for ourselves. Wouldn't you just like to ride out on a summer morning to look at the sunrise and see what lies over the next hilltop?'

'I thought that's what we've been doing.'

'Not entirely. We're doing all this because we're compelled to. What I was talking about was doing it just for fun.'

'I haven't done anything just for fun in years.'

'Didn't you rather enjoy threatening to crucify King Gethel of the Thulls? Ce'Nedra told me about that.'

Zakath laughed. 'That wasn't too bad,' he admitted. 'I wouldn't have done it, of course. Gethel was an idiot, but he was sort of necessary at that point.'

'It always comes to that, doesn't it? You and I do what's necessary, not what we'd really prefer to do. Neither of us sought this eminence, but we'll do what's necessary and what's expected of us. If we don't, this world will die, and good, honest men will die with it. I won't permit that if I can help it. I won't betray those good, honest men, and neither will you. You're too good a man yourself.'

'Good? Me?'

'You underestimate yourself, Zakath, and I think that very soon someone will come and teach you not to hate yourself any more.'

Zakath started visibly.

'You didn't think I knew?' Garion said, boring in relentlessly. 'But that's nearly over now. Your suffering and pain and remorse are almost done, and if you need

167

any instructions in how to be happy, look me up. After all, that's what friends are for, aren't they?'

A choked sob came from behind Zakath's visor.

The she-wolf had been standing between their horses. She looked up at Garion. 'Very well done,' she said. 'Perhaps one has misjudged you, young wolf. Perhaps you are not a puppy after all.'

'One can but do one's best,' Garion replied, also in the language of wolves. 'One hopes that one has not been too much a disappointment.'

'One feels that you have some promise, Garion.'

And that confirmed something that Garion had suspected for some time now. 'Thank you, Grandmother,' he said, sure at last just to whom he was speaking.

'And it took you so very, very long to say it?'

'It might have been considered impolite.'

'One believes that you have been too long with one's eldest daughter. She is, one has noticed, much caught up in propriety. One assumes you will continue to keep your discovery to yourself?'

'If you wish.'

'It might be wiser.' She looked at the palace gate. 'What is this place?'

'It is the palace of the king.'

'What are kings to wolves?'

'It is the custom among the man-things to pay respect to them, Grandmother. The respect is more to the custom than to the man-thing who wears the crown.'

'How very curious,' she sniffed.

At last, with a great deal of creaking and the clanking of chain, the drawbridge boomed down, and Baron Astellig and his knights led them into the palace courtyard.

As was the one in Vo Mimbre, the throne room here in Dal Perivor was a great, vaulted hall with sculptured buttresses soaring upward along the walls. Tall, narrow windows rose between the buttresses, and the light streaming through their stained glass panels was jeweled. The floor was polished marble, and on the red-carpeted stone platform at the far end stood the throne of Perivor, backed by heavy purple drapes. Flanking the draped wall hung the massive antique weapons of two thousand years of the royal house. Lances, maces, and huge swords, taller than any man, hung among the tattered war-banners of forgotten kings.

Almost bemused by the similarities, Garion half-expected to see Mandorallen in his gleaming armor come striding across the marble floor to greet them, flanked by red-bearded Barak and horse-maned Hettar. Once again, that strange sense of recurrence struck him. With a start he realized that in recounting past experiences to Zakath, he had in fact been reliving them. In some obscure way this seemed a kind of cleansing in preparation for the now almost inevitable meeting in the Place Which Is No More.

'And it please ye, Sir Knights,' Baron Astellig said to Garion and Zakath, 'let us approach the throne of King Oldorin that I may present ye to his Majesty. I will advise him of the diverse restrictions your quest hath lain upon ye.'

'Thy courtesy and consideration become thee, my Lord of Astellig,' Garion said. 'Gladly will we greet thy king.'

The three of them proceeded along the marble floor toward the carpeted platform. King Oldorin, Garion noticed, was a more robust-looking man than Korodullin of Arendia, but his eyes revealed a fearful lack of anything resembling thought.

A tall, powerfully built knight stepped in front of Astellig. 'This is unseemly, my Lord,' he said. 'Instruct thy companions to raise their visors that the king may behold those who approach him.'

'I will explain to his Majesty the reason for this necessary concealment, my Lord,' Astellig replied a bit stiffly. 'I assure thee that these knights, whom I dare to call friends, intend no disrespect to our Lord King.'

'I'm sorry, Baron Astellig,' the knight said, 'but I cannot permit this.'

The baron's hand went to his sword hilt.

'Steady,' Garion warned, placing one gauntleted hand on Astellig's arm. 'As all the world knows, it is forbidden to draw arms in the king's presence.'

'Thou art well-versed in propriety, Sir Knight,' the man barring their way said, sounding a bit less sure of himself now.

'I've been in the presence of kings before, my Lord, and I am conversant with the customary usages. I do assure thee that we mean no disrespect to his Majesty by our visored approach to the throne. We are compelled to it, however, by a stern duty which hath been lain upon us.'

The knight looked even more unsure of himself. 'Thou art well-spoken, Sir Knight,' he admitted grudgingly.

'An it please you then, Sir Knight,' Garion continued, 'wilt thou accompany Baron Astellig, my companion, and myself to the throne? A man of thine obvious prowess can easily prevent mischief.' A little flattery never hurt anything in difficult situations.

'It shall be as thou sayest, Sir Knight,' the knight decided.

The four of them approached the throne and bowed somewhat stiffly. 'My Lord King,' Astellig said.

'Baron,' Oldorin replied with an absent-seeming nod.

'I have the honor to present two stranger knights who have traveled here from afar in pursuit of a noble quest.'

The king looked interested. The word 'quest' rang bells in Mimbrate heads.

'As thou may have noticed, your Majesty,' Astellig continued, 'my friends are visored. This is not to be taken as a gesture of disrespect, but is a necessary concealment required by the nature of their quest. A foul evil is abroad in the world, and they journey with diverse companions to confront it. They each have some eminence in the world beyond the shores of our isle, and should they reveal their faces, they would instantly be recognized, and the evil one they seek would be forewarned of their coming and would seek to impede them. Thus it is that their visors must remain closed.'

'A reasonable precaution,' the king agreed. 'Greetings, Sir Knights, and well-met.'

'Thou art kind, your Majesty,' Garion said, 'and we are grateful to thee for thy gracious understanding of our circumstances. Our quest is fraught with perilous enchantments, and I do fear me that should we reveal our identities, we might well fail, and the whole world would suffer as a result.'

'I do fully understand, Sir Knight, and I will not press thee for further details of thy quest. The walls of any palace have ears, and some there are even here who might be in league with the villain thou seekest.'

'Wisely spoken, my King,' a rasping voice said from the back of the throne room. 'As I myself know full well, the powers of enchanters are myriad, and even the prowess of these two brave knights may not be sufficient to match them.'

Garion turned. The man who had spoken had absolutely white eyes.

'The wizard of whom I told thee,' Baron Astellig whispered to Garion. 'Be wary of him, Sir Knight, for he hath the king in thrall.'

'Ah, good Erezel,' the king said, his face lighting up, 'an it please thee, approach the throne. Mayhap in thy wisdom thou mayest advise these two questors concerning the possibility of avoiding the perils posed by the enchantments certain to be strewn in their path.'

'It shall be my pleasure, Lord King,' Naradas replied.

'You know who he is, don't you?' Zakath murmured to Garion.

'Yes.'

Naradas came down to the throne. 'If I may be so bold as to suggest it, Sir Knights,' he said in an unctuous tone, 'a great tourney is planned not long hence. Should you not participate, it might arouse suspicion in the minions the one you seek hath doubtless placed here. My first advice to you, therefore, is that you enter our tourney and thus avoid that mischance.'

'A most excellent suggestion, Erezel,' the empty-headed king approved. 'Sir Knights, this is Erezel, a great wizard and the closest advisor to our throne. Consider well his words, for they have great merit. We will, moreover, be greatly honored to have two such mighty men join with us in our forthcoming entertainment.'

Garion ground his teeth together. With that one inno-cent-seeming suggestion, Naradas had effectively achieved the delay he had been seeking for weeks now. There was no way out, however. 'We would be honored to join with thee and thy valiant knights in thy sport, your Majesty,' he said. 'Prithee, when are the games to begin?'

'Ten days hence, Sir Knight.'

CHAPTER THIRTEEN

The quarters to which they were escorted were again hauntingly familiar. The displaced Arends who had been washed ashore here so many centuries ago had, it appeared, lovingly recreated the royal palace at Vo Mimbre down to the last detail – even including its inconveniences. Durnik, ever practical, noticed this immediately. 'You'd think they'd have taken advantage of the opportunity to improve a few things,' he observed.

'There's a certain charm in archaism, dear,' Polgara said, smiling.

'It's nostalgic, perhaps, Pol, but a few modern touches wouldn't have hurt all that much. You *have* noticed that the baths are located down in the cellar, haven't you?'

'There's a point there, Lady Polgara,' Velvet agreed.

'It *was* much more convenient in Mal Zeth,' Ce'Nedra concurred. 'A bath in one's own apartments offers all sorts of opportunities for fun and mischief.'

Garion's ears turned bright red.

'I seem to be missing the more interesting parts of this conversation,' Zakath said slyly.

'Never mind,' Garion told him shortly.

And then the dressmakers arrived, and Polgara and the other ladies were whisked away to engage in that activity which, Garion had noticed, always seems to fill the feminine heart with a kind of dreamy bliss.

Immediately behind the dressmakers came the tailors, equally bent on making everyone look as old-fashioned as possible. Beldin, of course, adamantly refused their ministrations, even going so far as to show one insistent fellow a gnarled and very large fist to indicate that he was perfectly satisfied with the way he looked already.

Garion and Zakath, however, were under the constraint placed upon them by the Seeress of Kell, and so they remained buckled up in their armor.

When they were finally alone, Belgarath's expression grew grave. 'I want you two to be careful in that tournament,' he told the armored men. 'Naradas knows who we are, and he's already managed to delay us. He may try to go a little farther.' He looked sharply toward the door. 'Where are you going?' he demanded of Silk.

'I thought I'd nose around a bit,' the little thief said innocently. 'It never hurts to know what you're up against.'

'All right, but be careful — and don't let anything slip into your pockets by mistake. We're walking on some fairly shaky ground here. If someone sees you pilfering, we could all get into a great deal of trouble.'

'Belgarath,' Silk replied in an offended tone, 'no one has *ever* seen me steal anything.' And then he went out muttering to himself.

'Is he trying to say that he *doesn't* steal?' Zakath asked.

'No,' Eriond replied. 'Only that no one ever sees him doing it.' He smiled gently. 'He has a few bad habits, but we've been trying to break him of them.' It was the first time in quite a while that Garion had actually heard his young friend say anything. Eriond had grown increasingly more and more reticent — one might even say withdrawn. It was troubling. He had always been a strange boy, and he seemed to be able to perceive things that none of the rest of them could. A chill came over Garion as he remembered the fateful words of Cyradis at Rheon, 'Thy quest will be fraught with great peril, Belgarion, and one of thy companions shall lose his life in the course of it.'

And then, almost as if his memory had summoned her, the blindfolded Seeress of Kell emerged from the room in which the ladies had been conferring with their dressmakers. Immediately behind her came Ce'Nedra, clad only in a *very* short chemise. 'It's a perfectly suitable gown, Cyradis,' she was protesting.

'Suitable for thee perhaps, Queen of Riva,' the Seeress replied, 'but such finery is not for me.'

'Ce'Nedra!' Garion exclaimed in a shocked gasp, 'You're not dressed!'

'Oh, bother that!' she snapped. 'Everyone here has seen undressed women before. I'm just trying to reason with my mystical young friend here. Cyradis, if you don't put on the gown, I'll be very cross with you – and we really need to do something with your hair.'

The Seeress unerringly took the tiny queen in her arms and embraced her fondly. 'Dear, dear Ce'Nedra,' she said gently, 'thy heart is larger than thyself, and thy concern doth fill mine as well. I am content, however, in this simple garb. Mayhap in time my tastes will change, and then will I gladly submit to thy gentle ministrations.'

'There's absolutely no talking to her,' Ce'Nedra said, throwing her arms in the air. Then, with a charming flirt of the hem of her chemise, she stormed back into the room from which the two of them had emerged.

'You ought to feed her more,' Beldin told Garion. 'She's really very skinny, you know.'

'I sort of like her the way she is,' Garion replied. He looked at Cyradis. 'Will you sit, Holy Seeress?'

'If I may.'

'Of course.' He waved off Toth's almost instinctive move to aid his mistress and guided the girl to a comfortable chair.

'I thank thee, Belgarion,' she said. 'Thou art as kind as thou art brave.' She smiled, and it was like the sun coming up. She touched one hand to her hair. 'Doth this really look so ugly?' she asked.

'It's just fine, Cyradis,' he told her. 'Ce'Nedra sometimes exaggerates. and she has an absolute passion for making people over – me, usually.'

'And dost thou mind her efforts, Belgarion?'

'I suppose not. I'd probably miss them if she didn't try, at least.'

'Thou art caught in the snare of love, King Belgarion.

Thou art a mighty sorcerer, but methinks thy little queen hath a more powerful sorcery yet, for she holds thee in the palm of that tiny hand.'

'That's true, I suppose, but I don't really mind all that much.'

'If this gets any more cloying, I think I'll throw up,' Beldin said gruffly.

And then Silk returned.

'Anything?' Belgarath asked.

'Naradas beat you to the library. I stopped by there, and the man in charge—'

'Librarian,' Belgarath corrected absently.

'Whatever. Anyway, he said that as soon as Naradas arrived, he ransacked the library.'

'So that's it, then,' Belgarath said. 'Zandramas isn't on the island. She sent Naradas here to do her looking for her, it seems. Is he still looking?'

'Apparently not.

'That means he's found it, then.'

'And probably destroyed it to keep us from getting a look at it,' Beldin added.

'Nay, gentle Beldin,' Cyradis said. 'The chart ye seek doth still exist, but it is not in the place where ye propose to seek.'

'I don't suppose you could give us a few hints?' Belgarath asked her.

She shook her head.

'I didn't think so.'

'You said *the* chart,' Beldin said, approaching the subject obliquely. 'Does that mean there's only one copy?'

She nodded.

The dwarf shrugged. 'Oh, well,' he said. 'Looking for it gives us something to do while we're waiting for our two heroes here to go out and start denting other people's armor.'

'That brings up a point,' Garion said. He looked at Zakath. 'You're not particularly familiar with the lance, are you?'

'Not really, no.'

'Tomorrow morning, then, we'll have to go some place so that I can give you some instruction.'

'That seems like a sensible plan to me.'

The two of them arose early the following morning and left the palace on horseback. 'I think we'd better go out of town,' Garion said. 'There's a practice field near the palace, but there'll be other knights there. I'm not trying to be offensive, but the first few passes are usually very awkward. We're supposed to be great knights, so let's not let anybody get the idea that you're totally inept.'

'Thanks,' Zakath said drily.

'Do you enjoy public embarrassment?'

'Not really.'

'Let's do it my way, then.'

They rode out of the city and to a meadow a few miles away.

'You've got two shields,' Zakath noted. 'Is that customary.'

'The other one is for our opponent.'

'Opponent?'

'A stump or a tree probably. We need a target.' Garion reined in. 'Now,' he began, 'we're going to be involved in a formal tournament. The idea is not to kill anybody, since that's considered bad form. We'll probably be using blunted lances. That helps to keep down the fatalities.'

'But sometimes people *do* get killed, don't they?'

'It's not unheard of. The whole purpose of a formal joust is to knock the other fellow off his horse. You ride at him and aim your lance at the center of his shield.'

'And he does the same thing to me, I suppose.'

'Exactly.'

'It sounds painful.'

'It is. After a few passes, you'll probably be bruised from head to hip.'

'And they do this for entertainment?'

'Not entirely. It's a form of competition. They do it to find out who's the best.'

'Now *that* I can understand.'

'I thought the notion might appeal to you.'

They buckled the spare shield to a springy lower limb of a cedar tree. 'That's about the right height,' Garion said. 'I'll make the first couple of passes. Watch very closely. Then you can try.'

Garion had become quite proficient with the lance and he hit the shield squarely on both passes.

'Why do you stand up at the last second?' Zakath asked him.

'I wasn't actually standing so much as leaning forward. The idea is to brace your feet in the stirrups, lean forward, and hold your body rigid. That way the weight of the horse is added to your own.'

'Clever. Let me try it.'

Zakath completly missed the shield on his first attempt. 'What did I do wrong?' he asked.

'When you raised up and leaned forward, the point of your lance dipped. You have to adjust your point of aim.'

'Oh, I see. All right, let me try it again.' On the next pass he struck the shield a glancing blow that made it spin around the limb. 'Any better?' he asked.

Garion shook his head. 'You'd have killed him. When you hit the top of the shield that way, your lance is deflected upward, and it drives right into his visor. It breaks his neck.'

'I'll try it again.'

By noon, Zakath had made considerable progress.

'That's enough for today,' Garion said. 'It's starting to get hot out here.'

'I'm still all right,' Zakath objected.

'I was thinking about your horse.'

'Oh. He *is* lathered a bit, isn't he?'

'More than just a bit. Besides, I'm starting to get hungry.'

The day of the tourney dawned clear and sunny, and

throngs of the citizens of Dal Perivor streamed through the streets in bright-colored clothing toward the field where the festivities were to take place. 'A thought just occurred to me,' Garion said to Zakath as they left the palace. 'You and I aren't *really* interested in who gets proclaimed the winner of the tournament, are we?'

'I don't follow you.'

'We have something much more important to do, and assorted broken bones would probably hinder us. We make a few passes and unhorse a few knights and then allow ourselves to get knocked out of the saddle. We'll have satisfied the requirements of honor without putting ourselves in any serious danger of injury.'

'Are you suggesting that we deliberately lose?' Zakath asked incredulously.

'Approximately, yes.'

'I've never lost a contest of any kind in my whole life.'

'You're starting to sound more and more like Mandorallen every day,' Garion sighed.

'Besides,' Zakath went on, 'I think you're overlooking something. We're supposed to be mighty knights embarked on a noble quest. If we don't try our very best, Naradas will fill the king's ears with all sorts of innuendo and suspicion. If we win, on the other hand, we pull his teeth.'

'Win?' Garion snorted. 'You've learned very quickly in the past week or so, but the knights we'll be facing have been practicing all their lives. I don't think we're in any real danger of winning.'

'A compromise then?' Zakath asked slyly.

'What have you got in mind?'

'If we win the tournament, there's almost nothing the king won't grant us, right?'

'That's usually the way it works.'

'Wouldn't he be more than happy to let Belgarath have a look at that chart? I'm sure he knows where it is – or he can compel Naradas to produce it.'

'You've got a point there, I suppose.'

'You're a sorcerer. You can fix it so that we win, can't you?'

'Wouldn't that be cheating?'

'You're very inconsistent, Garion. First you suggest that we deliberately fall off our horses, and that's cheating, too, isn't it? I'll tell you what, my friend. I'm the Emperor of Mallorea. You have my imperial permission to cheat. Now, is there a way you can do it?'

Garion thought about it and then remembered something. 'Do you remember the time I told you that I had to stop a war in order to get Mandorallen and Nerina safely married?'

'Yes?'

'This is how I did it. Most lances break sooner or later. By the time this tournament is over, the lists will be ankle-deep in splinters. On the day I stopped that war, though, *my* lance would *not* break, and I sort of surrounded it with pure force. It was very effective. Nobody, not even the best knights in all of Mimbre, stayed on his horse that day.'

'I thought you said you conjured up a thunderstorm.'

'That was a little later. The two armies were facing each other across an open field. Not even Mimbrates would charge across a field where lightning was blowing big holes in the turf. They're not *that* stupid.'

'You've had a remarkable career, my young friend,' Zakath laughed.

'I had a bit of fun that day,' Garion admitted. 'It's not too often that one man gets to bully two complete armies. I got into a great deal of trouble about it later, though. When you tamper with the weather, you can't be sure just what the consequences are going to be. Belgarath and Beldin spent the next six months running around the world quieting things down. Grandfather was *very* cross when he got back. He called me all sorts of names, and 'blockhead' was about the mildest.'

'You mentioned something called "lists". What are they?'

'They sink posts into the ground and fasten a long,

180

heavy pole to the tops of them. The pole is about shoulder high on a horse. The knights who are jousting ride towards each other on opposite sides of the pole. I think the idea is to keep the horses from running into each other. Good horses are expensive. Oh, that reminds me of something else. We're going to have a certain advantage in this anyway. Our horses are quite a bit bigger and stronger than the local ones.'

'That's true, isn't it? I'll still feel more comfortable if you cheat, though.'

'I probably will, too. If we were to do it legitimately, we'd still pick up so many bruises that neither one of us would be able to get out of bed for a week, and we've got an appointment – if we can ever find out where it's supposed to take place.'

The tournament field was gaily decorated with bright-colored buntings and flapping pennons. A stand had been erected for the king, the ladies of the court, and members of the gentry too old to participate on the field. The commoners stood on the far side of the lists, watching avidly. A pair of gaily dressed jugglers were entertaining the crowd while the knights made their preparations. Brightly striped pavilions stood at either end of the lists – places for knights to have their armor repaired and places where the injured could suffer out of sight, since watching people groaning and writhing tends to dampen an otherwise enjoyable afternoon.

'I'll be right back,' Garion told his friend. 'I want to talk with Grandfather for a moment.' He dismounted and crossed the bright green turf to the end of the stand where Belgarath sat. The old man was wearing a snowy white robe and a disgruntled expression.

'Elegant,' Garion said.

'It's somebody's idea of a joke,' Belgarath said.

'Your obvious antiquity shines in your face, old friend,' Silk said impudently from just behind him. 'People instinctively want to make you as dignified-looking as possible.'

'Do you mind? What is it, Garion?'

181

'Zakath and I are going to cheat a little. If we win, the king will grant us a boon – like letting you look at that chart.'

'That might actually work, you know.'

'How do you cheat in a tournament?' Silk asked.

'There are ways.'

'Are you *sure* you'll win?'

'I can almost guarantee it.'

Silk jumped to his feet.

'Where are you going?' Belgarath demanded.

'I want to lay a few wagers.' And the little man scurried off.

'He never changes,' Belgarath observed.

'One thing, though. Naradas is here. He's a Grolim, so he'll know what we're doing. Please, Grandfather, keep him off my neck. I don't want him tampering with what I'm doing at some crucial moment.'

'I'll handle him,' Belgarath said bleakly. 'Go out there and do your best, but be careful.'

'Yes, Grandfather.' Garion turned and went back to where Zakath waited with their horses.

'We'll stand in the second or third rank,' Garion said. 'It's customary to let the winners of previous tournaments joust first. It makes us look properly modest, and it'll give you a chance to see how to approach the lists.' He looked around. 'We'll have to surrender our lances before we joust; and they'll give us each one of those blunted ones from that rack over there. I'll take care of them as soon as we get our hands on them.'

'You're a devious young man, Garion. What's Kheldar doing? He's running through those stands like a pickpocket hard at work.'

'As soon as he heard what we're planning, he went out to place a few wagers.'

Zakath suddenly burst out laughing. 'I wish I'd known. I'd have given him some money to wager for me as well.'

'Getting it back from him might have been a little difficult, though.'

Their friend, Baron Astellig, was unhorsed on the second pass. 'Is he all right?' Zakath asked with concern.

'He's still moving,' Garion said. 'He probably just broke one of his legs.'

'At least we won't have to fight him. I hate hurting friends. Of course, I don't have all that many friends.'

'You probably have more than you realize.'

After the third pass of the front rank, Zakath said, 'Garion, have you ever studied fencing?'

'Alorns don't use light swords, Zakath. Except for the Algars.'

'I know, but the theory is similar. If you twist your wrist or elbow at the last instant, you could knock your opponent's lance aside. Then you could correct your aim and smash into the center of his shield when his lance is completely out of position. He wouldn't have a chance at that point, would he?'

Garion considered it. 'It's highly unorthodox,' he said dubiously.

'So's using sorcery, isn't it? Would it work?'

'Zakath, you're using a fifteen-foot lance, and it weighs about two pounds a foot. You'd need arms like a gorilla to move it around that fast.'

'Not really. You don't really have to move it that far back and forth. Just a tap would do. Can I try it?'

'It's your idea. I'll be here to pick you up if it doesn't work.'

'I knew I could count on you.' Zakath's voice sounded excited – even boyish.

'Oh, Gods,' Garion murmured almost in despair.

'Anything wrong?' Zakath asked.

'No, I guess not. Go ahead and try it, if you feel that you have to.'

'What difference does it make? I can't get hurt, can I?'

'I wouldn't go entirely that far. Do you see that?' Garion pointed at a knight who had just been unhorsed and had come down on his back across the center pole of the lists, scattering bits and pieces of his armor in all directions.

'He's not really hurt, is he?'

'He's still moving – a little bit – but they'll need a black-smith to get him out of his armor before the physicians can go to work on him.'

'I still think it might work,' Zakath said stubbornly.

'We'll give you a splendid funeral if it doesn't. All right. It's our turn. Let's go get our lances.'

The blunted lances were padded at the tip with layer upon layer of woolly sheepskin tightly wrapped in canvas. The result was a round padded ball that looked totally humane, but which Garion knew would hurl a man from his saddle with terrific force, and it was not the impact of the lance that broke bones, but rather it was the violent contact with the ground. He was a bit distracted at the point when he began to focus his will, and so the best word he could come up with as a release for that will was 'Make it that way.' He was not entirely positive that it worked exactly as he had planned. His first opponent was hurled from his saddle at a point some five feet before Garion's lance touched his shield. Garion adjusted the aura of force around their lances. Zakath's technique, Garion saw with some surprise, worked flawlessly. A single, almost unnoticeable, twist of his forearm deflected his opponent's lance, and then his own blunted lance smashed directly into the center of the knight's shield. A man hurled forcefully from the back of a charging horse flies through the air for quite some distance, Garion noticed, and the crash when he hits the ground sounds much like that which might come from a collapsing smithy. Both their opponents were carried senseless from the field.

It was a bad day for the pride of Perivor. As their experience with their enhanced weapons increased, the Rivan King and the Emperor of Mallorea quite literally romped through the ranks of the steel-clad knights of Perivor, filling the dispensaries with row upon row of groaning injured. It was more than a rout. It soon reached disastrous proportions. At last, with even their unthinking Mimbrate heritage sobered by the realization

184

that they were facing an invincible pair, the knights of Perivor gathered and took counsel with each other. And then, en masse, they yielded.

'What a shame,' Zakath said regretfully. 'I was starting to enjoy this.'

Garion decided to ignore that.

As the two started back toward the stands to make the customary salute to the king, white-eyed Naradas came forward with an oily smile. 'Congratulations, Sir Knights,' he said. 'You are men of great prowess and extraordinary skill. You have won the field and the laurels of the day. Mayhap you have heard of the great prize of honor and glory that is to be bestowed upon the champions of this field?'

'No,' Garion said flatly. 'I can't say that we have.'

'You have contested this day for the honor of subduing a troublesome beast that betimes hath disturbed the peace of our fair kingdom.'

'What kind of beast?' Garion asked suspiciously.

'Why, a dragon, of course, Sir Knight.'

CHAPTER FOURTEEN

'He's tricked us again, hasn't he?' Beldin growled when they had returned to their quarters following the tourney. 'White-eyes is beginning to irritate me just a bit. I think I'll take some steps.'

'Too noisy,' Belgarath told him. 'The people here are not entirely Mimbrate.' He turned to Cyradis. 'There's a certain sound sorcery makes,' he said.

'Yes,' she replied. 'I know.'

'Can *you* hear it?'

She nodded.

'Are there other Dals here on the island who can hear it, as well?'

'Yes, Ancient Belgarath.'

'How about these counterfeit Mimbrates? They're at least half Dal. Is it possible that some of them might be able to hear it, too?'

'Entirely so.'

'Grandfather,' Garion said in a worried tone, 'that means that half the people in Dal Perivor heard what I did to the lances.'

'Not over the noise of the crowd, they didn't.'

'I didn't know that would make a difference.'

'Of course it does.'

'Well,' Silk said grimly, 'I won't use sorcery, and I can guarantee that there won't be any noise.'

'But there *will* be a certain amount of evidence, Kheldar,' Sadi pointed out, 'and since we're the only strangers in the palace, there might be some embarrassing questions if they find Naradas with one of your daggers sticking out of his back. Why don't you let me handle it? I can make things look much more natural.'

'You're talking about cold-blooded murder, Sadi,' Durnik accused.

'I appreciate your sensibilities, Goodman Durnik,' the eunuch replied, 'but Naradas has already tricked us twice and, each time he does, he delays us that much more. We have to get him out of the way.'

'He's right, Durnik,' Belgarath said.

'Zith?' Velvet suggested to Sadi.

He shook his head. 'She won't leave her babies – not even for the pleasure of biting someone. I have a few other things that are just as effective. They're not quite as fast perhaps, but they get the job done.'

'Zakath and I still have to come up against Zandramas,' Garion said glumly, 'and this time we'll have to do it alone – because of that stupid tournament.'

'It won't be Zandramas,' Velvet told him. 'Ce'Nedra and I spoke with some of the young ladies here at court while you two were out there being magnificent. They told us that this "fearsome beast" has been showing up from time to time for centuries now, and Zandramas has only been active for a dozen years, hasn't she? I really think the dragon you'll be fighting will be the real one.'

'I'm not so sure, Liselle,' Polgara disagreed. 'Zandramas can take the form of that dragon at any time. If the real one is asleep in her lair, it could very well be Zandramas who's been out there terrorizing the countryside this time – all as a part of the scheme to force a confrontation *before* we get to the place of the meeting.'

'I'll know which it is as soon as I get a look at it,' Garion said.

'How?' Zakath asked him.

'The first time we met, I cut off about four feet of her tail. If the one we run into out there has a stub tail, we'll know it's Zandramas.'

'Do we really *have* to go to this celebration tonight?' Beldin asked.

'It's expected, uncle,' Aunt Pol told him.

'But I haven't got a single solitary thing to wear, don't

y' know,' he said rogueishly, lapsing back into Feldegast's brogue.

'We'll take care of you, uncle,' she said ominously.

The affair that evening had been weeks in the planning. It was the grand finale of the tournament, and it involved dancing – in which Garion and Zakath, still in armor, could not participate. It involved a banquet – which visored, they could not eat. And it involved a great many flowery toasts to 'These mighty champions, who have lent luster to our remote isle by their presence here,' as the nobles in the court of King Oldorin vied with one another to heap extravagant praise on Garion and Zakath.

'How long is this likely to go on?' Zakath muttered to Garion.

'Hours.'

'I was afraid you might say that. Here come the ladies.'

Polgara, flanked by Ce'Nedra and Velvet, entered the throne room almost as if she owned it. Cyradis, strangely – or perhaps not – was not with them. Polgara, as usual, was gowned in royal blue velvet trimmed with silver. She looked magnificent. Ce'Nedra wore a cream-colored gown much like her wedding dress, although the seed pearls which had adorned her nuptial gown were missing. Her wealth of coppery-colored hair spilled down in curls over one shoulder. Velvet was gowned in lavender satin. Any number of the young knights of Perivor – those who could still walk after the day's entertainment – were hopelessly smitten by the sight of her.

'Time for some obscure introductions, I think,' Garion muttered to Zakath. Pleading the necessity for anonymity, the ladies had remained in their quarters since their arrival. Garion stepped forward and escorted them to the throne. 'Your Majesty,' he said to King Oldorin, bowing slightly, 'though I may not, by reason of our need for concealment, tell thee in fulsome detail of their lands of origin, it would be discourteous of me – to both thee and to the ladies themselves – not to present them. I have the honor to present her Grace, the Duchess of Erat.' That was safe.

Nobody on this side of the world would have the faintest idea where Erat was.

Polgara curtsied with exquisite grace, 'Your Majesty,' she greeted the king in her rich voice.

He rose to his feet with alacrity. 'Your Grace,' he replied with a deep bow. 'Thy presence here illuminates our poor palace.'

'And, your Majesty,' Garion went on, 'Her Highness, Princess Xera.' Ce'Nedra stared at him. 'Your real name might be too well-known,' he whispered to her.

Ce'Nedra recovered instantly. 'Your Majesty,' she said with a curtsy every bit as graceful as Polgara's. After all, a girl can't grow up in an imperial court without learning a *few* things.

'Your Highness,' the king responded. 'Thy beauty doth rob my poor tongue of speech.'

'Isn't he nice?' Ce'Nedra murmured.

'And lastly, your Majesty,' Garion concluded, 'but certainly not the least, the Margravine of Turia,' he introduced Velvet, making the name up on the spur of the moment.

Velvet curtsied. 'Your Majesty,' she said. When she straightened, she was smiling, leveling the full impact of her dimples upon him.

'My Lady,' the king faltered, bowing once again, 'thy smile doth stop my heart.' He looked around, a bit puzzled. 'Methinks I do remember another lady among thy companions, Sir Knight,' he said to Garion.

'A poor blind girl, your Majesty,' Polgara interceded, 'who hath but recently joined us. Courtly entertainments, I fear, would be lost on one who lives in darkness perpetual. She is in the care of the enormous man in our company, one of her family's faithful retainers, who hath guided and protected her since the melancholy occasion when the light of day forever vanished from her eyes.'

Two great tears of sympathy trickled down the king's cheeks. Arends, even transplanted ones, were, after all, an emotional people.

Then other companions entered, and Garion was glad

that his visor hid his grin. Beldin's face was like a thunder-cloud. His hair and beard had been washed and combed, and he wore a blue robe not unlike Belgarath's white one. Garion proceeded with a group of introductions as fraudulent as the previous ones, concluding with, 'And this, your Majesty, is Master Feldegast, a supremely talented jester, whose rare japes do lighten the weary miles for us all.'

Beldin scowled at him and then made a cursory bow. 'Ah, yer Majesty, 'tis overwhelmed I am by the splendor of yer city an' yer magnificent palace here. 'Tis a match fer Tol Honeth, Mal Zeth, an' Melcene — all of which places I have seen in th' plyin' of me trade an' demonstratin' me unspeakable talents, don't y' know.'

The king was grinning broadly. 'Master Feldegast,' he said, inclining his head. 'In a world full of sorrow, such men as thou art rare and precious.'

'Ah, isn't it grand of y' t' say it, yer Majesty?'

Then, with the formalities over, Garion and the others drifted away to mingle. A determined-looking young lady advanced on Garion and Zakath. 'You are the greatest knights on life, my Lords,' she greeted them with a curtsy, 'and the exalted stations of your companions do proclaim louder than words that ye are both men of high, mayhap even royal, rank.' She gave Garion a smoldering look. 'Art thou perchance betrothed, Sir Knight?' she asked.

Another one of those repetitions, Garion groaned inwardly. 'Married, my Lady,' he replied. This time he knew how to deal with the situation.

'Ah,' she said, her eyes clearly disappointed. Then she turned to Zakath. 'And thou, my Lord?' she asked, 'art thou espoused as well — or betrothed, perchance?'

'Nay, my Lady,' Zakath answered, sounding puzzled.

Her eyes brightened.

Garion stepped in at that point. 'It is time, my friend, for thee to consume yet another draft of that admittedly foul-tasting potion.'

'Potion?' Zakath asked in a baffled voice.

Garion sighed. 'Thy malady worsens, I perceive,' he said,

feigning a sorrowful voice. 'This forgetfulness of thine is, I fear me, a precursor of the more violent symptoms which will inevitably ensue. Pray to all seven Gods that we may conclude our quest 'ere the hereditary madness, the curse of thy family, o'erwhelms thee quite.'

The determined-looking young lady backed away, her eyes wide with fright.

'What *are* you talking about, Garion?' Zakath muttered.

'I've been through this before. The girl was looking for a husband.'

'That's absurd.'

'Not to her, it wasn't.'

And then the dancing started. Garion and Zakath drew off to one side to watch. 'It's a silly pastime, isn't it?' Zakath observed. 'I've never known why any sane man would choose to waste time on it.'

'Because the ladies love to dance,' Garion told him. 'I've never met one who didn't. It's in their blood, I think.' He looked toward the throne and saw that King Oldorin was unoccupied at the moment. He sat smiling and tapping his foot in time to the music. 'Let's find Belgarath and go talk with the king. This might be a good time to ask about that chart.'

Belgarath was leaning against one of the buttresses, watching the dancers with a slightly bored look on his face. 'Grandfather,' Garion said to him, 'nobody's talking to the king right now. Why don't we go ask him about that map?'

'Good idea. This party's likely to last well into the night, so there won't be much chance for a private audience.'

They approached the throne and bowed. 'Might we have a word with thee, your Majesty?' Garion asked.

'Of course, Sir Knight. Thou and thy companion are my champions, and it would be churlish of me indeed not to lend an ear to thee. What is this matter which concerns thee?'

'It is but a small thing, your Majesty. Master Garath

191

here—' Garion had dropped the 'Bel' in making the introduction. '— as I told thee earlier, is mine eldest advisor and he hath guided my steps since earliest childhood. In addition, he is a scholar of some note and hath recently turned his attention to the study of geography. There hath been a long-standing dispute among geographers concerning the configuration of the world of antiquity. By purest chance, Master Garath happened to hear of an ancient chart which, his informant assured him, is kept here in the palace in Dal Perivor. Beset by raging curiosity, Master Garath hath implored me to inquire of thee if thou knowest if such a chart doth indeed exist, and if perchance thou dost, if thou wilt give him permission to peruse it.'

'Indeed, Master Garath,' the king said, 'I do assure thee that thine informant was not in error. The chart you seek is one of our most prized relics, for it is the self-same chart which guided our ancestors to the shores of this isle eons ago. As soon as we have leisure, I will be most happy to provide thee access to it in furtherance of thy studies.'

Then Naradas stepped from behind the purple drape at the back of the throne. 'There will be, I fear me, scant time for studies for some while, your Majesty,' he said, sounding just a bit smug. 'Forgive me, my King, but I chanced to overhear thy last remark as I was hurrying to bring thee perhaps distressing news. A messenger hath arrived from the east advising that the foul dragon doth even now ravage the village of Dal Esta not three leagues from here. The beast is unpredictable in its depradations and may lurk in the forest for days 'ere it emerge again. It well may be that this tragic occurrence is to our advantage. Now is the time to strike. What better opportunity than this for our two brave champions to sally forth and rid us of this nuisance? And I do perceive that these powerful knights do rely heavily upon the advice of this ancient man, and it is fitting therefore that he should accompany them to guide their strategy.'

'Well spoken, Erezel,' the silly king agreed enthusiastically. 'I had feared me that flushing the beast from hiding

192

might have consumed weeks. Now it is accomplished in the space of a single night. Venture forth then, my champions and Master Garath. Rid my kingdom of this dragon, and no boon ye ask shall be denied thee.'

'Thy happy discovery was timely, Master Erezel,' Belgarath said. The words were bland, but Garion knew his grandfather well enough to recognize their implication. 'As his Majesty hath said, thou hast saved us much time this night. As soon as I have leisure, I will think of some way to thank thee properly.'

Naradas shrank back slightly, his face apprehensive. 'No thanks are necessary, Master Garath,' he said. 'I did no more than my duty to my king and his realm.'

'Ah yes,' Belgarath said, 'duty. We all have many duties, don't we? Commend me to the Child of Dark when next thou prayest to her. Advise her that, as is foreordained, we shall meet anon.'

Then he turned and, with Garion and Zakath close behind him, he strode out among the dancers and left the throne room. So long as he had been in the presence of strangers, the old man's expression had been neutral. Once they reached the deserted corridor, however, he began to swear savagely. 'I was right on the verge of getting my hands on that chart,' he fumed. 'Naradas has done it to me again.'

'Should I go back and get the others?' Garion asked.

'No. They'd all want to go along, and that'd only start an argument. We'll leave a note.'

'Again?'

'These repetitions are cropping up more and more regularly, aren't they?'

'Let's hope Aunt Pol doesn't react the same way this time.'

'What are you two talking about?' Zakath asked.

'Silk, Grandfather, and I slipped out of Riva when we went to meet Torak,' Garion explained. 'We left a note, but Aunt Pol didn't take it too well. As I understand it, there was a lot of swearing and a number of explosions.'

'Lady Polgara? She's the very soul of gentility.'

'Don't be deceived, Zakath,' Belgarath told him. 'Pol's got a vile temper when things don't go the way she wants them to go.'

'It must be a family trait,' Zakath said blandly.

'Are you trying to be funny? You two go down to the stables. Tell the grooms to saddle our horses and find out where this village is. I want to talk with Cyradis a moment before we leave. I'm going to get some straight answers out of that girl. I'll join you in the courtyard in a few minutes.'

It was perhaps ten minutes later when they mounted. Garion and Zakath took their lances from the rack at the stable wall, and then the three of them rode out of the palace compound. 'Any luck with Cyradis?' Garion asked Belgarath.

'Some. She told me that the dragon out there is *not* Zandramas.'

'It's the real one then?'

'Probably. She got cryptic on me then, though. She said that there's some other spirit influencing the dragon. That means you'll both have to be very careful. The dragon's very stupid normally, but if some spirit's guiding her, she might be a bit more perceptive.'

A shadow slunk from a dark side street. It was the she-wolf.

'How is it with you, little sister?' Garion greeted her formally. At the last instant, he avoided calling her 'Grandmother.'

'One is content,' she replied. 'You go to hunt. One will accompany you.'

'One must advise you that the creature we seek is not fit for eating.'

'One does not hunt only to eat.'

'We will be glad of your company then.'

'What did she say?' Zakath asked.

'She wants to go along.'

'Did you warn her that it's going to be dangerous?'

'I think she already knows.'

'It's up to her,' Belgarath shrugged. 'Trying to tell a wolf what to do is an exercise in futility.'

They passed out through the city gate and took the road to which one of the grooms had directed Garion. 'He said it's about eight miles,' Garion said.

Belgarath squinted up at the night sky. 'Good,' he said, 'there's a full moon. Let's try a gallop until we get to about a mile from that village.'

'How will we know when we're that close?' Zakath asked.

'We'll know,' Belgarath replied bleakly. 'There'll be all kinds of fire.'

'They don't *really* breathe fire, do they?'

'Yes, as a matter of fact, they do. You're both wearing armor, so that makes it a little safer. Her sides and belly are a bit softer than her back. Try to get your lances into her, then finish her off with your swords. Let's not drag this out. I want to get back to the palace and get my hands on that map. Let's ride.'

It was about an hour later when they saw the red glow of fire just ahead. Belgarath reined in. 'Let's go carefully,' he said. 'We'll want to pinpoint her location before we go charging in there.'

'One will go look,' the she-wolf said and loped off into the darkness.

'I'm glad she came along,' Belgarath said. 'For some reason it's comforting to have her around.'

Garion's visor concealed his smile.

The village of Dal Esta was perched on a hilltop, and they could see the sooty red flames shooting up out of burning barns and houses. They rode up the hill a ways and found the wolf waiting for them. 'One has seen the creature we seek,' she advised. 'It is feeding just now on the other side of that hill where the dens of the man-things are.'

'What's it feeding on?' Garion asked apprehensively.

'A beast such as the one upon which you sit.'

'Well?' Zakath asked.

'The dragon's on the other side of the village,' Belgarath told him. 'She's eating a horse just now.'

'A *horse*? Belgarath, this isn't a good time for surprises. Just how big is that thing?'

'About the size of a house – that's not counting the wings, of course.'

Zakath swallowed hard. 'Could we perhaps reconsider this? I haven't taken much joy in my life until recently. I'd sort of like to savor it a little longer.'

'I'm afraid we're committed now,' Garion told him. 'She doesn't fly very fast, and it takes her quite a while to get off the ground. If we can surprise her while she's eating, we might be able to kill her before she attacks.'

They rode carefully around the hill, noting the trampled crops and the carcasses of half-eaten cows. There were a few other dead things, as well – things at which Garion carefully avoided looking.

And then they saw it. 'Torak's teeth!' Zakath swore. 'It's bigger than an elephant!'

The dragon was holding down the carcass of a horse with its front claws, and she was not so much feeding as she was ravening.

'Give it a try,' Belgarath said. 'She's usually a bit unwary when she's eating. Be careful, though. Get clear of her as soon as you sink your lances into her. And don't let your horses go down. She'll kill them if they do, and a man on foot is at a serious disadvantage when he's fighting a dragon. Our little sister and I will slip around to the rear and attack her tail. She's sensitive there, and a few bites might distract her.' He dismounted, walked some distance away from the horses, and blurred into the shape of the great silver wolf.

'That still unnerves me,' Zakath admitted.

Garion had been looking carefully at the feeding dragon. 'Notice that she has her wings raised,' he said quietly. 'With her head down like that, they block her vision toward the rear. You go around to that side, and I'll go to this one. When we both get into position, I'll whistle. That's when we'll charge. Go in as fast as you can and try to stay behind that upraised wing. Sink your lance as deep into her as you can and leave it stuck in. A couple of lances hanging out of her should impede her movements a bit. Once you get the lance in, wheel and get out of there.'

'You're awfully cold-blooded about this, Garion.'

'In this kind of situation you almost have to be. If you stop to think about it, you'll never do it. This isn't the most rational thing we've ever done, you know. Good luck.'

'You, too.'

They separated and moved out slowly at some distance from the feeding dragon until they had flanked her on either side. Zakath dipped his lance twice to indicate that he was in position. Garion drew in a deep breath. He noticed that his hands were shaking slightly. He shook off all thought and concentrated on a spot just behind the dragon's front shoulder. Then he whistled shrilly.

They charged.

As far as it went, Garion's strategy worked quite well. The dragon's scaly hide, however, was much tougher than he had expected, and their lances did not penetrate as deeply as he might have wished. He wheeled Chretienne and rode away at a dead run.

The dragon shrieked, belching fire, and she tried to turn toward Garion. As he had hoped, the lances protruding from her sides impeded her movements. Then Belgarath and the she-wolf darted in, savagely biting and tearing at the scaly tail. Desperately, the dragon began to flap her sail-like wings. She rose ponderously into the air, screeching and belching out fire.

'She's getting away!' Garion threw the thought at his grandfather.

'She'll be back. She's a very vindictive beast.'

Garion rode past the dead horse and rejoined Zakath.

'The wounds we inflicted are probably mortal, aren't they?' the Mallorean said hopefully.

'I wouldn't count on it,' Garion replied. 'We didn't get the lances in deep enough, I'm afraid. We should have backed off another hundred yards to pick up more momentum. Grandfather says that we can expect her back.'

'*Garion,*' Belgarath's voice sounded in his mind, '*I'm going to do something. Tell Zakath not to panic.*'

'Zakath,' Garion said, 'Grandfather's going to use sorcery of some kind. Don't get excited.'

'What's he going to do?'

'I don't know. He didn't tell me.' Then Garion felt the familiar surge and rush of sound. The air around them turned a pale azure.

'Colorful,' Zakath said. 'What's it supposed to do?' His voice sounded nervous.

Belgarath came padding out of the darkness. 'Good enough,' he said in the language of wolves.

'What is it?' Garion asked.

'It's a kind of a shield. It'll protect you from the fire – at least partially. The armor should take care of the rest. You might get singed a bit, but the fire won't really hurt you. Don't get *too* brave, though. She still has claws and fangs.'

'It's a shield of sorts,' Garion told Zakath. 'It should help to protect us from the flame.'

Then from off to the east there was a scream and a sooty belch of fire up in the sky. 'Get ready!' Garion said sharply. 'She's coming back!' Cautioning the Orb to behave itself, he drew Iron-grip's sword. Zakath also pulled his broadsword from its sheath with a steely hiss. 'Spread out,' Garion said. 'Get far enough away so that she can only attack one of us at a time. If she comes at you, I'll attack her from behind. If she comes at me, you do the same. If you can manage it, try for her tail. She goes all to pieces when somebody attacks that. She'll try to turn around to protect it. Then whichever one of us is in front of her might be able to get a clear swing at her neck.'

'Right,' Zakath said.

They fanned out again, tensely awaiting the dragon's attack.

Their lances, Garion saw, had been bitten off, leaving

only short stumps protruding from the dragon's sides. It was upon Zakath that she fell, and the force of her strike knocked him out of his saddle. He floundered, trying to get to his feet as the dragon bathed him in flames.

Again and again he struggled, trying to get up, but he instinctively flinched back from each billow of flame, and the dragon's raking talons dug at him, making it impossible for him to regain his feet. Snakelike, the dragon's head darted forward, her cruel fangs screeching across his armor.

Garion discarded his strategy at that point. His friend needed immediate protection. He leaped from his saddle to run to Zakath's aid. 'I need some fire!' he barked at the Orb, and his sword immediately burst into bright blue flame. He knew that Torak had made the dragon invincible to common sorcery on the day he had created her, but he hoped that she might not be immune to the power of the Orb. He stepped in front of Zakath's struggling body and drove the dragon back with great, two-handed strokes. Iron-grip's sword sizzled each time it bit into her face, and she shrieked in pain with every stroke. She did not, however, flee.

'Get up!' Garion shouted to Zakath. 'Get on your feet!' Behind him he could hear the rattling of Zakath's armor as the Mallorean struggled to rise. Suddenly ignoring the pain Garion's blows were causing her, the dragon clawed at him with her talons, knocking him off-balance. He stumbled backwards and fell on top of Zakath. The dragon shrieked in triumph and lunged in. Desperately, Garion stabbed with his sword, and with a great, sizzling hiss, her bulging left eyeball collapsed. Even as he struggled to get back up again, a strange notion came to Garion. It was the same eye. Torak's left eye had been destroyed by the power of the Orb, and now the same thing had happened to the dragon. Despite the dreadful danger they were in, Garion was suddenly certain that they would win.

The dragon had fallen back, bellowing in pain and rage. Garion took advantage of that. He scrambled to his feet

199

and yanked Zakath up. 'Get around to her left side!' he barked. 'She's blind on that side now! I'll keep her attention! You swing at her neck!'

They separated, moving fast to get into position before the dragon could recover. Garion swung his great, blazing sword as hard as he could and opened a huge wound across the dragon's snout. The blood spurted out, drenching his armor, and the dragon answered his blow with a billow of flame that engulfed him. He ignored the fire and drove in, swinging stroke after stroke at her face. He could see Zakath directing two-handed blows at the snake-like neck, but the heavy, overlapping scales defeated his best efforts. Garion continued his attack with the burning sword. The half-blinded dragon clawed at him, and he struck at the scaly forepaw, half severing it. Injured now almost beyond endurance, the dragon began a grudging, step-by-step retreat.

'Keep on her!' Garion shouted to Zakath. 'Don't give her time to set herself again!'

Grimly, the pair drove the hideous beast back and back, alternating their blows. When Garion struck, the dragon turned her head to bathe him in fire. Then Zakath would swing at the unprotected back of her head. She would swivel her head to meet his attack, and then Garion would strike at her. Confused and frustrated by this deadly tactic, the dragon helplessly swung her head back and forth, her furnacelike breath singeing bushes and turf more often than it did her attackers. Finally, driven beyond her ability to bear the pain, she began to desperately flap her sail-like wings, clumsily attempting to rise from the earth.

'Don't let up!' Garion called. 'Keep pushing her!' They continued their savage attack. 'Try to get her wings!' Garion yelled. 'Don't let her get away!'

They switched their attack to the batlike wings, desperately striving to cripple the dragon's final option, but her armored skin defeated their purpose. Ponderously, she rose into the air, and still shrieking, belching flame and streaming blood from her many wounds, she flew off toward the east.

Belgarath had resumed his own form and he strode up to them, his face livid with rage. 'Are you two insane?' he almost screamed at them. 'I told you to be careful!'

'Things got a little out of hand there, Belgarath,' Zakath panted. 'We didn't have much choice in the matter.' He looked at the Rivan King. 'You saved my life again, Garion,' he said. 'You're starting to make a habit of that.'

'It sort of seemed like the thing to do,' Garion replied, sinking exhausted to the ground. 'We're still going to have to chase her down, though. If we don't, she'll only come back.'

'One does not think so,' the she-wolf said. 'One has had much experience with wounded beasts. You poked sticks into her, put out her eye, and cut her face and forepaw with fire. She will return to her den and remain there until she heals – or dies.'

Garion quickly translated for Zakath.

'It presents a problem, though,' the Emperor of Mallorea said dubiously. 'How are we going to persuade the king that we've driven her off for good? If we'd have killed her, we'd have no further obligation, but the king – with Naradas prompting him – might very well insist that we stay here until he's sure she's not coming back.'

Belgarath was frowning. 'I think Cyradis was right,' he said. 'The dragon wasn't behaving exactly right. Each time Garion hit her with that burning sword, she flinched momentarily.'

'Wouldn't you have?' Zakath asked him.

'This is a little different. The dragon herself wouldn't even feel fire. She was being directed by something – something that the Orb can injure. I'll talk it over with Beldin when we get back. As soon as you two get your breath, we'll round up the horses. I want to get back to Dal Perivor and have a look at that map.'

CHAPTER FIFTEEN

It was nearly dawn by the time they returned to the palace, and to their surprise, they found nearly everyone awake. A ripple of gasps ran through the throne room as Garion and Zakath entered. Garion's armor was scorched and red with the dragon's blood; Zakath's surcoat was charred, and great fang-marks scarred one side of his breastplate. The condition of their armor gave mute testimony to the seriousness of the encounter.

'My glorious champions!' the king exulted as they entered the throne room. It appeared to Garion at first that the king was leaping to a conclusion – that because they had returned alive, they had succeeded in killing the dragon.

'In all the years that this foul beast hath been ravaging this realm,' the king said, however, 'this is the first time anyone hath forced it to flee.' Then, noting Belgarath's puzzled look, he elaborated. 'Not two hours ago, we observed the dragon flying over the city, shrieking in pain and fright.'

'Which way did it go, your Majesty?' Garion asked.

'It was last seen flying out to sea, Sir Knight, and, as all men know, its lair lies somewhere to the west. The chastisement thou and thy valiant companion administered hath driven it from the realm. Doubtless it will seek shelter in its lair and lick its wound there. Now, an it please you, our ears hunger for an account of what transpired.'

'Let me,' Belgarath muttered. He stepped forward. 'Thy two champions, your Majesty, are modest men, as befits their nobility. They would, I do fear me, be reticent in their description of their exploit out of a desire not to appear boastful. Better, perhaps that I describe the encounter for them so that your Majesty and the members of thy court receive a truer version of what actually occurred.'

'Well said, Master Garath,' the king replied. 'True humility is the crown of any man of noble birth, but it doth, as thou sayest, oft-times obscure the truth of an encounter such as this night hath witnessed. Say on, I pray thee.'

'Where to begin?' Belgarath mused. 'Ah, well. As your Majesty knoweth, Master Erezel's timely warning that the dragon was ravaging the village of Dal Esta came not a moment too soon. Directly upon our departure from this very hall, we took to horse and rode post haste to the aforementioned village. Great fires burned there, graphic evidence of the dragon's fiery breath, and cattle and many of the inhabitants had already been slain and partially consumed by the beast – for whom all flesh is food.'

'Piteous,' the king sighed.

'His commiseration is all very pretty,' Zakath murmured to Garion, 'but I wonder if he'll be willing to dip into his treasury to aid the villagers in the reconstruction of their homes.'

'You mean actually to give back some of the taxes after he's gone to all the trouble of extorting them from his people?' Garion asked in mock surprise. 'What a shocking thing to suggest.'

'Carefully, thy champions reconnoitered the area around the village,' Belgarath was saying, 'and they soon located the dragon, which was at that very moment feeding on the bodies of a herd of horses.'

'I only saw one,' Zakath whispered.

'Sometimes he embellishes things to make his stories more exciting,' Garion whispered back.

Belgarath was warming to his subject now. 'Advised by me,' he said modestly, 'thy champions paused to take stock of the situation. At once we all perceived that the dragon's attention was wholly riveted upon its grisly feast, and of a certainty, because of its size and savagery, it had never been given reason to be wary. Thy champions separated and circled around the feeding dragon that they might attack one from either side, hoping thereby to drive their lances into its vitals. Cautiously, step by step, they moved, for though they are the bravest men on life, they are not foolhardy.'

There was absolute silence in the throne room as the king's court listened to the old man with that same breathless fascination Garion had seen before in the dining hall at Faldor's farm.

'Isn't he laying it on a bit thick?' Zakath whispered.

'It's a compulsion, I think,' Garion whispered back. 'Grandfather's never been able to let a good story rest on its own merits. He always feels the need for artistic enhancement.'

Certain now that he had his audience's full attention, Belgarath began to utilize all those subtle tricks of the storyteller's art. He altered pitch and volume. He changed cadences. Sometimes, his voice dropped to a whisper. He was obviously enjoying himself enormously. He described the simultaneous charge on the dragon in glowing detail. He told of the dragon's inital retreat, adding gratuitously a wholly fictional feeling of triumph in the hearts of the two knights and their belief that they had struck mortal blows with their lances. Though this last was not entirely true, it helped to heighten the suspense.

'I wish I'd seen *that* fight,' Zakath murmured. 'Ours was a lot more prosaic.'

The old man then went on to describe the dragon's vengeful return, and, just to make things interesting, he expanded hugely on Zakath's mortal peril. 'And then,' he went on, 'heedless of his own life, his stalwart companion leaped into the fray. Sick with the fear that his friend might already have received fatal injury and filled with righteous rage, he hurled himself into the very teeth of the beast with great two-handed strokes of his mighty blade.'

'Were you really thinking those things?' Zakath asked Garion.

'Approximately.'

'And then,' Belgarath said, 'though it may have been

some trick of the flickering light coming from the burning village, me thought I saw the hero's blade come all aflame. Again and again he struck, and each stroke was rewarded with rivers of bright blood and with shrieks of agony. And then, horror of horrors, a chance blow from the dragon's mighty talons hurled our champion back, and then he stumbled, and then he fell – full upon the body of his companion, who was still vainly striving to rise.'

Groans of despair came from the throng crowding the throne room, even though the presence of the two heroes plainly said that they had survived.

'I admit it freely,' Belgarath continued, 'that I felt dark despair in my heart. But as the savage dragon souught to slay our champions, the one – I may not say his name – plunged his burning sword into the very eye of the loathesome beast.'

There was a great roar of applause.

'Shrieking in pain, the dragon faltered and fell back. Our champions took advantage of this momentary opportunity to regain their feet. And then what a mighty battle ensued.' Belgarath proceeded in loving detail to describe at least ten times more sword strokes than Garion and Zakath had actually delivered.

'If I'd swung that sword that many times, my arms would have fallen off,' Zakath said.

'Never mind,' Garion said. 'He's enjoying himself.'

'At last,' Belgarath concluded, 'unable to any longer bear the dreadful punishment, the dragon, which had never known fear before, turned and cravenly fled from the field, to pass, as your Majesty hath said, directly over this fair city toward its hidden lair, where the fear it hath learned this night will, methinks, canker far more than the wounds it received. It will, I believe, never return to thy kingdom, your Majesty, for, stupid though it may be, it will not willingly return to the place which hath been the site of so much pain. And that, your Majesty, is exactly what happened.'

'Masterful!' the king said delightedly. And from the

assemblage there in the throne room came thunderous applause. Belgarath turned and bowed, signaling to Garion and Zakath to do likewise, generously permitting them to share in the adulation.

The nobles of the court, some of them with actual tears in their eyes, pressed forward to congratulate the trio, Garion and Zakath for their heroism and Belgarath for his lurid description of it. Naradas, Garion noticed, stood at the king's elbow, his dead white eyes burning with hatred. 'Brace yourselves,' Garion warned his friends. 'Naradas is planning something.'

When the hubbub had died down, the white-eyed Grolim stepped to the front of the dais. 'I, too, join my voice with these others in this hall to heap praise upon these mighty heroes and their brilliant advisor. Never hath this kingdom seen their match. Methinks, however, that caution is indicated here. I do fear me that Master Garath, fresh from the scene of this unutterably magnificent struggle and understandably exhilarated by what he hath witnessed, may have been too sanguine in his assessment of the dragon's present state of mind. Truly, most normal creatures would shun a place which hath been the locale of such desperate agony, but this foul, loathesome brute is no normal creature. Might it not be more probable that, given what we know of it, it will instead be consumed with rage and a hunger and a thirst for revenge? Should these mighty champions depart now, this fair and beloved kingdom would lie defenseless beneath the vengeful depradations of a creature consumed with hatred.'

'I *knew* he was going to do that,' Zakath grated.

'I am honor bound, therefore,' Naradas added, 'to advise his Majesty and the members of his court to consider long and well rather than make hasty decision concerning the disposition of these knights. We have seen that they are perhaps the only two on life who can face this monster with any hope of success. Of what other knights in all this land are there any of whom we can make the same statement with any degree of certainty?'

'What thou sayest may well be true, Master Erezel,' the king said with surprising coolness, 'but it would be churlish of me to hold them here against their will in view of the sacred nature of the quest in which they are engaged. We have delayed them here too long already. They have rendered us amply sufficient service. To insist on more would be ungrateful of us in the extreme. I thereby decree that tomorrow will be a day of celebration and of gratitude throughout the realm and shall culminate with a royal banquet at which we will honor these mighty champions and bid them a regretful farewell. I do perceive that the sun hath risen, and our champions are doubtless greatly fatigued by the rigors of the tourney of yesterday and by their encounter last night with the loathesome dragon. This day, therefore, will be a day of preparation, and tomorrow will be a day of joy and thanksgiving. Let us then to our beds for a time to refresh ourselves that we may more assiduously turn to our several tasks.'

'I thought he'd never get around to that,' Zakath said as the three of them moved through the packed throne-room. 'Right now I could sleep standing up.'

'Please don't,' Garion said. 'You're wearing armor, and you'd make an awful clatter when you toppled over. I don't want to be startled out of sleep. I'm as tired as you are.'

'At least you have someone to sleep with.'

'Two someones, actually, counting the puppy. Puppies take an unwholesome interest in toes, I've noticed.'

Zakath laughed.

'Grandfather,' Garion said, 'up until now, the king has blithely gone along with anything Naradas suggested. Did you tamper with him at all?'

'I made a couple of suggestions,' Belgarath admitted. 'I don't usually like to do that, but the situation was a bit unusual.'

It was in the corridor outside where Naradas caught up with them. 'You haven't won yet, Belgarath,' he hissed.

'No, probably not,' Belgarath admitted with aplomb, 'but then, neither have you, Naradas, and I imagine Zandramas – you've heard the name before, I trust – will be a bit cross with you when she finds out how miserably you've failed here. Maybe, if you start running right now, you can get away from her – for a while, at least.'

'This isn't the end of this, Belgarath.'

'Never thought it was, old boy.' Belgarath reached out and insultingly patted Naradas on the cheek. 'Run along now, Grolim,' he advised, 'while you still have your health.' He paused. 'Unless, of course, you'd like to challenge *me*. Considering your limited talents, I don't advise it, but that's entirely up to you.'

After one startled look at the Eternal Man, Naradas fled.

'I enjoy doing that to his kind,' Belgarath gloated.

'You *are* a dreadful old man, aren't you?' Zakath said.

'Never pretended not to be, Zakath,' Belgarath grinned. 'Let's go talk with Sadi. Naradas is starting to become an inconvenience. I think it's high time he left us.'

'You'll do anything, won't you?' Zakath asked as they continued down the corridor.

'To get the job done? Of course.'

'And when I interfered with you back in Rak Hagga, you could have blown me into nothingness, couldn't you?'

'Probably, yes.'

'But you didn't. Why not?'

'Because I thought I might need you, and I saw more in you than others did.'

'More than Emperor of half the world?'

'That's trash, Zakath,' Belgarath said scornfully. 'Your friend here is Overlord of the West, and he still has trouble getting his boots on the right feet.'

'I do *not*!' Garion objected vehemently.

'That's probably because you've got Ce'Nedra to help you figure it out. That's what you really need, Zakath – a wife, someone to keep you looking reasonably presentable.'

'I'm afraid that's quite out of the question, Belgarath,' Zakath sighed.

'We'll see,' the Eternal Man said.

The greetings they received in their quarters in the royal palace at Dal Perivor were not cordial.

'You old fool!' Polgara began, speaking to her father. Things deteriorated quite rapidly from there.

'You idiot!' Ce'Nedra shrieked at Garion.

'Please, Ce'Nedra,' Polgara said patiently, 'let *me* finish first.'

'Oh, of course, Lady Polgara,' the Rivan Queen agreed politely. 'Sorry. You have many more years of aggravation than I do. Besides, I can get *this* one alone in bed and give him a piece of my mind.'

'And you wanted *me* to get married?' Zakath asked Belgarath.

'It has its drawbacks,' Belgarath replied calmly. He looked around. 'The walls are still standing, I see, and there doesn't seem to be any evidence of explosions. Maybe, eventually, you'll grow up after all, Pol.'

'Another note?' she half-shrieked. 'A miserable note?'

'We were pressed for time.'

'The three of you went up against the dragon alone?'

'More or less – yes. The she-wolf was with us, however.'

'An *animal*? That's your idea of protection?'

'She was very helpful.'

At that point, Polgara began to swear – in several different languages.

'Why, Pol,' he objected mildly, 'you don't even know what those words mean – at least I *hope* you don't.'

'Don't underestimate me, old man. This isn't over yet. All right, Ce'Nedra, it's your turn.'

'I think I'd prefer to conduct my discussions with his Majesty in private – where I can be much more direct,' the tiny queen said in an icy tone.

Garion winced.

Then, surprisingly, Cyradis spoke. 'It was discourteous of thee, Emperor of Mallorea, to hurl thyself into mortal danger without first consulting me.' Belgarath, it appeared, had been characteristically obscure in his discussion with her before they had gone forth to face the dragon, conveniently forgetting to mention what they proposed to do.

'I beg thy forgiveness, Holy Seeress,' Zakath apologized, lapsing, perhaps unconsciously, into archaic language. 'The urgency of the matter was such that there was no time for consultation.'

'Nicely spoken,' Velvet murmured. 'We'll make a gentleman out of him yet.'

Zakath raised his visor and grinned at her – a surprisingly boyish grin.

'As it may be, Kal Zakath,' Cyradis continued sternly, 'know that I am wroth with thee for thy hasty and unthinking rashness.'

'I am covered with confusion, Holy Seeress, that I have offended thee, and I hope that thou canst find it in thy heart to forgive mine error.'

'Oh,' Velvet sighed, 'he'll be *just* fine. Kheldar, were you taking notes?'

'Me?' Silk sounded surprised.

'Yes. You.'

There were *far* too many things going on, and Garion was hovering on the verge of exhaustion. 'Durnik,' he said a bit plaintively, 'can you help me out of this?' He rapped his knuckles on the breastplate of his armor.

'If you wish.' Even Durnik's voice sounded cold.

'Does he really *have* to sleep with us?' Garion complained about midmorning.

'He's warm,' Ce'Nedra replied in a snippy tone, 'which is more than I can say for some others. Besides, he sort of fills the vacancy I have in my heart – in a small way, of course.'

The wolf puppy under the covers was enthusiastically licking Garion's toes, then, inevitably, fell to nibbling.

They slept for a goodly part of the day, rising about

midafternoon. They sent a servant to the king, asking to be excused from this night's festivities, pleading extreme fatigue.

'Wouldn't this be a good time to ask to see that map?' Beldin asked.

'I don't think so,' Belgarath replied. 'Naradas is getting desperate now. He knows how unforgiving Zandramas can be, so he'll do just about anything to keep us away from that chart. He still has the king's ear, and he'll come up with all kinds of excuses to stop us. Why don't we just let him wonder about what we're up to. It might help to keep him off-balance until Sadi has the chance to put him to sleep.'

The eunuch bowed a bit mockingly.

'There's an alternative, Belgarath,' Silk volunteered. 'I could slip around a bit and fish for information. If I can pinpoint the location of the map, a bit of burglary could solve our problem.'

'What if you got caught?' Durnik asked.

'Please, Durnik,' Silk said in a pained voice, 'don't be insulting.'

'It's got some possibilities,' Velvet said. 'Kheldar could steal a man's teeth even if the man had his mouth closed.'

'Better not chance it,' Polgara told her. 'Naradas is a Grolim, and he may very well have laid a few traps around that chart. He knows all of us, by reputation at least, and I'm sure he's fully aware of Silk's specialized talents.'

'Do we really have to kill him?' Eriond asked sadly, 'Naradas, I mean?'

'I don't think we have any choice, Eriond,' Garion said. 'As long as he's still alive, we'll be stumbling over him at every turn.' He frowned. 'It may be my imagination, but Zandramas seems very reluctant to leave the choice to Cyradis. If she can block us, she'll win by default.'

'Thy perception is not altogether awry, Belgarion,' Cyradis told him. 'Zandramas indeed hath done all in her power to thwart my task.' She smiled briefly. 'I tell thee truly, she hath caused me much vexation, and were the choice to be between her and thee, well might I be tempted to choose against her by way of retribution.'

'I never thought I'd hear that from one of the seers,' Beldin said. 'Are you actually coming down off that fence, Cyradis?'

She smiled again. 'Dear, gentle Beldin,' she said affectionately, 'our neutrality is not the result of whim, but of duty – a duty laid upon us before even thou wast born.'

Since they had slept most of the day, they talked well into the night. Garion awoke refreshed the next morning and prepared to face the day's festivities.

The nobles at the court of King Oldorin had utilized the previous day and probably half the night preparing speeches – long, flowery, and generally tedious speeches – in praise of 'our heroic champions'. Protected by his closed visor, Garion frequently found himself dozing – a languor brought on not by weariness, but by boredom. At one point he heard a light clang on the side of his armor.

'Ouch!' Ce'Nedra said, rubbing her elbow.

'What's the matter, dear?'

'Do you *have* to wear all that steel?'

'Yes, but you know I'm wearing it. What possessed you to try to gouge me in the ribs?'

'Habit, I suppose. Stay awake, Garion.'

'I wasn't sleeping,' he lied.

'Really? Why were you snoring then?'

Following the speeches, the king assessed the glassy-eyed condition of his court and called upon 'Good Master Feldegast' to lighten things up.

Beldin was at his outrageous best that day. He walked on his hands; he did astonishing back-flips; he juggled with amazing dexterity – all the while telling jokes in his lilting brogue. 'I hope I've managed in me small way t' add t' the festivities, yer Majesty,' he concluded the performance after bowing in response to the enthusiastic applause of the assemblage.

'Thou art truly a virtuoso, Master Feldegast,' the king complimented him. 'The memory of thy performance this day will warm many a dreary winter evening in this hall.'

'Ah, yer too kind t' say it, yer Majesty,' Beldin bowed.

Before the banquet got underway, Garion and Zakath went back to their quarters for a light meal, since they would be unable to eat in the main dining hall without raising their visors. As guests of honor, however, it was incumbent upon them to be present.

'I've never gotten very much entertainment out of watching other people eat,' Zakath said quietly to Garion after they had entered the banquet hall and taken their seats.

'If you want entertainment, watch Beldin,' Garion replied. 'Aunt Pol spoke very firmly with him last night. She told him to mind his manners today. You've seen the way he usually eats. The strain of behaving himself should come very close to making him fly apart.'

Naradas sat at the king's right elbow. His white eyes were uncertain – even slightly baffled. The fact that Belgarath had made no attempt to get his hands on the map obviously confused him.

And then the serving men began to bring in the banquet. The smells made Garion's mouth water, and he began to wish that he'd eaten a bit more earlier.

'I must talk with the king's chef before we leave,' Polgara said. 'This soup is exquisite.'

Sadi chuckled slyly.

'Did I say something amusing, Sadi?'

'Just watch, Polgara. I wouldn't want to spoil it for you.'

Suddenly there was a commotion at the head of the table. Naradas had half-risen, clutching at his throat with his hands. His white eyes were bulging, and he was making strangling noises.

'He's choking!' the king cried out. 'Someone help him!'

Several of the nobles near the head of the table leapt to their feet and began to pound the Grolim on the back. Naradas, however, continued to strangle. His tongue protruded from his mouth, and his face started to turn blue.

213

'Save him!' the king almost screamed.

But Naradas was beyond saving. He arched backward, stiffened, and toppled to the floor.

There were cries of dismay from all over the dining hall.

'How did you do that?' Velvet murmured to Sadi. 'I'd take an oath that you were never anywhere near his food.'

Sadi smirked wickedly. 'I didn't have to go near his food, Liselle,' he said. 'The other night I took a rather careful note of his customary place at the table. He always sits to the king's right. I slipped in here an hour or so ago and annointed his spoon with a little something that makes a man's throat swell shut.' He paused. 'I hope he enjoyed his soup,' he added. 'I know *I* certainly did.'

'Liselle,' Silk said, 'when we get back to Boktor, why don't you have a chat with your uncle. Sadi's out of work just now, and Javelin could use a man with his talents.'

'It snows in Boktor, Kheldar,' Sadi said with some distaste, 'and I really don't like snow that much.'

'You wouldn't necessarily have to be stationed in Boktor, Sadi. How would Tol Honeth suit you? You'd have to let your hair grow, though.'

Zakath leaned forward, chuckling. 'Brilliant, Sadi,' he added his congratulations, 'and so perfectly appropriate. Naradas poisoned *me* back in Rak Hagga, and you poisoned *him* here. I'll tell you what, I'll double any offer Javelin makes you if you'll come to work for me in Mal Zeth.'

'Zakath!' Silk exclaimed.

'The employment opportunities seem to be cropping up in all quarters of the world,' Sadi observed.

'Good men are hard to find, my friend,' Zakath told him.

The king, shaking and with his face white, was being slowly escorted from the room. As he passed their table, Garion could hear him sobbing.

Belgarath began to swear under his breath.

'What's the matter, father?' Polgara asked him.

'That idiot will be in mourning for weeks. I'll *never* get my hands on that map.'

CHAPTER SIXTEEN

Belgarath was still swearing when they returned to their quarters. 'I think I've outsmarted myself,' he fumed. 'We should have exposed Naradas before we killed him. There's no way to discredit him in the king's eyes now.'

Cyradis sat at the table eating a simple meal with Toth standing protectively over her. 'What hath thee wroth, Ancient One?' she asked.

'Naradas is no longer with us,' he replied, 'and now the king's in mourning for him. It could be weeks before he recovers his composure enough to show me that map.'

Her face grew distant and Garion seemed to hear the murmur of that strange group mind. 'I am permitted to aid thee in this, Ancient One,' she said. 'The Child of Dark hath violated the commandment we laid upon her when we assigned her this task. She sent her henchman here rather than coming to seek the chart herself. Thus certain strictures upon me are relaxed.' She leaned back in her chair and spoke briefly to Toth. He nodded and quietly left the room. 'I have sent for one who will assist us,' she said.

'What exactly are you going to do?' Silk asked her.

'It might be unwise of me to tell thee in advance, Prince Kheldar. Canst thou, however, discover the location of the remains of Naradas for me?'

'I should be able to do that,' he replied. 'I'll go ask around a bit.' Then he left the room.

'And when Prince Kheldar returns with the location of dead Naradas, thou, King of Riva, and thou, Emperor of Mallorea, go even unto the king and prevail upon him in the strongest of terms to accompany you at midnight to that place, for certain truths shall be revealed to him there which may lessen his grief.'

'Cyradis,' Beldin sighed, 'why must you always complicate things?'

She smiled almost shyly. 'It is one of my few delights, gentle Beldin. To speak obscurely doth cause others to ponder my words more carefully. The dawning of understanding in them causes me a certain satisfaction.'

'Not to mention the fact that it's very irritating.'

'That perhaps is also a part of the delight,' she agreed impishly.

'You know,' Beldin said to Belgarath, 'I think she's a human being after all.'

It was about ten minutes later when Silk returned. 'Found him,' he said a bit smugly. 'They've got him laid out on a bier in the chapel of Chamdar on the main floor of the palace. I looked in on him. He's really much, much more attractive with his eyes closed. The funeral's scheduled for tomorrow. It's summer, and he probably won't keep.'

'What would be thine estimate of the hour, Goodman?' Cyradis asked Durnik.

The smith went to the window and looked up at the stars. 'I make it about an hour before midnight,' he replied.

'Go then now, Belgarion and Zakath. Use all the powers of persuasion at your command. It is absolutely essential that the king be in that chapel at midnight.'

'We'll bring him, Holy Seeress,' Zakath promised her.

'Even if we have to drag him,' Garion added.

'I wish I knew what she was up to,' Zakath said as he and Garion walked down the hall outside. 'It might make the king a bit easier to persuade if we could tell him what to expect.'

'It might also make him sceptical,' Garion disagreed. 'I think Cyradis is planning something fairly exotic, and some people have difficulty accepting that sort of thing.'

'Oh, my, yes,' Zakath grinned.

'His Majesty does not wish to be disturbed,' one of the guards at the king's door said when they asked admission.

'Tell him please that it is a matter of extremest urgency,' Garion said.

'I'll try, Sir Knight,' the guard said dubiously, 'but he is much distraught at the death of his friend.'

The guard returned a few moments later. 'His Majesty consents to see thee and thy companion, Sir Knight, but prithee, be brief. His suffering is extreme.'

'Of course,' Garion murmured.

The king's private chambers were ornate. The king himself sat in a deeply cushioned chair reading a slender volume by the light of a single candle. His face looked ravaged, and there were signs that he had been weeping. He held up the book after they had presented themselves to him. 'A volume of consolation,' he said. 'It doth not offer much of that to me, however. How may I serve ye, Sir Knights?'

'We have come in part to offer thee our condolences, your Majesty,' Garion began carefully. 'Know that first grief is always sharpest. The passage of time will dull thy pain.'

'But never banish it entirely, Sir Knight.'

'Undoubtedly true, your Majesty. What we have come to ask of thee may seem cruel in the light of present circumstances, and we would not presume to intrude upon thee were the matter not of such supreme urgency – not to us so much as it is to thee.'

'Say on, Sir Knight,' the king said, a faint interest showing in his eyes.

'There are certain truths which must be revealed unto thee this very night, your Majesty,' Garion went on, 'and they can only be revealed in the presence of thy late friend.'

'Unthinkable, Sir Knight,' the king said adamantly.

'We are assured by the one who will reveal these truths that they may in some measure assuage thy sorrow. Erezel was thy dearest friend, and he would not have thee suffer needlessly.'

'Truly,' the king conceeded. 'He was a man with a great heart.'

217

'I'm sure,' Garion said.

'There is perhaps another, more personal reason for thee to visit the chapel where Master Erezel lies in state, your Majesty,' Zakath added. 'His funeral will be held, we are told, tomorrow. The ceremony will be attended by most of thy court. This night provides thee thy last opportunity to visit with him privately and to fix his well-loved features in thy memory. My friend and I will guard the chapel door to insure that thy communion with him and with his spirit shall be undisturbed.'

The king considered that. 'It may be even as thou sayest, Sir Knight,' he conceded. 'Though it wring my heart, I would indeed look upon his face one last time. Very well, then, let us repair to the chapel.' He rose and led them from the chamber.

The chapel of Chamdar, the Arendish God, was dimly lighted by a lone candle standing on the bier at the body's head. A gold-colored cloth covered the immobile form of Naradas to the chest, and his face was calm, even serene. Knowing what he did of the Grolim's career, Garion found that apparent serenity a mockery.

'We will guard the chapel door, your Majesty,' Zakath said, 'and leave thee alone with thy friend.' He and Garion stepped back out into the corridor and closed the door.

'You were very smooth back there,' Garion told his friend.

'You weren't so bad yourself, but smooth or rough, at least we got him here.'

They stood at the door awaiting Cyradis and the others. After about a quarter of an hour, they arrived.

'Is he in there?' Belgarath asked Garion.

'Yes. We had to do a bit of fast talking, but he finally agreed.'

Standing beside Cyradis was a figure robed and hooded in black. It appeared to be a woman, a Dal most likely, but it was the first time Garion had ever seen one of that race clad in any color but white. 'This is the one who will aid us,' the Seeress said. 'Let us go in unto the king, for the hour is nigh.'

Garion opened the door, and they filed in.

The king looked up in some surprise.

'Be not dismayed, King of Perivor,' Cyradis said to him, 'for, as thy champions have told thee, we have come to reveal truths to thee, truths which will lessen thy sorrow.'

'I am grateful for thine efforts, Lady,' the king replied, 'but that is scarce possible. My sorrow may neither be lessened nor banished. Here lieth my dearest friend, and my heart lieth on that cold bier with him.'

'Thine heritage is in part Dal, your Majesty,' she said to him, 'so thou art aware that many of us possess certain gifts. There are things the one you called Erezel did not tell thee 'ere he died. I have summoned one who will question him 'ere his spirit doth sink into the darkness.'

'A necromancer? Truly? I have heard of such, but have never seen the art practiced.'

'Knowest thou that one with such gifts cannot misspeak what the spirits reveal?'

'I understand so, yes.'

'I assure thee that it is true. Let us then probe the mind of this Erezel, and see what truths he will reveal to us.'

The dark-robed and hooded necromancer stepped to the bier and laid her pale, slender hands on Naradas' chest.

Cyradis began posing the questions. 'Who art thou?' she asked.

'My name was Naradas,' the figure in black replied in a halting, hollow voice. 'I was Grolim arch-priest of the Temple of Torak at Hemil in Darshiva.'

The king stared first at Cyradis and then at the body of Naradas in stunned astonishment.

'Whom didst thou serve?' Cyradis asked.

'I served the Child of Dark, the Grolim Priestess Zandramas.'

'Wherefore camest thou to this kingdom?'

'My mistress sent me hither to seek out a certain chart

and to impede the progress of the Child of Light to the Place Which Is No More.'

'And what means didst thou use to accomplish these ends?'

'I sought out the king of this isle, a vain and foolish man, and I beguiled him. He showed me the chart which I sought, and the chart revealed to me a wonder which my shadow conveyed immediately to my mistress. Now she knows precisely where the final meeting is to take place. I prevailed upon the king's gullibility and was able to lead him into various acts which delayed the Child of Light and his companions so that my mistress might arrive at the Place Which Is No More before him and thereby avoid the necessity of leaving the issue in the hands of a certain seeress whom my mistress distrusts.'

'How is it that thy mistress did not herself perform this task, which was lain upon *her* and not upon thee?' Cyradis' voice was stern.

'Zandramas had other concerns. I was her right hand, and all that I did was as if she had done the deeds herself.'

'His spirit doth begin to sink out of reach, Holy Seeress,' the necromancer said in a more normal tone of voice. 'Ask quickly, for soon I will no longer be able to wrest further answers from him.'

'What were these concerns of thy mistress which prevented her from seeking the answer to the last riddle herself as she was commanded to do?'

'A certain Grolim Hierarch from Cthol Murgos, Agachak by name, had come to Mallorea seeking the Place Which Is No More, hoping to supplant my Mistress. He was the last of our race with enough power to challenge her. She met him near the barrens of Finda and killed him there.' The hollow voice broke off, and then there came a despairing wail. 'Zandramas!' the voice cried. 'You said that I would not die! You promised, Zandramas!' The last word seemed to fall away into some unimaginable abyss.

The dark hooded necromancer's head slumped forward, and she was shuddering violently. 'His spirit has gone,

220

Holy Seeress,' she said in a weary voice. 'The midnight hour is past, and he can no longer be reached.'

'I thank thee,' Cyradis said simply.

'I but hope, Holy Seeress, that I have been able in some small way to aid thee in thine awesome task. May I retire now? for contact with this diseased mind hath distressed me beyond measure.'

Cyradis nodded briefly, and the necromancer quietly left the chapel.

The King of Perivor, his face ashen, but firmly set, walked to the bier. He took hold of the golden cloth which covered Naradas to the chest and hurled it to the floor. 'Some rag perhaps,' he said from between clenched teeth. 'I would not look upon the face of this foul Grolim more.'

'I'll see what I can find, your Majesty,' Durnik said sympathetically. He stepped out into the hall.

The rest stood silently by as the king, his back to the bier and his jaws clenching and unclenching, stared at the back wall of the chapel.

After a few moments, the smith returned with a torn piece of burlap, rusty and mildewed. 'There was a store-room just down the hall, your Majesty,' he said. 'This was plugging up a rat hole. Was it more or less what you had in mind?'

'Perfect, my friend. And it please thee, throw it over the face of that piece of carrion. I declare here unto ye all, there will *be* no funeral for this miscreant. Some ditch and a few spadefuls of earth shall be his grave.'

'More than a few spadefuls I think, your Majesty,' Durnik suggested prudently. 'He's corrupted your kingdom enough already. We wouldn't want him to pollute it any more, would we? I'll take care of it for you.'

'I like thee, my friend,' the king said. 'And it please thee, bury the Grolim face-down.'

'We'll see to it, your Majesty,' Durnik promised. He nodded to Toth, and the two of them roughly lifted the body of Naradas from the bier by the shoulders and dragged it from the chapel with its sandal-shod feet bouncing unceremoniously across the floor.

Silk stepped closer to Zakath. 'So now we know that Agachak is dead,' he said quietly to the Mallorean. 'Urgit will be delighted to hear it. I don't suppose you'd be willing to send a messenger to him to let him know about it?'

'The tensions between your brother and myself have not relaxed all *that* much, Kheldar.'

'Who *are* ye all?' the king demanded. 'Was this so-called quest of thine mere subterfuge?'

'The time hath come for us to reveal ourselves,' Cyradis said gravely. 'The need for concealment is now past, for the other spies Zandramas hath set in this place without the knowledge of Naradas cannot commune with her without his aid.'

'That's Zandramas, all right,' Silk said. 'She doesn't even trust herself.'

Garion and Zakath raised their visors with some relief. 'I know that your kingdom is isolated, your Majesty,' Garion said in his normal dialect. 'How much do you know of the outside world?'

'There are times when seafarers call upon this harbor,' the king replied. 'They bring us news as well as goods.'

'And what of the events that shaped the world in times past?'

'Our forebearers brought many books with them, Sir Knight, for the hours at sea are long and tedious. Among those volumes were those of history, which I have read.'

'Good,' Garion said. 'That should make things a bit easier to explain. I am Belgarion, King of Riva,' he introduced himself.

The king's eyes widened. 'The Godslayer?' he asked in an awed voice.

'You've heard about that, I see,' Garion said wryly.

'All the world hath heard of it. Didst thou indeed slay the God of Angarak?'

'I'm afraid so. My friend here is Kal Zakath, Emperor of Mallorea.'

The king began to tremble. 'What event is of such magnitude that it persuaded ye two to put aside thy hereditary enmity?'

'We'll get to that in a moment, your Majesty. The helpful fellow who's out burying Naradas is Durnik, the most recent disciple of the God Aldur. The short one there is Beldin, also a disciple, and the one with the whiskers is Belgarath the Sorcerer.'

'The Eternal Man?' The king's voice was choked.

'I wish you wouldn't throw that around so much, Garion,' Belgarath said in a pained tone. 'Sometimes it upsets people.'

'It saves time, Grandfather,' Garion replied. 'The tall lady with the lock of white hair is Belgarath's daughter, Polgara the Sorceress. The little one with the red hair is Ce'Nedra, my wife. The blond girl is the Margravine Liselle of Drasnia, niece to the Chief of Drasnian intelligence, and the blind-folded girl who exposed Naradas is the Seeress of Kell. The big fellow who's helping Durnik is Toth, her guide, and this one is Prince Kheldar of Drasnia.'

'The richest man in the world?'

'The reputation might be a trifle exaggerated, your Majesty,' Silk said modestly, 'but I'm working on it.'

'The young fellow with blond hair is named Eriond, a very close friend.'

'I am awed to be in such august company. Which of ye is the Child of Light?'

'That's the burden I bear, your Majesty,' Garion told him. 'Now, though it's largely a part of Alorn history and prophecy, you may know that from time to time in the past there have been meetings between the Child of Light and the Child of Dark. We're going toward the last one there's ever going to be. The meeting's going to decide the fate of the world. Our problem at the moment is discovering where the meeting's supposed to take place.'

'Thy quest then is even more awesome than I had imagined, King Belgarion. I will aid thee in whatsoever way I can. The foul Grolim Naradas misled me into hindering thee. Whatever small way in which I might assist thee may serve as partial recompense for that error. I will send forth my ships to seek out the place of the meeting for thee wheresoever it may be, from the beaches of Ebal to the reef of Korim.'

'The reef of *what*?' Belgarath exclaimed.

'Korim, Ancient Belgarath. It doth lie to the northwest of this isle. Its location is clearly marked upon that chart which thou hast sought. Let us repair to my chambers, and I will show thee.'

'I think we've just about come to the end of it, Belgarath,' Beldin said. 'As soon as you take a look at that map, you'll be able to go home.'

'What are you talking about?'

'That's the end of your task, old man. We certainly appreciate your efforts, though.'

'You wouldn't mind *too* much if I came along, would you?'

'That's up to you, of course, but we wouldn't want to keep you from anything important you've been neglecting.' Beldin's grin grew vicious. Needling Belgarath was one of his favorite forms of entertainment.

As they turned toward the chapel entrance, Garion saw the she-wolf sitting in the doorway. Her golden eyes were intent, and her tongue lolled out in a wolfly smile.

CHAPTER SEVENTEEN

They followed the king through the dimly lighted and deserted midnight halls of the palace at Perivor. A tense excitement filled Garion. They had won. No matter how hard Zandramas had tried to prevent it, they had still won. The answer to the riddle lay no more than a few yards away, and once it was answered, the meeting would take place. No power on earth could prevent it now.

'Stop that,' the voice in his mind told him. 'You have to be calm now – very calm. Try to think about Faldor's farm. That always seems to settle you.'

'Where have you—' Garion started, then broke off.

'Where have I what?'

'Never mind. The question always irritates you.'

'Amazing. You actually remembered something I said. Faldor's farm, Garion. Faldor's farm.'

He did as he had been told. Though the memories had seemed to fade over the years, they suddenly returned with startling clarity. He saw the shape of the place, the sheds and barns and the kitchen, smithy and dining hall on the lower floor, and the gallery on the second floor where the sleeping chambers were – all surrounding that central yard. He could hear the steely ring of Durnik's·hammer coming from the smithy and smell the warm fragrance of freshly baked bread coming from Aunt Pol's kitchen. He saw Faldor and old Cralto and even Brill. He saw Doroon and Rundorig and, last, Zubrette – blond and pretty and artfully deceitful. A vast kind of calm came over him, not unlike the calm that had engulfed him when he had stood in the tomb of the one-eyed God in the City of Endless Night so long ago.

'That's better,' the voice said. 'Try to hold on to that.

You're going to have to think very clearly in the next few days and you can't do that with your mind racing every which way. You can fly to pieces after it's all over.'

'That's if I'm still around.'

'We can hope.' Then the voice was gone.

The guards at the king's door admitted them, and the king went directly to a cabinet, unlocked it, and removed a roll of ancient, crackling parchment. 'It is much faded, I do fear me,' he said. 'We have tried to protect it from the light, but it is very old.' He went to a table and carefully unrolled the chart, weighting down the corners with books. Once again Garion felt the tense excitement as he held back slightly, reaching back into his memories of Faldor's farm to steady himself.

The King of Perivor pointed with his finger. 'Here lieth Perivor,' he told them, 'and here doth lie the reef of Korim.'

Garion knew that if he looked too long at that fateful spot on the map, the wild excitement and sense of triumph would return, so he merely glanced at it, then let his eyes rove over the rest of the map. The spellings were strangely archaic. His eyes automatically sought his own kingdom. 'Ryva' it was spelled. There was also 'Aryndia,' and 'Kherech' and 'Tol Nydra' as well as 'Draksnya' and 'Chthall Margose'.

'It's misspelled,' Zakath noted. 'The proper name is the Turim reef.'

Beldin began to explain, but Garion already knew the answer. 'Things change,' the dwarf said, 'and among those things is the way we say certain words. The sounds of words shift over the centuries. The name of that reef has probably changed several times over the last few thousand years. It's a common phenomenon. If Belgarath were to speak in the language the people spoke in the village where he grew up, for example, none of us would be able to understand him. I'd guess that for a time the reef was called Torim or something like that, and it finally settled into Turim. It may change again a few times. I've made a study of that sort of thing. You see, what happens is that—'

'*Will* you get on with it?' Belgarath demanded in exasperation.

'Aren't you interested in expanding your education?'

'Not at the moment, no.'

Beldin sighed. 'Anyway,' he continued, 'what we call writing is just a way to reproduce the sound of a word. As the sound changes, so does the spelling. The difference is easily explained.'

'Thine answer to the question was cogent, gentle Beldin,' Cyradis said, 'but in this particular case, the change of the sound was imposed.'

'Imposed?' Silk said, 'by who – whom?'

'It was the two prophecies, Prince Kheldar. In furtherance of their game, they altered the sound of the word to conceal the location from Ancient Belgarath and from Zandramas. These two were both required to solve the riddle 'ere the final meeting could take place.'

'Game?' Silk asked incredulously. 'They were playing games with something this important?'

'These two eternal awarenesses are not as we, Prince Kheldar. They contend with each other in myriad ways. Ofttimes, one will attempt to alter the course of a star, while the other strives to hold it in place. At other times, one will attempt to move a grain of sand while the other exerts all its energy to keep the grain motionless. Such struggles ofttimes consume whole eons. The riddle game they have played with Belgarath and Zandramas is but another of the ways they have used to formalize their contention, for should it ever come to pass that they confront each other directly, they would rend the universe apart.'

Garion suddenly remembered an image that had come to him in the throne room at Vo Mimbre just before he had exposed the Murgo Nachak to King Korodullin. He had seemed to see two faceless players seated at a game where the moves had been so complex that his mind could not follow them. With absolute certainty now he saw that he had caught a momentary glimpse of the higher reality Cyradis had just described. *'Did you do that on purpose?'* he asked the voice in his mind.

'Naturally. You needed a bit of encouragement to get you to do something that was necessary. You're a competitive sort of boy, so I thought the image of the great game might get you started.'

Then something else occurred to Garion. 'Cyradis,' he said, 'why is it that there are so many of *us* while Zandramas appears to be almost totally alone?'

'It hath ever been thus, Belgarion. The Child of Dark is solitary, even as was Torak in his pride. Thou, however, art humble. Thou hast never pushed thyself forward, for thou knowest not thine own worth. This is endearing in thee, Child of Light, for thou art not puffed up with thine own importance. The Prophecy of Dark hath ever chosen one and one only, and hath infused that one with all its power. The Prophecy of Light, however, hath chosen to disperse its power among many. Although thou art the principal bearer of the burden, all of thy companions share it with thee. The difference between the two prophecies is simple, but it is profound.'

Beldin was frowning. 'You're saying that it's sort of like the difference between absolutism and shared responsibility, then?'

'It is much as thou hast said. The difference is more complex, however.'

'I was just trying to be concise.'

'Now that's a first,' Belgarath said. Then he looked at the King of Perivor. 'Can you describe this reef to us, your Majesty?' he asked. 'The representation on the map isn't too precise.'

'Gladly, Ancient Belgarath. In my youth I sailed thither, for the reef is something of a marvel. Seafarers assert that there is none like it in all the world. It doth consist of a series of rocky pinnacles rising from the sea. The pinnacles themselves are easy to see and therefore to avoid. Other dangers, however, lurk beneath the surface. Savage currents and tides do rush through gaps in the reef, and the weather there is ever unsettled. By reason of these perils, the reef hath never been charted in any detail. All prudent sailors avoid it entirely, giving that dangerous obstruction wide berth.'

Durnik and Toth entered. 'We've taken care of it, Your Majesty,' Durnik reported. 'Naradas is safely in the ground now. He won't trouble you – or us – ever again. Did you want to know where we put him?'

'Methinks not, my friend. Thou and thy massive companion have done me a service this night. I implore thee, if ever I can do thee service in return, hesitate not to call upon me.'

'Cyradis,' Belgarath said, 'is this the last part of the riddle? Or are there other bits and pieces lurking about?'

'Nay, Ancient One. The game of the riddles is finished. Now the game of deeds doth begin.'

'Finally,' Belgarath said with some relief. Then he and Beldin fell to studying the map.

'Did we find it?' Durnik asked Silk. 'I mean, does the map show the location of Korim?'

Silk led him to the table. 'It's right here,' he said, pointing. 'This is a very old map. Modern maps misspell the name. That's why we had to come here.'

'We've been doing a lot of running around chasing after scraps of paper,' the smith observed.

'We have indeed, my friend. According to Cyradis, it's all been part of a game being played by the friend Garion's got inside his head and the other one, who's probably inside Zandramas' head.'

'I hate games.'

'I don't mind them.'

'That's becouse you're Drasnian.'

'That could be part of it, I suppose.'

'It's in the approximate location where the mountains of Korim were, Belgarath,' Beldin said, measuring off distances with his fingers. 'They were probably moved a bit when Torak cracked the world.'

'A lot of things were moved that day, as I recall.'

'Oh, yes,' Beldin agreed fervently. 'I had trouble standing up, and I'm built closer to the ground than you are.'

'You know something? I've noticed that myself. Your Majesty,' the old man addressed the king, 'could you be a bit more specific about the reef? Trying to land on the side of a rock pinnacle from a boat that's pitching around in the surf would be difficult and dangerous.'

'If memory doth serve me, Ancient Belgarath, I do seem to recall a few rocky beaches, built up, doubtless, from shards and boulders tumbled from the sides of the peaks and then pounded to bits by the restless sea. When the tide is low, this rubble, accumulated over the eons, doth rise above the surface of the sea, providing means whereby one may move freely from one pinnacle to the next.'

'Sort of like that land bridge from Morindland to Mallorea,' Silk recalled sourly. 'That wasn't a very pleasant trip.'

'Are there any landmarks of any kind?' Belgarath pressed. 'That reef goes on for quite a ways. It could take a lot of wading to find the exact place we need to reach.'

'I cannot attest to this from mine own true knowledge,' the king said cautiously, 'but certain seafarers have asserted that there appears to be a cave mouth on the north side of the highest pinnacle. On occasion, more adventurous ones have sought to go ashore to explore its depths, for, as is widely known, remote caves ofttimes serve as repositories for the ill-gotten gains of free-booters and pirates. The pinnacle, however, hath ever repulsed their most valiant efforts. Each time one of these brave souls attempts landing there, the sea becomes angry, and sudden storms do appear from a cloudless sky.'

'That's it, Belgarath,' Beldin chortled exultantly. 'Something's been going out of its way to keep casual explorers out of that cave.'

'*Two* somethings, I gather,' Belgarath agreed. 'You're right, though. We've finally located the exact place of the meeting. It's in that cave.'

Silk groaned.

'Art thou ill, Prince Kheldar?' the king inquired.

'Not yet, your Majesty, but I think I'm going to be.'

'Our Prince Kheldar has difficulties with caves, your Majesty,' Velvet explained, smiling.

'There's nothing difficult about it at all, Liselle,' the rat-faced little man disagreed. 'It's really very simple. Every time I see a cave, I go into an absolute panic.'

'I have heard of this malady,' the king said. 'One wonders what may be its mysterious source.'

'There's nothing mysterious about the source of mine, your Majesty,' Silk said drily. 'I know *exactly* where it came from.'

'If it is thine intent to dare the perilous reef, Ancient Belgarath,' the king said then, 'I will provide thee and thy companions with a stout ship to convey thee thither. I will give orders that the ship be ready to sail with the morning tide.'

'Your Majesty is very kind.'

'It is but small payment for the service thou hast rendered to me this night.' The king paused, his face reflective. 'It may be even as the spirit of foul Naradas proclaimed,' he mused. 'I may indeed be a vain and foolish man, but I am not immune to the promptings of gratitude. You all have preparations to make,' he said then. 'I will not delay you more. We shall meet again on the morrow 'ere you depart.'

'We thank you, your Majesty,' Garion said, his armor creaking as he bowed. Then he led the others from the chamber. He was not at all surprised to see the she-wolf sitting just outside the door.

'The time is exactly right, isn't it, Cyradis,' Polgara said to the Seeress once they were all out in the corridor. 'At Ashaba, you said it would be nine months until the meeting. As I make it, the exact time will be the day after tomorrow.'

'Thy calculations are correct, Polgara.'

'It works out precisely then. It should take us one full day

231

to reach the reef, and we'll go to the cave on the following morning.' Polgara smiled a bit wryly. 'All this time we've been fretting about arriving late, and now we get there precisely on time.' She laughed. 'What a waste of all that perfectly good worrying.'

'Well, now we know where and when,' Durnik said. 'All that's left to do is to go there and get on with it.'

'That sums it up, I'd say,' Silk agreed.

Eriond sighed, and Garion felt a chill suspicion that was not quite a certainty. *'Is it going to be he?'* he asked the dry voice. *'Is Eriond going to be the one who dies?'*

But the voice would not answer.

They entered their quarters with the wolf close behind them.

'It's been a long time getting here,' Belgarath said wearily. 'I'm getting a little old for these extended journeys.'

'Old?' Beldin snorted. 'You were born old. I still think you've got a few miles left in you, though.'

'I think that when we get home, I'll spend a century or so in my tower.'

'That's an idea. It should take you about that long to get it cleaned up – oh, one other thing, Belgarath. Why don't you fix that loose step?'

'I'll get around to it.'

'Aren't we all assuming that we're going to win?' Silk said. 'I think that making plans for the future at this point might be a bit premature – unless the Holy Seeress might see fit to let slip a hint or two about the outcome?' He looked at Cyradis.

'I would not be permitted to do that, Prince Kheldar – even if I knew the answer.'

'You mean you don't know?' he asked incredulously.

'The choice hath not yet been made,' she said simply. 'It may not be made until I stand in the presence of the Child of Light and the Child of Dark. Until that moment, the outcome doth still hang in the balance.'

'What good is it being a Seeress if you can't predict the future?'

'This particular Event is not susceptible to prediction, Kheldar,' she said tartly.

'I think we'd all better get some sleep,' Belgarath said. 'The next couple of days are going to be hectic.'

The she-wolf followed Garion and Ce'Nedra to their room and entered with them. Ce'Nedra looked a bit startled at that, but the wolf went directly to the bed and put her forepaws up on it to look critically at the puppy, who lay sleeping on his back with all four of his paws in the air.

The wolf gave Garion a slightly reproachful look. 'One notes that he has grown fat,' she said. 'Your mate has ruined him with overfeeding and pampering. He is no longer fit to be a wolf. He no longer even smells like a wolf.'

'One's mate bathes him from time to time,' Garion explained.

'Bathes,' the wolf said in a tone loaded with contempt. 'A wolf should be bathed only by the rain or in the course of swimming across a river.' She dropped to her haunches. 'One would ask a favor of your mate.'

'One will convey your request to her.'

'One had hoped you might. Ask your mate if she will continue to care for the young one. One believes you need not add that she has spoiled him so badly that he is unfit to be anything but a lap dog.'

'One will phrase your request cautiously.'

'What's she saying?' Ce'Nedra asked.

'She wants to know if you'd be willing to take care of the puppy.'

'Of course I will. I've wanted to do that all along.' Then she knelt and impulsively put her arms about the she-wolf's neck. 'I will care for him,' she promised.

'One notes that her scent is not unpleasant,' the wolf said to Garion.

'One has also noticed that.'

'One was fairly certain that you had.' Then the wolf rose to her feet and silently left the room.

'She's going to leave us now, isn't she?' Ce'Nedra said wistfully. 'I'm going to miss her.'

'What makes you think that?'

'Why else would she give up her baby?'

'I think there's a bit more to it than that. She's preparing for something.'

'I'm very tired, Garion. Let's go to bed.'

Later, in the velvet darkness as they lay close together in the bed, Ce'Nedra sighed. 'Two more days and I'll see my baby again. It's been so very, very long.'

'Try not to dwell on it, Ce'Nedra. You need your rest, and thinking too much about it will keep you awake.'

She sighed again, and after a few moments, she drifted off to sleep.

'Cyradis is not the only one who has to make a choice,' the voice in his mind told him. *'You and Zandramas also have choices to make.'*

'What choices are those?'

'You have to choose your successors. Zandramas has already chosen hers. You should be giving some thought to your last task as the Child of Light. It's going to be fairly significant.'

'I suppose that in a way, I'll sort of miss having that to carry around, but I'll be glad to get rid of it. Now I'll be able to go back to being ordinary again.'

'You never were ordinary, you know. You've been the Child of Light since the moment you were born.'

'I know I'm going to miss you.'

'Please don't get sentimental, Garion. I may stop by from time to time, just to see how you're doing. Now get some sleep.'

When he awoke the next morning, Garion lay in bed for quite some time. He had tried for very long not to think about something, but now he had no choice but to face it squarely. He had every reason in the world to hate Zandramas, but . . .

Finally, he slipped out of bed, dressed himself and went looking for Belgarath.

He found the old man in the central room, seated with Cyradis. 'Grandfather,' he said, 'I've got a problem.'

'There's nothing unusual about that. What's got you worked up this time?'

'Tomorrow, I'm going to meet Zandramas.'

'Why, do you know? I think you're right.'

'Please don't do that. This is serious.'

'Sorry, Garion. I'm feeling whimsical today.'

'I'm afraid that the only way we're going to be able to stop her is to kill her, and I'm not sure I'll be able to do that. Torak was one thing, but Zandramas is a woman.'

'Well, she *was*. I think her gender has become irrelevant now, though – even to herself.'

'I still don't think I'll be able to do it.'

'There will be no need, Belgarion,' Cyradis assured him. 'Another fate doth lie in store for Zandramas, no matter what my choice may be. Thou wilt not be required to shed her blood.'

A vast wave of relief came over Garion. 'Thank you, Holy Seeress,' he said. 'I've been afraid to face up to that. It's good to know that it's not one of the tasks I've got ahead of me. Oh, by the way, Grandfather, my friend up here—' He tapped his forehead. '– has been visiting again. Last night he told me that my final task will be to choose my successor. I don't suppose I could get you to help me, could I?'

'No Garion, I'm afraid not. I don't think I'm supposed to, am I, Cyradis?'

'Nay, Ancient Belgarath. That task lieth on the Child of Light alone.'

'I was afraid you might look at it that way,' Garion said glumly.

'Oh, one thing, Garion,' Belgarath said. 'The one you choose has a fair chance of becoming a God. Don't choose me. I'm not suited for the job.'

The others drifted in singly or in pairs. As each one entered, Garion considered their faces, trying to picture each of his friends as a divinity. Aunt Pol? No, that didn't seem right somehow, and that automatically excluded Durnik. He could not deprive her of her husband. Silk? That idea very nearly caused Garion to collapse in helpless laughter. Zakath? It had some possibilities. Zakath was an Angarak, and the new God would be the God of that race. Zakath was a bit unpredictable, however. Until recently, he had been obsessed with power. A sudden onset of Godhood might unsettle his mind and make him revert. Garion sighed. He'd have to think about it some more.

The servants brought in breakfast, and Ce'Nedra, obviously remembering her promise of the previous night, fixed a plate for the puppy. The plate contained eggs, sausage, and a generous dollop of jam. The she-wolf looked away with a shudder.

They deliberately avoided the subject of tomorrow's meeting as they ate. The meeting was inevitable now, so there was no point in talking about it.

Belgarath pushed back his plate with a look of contentment on his face. 'Don't forget to thank the king for his hospitality,' he told Garion.

And then the she-wolf came over and laid her head in the old man's lap. Belgarath looked startled. The wolf had usually avoided him. 'What is it, little sister?' he asked her.

Then, to everyone's astonishment, the wolf actually laughed and spoke quite plainly in the language of humans. 'Your brains have gone to sleep, old wolf,' she said to Belgarath. 'I thought you'd have known me weeks ago. Does this help?' A sudden blue nimbus surrounded her. 'Or this?' She shimmered, and then the wolf was gone. Standing in its place was a tawny-haired, golden-eyed woman in a brown dress.

'Mother!' Aunt Pol exclaimed.

'You're no more observant than your father, Polgara,' Poledra said reprovingly. 'Garion has known for quite some time now.'

Belgarath, however, was staring in horror at the puppy. 'Oh, don't be silly, old man,' his wife told him. 'You know that we're mated for life. The puppy was weak and sick, so the pack had to leave him behind. I cared for him, that's all.'

The smile on the face of the Seeress of Kell was gentle. 'This is the Woman Who Watches, Ancient Belgarath,' she said. 'Now is thy company complete. Know however, that she is ever with thee, as she has always been.'

Part Three

THE HIGH PLACES OF KORIM

THE KORIM REEF

PERIVOR

Dal Perivor

R. Perr

Dal
Estellr

To
Astelliy

THE HIGH PLACES OF KORIM

CHAPTER EIGHTEEN

Garion had seen his grandmother – or her image – several times, but the similarity of her features to Aunt Pol's seemed uncanny. There were differences, of course. Aunt Pol's hair, except for that white lock at her brow, was dark, almost black, and her eyes were a deep, deep blue. Poledra, on the other hand, had tawny hair, hovering nearly on the verge of being as blond as Velvet's, and her eyes were as golden as the eyes of a wolf. The features of the two women, however, were almost identical, as had been, the one time Garion had seen her image, the features of Aunt Pol's sister Beldaran. Belgarath, his wife, and his daughter had withdrawn to the far side of the room, and Beldin, his tears glistening through his scowl, had placed himself squarely between them and the others in the room to guard their privacy during their reunion.

'Who is she?' Zakath asked Garion in puzzlement.

'She's my Grandmother,' Garion replied simply. 'Belgarath's wife.'

'I didn't know he *had* a wife.'

'Where did you think Aunt Pol came from?'

'I guess I hadn't thought of that.' Zakath looked around, noting that both Ce'Nedra and Velvet were dabbing at their eyes with wispy little handkerchiefs.

'Why is everyone so misty-eyed?' he asked.

'We all thought that she had died in childbirth when Aunt Pol and her sister Beldaran were born.'

'And how long ago was that?'

'Aunt Pol is over three thousand years old,' Garion shrugged.

Zakath began to tremble. 'And Belgarath's been grieving all that time?'

'Yes.' Garion didn't really want to talk just then. All he wanted to do was to drink in the radiant faces of his family. The word came to him unbidden, and he suddenly remembered that bleak time after he had first learned that Aunt Pol was not, strictly speaking, his aunt. He had felt then so terribly alone – an orphan in the most dreadful sense of the word. It had taken years, but now everything was all right. His family was nearly complete. Belgarath, Poledra, and Aunt Pol did not speak, for speech was largely unnecessary. Instead they simply sat in chairs drawn closely together gazing into each others' faces and holding hands. Garion could only faintly begin to understand the intensity of their emotions. He did not, however, feel cut off from them, but rather seemed somehow to share their joy.

Durnik crossed the room to the rest of them. Even solid, practical Durnik's eyes shone with unshed tears. 'Why don't we leave them alone?' he suggested. 'It's a good time to get the packing done anyway. We have a ship to catch, you know.'

'She said you knew,' Ce'Nedra said accusingly to Garion when they had returned to their room.

'Yes,' he admitted.

'Why didn't you tell me?'

'She asked me to keep it to myself.'

'That doesn't apply to your own wife, Garion.'

'It doesn't?' he asked in feigned surprise. 'When did they pass that rule?'

'I just made it up,' she admitted. 'Oh, Garion,' she said then, throwing her arms about his neck and kissing him, 'I do love you.'

'I certainly hope so. Shall we pack?'

The corridors of the royal palace here in Perivor were cool as Garion and Ce'Nedra returned to the central room, and the arched embrasures admitted golden morning sunlight as if even the elements were bestowing a benediction on what was, after all, a special, even sacred, day.

When they had all gathered once again, Belgarath and

his wife and daughter had composed themselves enough so that they welcomed company.

'Would you like to have me introduce them, Mother?' Aunt Pol asked.

'I know all of them, Polgara,' Poledra replied. 'I've been with you for quite some time, remember?'

'Why didn't you tell me?'

'I wanted to see if you could figure it out for yourself. You disappointed me just a bit, Polgara.'

'Mother,' Aunt Pol protested, 'not in front of the children.'

They both laughed that same warm, rich laugh. 'Ladies and gentlemen,' Polgara said then, 'this is my mother, Poledra.'

They crowded around the tawny-haired legend. Silk extravagantly kissed her hand. 'I suppose, Lady Poledra,' he said slyly, 'we should congratulate Belgarath. All things considered, I think *you* got the worst of that bargain. Your daughter's been trying to reform him for about three eons now without much notable success.'

Poledra smiled. 'One has perhaps greater resources at one's command than one's daughter, Prince Kheldar.' She lapsed, it seemed, unconsciously into her previous mode of speech.

'All right, Poledra,' Beldin growled, stumping forward, 'what *really* happened? After the girls were born, our Master came to us and told us that you were no longer with us. We all thought He meant that you had died. The twins cried for two straight months, and that left me to try to cope with the babies. What really happened?'

'Aldur didn't lie to you, Beldin,' she replied calmly. 'In a very real sense, I *was* no longer with you. You see, shortly after the girls were born, Aldur and UL came to me. They said they had a great task for me but that it would involve an equally great sacrifice. I would have to leave you all behind to prepare for the task. At first, I refused, but when they explained the task to me, I had no choice but to agree. I turned my back on the Vale and went with UL to Prolgu to receive instruction. From time to time He'd relent and let me go unobserved out into the world to see how my family was doing.' She looked rather firmly at Belgarath. 'You and I have much to discuss, Old Wolf,' she told him.

Belgarath winced.

'I don't suppose you could give us some enlightenment about this momentous task?' Sadi suggested mildly.

'I'm afraid not.'

'I didn't think so,' the eunuch murmured.

'Eriond,' Poledra said then, greeting the blond-haired young man.

'Poledra,' he responded. Eriond, as always, seemed unsurprised by this turn of events. Eriond, Garion had noticed, was never surprised.

'You've grown since we last met,' she noted.

'I suppose I have,' he agreed.

'Are you ready?'

The question sent a chill through Garion as he suddenly remembered the strange dream he had had the night before his true identity had been revealed.

There was a polite knock on the door. Durnik answered it and found an armored knight standing outside. 'His Majesty hath dispatched me to advise thee and thy companions that thy ship awaiteth thee in the harbor, my Lord,' the knight said.

'I'm not a—' Durnik started.

'Let it lie, Durnik,' Silk told him. 'Sir Knight,' he said to the armored man at the door, 'where might we find his Majesty? We would take our leave of him and thank him for his many kindnesses.'

'His Majesty doth await thee and thy companions at the harbor, my Lord. He would bid you all farewell there and see you off on the great adventure which doth lie in store for ye.'

'We will make haste then, Sir Knight,' the little man promised. 'It were discourteous of us in the extreme to keep one of the paramount monarchs of the world awaiting our arrival. Thou hast performed thine appointed task in

244

manner which does thee credit, Sir Knight, and we are all in thy debt.'

The knight bowed, beaming. Then he went back down the hallway.

'Where did you ever learn to speak like that, Kheldar?' Velvet asked in some surprise.

'Ah, dear Lady,' Silk replied with outrageous extravagance, 'knowest thou not that the poet doth lurk beneath the most common exterior? An it please thee, I will deliver unto thee fullsome compliments upon thine every ravishing and unsurpasséd part.' He eyed her up and down suggestively.

'Kheldar!' she exclaimed, blushing bright red.

'That's sort of fun, you know,' Silk said, referring to the archaic speech – at least Garion *hoped* that was what he was referring to. 'Once you learn how to wrap your tongue around the 'hath's', and 'doth's' and 'foreasmuches', it has a certain ring and cadence to it, doesn't it?'

'We're surrounded by charlatans, mother,' Polgara sighed.

'Belgarath,' Durnik said seriously, 'there's not much point in taking the horses, is there? What I mean is that we're going to be clambering over rocks and wading in surf when we get to the reef. Wouldn't the horses just be in the way?'

'You're probably right, Durnik,' the old man agreed.

'I'll go down to the stables and talk with the grooms,' the smith said. 'The rest of you go on ahead. I'll catch up.' He turned and left the room.

'An eminently practical man,' Poledra observed.

'The poet, however, doth lurk beneath that most practical of exteriors, Mother,' Polgara smiled, 'and thou wouldst not believe how much pleasure I take in that aspect of him.'

'I think it's time for us to get off this island, Old Wolf,' Poledra said wryly. 'Two more days and they'll all be sitting around composing bad poetry.'

Servants arrived then to carry their packs to the harbor,

245

and Garion and his companions trooped through the halls of the palace and out into the streets of Dal Perivor. Although the morning had dawned bright and sunny, a bank of heavy clouds had begun to build up off to the west, heavy, purple clouds that spoke eloquently of the likelihood of bad weather over Korim.

'I suppose we should have known,' Silk sighed. 'Once – just once – I'd like to see one of these stupendous events happen in good weather.'

Garion fully understood what lay behind the apparently light-hearted banter. None of them approached tomorrow without a certain apprehension. The pronouncement Cyradis had made at Rheon that one of them would not survive the meeting lay heavily on each of their minds, and in the fashion as old as man himself, each tried to make light of his fears. That reminded him of something, and he dropped back to have a word with the Seeress of Kell. 'Cyradis,' he said to the blindfolded girl, 'should Zakath and I wear our armor when we get to the reef?' He plucked at the front of the doublet he had put on with some relief that morning in the hope that he might never again be obliged to encase himself in steel. 'What I'm getting at is that if the meeting is going to be entirely spiritual, there's no real need for it, is there? But if there's a possibility of some fighting, we should probably be prepared, shouldn't we?'

'Thou art as transparent as glass, Belgarion of Riva,' she said, chiding him gently. 'Thou thinkest to trick answers from me to questions which I am forbidden to discuss with thee. Do as it pleaseth thee, King of Riva. Prudence, however, doth suggest that a bit of steel here and there in thine apparel might not be inappropriate when approaching a situation where surprises might await thee.'

'I will be guided by thee,' Garion grinned. 'Thy prudent advice seemeth me the course of wisdom.'

'Makest thou a rather feeble attempt at humor, Belgarion?'

'Would I do that, Holy Seeress?' He grinned at her

and strode back to where Belgarath and Poledra walked hand in hand just behind Zakath and Sadi. 'Grandfather, I think I just managed to sneak an answer out of Cyradis,' he said.

'That might be a first,' the old man replied.

'I think there might be some fighting when we get to the reef. I asked her if Zakath and I should wear armor when we get there. She didn't answer me directly, but she said that it might not be a bad idea — just in case.'

'You might want to pass that on to the others. Let's not have them walking into something blind.'

'I'll do that.'

The king, along with most of his gaily-clad court, awaited them on a long wharf extending out into the choppy waters of the harbor. Despite the temperate morning, the king wore an ermine robe and a heavy gold crown. 'Gladly do I greet thee and thy noble companions, Belgarion of Riva,' he declaimed, 'and in sadness do I await thy departure. Many here have pled with me that I might permit them also to speak to this matter, but in thy behalf I have steadfastly refused such permission, knowing full well the urgency of thy quest.'

'Thou art a true and faithful friend, your Majesty,' Garion said with genuine gratitude at being spared a morning of windy speeches. He clasped the king's hand warmly. 'Know that if the Gods grant us victory on the morrow, we will return straightway to this happy isle so that we may more fulsomely express our gratitude to thee and the members of thy court who have all treated us with such noble courtesy.' Besides, they had to come back for the horses anyway. 'And now, your Majesty, our fate awaits us. We must, with scant and niggard farewell, take ship to go forth with resolute hearts to meet that fate. An it please the Gods, we shall return anon. Goodbye, my friend.'

'Fare thee well, Belgarion of Riva,' the king said in a voice near to tears. 'May the Gods grant thee and thy companions victory.'

'Pray that it may be so.' Garion turned with a rather

melodramatic swirl of his cloak and led his friends up the gangway. He glanced back over his shoulder and saw Durnik pushing his way through the crowd. That would help. As soon as the smith was on board, Garion could give the order to cast off all lines and thus avoid the necessity of more extended farewells shouted across the ship's rail.

Directly behind Durnik came the several carts carrying their packs. Their belongings were quickly transferred to the ship, and Garion went aft to speak with the captain, a grizzled old seaman with a weathered face.

Unlike western vessels, whose bare plank decks were usually holy-stoned into some semblance of whiteness, the quarter-deck and its surrounding railings were finished with a dark, glossy varnish, and snowy ropes hung in neat coils from highly polished belaying pins. The effect was almost ostentatiously neat, evidence that the vessel's master took great pride in his ship. The captain himself wore a somewhat weathered blue doublet. He was, after all, in port. A jaunty velvet cap was cocked rakishly over one of his ears.

'I guess that's everything, Captain,' Garion said. 'We may as well cast off and get clear of the harbor before the tide turns.'

'You've been to sea before I see, young master,' the captain said approvingly. 'I hope your friends have as well. It's always a trial to have landsmen aboard. They never seem to realize that throwing up into the wind isn't a good idea.' He raised his voice to an ear-splitting bellow. 'Cast off all lines! Prepare to make sail!'

'Your speech doesn't seem to be that of the island, Captain,' Garion observed.

'I'd be surprised if it were, young master. I'm from the Melcene Islands. About twenty years ago, there were some ugly rumors about me being circulated in some quarters back home, so I thought it might be prudent to absent myself for a while. I came here. You wouldn't believe what these people were calling a ship when I got here.'

'Sort of like a sea-going castle?' Garion suggested.

'You've seen them then?'

'In another part of the world.'

'Make sail!' the captain roared at his crew. 'There, young master,' he grinned at Garion. 'I'll have you out of earshot in no time at all. That should spare us all that drasty eloquence. Where was I? Oh, yes. When I got here, the ships of Perivor were so top-heavy that a good sneeze would capsize them. Would you believe it only took me five years to explain that to these people?'

'You must have been amazingly eloquent, Captain,' Garion laughed.

'A bout or two with belaying pins helped a bit,' the captain conceeded. 'Finally I had to issue a challenge, though. None of these blockheads can refuse a challenge, so I proposed a race around the island. Twenty ships started out, and only mine finished. They started listening about then. I spent the next five years in the yards supervising construction. Then the king finally let me go back to sea. I got me a baronetcy out of it – not that it matters. I think I've even got a castle somewhere.'

A brazen blast came from the wharf as, in true Mimbrate fashion, the knights of the king's court saluted them on their horns. 'Isn't that pitiful?' the captain said. 'I don't think there's a man on the whole island who can carry a tune.' He looked appraisingly at Garion. 'I heard tell that you're making for the Turim reef.'

'Korim reef,' Garion corrected absently.

'You've been listening to the landsmen, I see. They can't even pronounce the name right. Anyway, before you get your mind set in stone about where you want to land, send for me. There's some very ugly water around that reef. It's not the sort of place where you want to make mistakes, and I've got some fairly accurate charts.'

'The king told us there weren't any charts of the reef.'

The captain winked slyly. 'The rumors I mentioned earlier stirred some ship-captains to try to follow me,' he admitted, 'although "chase" would probably be a more accurate word. Rewards cause that sort of thing

249

sometimes. Anyhow, I was passing near the reef in calm weather once, and I decided to take some soundings. It never hurts to have a place to hide where others are afraid to follow you.'

'What's your name, Captain?' Garion asked him.

'Kresca, young master.'

'I think we can drop that. Garion will do just fine.'

'Whatever you like, Garion. Now get off my quarter-deck so I can maneuver this old tub out of the harbor.'

The speech was different, and it was half-way around the world, but Captain Kresca was so much like Barak's friend Greldik that Garion felt suddenly very secure. He went below to join the others. 'We've had a bit of luck,' he told them. 'Our captain is a Melcene. He's not overburdened with scruples, but he *has* got charts of the reef. He's probably the only man in these waters who does. He's offered to advise us when the time comes to decide on where we want to land.'

'That was helpful of him,' Silk said.

'Maybe, but I think his main concern is not ripping the bottom out of his ship.'

'I can relate to that,' Silk said. '– As long as I'm on board, anyway.'

'I'm going back up on deck,' Garion said then. 'Staying in a stuffy compartment on the first day of a voyage always makes me a little queasy for some reason.'

'And *you're* the ruler of an island?' Poledra said.

'It's just a question of getting adjusted, Grandmother.'

'Of course.'

The sea and sky were unsettled. The heavy cloud-bank was still coming in from the west, sending long, ponderous combers rolling in from that direction, waves which had in all probability started somewhere off the east coast of Cthol Murgos. Although, as king of an island nation, Garion knew that the phenomenon was not unusual, he nonetheless felt a certain sense of superstitious apprehension when he saw that the surface winds were moving westward while those aloft as proclaimed by the movement

250

of the clouds, moved east. He had seen this happen many times before, but this time he could not be positive that the weather was responding to natural causes or to something else. Idly, he wondered what those two eternal awarenesses might have done had he and his friends not found a ship. He had a momentary vision of the sea parting to provide a broad highway across its bottom, a highway littered with startled fish. He began to feel less and less in charge of his own destiny. Even as he had on the long trek to Cthol Mishrak, he became increasingly certain that the two prophecies were herding him toward Korim for a meeting which, though he himself might not have chosen it, was the ultimate Event toward which the entire universe had been yearning since the beginning of days. A plaintive 'why me?' hovered on his lips.

And then Ce'Nedra was there, burrowing under his arm as she had during those first few heady days when they had finally discovered that they did, in fact, love each other. 'What are you thinking about, Garion?' she asked softly. She had changed out of the antique green satin gown she had worn at the palace and now wore a gray dress of utilitarian wool.

'I'm not, really. Probably worrying comes a lot closer.'

'What's there to worry about? We're going to win, aren't we?'

'That hasn't been decided yet.'

'Of course you're going to win. You always do.'

'This time's a little different, Ce'Nedra.' He sighed. 'It's not just the meeting, though. I've got to choose my successor, and the one I choose is going to be the new Child of Light – and most probably a God. If I pick the wrong person, it's possible that I'll create a God who'll be an absolute disaster. Could you imagine Silk as a God? He'd be out there picking the pockets of the other Gods and inscribing off-color jokes in the constellations.'

'He doesn't really seem to have the right kind of temperament for it,' she agreed. 'I *like* him well enough, but I'm afraid UL might disapprove very strongly. What else is bothering you?'

'You know what else. One of us isn't going to live through tomorrow.'

'You don't really have to concern yourself about that, Garion,' she said wistfully. 'It's going to be me. I've known that from the very beginning.'

'Don't be absurd. I can make sure it's not you.'

'Oh? How?'

'I'll just tell them that I won't make the choice if they hurt you in any way.'

'Garion!' she gasped. 'You can't do that! You'll destroy the universe if you do!'

'So what? The universe doesn't mean anything to me without you, you know.'

'That's very sweet, but you can't do it. You wouldn't do it anyway. You've got too great a sense of responsibility.'

'What makes you think you're going to be the one?'

'The tasks, Garion. Every one of us has a task — some of us more than one. Belgarath had to find out where the meeting's going to take place. Velvet had to kill Harakan. Even Sadi had a task. He had to kill Naradas. I have no task — except to die.'

Garion decided at that point to tell her. 'You *did* have a task, Ce'Nedra,' he told her, 'and you did it very well.'

'What are you talking about?'

'You wouldn't remember it. After we left Kell, you were very drowsy for several days.'

'Yes, I remember that.'

'It wasn't because you were sleepy. Zandramas was tampering with your mind. She's done it before. You remember that you got sick on your way to Rak Hagga?'

'Yes.'

'It was a different kind of sickness, but it was Zandramas again. She's been trying to take control of you for more than a year now.'

Ce'Nedra stared at him.

'Anyway, after we left Kell, she managed to put your

mind to sleep. You wandered off and, out there in the forest, you thought you met Arell.'

'Arell? She's dead.'

'I know, but you thought you met her all the same, and she gave you what you thought was our baby. Then this supposed Arell asked you some questions, and you answered them.'

'What kind of questions?'

'Zandramas had to find out where the meeting was supposed to take place, and she couldn't go to Kell. She posed as Arell so she could ask you those questions. You told her about Perivor, about the map and about Korim. That was your task.'

'I betrayed you?' Her look was stricken.

'No. You saved the universe. Zandramas absolutely *has* to be at Korim at the right time. Somebody had to tell her where to go, and that was *your* task.'

'I don't remember any of this.'

'Of course not. Aunt Pol erased the memory of it from your mind. It wasn't really your fault, and you'd have been overcome with remorse if you'd been able to remember what happened.'

'I still betrayed you.'

'You did what had to be done, Ce'Nedra.' Garion smiled a bit wistfully. 'You know, both sides in this have been trying to do the same thing. We – and Zandramas, of course – have been trying to find Korim and to keep the other side from finding out where it is so that we can win by default. It was never going to happen that way, though. The meeting absolutely *has* to take place before Cyradis can choose. The Prophecies weren't going to let it happen any other way. Both sides have wasted a great deal of effort trying to do something that simply could not be done. We should have all realized that from the very beginning. We could have saved ourselves a lot of trouble. About the only consolation I have is that Zandramas wasted a lot more effort than we did.'

'I'm still certain that it's going to be me.'

'Nonsense.'

'I just hope they let me hold my baby before I die,' she said sadly.

'You're *not* going to die, Ce'Nedra.'

She ignored him. 'I want you to take care of yourself, Garion,' she said firmly. 'Be sure that you eat right, dress warmly in winter, and make sure that our son doesn't forget me.'

'Ce'Nedra, will you stop this?'

'One last thing, Garion,' she plowed on relentlessly. 'After I've been gone for a while, I want you to marry again. I don't want you moping around the way Belgarath has for the last three thousand years.'

'Absolutely not. Besides, nothing's going to happen to you.'

'We'll see. Promise, Garion. You weren't meant to be alone, and you need somebody to take care of you.'

'Have you almost finished with this?' It was Poledra. She stepped out from behind the foremast in a businesslike way. 'It's all very pretty and sweetly melancholy, I'm sure, but isn't it just a trifle overdramatic? Garion's right, Ce'Nedra. Nothing's going to happen to you, so why don't you fold up all this nobility and put it away in a closet someplace?'

'I know what I know, Poledra,' Ce'Nedra said stubbornly.

'I hope you won't be too disappointed when you wake up the day after tomorrow and find that you're in perfect health.'

'Who's it going to be, then?'

'Me,' Poledra said simply. 'I've known about it for over three thousand years now, so I've had time to get used to it. At least I have this day with the ones I love before I have to leave for good. Ce'Nedra, that wind is very chilly. Let's go below before you catch cold.'

'She's just like your Aunt Pol, isn't she?' Ce'Nedra said over her shoulder as Poledra firmly led her toward the stair leading below decks.

'Naturally,' Garion called back.

'It's started, I see,' Silk said from not far away.

'What's started?'

'The gushy farewells. Just about everybody's convinced that he's the one who won't see the sun go down tomorrow. I'd imagine that they'll all come up here one by one to say good-bye to you. I thought I'd be first – sort of to get it out of the way – but Ce'Nedra beat me to it.'

'You? Nothing could kill you, Silk. You're too lucky.'

'I've made my own luck, Garion. It's not that hard to tamper with dice.' The little man's face grew reflective. 'We've really had some good times, haven't we? I think they outweigh the bad ones, and that's about all a man can hope for.'

'You're as maudlin as Ce'Nedra and my grandmother were.'

'It does sort of seem that way, doesn't it? And that's very unbecoming. Don't be too sad about it, Garion. If I *do* happen to be the one, it should spare me the discomfort of making a *very* unpleasant decision.'

'Oh? What decision is that?'

'You know my views on marriage, don't you?'

'Oh, yes. You've spoken on the subject many, many times.'

Silk sighed. 'All that to the contrary, I think I'm going to have to make up my mind about Liselle.'

'I wondered how long that would take you.'

'You knew?' Silk looked surprised.

'Everybody knew, Silk. She set out to get you, and she did exactly that.'

'That's depressing – to get trapped finally when I'm in my dotage.'

'I'd hardly say you're *that* far gone.'

'I must be to even be considering something like this,' Silk said moodily. 'Liselle and I could continue to go on the way we have been, I suppose, but sneaking down hallways to her bedroom in the middle of the night seems a little disrespectful for some reason, and I'm too fond of her for that.'

'Fond?'

'All right then,' Silk snapped. 'I'm in love with her. Does it make you feel better to have me come right out and say it?'

'I just wanted to get it clear, that's all. Is this the first time you've admitted it – even to yourself?'

'I've been trying to avoid that. Do you suppose we could talk about something else?' He looked around. 'I wish he'd go find another piece of air to fly in,' he said in a grouchy tone of voice.

'Who?'

'That blasted albatross. He's back again.' Silk pointed. Garion turned and saw the white sea-bird with its enormous wings on station once more just ahead of the bow-sprit. The cloud bank to the west had grown more and more purple as the morning had progressed, and against that backdrop the snowy bird seemed almost to glow with an unearthly incandescence.

'That's very strange,' Garion said.

'I just wish I knew what he was up to,' Silk said. 'I'm going below. I don't want to look at him any more.' He took Garion's hand in his. 'We've had fun,' he said gruffly. 'Take care of yourself.'

'You don't have to leave.'

'I have to make room for all the others waiting in line to see you, your Majesty,' Silk grinned. 'I think you're in for a depressing day. I'm going to go find out if Beldin's found an ale barrel yet.' With a jaunty wave, the little man turned and went to the stairway leading below.

Silk's prediction proved to be all too accurate. One by one, Garion's friends came up on deck to take leave of him, each firmly convicted that *he* would be the one to die. All in all, it was a very gloomy day.

It was almost twilight when the last of the self-composed epitaphs had been completed. Garion leaned on the rail, looking back at the phosphorescent wake glowing behind their ship.

'Bad day, I take it?' It was Silk again.

'Dreadful. Did Beldin find any ale?'

'I don't recommend any of that for you. You'll need your wits about you tomorrow. I just came up to make sure that all the gloom your friends have been piling on you doesn't make you start thinking about drowning yourself.' Silk frowned. 'What's that?' he asked.

'What's what?'

'That booming noise.' He looked toward the bow. 'There it is,' he said tensely.

The purple sky had turned almost black with the onset of evening, a black pierced here and there with patches of angry red, the light of the setting sun glowing through the clouds. There was a rusty-colored blur low on the horizon, a blur that seemed to be wearing a white necklace of frothy surf.

Captain Kresca came forward with the rolling walk of a man who spends little time ashore. 'That's it, good masters,' he told them. 'That's the reef.'

Garion stared out at the Place Which is No More, his thoughts and emotions stumbling over each other.

And then the albatross gave a strange cry, a cry that seemed almost triumphant. The great pearly white bird dipped its pinions once, then continued toward Korim on seemingly motionless wings.

CHAPTER NINETEEN

Oskatat the Seneschal moved with a certain deliberate speed through the corridors of the Drojim Palace toward the throne room of Urgit, high King of Cthol Murgos. Oskatat's scarred face was bleak, and his mind was troubled. He stopped before the closely guarded door to the throne room. 'I will speak with his Majesty,' he declared.

The guards hastily opened the door for him. Although by mutual agreement between himself and King Urgit, Oskatat still bore only the title of Seneschal, the guards, like everyone else in the palace, recognized the fact that he was second only to the king himself in authority in Cthol Murgos.

He found his rat-faced monarch engaged in light conversation with Queen Prala and Queen Mother Tamazin, Oskatat's own wife. 'Ah, there you are, Oskatat,' Urgit said. 'Now my little family is complete. We've been discussing some extensive remodeling of the Drojim Palace. All these jewels and the tons of gold on the ceilings are in terribly bad taste, wouldn't you say? Besides, I need the money I'll be able to get for all that trash for the war effort.'

'Something important has come up, Urgit,' Oskatat told his king. By royal command, Oskatat always called his king by his first name in private conversations.

'That's depressing,' Urgit said, sprawling deeper into the cushions on his throne. Taur Urgas, Urgit's supposed father, had scornfully rejected such comforts as cushions, preferring to set an example of Murgo hardihood by sitting for hours on cold stone. About all that brainless gesture had gained the mad king had been a fistula which added quite noticeably in the later years of his life to his irritability.

'Sit up straight, Urgit,' Lady Tamazin, the king's mother, said absently.

'Yes, mother,' Urgit replied, straightening slightly on his throne. 'Go ahead, Oskatat,' he said, 'but please drop it on me gently. Lately I've noticed that "important things" usually turn out to be disasters.'

'I've been in contact with Jaharb, Chief Elder of the Dagashi,' Oskatat reported. 'At my request, he's been trying to pinpoint the location of Agachak the Hierarch. We've finally found him – or at least found the port he sailed from when he left Cthol Murgos.'

'Astonishing,' Urgit said with a broad grin. 'For once you've actually brought me some good news. So Agachak has left Cthol Murgos. We can hope that it's his intention to sail off the edge of the world. I'm glad you told me about this, Oskatat. I'll sleep much better now that that walking corpse no longer contaminates what's left of my kingdom. Were Jaharb's spies able to find out his intended destination?'

'He's bound for Mallorea, Urgit. Judging from his actions, he appears to believe that the Sardion is there. He went to Thull Mardu and pressured King Nathel into accompanying him.'

Urgit suddenly laughed uproariously. 'He actually did it!' he exclaimed with delight.

'I don't quite follow you.'

'I suggested to him once that he take Nathel instead of me when he went after the Sardion. Now he's saddled himself with that cretin. I'd give a great deal to listen to some of their conversations. If he happens to succeed, he'll make Nathel Overking of Angarak, and Nathel can't even tie his own shoes.'

'You don't actually think Agachak will succeed, do you?' Queen Prala said, a slight frown creasing her flawless brow. Queen Prala was several months gone with child, and she'd taken to worrying about things lately.

'Win?' Urgit snorted. 'He hasn't got a chance. He has to get past Belgarion first – not to mention Belgarath and Polgara. They'll incinerate him.' He smiled sardonically. 'It's so nice to have powerful friends.' He stopped, frowning slightly. 'We really ought to warn Belgarion, though – and Kheldar,' he added. He sprawled down into his cushions again. 'The last we heard, Belgarion and his friends had left Rak Hagga with Kal Zakath. Our best guess was that they were going to Mal Zeth, either as guests or as prisoners.' He pulled at his long, pointed nose. 'I know Belgarion well enough to know that he's not the sort to stay a prisoner for very long, though. Zakath probably knows where he is, however. Oskatat, is there any way we can get a Dagashi to Mal Zeth?'

'We could try, Urgit, but our chances of success wouldn't be too good, and a Dagashi might have some difficulty getting in to see the Emperor. Zakath's got a civil war on his hands, so he's likely to be a bit preoccupied.'

'That's true, isn't it?' Urgit tapped his fingers on the arm of his throne. 'He's still keeping abreast of what's happening here in Cthol Murgos, though, wouldn't you say?'

'Undoubtedly.'

'Why not let *him* be our messenger to Belgarion then.'

'You're moving a little fast for me, Urgit,' Oskatat confessed.

'What's the nearest town occupied by the Malloreans?'

'They still have a reduced garrison at Rak Cthaka. We could overwhelm them in a few hours, but we haven't wanted to give Zakath any reason to return to Cthol Murgos in force.'

Urgit shuddered. 'I'm very strongly inclined toward that line of thinking myself,' he admitted, 'but I owe Belgarion several favors, and I want to protect my brother as much as I can. I'll tell you what you do, Oskatat. Take about three army corps and run on down to Rak Cthaka. Malloreans out in the countryside will run off to Rak Hagga to pass the word on to Kal Zakath that we're beginning to attack his cities. That should get his attention. Mill around outside the city for a while, then surround the place. Ask for a parlay with the garrison commander. Explain the situation to him. I'll compose a letter to Kal Zakath pointing out a certain community of interest in this affair. I'm sure he doesn't want Agachak in Mallorea any more than I want the old magician here in Cthol Murgos. I'll suggest in the strongest terms that he pass the word on to Belgarion. The word he'll have already received about our hostile actions will guarantee that he'll at least look at my letter. He'll get in touch with Belgarion, and then we can both sit back and watch the Godslayer solve our problem for us.' He grinned suddenly. 'Who knows? This might even be the first step toward a reconciliation between his Imperial Implacableness and me. I really think it's time for Angaraks to stop killing each other.'

'Can't you squeeze any more speed out of her?' King Anheg demanded of Captain Greldik.

'Of course, Anheg,' Greldik growled. 'I could crowd on more sail, and we'll be as swift as an arrow – for about five minutes. Then the masts will break, and we'll go back to rowing. Which shift should I put you down for?'

'Greldik, have you ever heard the term *"lèsé majesty"*?'

'You've mentioned it frequently, Anheg, but you should take a look at maritime law sometime. When we're on board this ship and at sea, I have even more absolute authority than you've got in Val Alorn. If I tell you to row, you'll row – or swim.'

Anheg walked away, muttering curses under his breath.

'Any luck?' Emperor Varana asked as the Alorn king approached the bow.

'He told me to mind my own business,' Anheg grunted. 'Then he offered to let me man an oar if I was in such a hurry.'

'Have you ever manned an oar before?'

'Once. Chereks are a sea going people, and my father thought it would be educational for me to make a voyage as a deckhand. I didn't mind the rowing so much. It was the flogging that irritated me.'

'They actually flogged the crown prince?' Varana asked incredulously.

'It's very hard to see an oarsman's face when you're coming up behind him,' Anheg shrugged. 'The oarsmaster was trying to get more speed out of us. We were pursuing a Tolnedran merchantman at the time, and we didn't want her to reach the safety of Tolnedran territorial waters.'

'Anheg!' Varana exclaimed.

'That was years ago, Varana. I've given orders now that Tolnedran vessels are not to be molested – at least not in the sight of witnesses. The whole point of this is that Greldik's probably right. If he puts on all sail, the wind will uproot his masts, and you and I'll both wind up rowing.'

'We don't have much chance of catching up with Barak, then, do we?'

'I'm not so sure. Barak's not nearly as good a sailor as Greldik is, and that oversized tub of his isn't very responsive to the helm. We're gaining on him every day. When he gets to Mallorea, he's going to have to stop in every port to ask questions. Most Malloreans wouldn't recognize Garion if he walked up and spat in their eyes. Kheldar's another matter, though. I understand that the little thief has branch offices in most of the cities and towns in Mallorea. I know how Barak thinks. As soon as he gets to Mallorea, he's going to go looking for Silk, since Silk and Garion are obviously going to be together. I don't have to ask about Silk, though. All I've got to do is describe the *Seabird* to waterfront loafers in just a few towns. For the price of a few tankards of ale, I'll be able to follow Barak wherever he goes. Hopefully, we'll catch up with him before he finds Garion and ruins everything. I just wish that blind girl hadn't told him he couldn't go along. The fastest way I know of to get Barak to do something is to forbid him to do it. If he were with Garion, at least Belgarath would be there to keep him under control.'

'How do you propose to stop him even if we do catch up

with him? His ship may be slower than this one, but it's also bigger, and it carries more men.'

'Greldik and I have worked that out,' Anheg replied. 'Greldik's got a special piece of equipment in his forward hold. It bolts to the bow of this ship. If Barak refuses to come about when I order him to, Greldik's going to ram him. He won't go very fast in a sinking ship.'

'Anheg, that's monstrous!'

'So's what Barak's trying to do. If he succeeds in breaking through to Garion, Zandramas will win, and we'll all end up under the heel of somebody worse than Torak was. If I have to sink *Seabird* to avoid that, I'll do it ten times over.' He sighed. 'I'll miss my cousin, though, in case he gets drowned,' he admitted.

Queen Porenn of Drasnia had summoned Margrave Khendon, the chief of her intelligence service, to her private chambers that morning and issued her commands in no uncertain terms. 'Every one of them, Javelin,' she had said in a peremptory tone. 'I want every single spy out of this wing of the palace for the rest of the day.'

'Porenn!' Javelin had gasped. 'That's unheard of!'

'Not really. You just heard it – from me. Tell your people to sweep all the unofficial spies out as well. I want this wing of the palace totally unpopulated within the hour. I have spies of my own, Javelin, and I know where all the usual hiding places are. Clean out every one of them.'

'I'm bitterly disappointed in you, Porenn. Monarchs simply don't treat the intelligence service in this fashion. Have you any idea of what this is going to do to my people's morale?'

'Frankly, Khendon, I couldn't care less about the morale of your professional snoops. This is a matter of supreme urgency.'

'Has my service ever failed you, your Majesty?' Javelin's tone was a bit offended.

'Twice that I recall. Didn't the Bear Cult infiltrate your

service? And didn't your people fail abysmally to warn me about General Haldar's defection?'

Javelin had sighed. 'All right, Porenn, sometimes a few minor things have escaped us.'

'You call Haldor's going over to the Bear-cult minor?'

'You're being unnecessarily critical, Porenn.'

'I want this wing cleared, Javelin. Would you like to have me summon my son? We'll draw up a proclamation making the prohibition against spying on the royal family permanent.'

'You wouldn't!' Javelin's face had turned absolutely white. 'The whole service would collapse. The right to spy on the royal family has always been the highest reward for exemplary service. Most of my people jump at the chance.' He frowned slightly. 'Silk's turned it down three times already, though,' he added.

'Then clear them out, Javelin – and don't forget the closet hidden behind the tapestry in the corridor just outside.'

'How did you find out about *that*?'

'I didn't. Kheva did, actually.'

Javelin had groaned.

A few hours after that, Porenn sat impatiently in her sitting room with her son, King Kheva. Kheva was maturing rapidly now. His voice had settled into a resonant baritone, and a downy beard had begun to sprout on his cheeks. His mother, in somewhat marked contrast to most regents, had been gradually introducing him into state councils and negotiations with foreign powers. It would not be long now until she could gently guide him to the forefront and gradually withdraw herself from her unwanted position of authority. Kheva would be a good king, she thought. He was very nearly as shrewd as his father had been and he had that most necessary trait in a reigning monarch, good sense.

There was a rather heavy-handed pounding on the sitting-room door. 'Yes?' Porenn replied.

'It's me, Porenn,' a brash-sounding voice said, 'Yarblek.'

'Come in, Yarblek. We've got something to talk about.'

Yarblek pushed the door open, and he and Vella entered. Porenn sighed. During the course of her visit to Gar og Nadrak, Vella had reverted. She had shed the shallow veneer of gentility Porenn had labored so long to create, and her garb indicated that she had once again become the wild, untameable creature she had always been before.

'What's all the rush, Porenn?' Yarblek said gruffly, dumping his shabby felt coat and shaggy hat in the corner. 'Your messenger almost killed his horse getting to me.'

'Something urgent has come up,' the Queen of Drasnia replied. 'I think it concerns us all. I want you to keep it in strictest confidence, however.'

'Confidence,' Yarblek laughed derisively. 'You know there aren't any secrets in your palace, Porenn.'

'There is this time,' Porenn said a bit smugly. 'This morning I ordered Javelin to clear all the spies out of this wing of the palace.'

Yarblek grinned. 'How did he take it?'

'Badly, I'm afraid.'

'Good. He's been getting just a little too sure of himself lately. All right, let's get down to business. What's this problem?'

'In a moment. Did you find out what Drosta's been up to?'

'Of course. He's trying to make peace with Zakath. He's been dealing – at a distance – with the Mallorean who's in charge of their Bureau of Internal Affairs; Brador, I think his name is. Anyway, Drosta's been letting Mallorean agents funnel through Gar og Nadrak to infiltrate the west.'

It was Yarblek's tone of voice more than anything that warned Porenn that there was more. 'All of it, Yarblek. You're holding things back.'

Yarblek sighed. 'I *hate* dealing with a clever woman,' he complained. 'It seems so unnatural for some reason.' Then he prudently skipped out of the range of Vella's daggers. 'All right,' he gave up. 'Zakath needs money and lots of it to deal with the wars he's got on two different fronts. Drosta's cut the import duties on Mallorean carpets – at least to the merchants who pay taxes to Mal Zeth. Those Malloreans have been scalping Silk and me in the Arendish markets.'

'I assume you took advantage of that information?'

'Naturally.' He thought a moment. 'Here's your chance to make a tidy profit, Porenn,' he suggested. 'Drosta's cut the import duties to the Malloreans by fifteen percent. You could raise *your* duties by the same amount. You'll make money, and Silk and I can stay competitive.'

'I think you're trying to swindle me, Yarblek,' Porenn said suspiciously.

'Me?'

'We'll talk about it later. Now, listen very carefully. This is the reason I sent for you. Barak, Mandorallen, Hettar, Lelldorin, and Relg are sailing to Mallorea. We're not entirely positive, but we think they plan to intrude themselves in Belgarion's quest. You were there at Rheon, and you know that that Dalasian Seeress told us. Those hotheads absolutely *have* to stay out of it.'

'I'll certainly agree about that.'

'How fast can you get a message to your people in Mallorea?'

'A few weeks. Maybe a little faster if I make it a top priority.'

'This matter has the highest priority, Yarblek. Anheg and Varana are chasing Barak, but we can't be sure they'll catch him in time. We have to delay Barak, and the best way to do that is to feed him misinformation. I want you to instruct your people in Mallorea to tell Barak lies. Keep him going off in the wrong direction every chance you get. Barak will be following Kheldar, so he'll be checking in at every one of your branch offices in Mallorea for information. If Kheldar and the others are going to Maga Renn or Penn Daka, have your people tell Barak that he's going to Mal Dariya.'

'I know the procedure, Porenn,' Yarblek said. He squinted at her speculatively. 'You'll be turning authority

here in Drasnia over to his Majesty here fairly soon, won't
you?' he asked her.

'In a few years, yes.'

'When this business in Mallorea is concluded, I think
Silk and I might want to have a long discussion with you.'

'Oh?'

'What's your feeling about accepting a junior partner-
ship in our operation – after your obligations here in
Boktor have all been satisfied?'

'I'm very flattered, Yarblek. What possessed you to raise
such a possibility?'

'You're very shrewd, Porenn, and you've got all sorts of
contacts. We might even be prepared to go as high as a five
percent share.'

'Absolutely out of the question, Yarblek,' King Kheva
interrupted surprisingly. 'The percentage would have to be
at least twenty.'

'*Twenty?*' Yarblek almost screamed.

'I have to protect my mother's interests,' Kheva said
blandly. 'She won't always be young, you know, and I'd
hate to see her spend her declining years scrubbing floors.'

'This is highway robbery, Kheva!' Yarblek's face had
turned bright red.

'I'm not holding a knife to your throat, Yarblek,' Kheva
said. 'It might really be better in the long run if mother
went into business for herself anyway. She should be able
to do very well – particularly in view of the fact that all
members of the royal family are exempt from Drasnian
import duties.'

'I think you just stabbed yourself in the hand, Yarblek,'
Vella smirked. 'As long as you're getting bad news today
anyway, I might as well add my share. When this is all over,
I want you to sell me.'

'Sell you? To whom?'

'I'll tell you when the time comes.'

'Has he got any money?'

'I really don't know, but that doesn't matter. I'll pay you
your share of the price myself.'

'You must really think a lot of him to make that kind of an offer.'

'You have absolutely no idea, Yarblek. I was made for this man.'

'We were told to stay here, Atesca,' Brador said stubbornly.

'That was before this long silence,' General Atesca said, nervously pacing up and down in the large pavilion they shared. Atesca wore his uniform and his gold-inlaid steel breastplate. 'The Emperor's well-being and safety are *my* responsibility.'

'They're as much mine as they are yours.' Brador was absently rubbing the furry tummy of the half-grown cat lying ecstatic in his lap.

'All right, why aren't you doing something about it then? We haven't had word of him in weeks. Not even your intelligence network can tell us where he is.'

'I know that, Atesca, but I'm not going to disobey an imperial command just because you're getting nervous — or bored.'

'Why don't you stay here and take care of the kittens, then?' Atesca said acidly. 'I'm going to move the army out tomorrow morning.'

'I didn't deserve that, Atesca.'

'Sorry, Brador. This long silence is making me a little edgy, and I'm losing my grip on civility.'

'I'm as concerned as you are, Atesca,' Brador said, 'but all of my training rises up in protest at the notion of flying directly in the face of an imperial command.' The kitten in Brador's lap nuzzled at his fingers affectionately. 'You know,' he said, 'I think that when his Majesty returns, I'll ask him if I can have this kitten. I'm really growing rather fond of her.'

'That's up to you,' Atesca said. 'Trying to find homes for two or three litters of kittens every year might keep you out of trouble.' The broken-nosed general tugged thoughtfully at one earlobe. 'How about a compromise?' he suggested.

'I'm always willing to listen.'

'All right. We know that Urvon's army has largely disbanded, and there's fairly strong presumptive evidence that Urvon is dead.'

'I'd say so, yes.'

'And Zandramas has moved her forces into the Dalasian protectorates.'

'That's what my people report.'

'Now then, we're both senior officials in his Majesty's government, aren't we?'

'Yes.'

'Doesn't that mean that we're expected to use our own initiative to take advantage of tactical situations that arise in the field without consulting Mal Zeth?'

'I suppose so. You've spent more time in the field than I have, though.'

'It's standard practice, Brador. All right, then. Darshiva is virtually undefended. What I'm suggesting is that we restore order across the river in Peldane and move in to occupy Darshiva. That way we cut Zandramas off from her base of support. We set up a main line of resistance along the edge of those mountains to repel her forces if they try to return. We'll have effectively brought these two provinces back under imperial control. We might even get a few medals out of it.'

'His Majesty *would* be rather pleased if that happened, wouldn't he?'

'He'd be overjoyed, Brador.'

'I still don't see how occupying Darshiva is going to get us any closer to locating his Majesty.'

'That's because you're not a military man. We have to keep track of the enemy. In this case, that means the Darshivan army. Standard military proceedure in such situations is to send out patrols in force to make contact with the enemy to determine his strength and probable intentions. If those patrols should just *happen* to encounter the Emperor in the process, well—' he spread his hands eloquently.

'You'd have to brief the officers in command of those patrols rather thoroughly,' Brador pointed out cautiously. 'A green lieutenant might get flustered and blurt out things we'd rather not have the emperor aware of.'

'I said patrols in *force*, Brador,' Atesca smiled. 'I was thinking along the lines of full brigades. A brigade is commanded by a colonel, and I've got a number of fairly intelligent colonels.'

Brador grinned at his friend. 'When do we start?' he asked.

'Did you have anything planned for tomorrow morning?'

'Nothing that I can't postpone,' Brador said.

'But *why* didn't you know it was coming?' Barak demanded of Drolag, his bosun. The two of them stood on the aft deck with the wind-driven rain sheeting almost horizontally across the rail to tear at their beards.

Drolag mopped at his face with one hand. 'I haven't got the faintest idea, Barak,' he admitted. 'That leg has never failed me before.' Drolag was one of those unfortunates who at some time in the past had broken one of his legs – in Drolag's case it had happened in a tavern brawl. He had discovered not long after the bone had knit that the leg was extraordinarily sensitive to weather changes. He was able to predict the onset of bad weather with uncanny accuracy. His shipmates always watched him very closely. When Drolag winced with every step, they began searching the horizons for oncoming storms; when he limped, they shortened sail and began rigging safety lines; and when he fell down with a surprised cry of pain, they immediately battened down all hatches, rigged the sea anchor, and went below. Drolag had turned a temporary inconvenience into a lifetime career. He always commanded top pay, and nobody ever expected him to do any real work. All he had to do was pace the deck where everybody could watch him. The miraculous leg even made it possible for him to predict with some degree of certainty just exactly when a given storm would hit. But not this time. The storm that swept the *Seabird*'s decks with wind and pelting rain had come unannounced, and Drolag was as surprised by its arrival as any man on board.

'You didn't get drunk and fall down and break it again, did you?' Barak demanded suspiciously. Barak had very little knowledge of human anatomy – except about where to hit someone with an axe or to run a sword through him which would have the desired, and usually fatal, results. The big red-bearded man reasoned somewhat foggily that if Drolag had achieved his weather sensitivity by breaking his leg, a second break might very well have taken it away again.

'No, of course I didn't, Barak,' Drolag said disgustedly. 'I'm not going to risk my livelihood for a few tankards of bad ale.'

'How did the storm sneak up on you, then?'

'I don't know, Barak. Maybe it's not a natural storm. Some wizard may have summoned it. I don't know if my leg would react to something like that.'

'That's always an easy excuse, Drolag,' Barak scoffed. 'Any time an ignorant man can't explain something, he blames it on magic.'

'I don't have to take this, Barak,' Drolag said hotly. 'I earn my way, but I'm not responsible for supernatural forces.'

'Go below, Drolag,' Barak told him. 'Have a long talk with your leg and see if it can come up with a better excuse.'

Drolag staggered down the pitching deck talking to himself.

Barak was in a foul humor. Everything seemed to be conspiring to delay him. Not long after he and his friends had witnessed Agachak's unpleasant demise, *Seabird* had struck a submerged log and sprung a seam. It had only been by dint of herculean bailing that they had been able to limp down river to Dal Zerba and to haul the leaky ship up onto a mud-bar for repairs. That chore had cost them two weeks, and now this storm from nowhere added to the delay. Then Unrak came up from below, trailed by the dull-faced King of the Thulls. Unrak looked around with the wind clawing at his bright red hair. 'It doesn't seem to be letting up, does it, father?' he observed.

'Not noticeably.'

'Hettar wants to talk with you.'

'I've got to steer this big brute.'

'The mate can do it, father. All he has to do is keep her bow into the wind. Hettar's been studying that map, and he thinks we're in danger.'

'From this little storm? Don't be silly.'

'Is *Seabird*'s bottom strong enough to take on rocks?'

'We're in deep water.'

'Not for long, I don't think. Just come below, father. Hettar can show you.'

Grumbling, Barak turned the tiller over to the first mate and followed his son to the companionway leading below. Nathel, the King of the Thulls, trailed along behind them, his face incurious. Nathel was a bit older than Unrak, but he had taken to following Barak's red-haired son about like a stray puppy. Unrak was none too gracious to his unwanted companion.

'What's this all about, Hettar?' Barak demanded of his friend as he entered the cramped cabin.

'Come over here and have a look,' the tall Algar said.

Barak strode to the bolted-down table and looked down at the map.

'We left Dal Zerba yesterday morning, right?'

'Yes. We'd have gotten away sooner if somebody'd been paying attention to what was lying under the surface of that river. I think I'll find out who was on bow watch that day and have him keel-hauled.'

'What's keel-hauled?' Nathel asked Unrak.

'Something very unpleasant,' the red-haired boy replied.

'I'd rather you didn't tell me, then. I don't like unpleasant stuff.'

'Whatever you want, your Majesty.' Unrak *did* have a *few* manners.

'Couldn't you just call me Nathel?' the Thull asked

272

plaintively. 'I'm not really a king anyway. Mother's the one who makes all the decisions.'

'Anything you want, Nathel.' Unrak said it with a certain pity.

'How far would you estimate we've come since yesterday?' Hettar asked Barak.

'Oh, maybe twenty leagues. We had to heave to last night because we're in strange waters.'

'That puts us almost right here, doesn't it?' Hettar pointed at an ominous symbol on the map.

'We aren't anywhere near that reef, Hettar. We came about to southeast as soon as we came out of that estuary at the mouth of the river.'

'But we haven't been *going* southeast, Barak. There seems to be a current that comes down along the west coast of Mallorea, and it's a fairly strong one. I've checked a few times. Your bow is pointed southeast, but the *Seabird* has been drifting sideways almost due south because of that current.'

'When did you suddenly become such an expert on sailing?'

'I don't have to be, Barak. Take a stick of wood and throw it off your starboard side. Your ship will catch up with the stick in just a few minutes. We're definitely drifting south in spite of whichever direction your bow is pointed. I'd guess that within an hour we'll be able to hear the surf breaking on that reef.'

'I do confirm that our friend speaketh truth, my Lord of Trellhiem,' Mandorallen assured him. 'I myself have witnessed his experiment with the stick. Truly, we are tending southward.'

'What can we do?' Lelldorin asked a bit apprehensively.

Barak stared gloomily at the map. 'We don't have any choice,' he said. 'We can't get back out into open sea in this storm. We'll have to drop both anchors and hope that we can find a bottom that'll hold us. Then we sit tight and ride it out. What's the name of that reef, Hettar?'

'Turim,' the Algar replied.

CHAPTER TWENTY

Like almost every other ship's cabin in all the world, the one on Captain Kresca's vessel was low and had dark-stained beams overhead. The furniture was bolted to the floor, and oil lamps swung from the beams as the ship, swinging at anchor, rolled heavily in the combers coming in off the Sea of the East. Garion rather liked being at sea. There was a calmness, a kind of suspension of care out on deep water. When he was ashore it seemed that he was always scurrying from place to place through crowds of people, all filling his ears with distractions. At sea, however, there was time to be alone with his thoughts, and the even, patient roll of waves and the slow movement of the sky made those thoughts long and deep.

Their evening meal had been simple, a hearty bean soup and thick slices of dark, rich bread, and they sat on the benches around the plain table after they had eaten, talking idly and awaiting the arrival of the captain, who had promised to join them as soon as he had secured his ship.

The half-grown wolf lay under the table near where Ce'Nedra sat, and his eyes had a studied, pleading look in them. Ce'Nedra slipped him tidbits when she thought no one was watching her. Wolves are not stupid, after all.

'The surf seems to be heavy,' Zakath said, cocking his head to one side to listen to the booming of the waves against the rocks of the reef. 'That's likely to cause some problems when we try to land, isn't it?'

'I rather doubt it,' Belgarath said. 'This storm has probably been brewing since the day the earth was made. It's not going to interfere with us in any way.'

'Aren't you being just a little fatalistic, Belgarath?' Beldin suggested, 'and perhaps slightly overconfident?'

'I don't think so. The two prophecies *must* have this meeting. They've been coming toward this place since the beginning of time. They're not going to let anything interfere with the arrival of anyone who's supposed to be here.'

'Why raise a storm like this, then?'

'The storm wasn't designed to hinder us – or Zandramas.'

'What is its purpose?'

'It's probably out there to keep others away. There are only certain people who are supposed to be on that reef tomorrow. The prophecies are going to see to it that no one else can set foot on it until after our business has been completed.'

Garion looked at Cyradis. The blindfolded girl's face was calm, even serene. The half-concealment of the strip of cloth across her eyes had always at least partially concealed her features from him. In this light, however, he suddenly realized just how extraordinarily beautiful she really was. 'That raises something rather interesting, Grandfather,' he said. 'Cyradis, didn't you tell us that the Child of Dark has always been solitary? Doesn't that mean that she'll have to face us alone tomorrow?'

'Thou hast misread my meaning, Belgarion of Riva. Thou and each of thy companions have had your names writ large in the stars since the beginning of days. Those who will accompany the Child of Dark, however, are of no moment. Their names do not stand in the book of the heavens. Zandramas is the only emissary of the dark prophecy of any significance. The others she will bring with her were doubtless chosen at random, and their numbers are limited to match your force.'

'A fair fight, then,' Velvet murmured approvingly. 'I think we can probably cope.'

'That doesn't bode too well for me, though,' Beldin said. 'Back at Rheon, you rather carefully listed the people who were supposed to come here with Garion. As I recall, my name wasn't on the list. Do you suppose they forgot to send me an invitation?'

'Nay, gentle Beldin. Thy presence here is necessary now. Zandramas hath included in her forces one who is beyond the prophecies. Thou art here to offset that one, though in numbers only.'

'Zandramas can't ever play a game without cheating, can she?' Silk said.

'Can you?' Velvet asked him.

'That's different. I'm only playing for worthless counters – bits and pieces of unimportant metal. The stakes in this game are a lot higher.'

The cabin door opened, and Captain Kresca entered with several rolls of parchment under his arm. He had changed out of his doublet and now wore a tar-stained canvas sea-coat and no hat. Garion saw that his short-cropped hair was as silvery as Belgarath's, a startling contrast to his deeply tanned and weathered face. 'The storm seems to be abating,' he announced. 'At least around the reef it is. I don't think I've ever seen a storm like this.'

'I'd be surprised if you had, Captain,' Beldin told him. 'As closely as we can determine, this is the first one – and probably the last – of its kind.'

'I think you're wrong, friend,' Captain Kresca disagreed. 'There's nothing new in the way of weather in the world. It's all happened before.'

'Just let it lie,' Belgarath said quietly to Beldin. 'He's a Melcene. He's not really prepared for this sort of thing.'

'All right,' the captain said, pushing their soup bowls out of the way and laying his charts on the table. 'We're here.' He pointed. 'Now, which part of the reef was it you propose to land on?'

'The highest pinnacle,' Belgarath told him.

Kresca sighed. 'I might have known,' he said. 'That's the one part of the reef where my charts aren't too accurate. About the time I got to taking soundings around that one, a squall came out of nowhere, and I had to back off.' He thought about it. 'No matter,' he decided. 'We'll stand a half-mile or so off shore and go in with the long-boat. There's something you ought to know about that part of the reef, though.'

'Oh?' Belgarath said.

'I think there are some people there.'

'I sort of doubt it.'

'I don't really know of any other creature that builds fires, do you? There's a cave on the north side of that pinnacle, and sailors have been seeing the light of fires coming out of the mouth of it for years now. It's my guess that there's a band of pirates living in there. It wouldn't be all that hard for them to come out in small boats on dark nights and waylay merchantmen in the straits on the landward side of the reef.'

'Can you see the fire from where we are right now?' Garion asked him.

'I'd guess so. Let's go topside and have a look.'

The ladies, Sadi, and Toth remained in the cabin, and Garion and his other friends followed Captain Kresca up the companionway to the deck. The wind which had been howling through the rigging when the sailors had dropped anchor had fallen off, and the surf along the reef was no longer frothy.

'There,' Kresca said, pointing. 'It's not quite as visible from this angle, but you can make it out. When you're standing out to sea from the cave-mouth, it's really bright.'

Dimly, Garion could see a sooty red glow a short way up the side of a bulky-looking peak jutting up out of the sea. The other rocks that formed the reef appeared to be little more than slender spires, but the central peak had a different shape. For some reason, it reminded Garion of the truncated mountain which was the site of far-off Prolgu in Ulgoland.

'Nobody's ever explained to my satisfaction how the top of that mountain got sliced off like that,' Kresca said.

'It's probably a very long story,' Silk told him. The little man shivered. 'It's still a little chilly out here,' he noted. 'Why don't we go below again?'

Garion fell back to walk beside Belgarath. 'What's making that light, Grandfather?' he asked quietly.

'I'm not entirely sure,' Belgarath replied, 'but I think it might be the Sardion. We know it's in that cave.'

'We do?'

'Of course we do. At the time of the meeting, the Orb and the Sardion have to come into each others' presence in the same way you and Zandramas do. That Melcene scholar who stole the Sardion – the one Senji told us about – sailed around the southern tip of Gandahar and disappeared into these waters. That was all too convenient to be mere coincidence. The Sardion was controlling the scholar, and the scholar delivered the stone to the precise place it wanted to go. It's probably been waiting for us in that cave for about five hundred years.'

Garion looked back over his shoulder. The hilt of his sword was covered by the leather sleeve, but he was still fairly certain that he'd be able to see the muted glow of the Orb. 'Doesn't the Orb usually react to the presence of the Sardion?' he asked.

'We may not be close enough yet, and we're still at sea. Open water confuses the Orb. Then, too, maybe it's trying to conceal itself from the Sardion.'

'Could it actually think its way through that complex an idea? It's usually fairly childish, I've noticed.'

'Don't underestimate it, Garion.'

'Everything's fitting together, then, isn't it?'

'It all has to, Garion. Otherwise what's going to happen tomorrow couldn't happen.'

'Well, father?' Polgara asked as they re-entered the cabin.

'There's a fire of some kind in that cave, all right,' he told her. His fingers, however, were telling her something else. – *We'll talk about it in more detail after the captain leaves*. – He turned toward Kresca. 'When's the next low tide?' he asked the seaman.

Kresca squinted, calculating. 'We just missed one,' he said. 'The tide's coming in now. The next low tide will come about day-break and, if my observations are correct, it should be a neap tide. Well, I'll leave you to get some rest now. I sort of gather that you've got a full day ahead of you tomorrow.'

'Thank you, Captain Kresca,' Garion said, shaking the seaman's hand.

'Don't mention it, Garion,' Kresca grinned. 'The King of Peldane paid me very handsomely for this voyage, so being helpful doesn't really cost me anything.'

'Good,' Garion grinned back. 'I like to see friends get ahead in the world.'

The captain laughed and went back out with a hearty wave.

'What was he talking about?' Sadi asked. 'What's a neap tide?'

'It only happens a few times a year,' Beldin explained. 'It's an extreme low tide. It has to do with the positions of the sun and moon.'

'Everything seems to be going out of its way to make tomorrow a very special day,' Silk observed.

'All right, father,' Polgara said crisply. 'What's the story on the fire in that cave?'

'I can't be positive, Pol, but I rather strongly suspect that it's not a group of pirates – not after all the trouble the prophecies have gone to, keep people away from the cave.'

'What do you think it is, then?'

'It's probably the Sardion.'

'Would it give off a red glow?'

He shrugged. 'The Orb glows blue. I suppose there's a sort of logic to the Sardion's glowing a different color.'

'Why not green?' Silk asked.

'Green's an in-between color,' Beldin told him. 'It's a mixture of blue and yellow.'

'You're a real gold mine of useless information, you know that, Beldin?' Silk said.

'There's no such thing as useless information, Kheldar,' Beldin sniffed.

'All right,' Zakath said, 'how are we going to go about this?'

'Cyradis,' Belgarath said to the Seeress, 'I'm guessing about this, but I think I'm fairly close. Nobody is going to reach that cave first, are they? What I mean is that the prophecies aren't going to let Zandramas get there before we do – or let us get there first either.'

'Astounding,' Beldin murmured. 'That actually sounded like real logic. Aren't you feeling well, Belgarath?'

'Would you please?' Belgarath growled. 'Well, Cyradis?'

She paused, her expression distant. Garion seemed to hear that faint choral murmuring. 'Thy reasoning is correct, Ancient One. The same perception came to Zandramas some time ago, so I am not revealing anything unto thee which she doth not already know. Zandramas, however, hath rejected the fruits of her reasoning and hath striven to circumvent her conclusions.'

'Very well, then,' Zakath said, 'since we're all going to get there at the same time anyway, and since everybody knows about it, there's not much point in being coy, is there? I say we just land on the beach and march straight to the cave.'

'Stopping only long enough for you and me to put on our armor,' Garion added. 'It probably wouldn't be a good idea to dress up here on board ship. It might make Kresca nervous.'

'Your plan sounds good to me, Zakath,' Durnik agreed.

'I'm not so sure,' Silk said dubiously. 'There's a certain advantage to sneaking.'

'Drasnians,' Ce'Nedra sighed.

'Listen to his reasons before you throw the notion out, Ce'Nedra,' Velvet suggested.

'It's sort of like this,' Silk went on. 'Zandramas *knows* – deep down – that she can't beat us to that cave, but she's been trying for months all the same, hoping that there's some way she can by-pass the rules. Now, let's try to think the way she does.'

'I'd sooner take poison,' Ce'Nedra said with a shudder.

'It's only for the sake of understanding your opponent, Ce'Nedra. Now, Zandramas has been hoping against hope that she can beat us to that cave and avoid the necessity of coming up against Garion. He *did* kill Torak, after all, and nobody in his right mind would willingly confront the Godslayer.'

'I'm going to have that removed from my title when I get back to Riva,' Garion said sourly.

'You can do that later,' Silk told him. 'What would Zandramas most likely feel if she arrived at the cavemouth, looked around, and didn't see us?'

'I think I see where you're going, Kheldar,' Sadi said admiringly.

'You would,' Zakath said drily.

'It's really rather brilliant, you know, Kal Zakath,' the eunuch said. 'Zandramas is going to feel a wild exultation. She'll believe that she's succeeded in circumventing the prophecies and that she's won in spite of them.'

'Then what's going to happen to her when we all step out from behind a boulder and she finds out that she still has to face Garion and submit to the choice of Cyradis after all?' Silk asked.

'She's probably going to be very disappointed,' Velvet said.

'I think disappointment might be too mild a term,' Silk suggested. 'I think chagrin might come closer. Couple that with exasperation and a healthy dose of fear, and we'll be looking at somebody who's not going to be thinking too clearly. We're fairly sure there's going to be a fight when we get there, and you've always got an advantage in a fight when the opposing general is distracted.'

'It's sound tactical reasoning, Garion,' Zakath conceeded.

'I'll go along with it,' Belgarath said. 'If nothing else, it should give me the opportunity to pay Zandramas back for all the times she's upset me. I think I still owe her just a bit for slicing pieces out of the Ashabine Oracles.

I'll talk with Captain Kresca early tomorrow morning and find out if there's a beach on the east side of the peak. With a neap tide, our chances should be pretty good. Then we'll work our way up along the side of the peak, staying out of sight. We'll take cover near the cave mouth and wait for Zandramas to put in an appearance. Then we'll step out and surprise her.'

'I can add an even bigger advantage,' Beldin said. 'I'll scout on ahead and let you know when she lands. That way, you'll be ready for her.'

'Not as a hawk, though, Uncle,' Polgara suggested.

'Why not?'

'Zandramas isn't stupid. A hawk wouldn't have any business on that reef. There wouldn't be anything there for him to eat.'

'Maybe she'll think the storm blew me out to sea.'

'Do you want to risk your tail feathers on a maybe? A seagull, Uncle.'

'A seagull?' he objected. 'But they're so stupid – and so dirty.'

'*You?* Worried about dirt?' Silk asked him, looking up. Silk had been busily counting on his fingers.

'Don't push it, Kheldar,' Beldin growled ominously.

'What day of the month was Prince Geran born on?' Silk asked Ce'Nedra.

'The seventh, why?'

'We appear to have another one of those things that's setting out to make tomorrow very special. If I've counted right, tomorrow will be your son's second birthday.'

'It can't be!' she exclaimed. 'My baby was born in the winter time.'

'Ce'Nedra,' Garion said gently, 'Riva's up near the top of the world. This reef is near the bottom. It *is* winter in Riva right now. Count up the months since Geran was born – the time he spent with us before Zandramas stole him, the time we spent marching on Rheon, the trip to Prolgu then to Tol Honeth and on to Nyissa and all those other places where we had to stop. I think if you count rather closely, you'll find that it *has* been very close to two years.'

She frowned, ticking the months off. Finally, her eyes went very wide. 'I think he's right!' she exclaimed. 'Geran will be two years old tomorrow!'

Durnik laid his hand on the little queen's arm. 'I'll see if I can make something for you to give him as a present, Ce'Nedra,' he said gently. 'A boy ought to have a birthday present after he's been separated from his family for so long.'

Ce'Nedra's eyes filled with tears. 'Oh, Durnik!' She wept, embracing him. 'You think of everything.'

Garion looked at Aunt Pol, his fingers moving slightly. —*Why don't you ladies take her in and put her to bed?*—he suggested.—We're all through here, and if she thinks too much about this, she's going to get herself worked up.—Tomorrow's going to be hard enough for her anyway.—

—*You might be right.*—

After the ladies had left, Garion and the other men sat around the bolted-down table reminiscing. They covered in some detail the various adventures they had shared since that wind-tossed night so long ago when Garion, Belgarath, Aunt Pol and Durnik had crept out through the gate of Faldor's farm into the world where the possible and the impossible inexorably merged. Again, Garion felt that sense of cleansing, coupled with something else. It was as if, by recapitulating all that had happened in their long journey to the reef lying out there in the darkness, they were somehow bringing everything into focus to strengthen their resolve and their sense of purpose. It seemed to help for some reason.

'I think that's about enough of that,' Belgarath said finally, rising to his feet. 'Now we all know what's behind us. It's time to pack all that away and start looking ahead. Let's get some sleep.'

Ce'Nedra stirred restlessly when Garion slipped into bed. 'I thought you were going to stay up all night,' she said sleepily.

'We were talking.'

'I know. I could hear the murmur of voices even in here. And men think women talk all the time.'

'Don't you?'

'Probably, but a woman can talk while her hands are busy. A man can't.'

'You might be right.'

There was a moment of silence. 'Garion,' she said.

'Yes, Ce'Nedra?'

'Can I borrow your knife – the little dagger Durnik gave you when you were a boy?'

'If you want something cut, point it out. I'll cut it for you.'

'It's nothing like that, Garion. I just want to have a knife tomorrow.'

'What for?'

'As soon as I see Zandramas, I'm going to kill her.'

'Ce'Nedra!'

'I have every right to kill her, Garion. You told Cyradis you didn't think you could do it because Zandramas is a woman. I don't suffer from the same kind of delicacy as you do. I'm going to carve out her heart – if she has one – slowly.' She said it with a fierceness he had never heard in her voice before. 'I want blood, Garion! Lots of blood, and I want to hear her scream as I twist the knife in her. You'll lend me your dagger, won't you?'

'Absolutely not!'

'That's all right, Garion,' she said in an icy tone. 'I'm sure Liselle will lend me one of hers. Liselle's a woman and she knows how I feel.' Then she turned her back on him.

'Ce'Nedra,' he said placatingly.

'Yes?' Her tone was sulky.

'Be reasonable, dear.'

'I don't want to be reasonable. I want to kill Zandramas.'

'I'm not going to let you put yourself in that kind of danger. We have much more important things to do tomorrow.'

She sighed. 'I suppose you're right. It's just—'

'Just what?'

She turned back and put her arms around his neck. 'Never mind, Garion,' she said. 'Let's go to sleep now.' She nestled down against him, and after a few moments her regular breathing told him that she had drifted off.

'*You should have given her the knife,*' the voice in his mind told him. '*Silk could have stolen it back from her sometime tomorrow.*'

'*But—*'

'*We've got something else to talk about, Garion. Have you been thinking about your successor?*'

'*Well – sort of. It doesn't really fit any of them, you know.*'

'*Have you given serious consideration to each of them?*'

'*I suppose I have, but I haven't been able to make any decisions yet.*'

'*You're not supposed to make your choice yet. All you had to do was think about each one of them and get them all firmly fixed in your mind.*'

'*When do I make the choice then?*'

'*At the last possible moment, Garion. Zandramas might be able to hear your thoughts, but she can't hear what you haven't decided yet.*'

'*What if I make a mistake?*'

'*I really don't think you can, Garion. I really don't.*'

Garion's sleep was troubled that night. His dreams seemed chaotic, disconnected, and he woke often only to sink back into restless doze. There was at first a kind of distorted recapitulation of the strange dreams which had so disturbed him that night long ago on the Isle of the Winds just before his life had been unalterably changed. The question, 'are you ready?' seemed to echo again and again in the vaults of his mind. Again, he faced Rundorig with Aunt Pol's matter-of-fact instruction to kill his boyhood friend roaring in his mind. And then the boar he had encountered in the snowy wood outside Val Alorn was there, pawing at the snow, its eyes aglow with rage and

285

hate. 'Are you ready?' Barak asked him before releasing the beast. Then he stood on the colorless plain surrounded by the pieces of the incomprehensible game trying to decide which piece to move while the voice in his mind urged him to hurry.

The dream subtly changed and took on a different tone. Our dreams, no matter how bizarre, have a familiarity to them, since they are formed and shaped by our own minds. Now it seemed as if Garion's dreams were being formed by a different and unfriendly awareness almost in the same way that Torak had intruded Himself in dreams and in thoughts before the meeting at Cthol Mishrak.

Again he faced Asharak the Murgo in the loamy Wood of the Dryads, and once again he unleashed his will with that single, open-handed slap and the fatal word, 'burn!' This was a familiar nightmare. It had haunted Garion's sleep for years. He saw Asharak's cheek begin to seethe and smoke. He heard the Grolim shriek and saw him clutch at his burning face. He heard the dreadful plea, 'Master, have mercy!' He spurned that plea and intensified the flame, but this time the act was not overlaid with the sense of self-loathing which had always accompanied the dream, but a kind of cruel exultation, a hideous joy as he watched his enemy writhe and burn before him. Deep within him something cried out, trying to repudiate that unholy joy.

And then he was at Cthol Mishrak, and his flaming sword slid again and again into the body of the One-Eyed God. Torak's despairing 'Mother!' did not this time fill him with pity but with a towering satisfaction. He felt himself laughing, and the savage, unpitying laughter erased his humanity.

Soundlessly shrieking in horror, Garion recoiled, not so much from the awful images of those whom he had destroyed, but more from his own enjoyment of their despairing agony.

CHAPTER TWENTY-ONE

They were a somber group when they gathered in the main cabin before daybreak the following morning. With a sudden, even surprising, insight, Garion was very certain that the nightmares had not been his alone. Insight and intuitive perception were not normal for Garion. His sensible Sendarian background rejected such things as questionable, even in some peculiar way immoral. *'Did you do that?'* he asked the voice.

'No. Rather surprisingly, you came up with it all on your own. You seem to be making some progress – slowly, of course, but progress all the same.'

'Thanks.'

'Don't mention it.'

Silk looked particularly shaken as he entered the cabin. The little man's eyes were haunted, and his hands were shaking. He slumped onto a bench and buried his face in his hands. 'Have you got any of that ale left?' he asked Beldin in a hoarse voice.

'A little quivery this morning, Kheldar?' the dwarf asked him.

'No,' Garion said. 'That's not what's bothering him. He had some bad dreams last night.'

Silk raised his face sharply. 'How did you know that?' he demanded.

'I had some myself. I got to relive what I did to Asharak the Murgo, and I killed Torak again – several times. It didn't get any better as we went along.'

'I was trapped in a cave,' Silk said with a shudder. 'There wasn't any light, but I could feel the walls closing in on me. I think the next time I see Relg, I'm going to hit him in the mouth – gently, of course. Relg's sort of a friend.'

'I'm glad I wasn't the only one,' Sadi said. The eunuch had placed a bowl of milk on the table, and Zith and her babies were gathered around it, lapping and purring. Garion was a bit surprised to note that no one really paid any attention to Zith and her brood any more. People, it seemed, could get used to almost anything. Sadi rubbed his long-fingered hand over his shaved scalp. 'It seemed to me that I was adrift in the streets of Sthiss Tor, and I was trying to survive by begging. It was ghastly.'

'I saw Zandramas sacrificing my baby,' Ce'Nedra said in a stricken voice. 'There was crying and so much blood – so very much blood.'

'Peculiar,' Zakath said. 'I was presiding over a trial. I had to condemn a number of people. There was one of them I cared a great deal about, but I was forced to condemn her anyway.'

'I had one, too,' Velvet admitted.

'I rather expect we all did,' Garion told them. 'The same thing happened to me on the way to Cthol Mishrak. Torak kept intruding in my dreams.' He looked at Cyradis. 'Does the Child of Dark always fall back on this?' he asked her. 'We've found that events keep repeating themselves when we're leading up to one of these meetings. Is this one of those events that keeps happening over and over again?'

'Thou art very perceptive, Belgarion of Riva,' the Seeress told him. 'In all the uncounted eons since these meetings began, thou art the first Child of either Light or Dark to have realized that the sequence must be endlessly repeated until the division hath ended.'

'I not sure I can take much credit for it, Cyradis,' he admitted. 'As I understand it, the meetings are getting closer and closer together. I'm probably the first in history to have been the Child of Light – or Dark – during *two* meetings, and even then it took me a while to realize that it was happening. The nightmares are part of that pattern then?'

'Thy guess is shrewd, Belgarion,' she smiled gently.

'Unfortunately, it is not correct. It seemeth me a shame to waste such a clever perception, though.'

'Are you trying to be funny, Holy Seeress?'

'Would I do that, noble Belgarion?' she said, perfectly imitating Silk's inflection.

'You could spank her,' Beldin suggested.

'With that human mountain standing guard over her?' Garion said, grinning at Toth. His eyes narrowed. 'You're not permitted to help us with this, are you Cyradis?' he asked her.

She sighed and shook her head.

'That's all right, Holy Seeress,' he said. 'I think we can come up with a workable answer to the question by ourselves.' He looked at Belgarath. 'All right,' he said. 'Torak tried to frighten me with nightmares, and now it looks as if Zandramas is trying to do the same thing, except that this time, she's doing it to all of us. If it's not one of those usual repetitions, what is it?'

'That boy's beginning to develop a rather keen analytical mind, Belgarath,' Beldin said.

'Naturally,' the old man said modestly.

'Don't wrench your shoulder out of its socket trying to pat yourself on the back,' Beldin said sourly. He rose to his feet and started pacing up and down, his forehead creased in thought. 'Now then,' he began, 'first; this isn't just one of the tedious repetitions that have been dogging us since the beginning, right?'

'Right,' Belgarath agreed.

'Second; it happened in about the same way last time.' He looked at Garion. 'Right?' he asked.

'Right,' Garion said.

'That's only two times. Twice can be a coincidence, but let's assume that it's not. We know that the Child of Light always has companions, but that the Child of Dark is always solitary.'

'So Cyradis tells us,' Belgarath agreed.

'She doesn't have any reason to lie to us. All right, if the Child of Light has companions but the Child of

289

Dark is alone, wouldn't that put the Dark at a serious disadvantage?'

'You'd think so.'

'But the two have always been so evenly matched that not even the Gods can predict the outcome. The Child of Dark is using something to offset the apparant advantage of our side. I think these nightmares might be part of it.'

Silk rose and came over to Garion. 'Discussions like this make my head ache,' he said quietly. 'I'm going up on deck for a while.' He left the cabin, and for no apparent reason the gangly young wolf followed him.

'I don't really think a few nightmares would make that much difference, Beldin,' Belgarath disagreed.

'But what if the nightmares are only a part of it, Old Wolf?' Poledra asked him. 'You and Pol were both at Vo Mimbre, and that was one of these meetings, too. You two have been companions of the Child of Light twice already. What happened at Vo Mimbre?'

'We *did* have nightmares,' Belgarath conceded to Beldin.

'Anything else?' the dwarf asked intently.

'We saw things that weren't there, but that could have come from all the Grolims in the vicinity.'

'And?'

'Everybody went sort of crazy. It was all we could do to keep Brand from trying to attack Torak with his teeth, and at Cthol Mishrak I entombed Belzedar in solid rock, and then Pol wanted to dig him up so that she could drink his blood.'

'Father! I did *not*!' she objected.

'Oh, really? You were *very* angry that day, Pol.'

'It fits the same pattern, Old Wolf,' Poledra said somberly. 'Our side fights with normal weapons. Garion's sword might be a little abnormal, but it's still just a sword.'

'You wouldn't say that if you'd been at Cthol Mishrak,' her husband told her.

'I *was* there, Belgarath,' she replied.

'You *were*?'

'Of course. I was hiding in the ruins watching. Anyway, the Child of Dark doesn't attack the body; it attacks the mind. That's how it manages to keep everything so perfectly balanced.'

'Nightmares, hallucinations, and ultimately madness,' Polgara mused. 'That's a formidable array of things to throw against us. It might even have worked — if Zandramas hadn't been so clumsy.'

'I don't quite follow that, Pol,' Durnik said.

'She blundered,' Polgara shrugged. 'If only one person has a nightmare, he'll probably try to shrug it off and he certainly won't mention it on the morning of the meeting. Zandramas sent nightmares to all of us, though. This conversation probably wouldn't have taken place if she hadn't.'

'It's nice to know that she can stumble, too,' Belgarath said. 'All right then, we know that she's been tampering with us. The best way to defeat that tactic is to put those nightmares out of our minds.'

'*And* to be particularly wary if we start seeing things that shouldn't be there,' Polgara added.

Silk and the wolf came back down the stairs to the cabin. 'We've got absolutely beautiful weather this morning,' he reported happily, bending slightly to scratch the pup's ears.

'Wonderful,' Sadi murmured drily. Sadi was carefully annointing his small dagger with a fresh coating of poison. He was wearing a stout leather jerkin and leather boots that reached to mid thigh. Back in Sthiss Tor, Sadi had appeared, despite his slender frame, to be soft, even in some peculiar way, flabby. Now, however, he looked lean and tough. A year or more without drugs and with an enforced regimen of hard exercise had changed him a great deal.

'It's perfect,' Silk told him. 'We have fog this morning, ladies and gentlemen,' he said, 'a nice, wet gray fog almost thick enough to walk on. That fog would be a burglar's delight.'

'Trust Silk to think of that.' Durnik smiled. The smith

wore his usual clothing, but he had given Toth his axe, while he himself carried the dreadful sledge with which he had driven off the demon Nahaz.

'The prophecies are leading us around by the noses again,' Beldin said irritably, 'but at least it appears that we made the right decision last night. A good thick fog makes sneaking almost inevitable.' Beldin looked the same as always, tattered, dirty, and very ugly.

'Maybe they're just trying to help,' Velvet suggested. Velvet had shocked them all when she had entered the cabin a half-hour earlier. She wore tight-fitting leather clothing not unlike that normally worn by the Nadrak dancer, Vella. It was a peculiarly masculine garb and bleakly businesslike. 'They've done a great deal to assist Zandramas. Maybe it's our turn to get a little help.'

'*Is she right?*' Garion asked the awareness that shared his mind. '*Are you and your opposite helping us for a change?*'

'*Don't be silly, Garion. Nobody's been helping anybody. That's forbidden at this particular stage of the game.*'

'*Where did the fog come from then?*'

'*Where does fog usually come from?*'

'*How would I know?*'

'*I didn't think so. Ask Beldin. He can probably tell you. The fog out there is perfectly natural.*'

'Liselle,' Garion said, 'I just checked with my friend. The fog isn't the result of any playing around. It's a natural result of the storm.'

'How disappointing,' she said.

Ce'Nedra had risen that morning fully intent on wearing a Dryad tunic. Garion had adamantly rejected that idea, however. She wore instead a simple gray wool dress with no petticoats to hinger her movements. She was quite obviously stripped down for action. Garion was fairly certain that she had at least one knife concealed somewhere in her clothing. 'Why don't we get started?' she demanded.

'Because it's still dark, dear,' Polgara explained patiently.

'We have to wait for at least a little bit of light.' Polgara and her mother wore almost identical plain dresses, Polgara's gray, and Poledra's brown.

'Garion,' Poledra said then, 'why don't you step down to the galley and tell them that we'll have breakfast now? We should all eat something, since I doubt that we'll have time or maybe even the need for lunch.' Poledra sat at Belgarath's side, and the two of them were almost unconsciously holding hands. Garion was a bit offended at her suggestion. He *was* a king, after all, not an errand boy. Then he realized just how silly that particular thought was. He started to rise.

'I'll go, Garion,' Eriond said. It was almost as if the blond young man had seen into his friend's thoughts. Eriond wore the same simple brown peasant clothes he always wore, and he had nothing even resembling a weapon.

As the young man went out through the cabin door, Garion had an odd thought. Why was he paying so much attention to the appearance of each of his companions? He had seen them all before, and for the most part, he had seen the clothing they wore this morning so many times that the garments should not even have registered on his mind. Then with dreadful certainty, he knew. One of them was going to die today, and he was fixing them all in his mind so that he could remember for the rest of his life the one who was to make that sacrifice. He looked at Zakath. His Mallorean friend had shaved off his short beard. His slightly olive skin was no longer pale, but tanned and healthy-looking save for the slighter pitch on his chin and jaw. He wore simple clothing much like Garion's own, since as soon as they reached the reef, the two of them would be putting on their armor.

Toth, his face impassive, was dressed as always — a loin-cloth, sandals, and that unbleached wool blanket slung across one shoulder. He did not, however, have his heavy staff. Instead, Durnik's axe lay in his lap.

The Seeress of Kell was unchanged. Her hooded white robe gleamed, and her blindfold, unwrinkled and

293

unchanged, smoothly covered her eyes. Idly, Garion wondered if she removed the cloth when she slept. A chilling thought came to him then. What if the one they would lose today was going to be Cyradis? She had sacrificed everything for her task. Surely the two prophecies could not be so cruel as to require one last, supreme sacrifice from this slender girl.

Belgarath, of course, was unchanged and unchangeable. He still wore the mismatched boots, patched hose, and rust-colored tunic he had worn when he had appeared at Faldor's farm as Mister Wolf the storyteller. The one difference about the old man was the fact that he did not hold a tankard in his free hand. At supper the previous evening, he had almost absently drawn himself one that brimmed with foaming ale. Poledra, just as absently, had firmly removed it from his hand and had emptied it out a port-hole. Garion strongly suspected that Belgarath's drinking days had come rather abruptly to an end. He decided that it might be refreshing to have a long conversation with his Grandfather when the old man was completely sober.

They ate their breakfast with hardly any conversation, since there was nothing more to say. Ce'Nedra dutifully fed the puppy, then looked rather sadly at Garion. 'Take care of him, please,' she said.

There was no point in arguing with her on that score. The idea that she would not survive this day was so firmly fixed in her mind that no amount of talking would erase it. 'You might want to give him to Geran,' she added. 'Every boy should have a dog, and caring for him will teach our son responsibility.'

'I never had a dog,' Garion said.

'That was unkind of you, Aunt Pol,' Ce'Nedra said, lapsing unconsciously – or perhaps not – into that form of address.

'He wouldn't have had time to look after one, Ce'Nedra,' Polgara replied. 'Our Garion has had a very busy life.'

'Let's hope that it gets less so when this is all over,' Garion said.

After they had eaten, Captain Kresca entered the cabin carrying a map. 'This isn't very precise,' he apologized. 'As I said last night, I was never able to take very accurate soundings around that peak. We can inch our way to within a few hundred yards of the beach, and then we'll have to take to the long-boat. This fog is going to make it even more complicated, I'm afraid.'

'Is there a beach along the east side of the peak?' Belgarath asked him.

'A very shallow one,' Kresca replied. 'The neap tide should expose a bit more of it, though.'

'Good. There are a few things we'll need to take ashore with us.' Belgarath pointed at the two stout canvas bags holding the armor Garion and Zakath would wear.

'I'll have some men stow them in the boat for you.'

'When can we get started?' Ce'Nedra asked impatiently.

'Another twenty minutes or so, little lady.'

'So long?'

He nodded. 'Unless you can figure out a way to make the sun come up early.'

Ce'Nedra looked quickly at Belgarath.

'Never mind,' he told her.

'Captain,' Poledra said, 'could you have someone look after our pet?' She pointed at the wolf. 'He's a bit over-enthusiastic sometimes, and we wouldn't want him to start howling at the wrong time.'

'Of course, Lady.' Kresca, it appeared, had not spent enough time ashore to recognize a wolf when he saw one.

'Inching' proved to be a very tedious process. The sailors raised the anchors and then manned the oars. After every couple of strokes, they paused while a man in the bow heaved out the lead-weighted sounding line.

'It's slow,' Silk observed in a low voice as they all stood on deck, 'but at least it's quiet. We don't know who's on that reef, and I'd rather not alert them.'

'It's shoaling, Captain,' the man with the sounding line reported, his voice no louder than absolutely necessary. The obviously warlike preparations of Garion and his friends had stressed the need for quiet louder than any words. The sailor cast out his line again. There was that interminable-seeming wait while the ship drifted up over the weighted line. 'The bottom's coming up fast, Captain,' the sounder said then. 'I make it two fathoms.'

'Back your oars,' Kresca commanded his crew in a low voice. 'Drop the hook. This is as close as we can go.' He turned to his mate. 'After we get away in the long-boat, back out about another hundred yards and anchor there. We'll whistle when we come back — the usual signal. Guide us in.'

'Aye, aye, Cap'n.'

'You've done this before, I see,' Silk said to Kresca.

'A few times, yes,' Kresca admitted.

'If all goes well today, you and I might want to have a little talk. I have a business proposition that I think might interest you.'

'Is that all you ever think about?' Velvet asked him.

'A missed opportunity is gone forever, my dear Liselle,' he replied with a certain pomposity.

'You're incorrigible.'

'I suppose you could say that, yes.'

An oil-soaked wad of burlap in the hawsehole muffled the rattling of the anchor chain as the heavy iron hook sank down through the dark water. Garion felt rather than heard the grating of the points of the anchor on the rocks lying beneath the heavy swells.

'Let's board the longboat,' Kresca said. 'The crew will lower her after we're all on board.' He looked apologetically at them. 'I'm afraid you and your friends are going to have to help with the rowing, Garion. The longboat only holds so many people.'

'Of course, Captain.'

'I'll come along to make sure you get ashore safely.'

'Captain,' Belgarath said then, 'once we're ashore, stand your ship out to sea a ways. We'll signal you when we're ready to be picked up.'

'All right.'

'If you don't see a signal by tomorrow morning, you might as well go on back to Perivor, because we won't be coming back.'

Kresca's face was solemn. 'Is whatever it is you're planning to do on that reef really *that* dangerous?' he asked.

'Probably even more so,' Silk told him. 'We've all been trying very hard not to think about it.'

It was eerie rowing across the oily-seeming black water with the grayish tendrils of fog rising from the heavy swells. Garion was suddenly reminded of that foggy night in Sthiss Tor when they had crossed the River of the Serpent with only the unerring sense of direction of the one-eyed assassin Issus to guide them. Idly, as he rowed, Garion wondered whatever had happened to Issus.

After every ten stokes or so, Captain Kresca, who stood in the stern at the tiller, signaled for them to stop, and he cocked his head, listening to the sound of the surf. 'Another couple hundred yards now,' he said in a low voice. 'You there,' he said to the sailor in the bow who held another sounding line, 'keep busy with that lead. I don't want to hit any rocks. Sing out if it starts shoaling.'

'Aye, aye, Cap'n.'

The longboat crept on through dark and fog toward the unseen beach where the long wash and slither of the waves on graveled shingle made that peculiar grating sound as each wave lifted pebbles from the beach to carry them up to the very verge of land and then, with melancholy and regretful note, to draw them back again as if the ever-hungry sea mourned its inability to engulf the land and turn all the world into one endless ocean where huge waves, unimpeded, could roll thrice around the globe.

The heavy fog bank lying to the east began to turn lighter and lighter as dawn broke over the dark, mist-obscured waves.

'Another hundred yards,' Kresca said tensely.

'When we get there, Captain,' Belgarath said to him, 'keep your men in the boat. They won't be permitted to land anyway, and they'd better not try. We'll push you back out as soon as we get ashore.'

Kresca swallowed hard and nodded.

Garion could hear the surf more clearly now and catch the seaweed-rank smell of the meeting of sea and land. Then, just before he was able to make out the dark line of the beach through the obscuring fog, the heavy, dangerous swells flattened, and the sea around the longboat became as flat and slick as a pane of glass.

'That was accommodating of them,' Silk observed.

'Shh,' Velvet told him, laying one finger to her lips. 'I'm trying to listen.'

The bow of the longboat grated on the gravel strand, and Durnik stepped out of the boat and drew it farther up onto the pebbles. Garion and his friends also stepped out into the ankle-deep water and waded ashore. 'We'll see you tomorrow morning, Captain,' Garion said quietly as Toth prepared to push the boat back out. 'I hope,' he added.

'Good luck, Garion,' Kresca said. 'After we're all back on board, you'll have to tell me what this was all about.'

'I may want to forget about it by then,' Garion said ruefully.

'Not if you win,' Kresca's voice came back out of the fog.

'I like that man,' Silk said. 'He's got a nice optimistic attitude.'

'Let's get off this open beach,' Belgarath said. 'In spite of what Garion's friend told him, I sense a certain tenuousness about this fog. I'll feel a lot better if we've got some rocks to hide behind.'

Durnik and Toth picked up the two canvas bags containing the armor, and Garion and Zakath drew their swords and led the way up from the gravel strand. The mountain they approached seemed composed of speckled granite, fractured into unnatural blocks. Garion had seen enough granite in the mountains here and there around the world to know that the stone usually crumbled and weathered into rounded shapes. 'Strange,' Durnik murmured, kicking with one still-wet boot at the perfectly squared-off edge of one of the blocks. He lowered the canvas bag and drew his knife. He dug for a moment at the rock with his knife-point. 'It's not granite,' he said quietly. 'It *looks* like granite, but it's much too hard. It's something else.'

'We can identify it later,' Beldin told him. 'Let's find some cover just in case Belgarath's suspicion turns out to be accurate. As soon as we get settled, I'll drift around the peak a few times.'

'You won't be able to see anything,' Silk predicted.

'I'll be able to hear, though.'

'Over there,' Durnik said, pointing with his sledge. 'It looks as if one of these blocks got dislodged and rolled down to the beach. There's a fairly large niche there.'

'Good enough for now,' Belgarath said. 'Beldin, when you make the change, do it very slowly. I'm sure Zandramas landed at almost the exact same time we did, and she'll hear you.'

'I know how it's done, Belgarath.'

The niche in the side of the strange, stair-stepped peak was more than large enough to conceal them, and they moved down into it cautiously.

'Neat,' Silk said. 'Why don't you all wait here and catch your breath? Beldin can turn into a seagull and go have a look around the island. I'll go on ahead and pick out a trail for us.'

'Be careful,' Belgarath told him.

'Someday you're going to forget to say that, Belgarath, and it'll probably wither every tree on earth.' The little man climbed back up out of the niche and disappeared into the fog.

'You *do* say that to him a lot, you know,' Beldin said to Belgarath.

'Silk's an enthusiast. He needs frequent reminding. Did you plan to leave sometime during the next hour?'

Beldin spat out a very unflattering epithet, shimmered very slowly, and sailed away.

'Your temper hasn't improved much, Old Wolf,' Poledra said to him.

'Did you think it might have?'

'Not really,' she replied, 'but there's always room for hope.'

Despite Belgarath's premonition, the fog hung on. After about a half-hour, Beldin returned. 'Somebody's landed on the west beach,' he reported. 'I couldn't see them, but I could certainly hear them. Angaraks seem to have some trouble keeping their voices down – sorry, Zakath, but it's the truth.'

'I'll issue an imperial command that the next three or four generations converse in whispers, if you'd like.'

'No, that's all right, Zakath.' The dwarf grinned. 'As long as I'm on the opposite side from at least *some* Angaraks, I like to be able to hear them coming. Did Kheldar make it back yet?'

'Not yet,' Garion told him.

'What's he doing? These stone blocks are much too big to steal.'

Then Silk slipped over the edge of the niche and dropped lightly to the stone floor. 'You're not going to believe this,' he said.

'Probably not,' Velvet said, 'but why don't you go ahead and tell us anyway?'

'This peak is man-made – or at least *something* made it. These blocks encircle it like terraces, all straight and smooth. The thing forms steps up to that flat place on top. There's an altar up there and a huge throne.'

'So *that's* what it meant!' Beldin exclaimed, snapping his fingers. 'Belgarath, have you ever read the Book of Torak?'

'I've struggled through it a few times. My Old Angarak isn't really all that good.'

'You can speak Old Angarak?' Zakath asked with some surprise. 'It's a forbidden language here in Mallorea. I suspect Torak was changing a few things, and he didn't want anyone to catch him at it.'

300

'I learned it before the prohibition went into effect. What's the point of this, Beldin?'

'Do you remember that passage near the beginning – in the middle of all that conceited blather – when Torak said He went up into the High Places of Korim to argue with UL about the creation of the world?'

'Vaguely.'

'Anyway, UL didn't want anything to do with it, so Torak turned his back on His father and went down and gathered up the Angaraks and led them back to Korim. He told them what he had in mind for them, and then, in true Angarak fashion, they fell down on their faces and started butchering each other as sacrifices. There's a word in that passage, "Halagachak". It means "temple" or something like that. I always thought that Torak was speaking figuratively, but He wasn't. This peak is that temple. The altar up there more or less confirms it, and these terraces were where the Angaraks stood to watch while the Grolims sacrificed people to their God. If I'm right, this is also the place where Torak spoke with His father. Regardless of how you feel about old burnt-face, this is one of the holiest places on earth.'

'You keep talking about Torak's father,' Zakath said, looking puzzled. 'I didn't know that the Gods *had* fathers.'

'Of course They do,' Ce'Nedra said loftily. 'Everybody knows that.'

'I didn't.'

'UL is Their father,' she said in a deliberately off-hand manner.

'Isn't He the God of the Ulgos?'

'Not by choice exactly,' Belgarath told him. 'The original Gorim more or less bullied Him into it.'

'How do you bully a God?'

'Carefully,' Beldin said. 'Very, very carefully.'

'I've met UL,' Ce'Nedra supplied gratuitously. 'He sort of likes me.'

'She can be very irritating at times, can't she?' Zakath said to Garion.

301

'You've noticed.'

'You don't have to like me,' she said with a toss of her curls, 'either one of you. As long as the Gods like a girl, she'll do all right.'

Garion began to have some hope at that point. If Ce'Nedra was willing to banter with them, it was a fair indication that she did not take her supposed intimations of her own incipient demise all that seriously. He *did*, however, wish that he could get that knife away from her.

'During the course of your fascinating explorations, did you by any chance happen to locate that cave?' Belgarath asked Silk. 'I more or less thought that's why you were out there sneaking around in the fog.'

'The cave?' Silk said. 'Oh, that's around on the north side. There's a sort of amphitheater in front of it. It's almost exactly in the middle of that face. I found that in the first ten minutes.'

Belgarath glared at him.

'It's not exactly a cave, though,' Silk added. 'There may be a cave back inside the peak, but the opening is more like a wide doorway. It's got pillars on each side and a familiar face above the lintel.'

'Torak?' Garion said with a sinking feeling.

'None other.'

'Hadn't we better get started then?' Durnik suggested. 'If Zandramas is already on the island . . .' He spread his hands.

'So what?' Beldin said.

They all stared at the grotesque little hunchback.

'Zandramas can't go into the cave until we get there, can she?' he asked Cyradis.

'Nay, Beldin,' she replied. 'That is forbidden.'

'Good. Let her wait, then. I'm sure she'll enjoy the anticipation. Did anybody think to bring anything to eat? I may have to be a seagull, but I *don't* have to eat raw fish.'

CHAPTER TWENTY-TWO

They waited for almost an hour until Beldin decided that by now Zandramas must be keyed to a fever pitch. Garion and Zakath took advantage of the delay to put on their armor. 'I'll take a look,' the dwarf said finally. He slowly slipped into the shape of a seagull and drifted away into the fog. When he returned, he was chuckling evilly. 'I've never heard a woman use that kind of language,' he said. 'She even puts you to shame, Pol.'

'What's she doing?' Belgarath asked him.

'She's standing outside the cave mouth – or door, or whatever you want to call it. She had about forty Grolims with her.'

'*Forty?*' Garion exclaimed. He turned on Cyradis. 'I though you said we'd be evenly matched,' he accused.

'Art thou not a match for at least five, Belgarion?' she asked simply.

'Well—'

'You said *had*,' Belgarath said to his brother.

'I'd say that our star-speckled friend tried to force several of her Grolims to push through whatever it is that has the door sealed against her. I'm not sure if it was the force holding the door or if Zandramas lost her temper when the Grolims failed. About five of them are noticeably dead at the moment, and Zandramas is stalking about outside inventing swearwords. All of her Grolims have purple linings on the inside of their hoods, by the way.'

'Sorcerers, then,' Polgara said bleakly.

'Grolim sorcery is not all that profound,' Beldin shrugged.

'Could you see if she's got those lights under her skin?' Garion asked.

'Oh, my, yes. Her face looks like a meadow full of fireflies on a summer evening. I saw something else, too. That albatross is out there. We nodded, but we didn't have time to stop and speak.'

'What was he doing?' Silk asked suspiciously.

'Just hovering. You know how albatrosses are. I don't think they move their wings more than once a week. The fog is starting to thin. Why don't we just ease around and stand on one of these terraces just above that amphitheater and let this murk dissipate. Seeing a group of dark figures emerging out of the fog should give her quite a turn, wouldn't you think?'

'Did you see my baby?' Ce'Nedra asked, her heart in her voice.

'He's hardly a baby any more, little girl. He's a sturdy little lad with curls as blond as Eriond's used to be. I gathered from his expression that he's not very fond of the company he's in, and judging from the look of him, he's going to grow up to be as bad-tempered as the rest of his family. Garion could probably go down there and hand him the sword, and then we could all sit back and watch him deal with the problem.'

'I'd rather not have him start killing people until after he loses his baby teeth,' Garion said firmly. 'Is there anybody else there?'

'Judging from his wife's description, the Archduke Otrath is among the group. He's wearing a cheap crown and sort of second-hand royal robes. There's not too much in the way of intelligence in his eyes.'

'That one is mine,' Zakath grated. 'I've never had the opportunity to deal with high treason on a personal level before.'

'His wife will be eternally in your debt,' Beldin grinned. 'She might even decide to journey to Mal Zeth to offer her thanks – among other things – in person. She's a lush wench, Zakath. I'd advise that you get plenty of rest.'

'Methinks I care not for the turn this conversation hath

taken,' Cyradis said primly. 'The day wears on. Let us proceed.'

'Anythin' yer heart desires, me little darlin',' Beldin grinned.

Cyradis smiled in spite of herself.

Again they all spoke with that jocular bravado. They were approaching what was probably the most important Event in all of time, and making light of it was a natural human response.

Silk led the way out of the niche, his soft boots making no sound on the wet stones under their feet. Garion and Zakath, however, had to move with some care to avoid clinking. The sharply mounting stone terraces were each uniformly about ten feet tall, but at regular intervals there were stairways leading from one terrace to the one above. Silk led them up about three levels and then began circling the truncated pyramid. When they reached the northeast corner, he paused. 'We'd better be very quiet now,' he whispered. 'We're only about a hundred yards from that amphitheater. We don't want some sharp-eared Grolim to hear us.'

They crept around the corner and made their way carefully along the north face for several minutes. Then Silk stopped and leaned out over the edge to peer down into the fog. 'This is it,' he whispered. 'The amphitheater's a rectangular indentation in the side of the peak. It runs from the beach up to that portal or whatever you want to call it. If you look over the edge, you'll see that the terraces below us break off back there a ways. The amphitheater is right below us. We're within a hundred yards of Zandramas right now.'

Garion peered down into the fog, almost wishing that by a single act of will he could brush aside the obscuring mist so that he could look at the face of his enemy.

'Steady,' Beldin whispered to him. 'It's going to come soon enough. Let's not spoil the surprise for her.'

Disjointed voices came up out of the fog – harsh, gutteral Grolim voices. The fog seemed to muffle them, so Garion could not pick out individual words, but he didn't really have to.

They waited.

The sun by now had risen above the eastern horizon, and its pale disk was faintly visible through the fog and the roiling cloud that was the aftermath of the storm. The fog began to eddy and swirl. Gradually the mist overhead dissolved, and now Garion could see the sky. A thick blanket of dirty-looking scud lay over the reef but extended only a few leagues to the east. Thus it was that the sun, low on the eastern horizon, shone on the underside of the clouds and stained them an angry reddish orange with its light. It looked almost as if the sky had taken fire.

'Colorful,' Sadi murmured, nervously passing his poisoned dagger from one hand to the other. He set his red leather case down and opened it. Then he took up the earthenware bottle, worked the stopper out, and laid it on its side. 'There should be mice on this reef,' he said, 'or the eggs of sea-birds. Zith and her babies will be all right.' Then he straightened, carefully putting a small bag he had taken from the case in the pocket of his tunic. 'A little precaution,' he whispered by way of explanation.

The fog now lay beneath them like a pearly gray ocean in the shadow of the pyramid. Garion heard a strange, melancholy cry and raised his eyes. The albatross hovered on motionless wings above the fog. Garion peered intently down into the obscuring mist, almost absently working the leather sleeve off the hilt of his sword. The Orb was glowing faintly, and its color was not blue, but an angry red, almost the color of the burning sky.

'That confirms it, Old Wolf,' Poledra said to her husband. 'The Sardion's in that cave.'

Belgarath, his silvery hair and beard glowing red in the light reflected from the clouds overhead, grunted.

The fog below began to swirl, its surface looking almost like an angry sea. It thinned even more. Garion could now see shadowy forms beneath them, hazy, indistinct, and uniformly dark.

The fog was now no more that a faintly obscuring haze.

'Holy sorceress!' a Grolim voice exclaimed in alarm. 'Look!'

A hooded figure in a shiny black satin robe spun about, and Garion looked full into the face of the Child of Dark. He had heard the lights beneath her skin described several times, but no description had prepared him for what he now saw. The lights in Zandramas' face were not stationary, but swirled restlessly beneath her skin. In the shadow of the ancient pyramid, her features were dark, nearly invisible, but the swirling lights made it appear, in the cryptic words of the Ashabine Oracles, as if 'all the starry universe' were contained in her flesh.

Behind him he heard the sharp hiss of Ce'Nedra's indrawn breath. He turned his head and saw his little queen, dagger in hand and eyes ablaze with hatred, starting toward the stairs leading down into the amphitheater. Polgara and Velvet, obviously aware of her desperate plan, quickly restrained and disarmed her.

Then Poledra stepped to the edge of the terrace. 'And so it has come at last, Zandramas,' she said in a clear voice.

'I was but waiting for thee to join thy friends, Poledra,' the sorceress replied in a taunting tone. 'I was concerned for thee, fearing that thou hadst lost thy way. Now it is complete, and we may proceed in orderly fashion.'

'Thy concern with order is somewhat belated, Zandramas,' Poledra told her, 'but no matter. We have all, as was foretold, arrived at the appointed place at the appointed time. Shall we put aside all this foolishness and go inside? The universe must be growing impatient with us.'

'Not just yet, Poledra,' Zandramas replied flatly.

'How tiresome,' Belgarath's wife said wearily. 'That's a failing in thee, Zandramas. Even after something obviously isn't working, thou must continue to try. Thou hast twisted and turned and tried to evade this meeting, but all in vain. And all of thine evasion hath only brought thee more quickly to this place. Thinkest thou not that it is time to forgo thine entertainments and to go along gracefully?'

'I do not think so, Poledra.'

Poledra sighed. 'All right, Zandramas,' she said in a resigned tone, 'as it pleaseth thee.' She extended her arm, pointing at Garion. 'Since thou art so bent on this, thus I summon the Godslayer.'

Slowly, deliberately, Garion reached back across his shoulder and wrapped his hand about the hilt of his sword. It made an angry hiss as it slid from its sheath and it was already flaming an incandescent blue as it emerged. Garion's mind was icy calm now. All doubt and fear were gone, even as they had been at Cthol Mishrak, and the spirit of the Child of Light possessed him utterly. He took the sword hilt in both hands and slowly raised it until the flaming blade was pointed at the fiery clouds overhead. 'This is thy fate, Zandramas!' he roared in an awful voice, the archaic words coming unbidden to his lips.

'That has yet to be determined, Belgarion.' Zandramas' tone was defiant, as might be expected, but there was something else behind it. 'Fate is not always so easily read.' She made an imperious gesture, and her Grolims formed up into a phalanx around her and began to intone a harsh chant in an ancient and hideous language.

'Get back!' Polgara warned sharply, and she, her parents, and Beldin stepped to the edge of the terrace.

Flickering faintly, an inky shadow began to appear at the very edge of Garion's vision, and he began to feel an obscure sense of dread. 'Watch yourselves,' he quietly warned his friends. 'I think she's starting one of those illusions we were talking about last night.' Then he felt a powerful surge and head a roar of sound. A wave of sheer darkness rolled out from the extended hands of the Grolims massed around Zandramas, but the wave shattered into black fragments that sizzled and skittered around the amphitheater like frightened mice as the four sorcerers blew it apart almost contemptuously with a single word spoken in unison. Several of the Grolims collapsed writhing to the stone floor, and most of the rest of them staggered back, their faces suddenly pasty white.

Beldin cackled evilly. 'An' would ye like t' try it again, darlin'?' he taunted Zandramas. 'If that's yer intent, ye should have brought more Grolims. Yer usin' 'em up at a fearful rate, don't y' know.'

'I *wish* you wouldn't do that,' Belgarath said to him.

'So does *she*, I'll wager. She takes herself very seriously, and a little ridicule always sets that sort off their pace.'

Without changing expression, Zandramas hurled a fireball at the dwarf, but he brushed it aside as if it were no more than an annoying insect.

Garion quite suddenly understood. The sudden sheet of darkness and the fireball were not intended seriously. They were no more than subterfuge, a way to distract attention from that shadow at the edge of vision.

The Sorceress of Darshiva smiled a chill little smile. 'No matter,' she shrugged. 'I was only testing you, my droll little hunchback. Keep laughing, Beldin. I like to see people die happy.'

'Truly,' he agreed. 'Smile a bit yerself, me darlin', an' have a bit of a look around. Y' might say goodbye t' the sun while yer at it, fer I don't think ye'll be seein' it fer much longer.'

'Are all these threats really necessary?' Belgarath asked wearily.

'It's customary,' Beldin told him. 'Insults and boasting are a common prelude to more serious business. Besides, she started it.' He looked down at Zandramas' Grolims, who had started to move menacingly forward. 'I guess it's time, though. Shall we go downstairs then and prepare a big pot of Grolim stew? I like mine chopped rather fine.' He extended his hand, snapped his fingers, and wrapped the hand around the hilt of a hook-pointed Ulgo knife.

With Garion in the lead, they walked purposefully to the head of the stairs and started down as the Grolims, with a variety of weapons in their hands, rushed to the bottom.

'Get back!' Silk snapped at Velvet, who had resolutely joined them with one of her daggers held professionally low.

'Not a chance,' she said crisply. 'I'm protecting my investment.'

'What investment?'

'We can talk about it later. I'm busy right now.'

The Grolim leading the charge was a huge man, almost as big as Toth. He was swinging a massive axe, and his eyes were filled with madness. When he was perhaps five feet from Garion, Sadi stepped up to the Rivan King's shoulder and hurled a fistfull of strangely colored powder full into the ascending Grolim's face. The Grolim shook his head, pawing at his eyes. Then he sneezed. And then his eyes filled with horror, and he screamed. Howling in terror, he dropped his axe, spun, and bolted back down, shouldering his companions off the steps as he fled. When he reached the floor of the amphitheater, he did not stop, but ran toward the sea. He floundered out into waist-deep water and then stepped off the edge of an unseen terrace lurking beneath the surface. It did not appear that he knew how to swim.

'I thought you were out of that powder,' Silk said to Sadi even as he made a long, smooth, overhand cast with one of his daggers. A Grolim stumbled back, plucking at the dagger hilt protruding from his chest, missed his footing, and fell heavily backward down the stairway.

'I always keep a bit for contingencies,' Sadi replied, ducking under a sword swipe and deftly slicing a Grolim across the belly with his poisoned dagger. The Grolim stiffened, then slowly toppled out off the side of the staircase. A number of black-robed men, seeking to surprise them from the rear, were clambering up the rough sides of the stairway. Velvet knelt and cooly drove one of her daggers into the upturned face of a Grolim on the verge of reaching the top. With a hoarse cry he clutched at his face and fell backward, sweeping several of his companions off the wall as he plunged down.

Then the blond Drasnian girl darted to the other side of the stairs, shaking out her silken cord. She deftly looped it about the neck of a Grolim in the act of scrambling up onto the steps. She stepped under his flailing arms, turned until they were back to back, and leaned forward. The helpless Grolim's feet came up off the step, and he clutched at the cord about his neck with both hands. His feet kicked futilely at the air for a few moments, his face turning black, and then he went limp. Velvet turned back, unlooped her cord, and cooly kicked the inert body off the edge.

Durnik and Toth had moved up to take positions beside Garion and Zakath, and the four of them moved implacably down the stairs, step by step, chopping and smashing at the black-robed figures rushing up to meet them. Durnik's hammer seemed only slightly less dreadful than the sword of the Rivan King. The Grolims fell before them as they moved inexorably down the stairs. Toth was chopping methodically with Durnik's axe, his face as expressionless as that of a man felling a tree. Zakath was a fencer, and he feinted and parried with his massive, though nearly weightless sword. His thrusts were quick and usually lethal. The steps below the dreadful quartet were soon littered with twisted bodies and were running with rivulets of blood.

'Watch your footing,' Durnik warned as he crushed another Grolim's skull. 'The steps are getting slippery.'

Garion swept off another Grolim head. It bounced like a child's ball down the steps even as the body toppled off the side of the stairway. Garion risked a quick look back over his shoulder. Belgarath and Beldin had joined Velvet to help the girl repel the black-robed men scrambling up the sides of the steps. Beldin seemed to take vicious delight in driving his hook-pointed knife into Grolim eyes, then, with a sharp twist and a jerk he would pull out sizable gobs of brains. Belgarath, his thumbs tucked into his rope belt, waited calmly. When a Grolim's head appeared above the edge of the stair, the old man would draw back his foot and kick the priest of Torak full in the face. Since it was a thirty-foot drop from the stairs to the stones of the amphitheater, few of the Grolims he kicked off the side of the stairs tried the climb a second time.

When they reached the foot of the stairs, scarcely any of Zandramas' Grolims survived. With his usual prudence, Sadi darted around first one side of the stairway and then the other, cooly sinking his poisoned dagger into the bodies of those Grolims who had fallen to the amphitheater floor, the inert dead as well as the groaning injured.

Zandramas seemed somewhat taken aback by the sheer violence of her foes' descent. She held her ground nonetheless, drawing herself up in scornful defiance. Standing behind her, his mouth agape with terror, stood a man in a cheap crown and somewhat shopworn regal robes. His features bore a faint resemblance to those of Zakath, so Garion assumed that he was the Archduke Otrath. And then at last, Garion beheld his own young son. He had avoided looking at the boy during the bloody descent, since he had been unsure of what his own reaction might have been at a time when his concentration was vital. As Beldin had said, Geran was no longer a baby. His blond curls gave his face a softness, but there was no softness in his eyes as he met his father's gaze. Geran was quite obviously consumed with hatred for the woman who firmly held his arm in her grasp.

Gravely, Garion raised his sword to his visor in salute, and, just as gravely, Geran lifted his free hand in response.

Then the Rivan King began an implacable advance, pausing only long enough to kick an unattached Grolim head out of his way. The uncertainty he had felt back in Dal Perivor had vanished now. Zandramas stood no more than a few yards away, and the fact that she was a woman no longer mattered. He raised his flaming sword and continued his advance.

The flickering shadow along the periphery of his vision grew darker, and he hesitated as his sense of dread increased. Try though he might, he could not stifle it. He faltered.

The shadow, vague at first, began to coalesce into a hideous face that towered behind the black-robed sorceress. The eyes were soullessly blank, and the mouth gaped open in an expression of unspeakable loss as if the owner of the face had been plunged into a horror beyond imagining from a place of light and glory. That loss however, bespoke no compassion or gentleness, but rather expressed the implacable need of the hideous being to find others to share its misery.

'Behold the King of Hell!' Zandramas cried triumphantly. 'Flee now and live a few moments longer 'ere he pulls you all down into eternal darkness, eternal flames, and eternal despair.'

Garion stopped. He could not advance on that ultimate horror.

And then a voice came to him out of his memories, and with the voice there came an image. He seemed to be standing in a damp clearing in a forest somewhere. A light, drizzling rain was falling from a heavy, nighttime sky, and the leaves underfoot were wet and soggy. Eriond, all unconcerned, was speaking to them. It had happened, Garion realized, just after their first encounter with Zandramas, who had assumed the shape of the dragon to attack them. 'But the fire wasn't real,' the young man was explaining. 'Didn't you all know that?' He looked slightly surprised at their failure to understand. 'It was only an illusion. That's all evil ever really is – an illusion. I'm sorry if any of you were worried, but I didn't have time to explain.'

That was the key, Garion understood now. Hallucination was the product of derangement; illusion was not. He was not going mad. The face of the King of Hell was no more real than had been the illusion of Arell which Ce'Nedra had encountered in the forest below Kell. The

313

only weapon the Child of Dark had to counter the Child of Light with was illusion, a subtle trickery directed at the mind. It was a powerful weapon, but very fragile. One ray of light could destroy it. He started forward again.

'Garion!' Silk cried.

'Ignore the face,' Garion told him. 'It isn't real. Zandramas is trying to frighten us into madness. The face isn't there. It doesn't even have as much substance as a shadow.'

Zandramas flinched, and the enormous face behind her wavered and vanished. Her eyes darted this way and that, lingering, Garion seemed to perceive, upon the portal leading into the cave. As surely as if he could see it, Garion *knew* that there was something in that cave — something which was Zandramas' last line of defense. Then, seemingly all unconcerned by the obliteration of the weapon which had always served the Child of Dark so well, she made a quick gesture to her remaining Grolims.

'No.' It was the light, clear voice of the Seeress of Kell. 'I cannot permit this. The issue must be decided by the Choice, not by senseless brawling. Put up thy sword, Belgarion of Riva, and withdraw thy minions, Zandramas of Darshiva.'

Garion found that the muscles of his legs had suddenly cramped, and that he could no longer move even one step. Painfully, he twisted around. He saw Cyradis descending the stairs, guided now by Eriond. Immediately behind her came Aunt Pol, Poledra, and the Rivan Queen.

'The task you both share here,' Cyradis continued in an echoing choral voice, 'is not to destroy each other, for should it come to pass that one of you destroyeth the other, your tasks will remain uncompleted, and I also will be unable to complete mine. Thus, all that is, all that was, and all that is yet to be will forever perish. Put up thy sword, Belgarion, and send away thy Grolims, Zandramas. Let us go even into the Place Which Is No More and make our choices. The universe grows weary of our delay.'

314

Regretfully, Garion sheathed his sword, but the Sorceress of Darshiva's eyes narrowed. 'Kill her,' she commanded her Grolims in a chillingly flat voice. 'Kill the blind Dalasion witch in the name of the new God of Angarak.'

The remaining Grolims, their faces filled with religious exaltation, started toward the foot of the stairs. Eriond sighed and resolutely stepped forward to place his body in front of that of Cyradis.

'That will not be necessary, Bearer of the Orb,' Cyradis told him. She bowed her head slightly, and the choral voice swelled to a crescendo. The Grolims faltered, and then began to grope around, staring with unseeing eyes at the daylight around them.

'It's the enchantment again,' Zakath whispered, 'the same one that surrounded Kell. They're blind.'

This time, however, what the Grolims saw in their blindness was not the vision of the Face of God the gentle old priest of Torak they had met in the sheep-camp above Kell had seen, but something altogether different. The enchantment, it appeared, could cut two ways. The Grolims cried out first in alarm, then in fright. Then their cries became screams, and they turned, stumbling over each other and even crawling on hands and knees to escape that which they saw. They scrambled blindly down to the water's edge, obviously bent on following the hulking Grolim into whose face Sadi had thrown that strange powder of his. They floundered out into the now gently rolling waves, and one by one stepped off into deep water.

A few could swim, but not very many. Those who could swam desperately out to sea and inevitable death. Those who could not sank beneath the surface, their imploring hands reaching upward even after their heads had gone under. Columns of bubbles rose to the top of the dark water for a few moments, and then they stopped.

The albatross, its great wings motionless, drifted over them for a moment and then returned to hover over the amphitheater.

CHAPTER TWENTY-THREE

'And now art thou, as thou hast ever chosen to be, alone, Child of Dark,' Cyradis said sternly.

'The ones who were here with me were of no moment, Cyradis,' Zandramas replied indifferently. 'They have served their purpose, and I no longer need them.'

'Art thou then ready to enter through the portal into the Place Which Is No More to stand in the presence of the Sardion, there to make thy choice?'

'Of course, Holy Seeress,' Zandramas acquiesced with surprising mildness. 'Gladly will I join with the Child of Light that together we may enter the Temple of Torak.'

'Watch her, Garion,' Silk whispered. 'The whole tone of this is wrong. She's up to something.'

But Cyradis, it appeared, had also detected the ruse. 'Thy sudden acceptance is puzzling, Zandramas,' she said. 'Vainly hast thou striven for all these weary months to avoid this meeting, and now thou wouldst rush eagerly into the grotto. What hath so altered thee? Doth perchance some unseen peril lurk within yon grot? Seekest thou still to lure the Child of Light to his doom, thinking thereby to avoid the necessity of the Choice?'

'The answer to thy question, blind witch, doth lie behind that portal,' Zandramas replied in a harsh voice. She turned her glittering face toward Garion. 'Surely the great Godslayer is without fear,' she said. 'Or is he who slew Torak become of a sudden timid and fearful? What threat could I, a mere woman, pose to the mightiest warrior in the world? Let us then investigate this grotto together. Confidently will I deliver my safety into thy hands, Belgarion.'

'It may not be so, Zandramas,' the Seeress of Kell

declared. 'It is too late now for subterfuge and deceit. Only the Choice will free thee now.' She paused and briefly bowed her head. Again Garion heard that choral murmuring. 'Ah,' she said at last, 'now we understand. The passage in the Book of the Heavens was obscure, but now it is clear.' She turned toward the portal. 'Come forth, Demon Lord. Lurk not in darkness awaiting prey, but come forth that we may see thee.'

'*No!*' Zandramas cried hoarsely.

But it was too late. Reluctantly, almost as if being driven, the battered and half-crippled dragon limped out of the grotto, roaring and belching billows of flame and smoke.

'Not again,' Zakath groaned.

Garion, however, saw more than just the dragon. Even as in the snow-clogged forest outside Val Alorn when he had seen the image of Barak superimposed upon that of the dreadful bear rushing to his rescue after he had speared the boar when he was no more than fourteen, he now saw the form of the Demon Lord Mordja within the shape of the dragon. Mordja, arch-foe of Nahaz, the demon who had borne the shrieking Urvon into the eternal pit of Hell. Mordja, who with a half-dozen snakelike arms grasped a huge sword – a sword which Garion recognized all too well. The Demon Lord, encased in the form of the dragon, strode forward with monstrous step wielding Cthrek Goru, Torak's dread sword of shadows.

The burning red clouds overhead erupted with lightning as the hideously twinned beast came at them. 'Spread out!' Garion shouted. 'Silk! Tell them what to do!' He drew a deep breath as great bolts of lightning streaked down from the roiling red sky above to crash against the sides of the terraced pyramid with earth-shattering claps of thunder. 'Let's go!' Garion cried to Zakath as he once more drew Iron-grip's sword. But then he paused, dumbfounded. Poledra, as calmly as she would if crossing a meadow, approached the awful monstrosity. 'Thy master is the Lord of Deception, Mordja,' she said to the suddenly

317

immobilized creature before her, 'but it is time for deceit to end. Thou wilt speak only truth. What is thy purpose here? What is the purpose of all of thy kind in this place?'

The Demon Lord, frozen within the form of the dragon, snarled its hatred as it twisted and writhed, attempting to break free.

'Speak, Mordja,' Poledra commanded. Did *anyone* have that kind of power?

'I *will* not.' Mordja spat out the words.

'Thou wilt,' Garion's grandmother said in a dreadfully quiet voice.

Mordja shrieked then, a shriek of total agony.

'What is thy purpose?' Poledra insisted.

'I serve the King of Hell!' the demon cried.

'And what is the purpose of the King of Hell here?'

'He would possess the stones of power,' Mordja howled.

'And why?'

'That he may break his chains, the chains in which accursed UL bound him long 'ere any of this was made.'

'Wherefore hast thou then aided the Child of Dark, and wherefore didst thy foe Nahaz aid the Disciple of Torak? Didst not thy Master know that each of them sought to raise a God? A God which would even more securely bind him?'

'What they sought was of no moment,' Mordja snarled. 'Nahaz and I contended with each other, in truth, but our contention was *not* on behalf of mad Urvon or sluttish Zandramas. In the instant that either of them gained Sardion would the King of Hell reach forth with my hands – or with the hands of Nahaz – and seize the stone. Then, using its power, would the one of us or the other wrest Cthrag Yaska from the Godslayer and deliver both stones to our Master. In the instant that *he* took up the two stones would *he* become the new God. His chains would break and he would contend with UL as an equal – nay, an even mightier – God, and all that is, was, or will be would be his and his alone.'

'And what then was to be the fate of the Child of Dark or the Disciple of Torak?'

'They were to be our rewards. Even now doth Nahaz feed eternally upon mad Urvon in the darkest pit of Hell, even as I shall feed upon Zandramas. The ultimate reward of the King of Hell is eternal torment.'

The Sorceress of Darshiva gasped in horror as she heard her soul's fate so cruelly pronounced.

'Thou canst not stop me, Poledra,' Mordja taunted, 'for the King of Hell hath strengthened my hand.'

'Thy hand, however, is confined in the body of this rude beast,' Poledra said. 'Thou hast made thy choice, and in *this* place, a choice, once made, cannot be unmade. Here wilt thou contend alone, and thine only ally will *not* be the King of Hell, but no more than this mindless creature which thou hast chosen.'

The demon raised its dreadful, fang-filled muzzle with a great howl, and it struggled, heaving its vast shoulders this way and that as it desperately tried to wrench itself free of the shape which enclosed it.

'Does this mean we have to fight them *both?*' Zakath asked Garion in a shaking voice.

'I'm afraid so.'

'Garion, have you lost your mind?'

'It's what we do, Zakath. At least Poledra has limited Mordja's power – I don't know how, but she has. Since he doesn't have his full powers, we at least have a chance against him. Let's get at it.' Garion clapped down his visor and strode forward, swinging his flaming sword before him.

Silk and the others had separated, and they were approaching the dragon from the sides and from the rear.

As he and Zakath warily moved in, Garion saw something that might be an even greater advantage. The melding of the primitive mind of the dragon and the age-old one of the demon was not complete. The dragon, with stubborn stupidity, could only focus her single eye upon those enemies who stood directly before her, and

319

she charged on, unmindful of Garion's friends moving toward her flanks. Mordja, however, was all too much aware of the dangers advancing from the sides and from the rear. The division of the unnaturally joined mind of the vast, bat-winged creature gave it a kind of uncharacteristic hesitation, indecision even. Then Silk, the sword of a fallen Grolim in his hands, darted in from the rear and chopped manfully at the writhing tail.

The dragon bellowed in pain, and flames burst from her gaping mouth. Overriding what little control Mordja exerted upon her, she wheeled clumsily to respond to Silk's attack. The little thief, however, skipped nimbly out of her way even as the others dashed in to attack her flanks. Durnik rhythmically hammered on one exposed flank while Toth chopped no less rhythmically at the other.

A desperate plan came unbidden to Garion as he saw that the dragon had turned almost completely around to meet Silk's attack. 'Work on her tail!' he shouted to Zakath. He backed off a few paces to give himself running room, then lumbered forward, his movements made awkward by his armor. He leaped over the slashing tail and ran up the dragon's back.

'Garion!' he heard Ce'Nedra scream in horror. He ignored her frightened cry and continued to scramble up the scaly back until he was finally able to plant his feet on the dragon's shoulders between the bat-like wings. The dragon, he knew, would not fear or even feel the strokes of his burning sword. Mordja, however, would. He raised Iron-grip's sword and struck a two-handed blow at the base of the scaly neck. The dragon, weaving her fearsome head and breathing fire and smoke as she sought out those who were attacking her, paid no heed. Mordja, however, screamed in agony as the power of the Orb seared him. That was their advantage. Left to herself, the dragon was incapable of meeting their many-pronged attack. It was the added intelligence of the Demon Lord that made her so dangerous in this situation, but Garion had seen evidence in the past that the Orb could inflict intolerable agony upon a demon. In that respect, it had even more power than did a God. Demons fled from the presence of the Gods, but they could not flee from the chastisement of Aldur's Orb. 'Hotter!' he commanded the stone as he raised his blade again. He struck and struck and struck again. The great blade no longer bounced off the dragon's scales but seared its way through them to bite into the dragon's flesh. The half-indistinct image of Mordja, encased in the dragon, shrieked as the sword cut into *his* neck even as it slashed at that of the dragon. Almost in mid-stroke, Garion reversed his sword and, grasping the cross-piece of the hilt, drove it down into the dragon's back between the vast shoulders.

Mordja screamed.

Garion wrenched the sword back and forth, tearing the wound even wider.

Even the dragon felt that. She screamed.

Garion raised his sword again, and once again sank it into the bleeding wound, deeper this time.

The dragon and Mordja screamed in unison.

Ludicrously, Garion remembered a time in his bygone youth when he had watched old Cralto digging holes for fence posts. He consciously imitated the old farm-worker's rhythmic motion, raising his reversed sword high overhead as Cralto had his shovel, and driving the blade down into the dragon's flesh. With each driving blow the wound grew deeper, and blood gushed and spurted from the quivering flesh. He momentarily saw the white of bone and altered his point of aim. Not even Iron-grip's sword could shear through that tree-trunk sized backbone.

His friends had momentarily fallen back, astonished at the Rivan King's insane-appearing audacity. Then they saw that the dragon's almost serpentlike head was raised high in the air as she tried desperately to writhe her neck around to bite at the tormenter digging a huge hole between her shoulder-blades. They rushed back into the attack, hacking and stabbing at the softer scales covering

321

the dragon's throat, belly and flanks. Darting in and out quickly to avoid being trampled by the huge beast, Silk, Velvet, and Sadi attacked the unprotected underside of the distracted dragon. Durnik was steadily pounding on the dragon's side, methodically breaking ribs one by one as Toth chopped at the other side. Belgarath and Poledra, once again as wolves, were gnawing on the writhing tail.

Then Garion saw what he had been searching for – the hawser-like tendon leading down into one of the dragon's huge wings. 'Hotter!' he shouted again at the Orb.

The sword flared anew, and this time Garion did not strike. Instead he set the edge of his weapon against the tendon and began to saw back and forth with it, burning through the tough ligament rather than chopping. The tendon, finally severed, snapped, its cut ends slithering snakelike back into the bleeding flesh.

The bellow of pain that emerged from that flame-filled mouth was shattering. The dragon lurched, then fell, thrashing its huge limbs in terrible agony.

Garion was thrown clear when the dragon fell. Desperately he rolled, trying to get away from those flailing claws. Then Zakath was there, yanking him to his feet. 'You're insane, Garion!' he shouted in a shrill voice. 'Are you all right?'

'I'm fine,' Garion said in a tight voice. 'Let's finish it.'

Toth, however, was already there. In the very shadow of the dragon's huge head he stood, his feet planted wide apart, chopping at the base of the dragon's throat. Great gushes of blood spurted from severed arteries as the huge mute, his heavy shoulders surging, sought to find and cut the barrel-like windpipe. Despite the concerted efforts of Garion and his friends, there had been little more than pain before. Toth's single-minded attack, however, threatened the dragon's very life. Were he to succeed in severing or even broaching the thick gristle of that windpipe, the dragon would die, choking for lack of breath or drowning in her own blood. She clawed her way back onto her forelegs and reared high over the huge mute.

'Toth!' Durnik shouted. 'Get out of there! She's going to strike!'

But it was not the fanged mouth that struck. Dimly, within the bleeding body of the dragon, Garion saw the indistinct shape of Mordja desperately raise Cthrek Goru, the sword of shadows. Then the Demon Lord thrust out with the sword. The blade, as if insubstantial, emerged from the dragon's chest and, as smoothly, plunged into Toth to emerge from his back. The mute stiffened, then slid limply off the sword, unable even in death to cry out.

'No!' Durnik roared in a voice filled with indescribable loss.

Garion's mind went absolutely cold. 'Keep her teeth off me,' he told Zakath in a flat, unemotional tone. Then he dashed forward, reversing his sword once again in preparation for a thrust such as he had never delivered before. He aimed that thrust not at the wound Toth had opened but at the dragon's broad chest instead.

Cthrek Goru flickered out to ward him off, but Garion parried that desperate defensive stroke, then set his shoulder against the massive crosspiece of his sword's hilt. He fixed the now-shrinking demon with a look of pure hatred and then he drove his sword into the dragon's chest with all his strength, and the great surge as the Orb unleashed its power almost staggered him.

The sword of the Rivan King slid smoothly into the dragon's heart, like a stick into water.

The awful bellowing from both the dragon and the Demon Lord broke off suddenly in a kind of gurgling sigh.

Grimly, Garion wrenched his sword free and stepped clear of the convulsing beast. Then, like a burning house collapsing in on itself, the dragon crumpled to the ground, twitched a few times, and was still.

Garion wearily turned.

Toth's face was calm, but blind Cyradis knelt on one side of his body and Durnik on the other. They were both weeping openly.

High overhead, the albatross cried out once, a cry of pain and loss.

Cyradis was weeping, her blindfold wet with her tears.

The smoky-looking orange sky roiled and tumbled overhead, and inky black patches lay in the folds of the clouds, shifting, coiling, and undulating as the clouds, still stained on their undersides by the new-risen sun, writhed in the sky above and flinched and shuddered as they begot drunken-appearing lightning that staggered down through the murky air to strike savagely at the altar of the One-eyed God on the pinnacle above.

Cyradis was weeping.

The sharply regular stones that floored the amphitheater were still darkly wet from the clinging fog that had enveloped the reef before dawn and the downpour of yesterday. The white speckles in that iron-hard stone glittered like stars under their sheen of moisture.

Cyradis was weeping.

Garion drew in a deep breath and looked around the amphitheater. It was not as large perhaps as he had first imagined – certainly not large enough to contain what had happened here – but then, all the world would probably not have been large enough to contain that. The faces of his companions, bathed in the fiery light from the sky and periodically glowing dead white in the intense flashes of the stuttering lightning, seemed awed by the enormity of what had just happened. The amphitheater was littered with dead Grolims, shrunken black patches lying on the stones or sprawled in boneless-looking clumps on the stairs. Garion heard a peculiar, voiceless rumble that died off into something almost like a sigh. He looked incuriously at the dragon. Its tongue protruded from its gaping mouth, and its reptilian eye stared blankly at him. The sound he had heard had come from that vast carcass. The beast's entrails, still unaware that they, like the rest of the dragon were dead, continued their methodical work of digestion. Zandramas stood frozen in shock. The beast she had raised and the demon she had sent to possess it were both dead, and her desperate effort to evade the necessity of standing powerless and defenseless in the place of the Choice had crumbled and fallen as a child's castle of sand crumbles before the encroaching waves. Garion's son looked upon his father with unquestioning trust and pride, and Garion took a certain comfort in that clear-eyed gaze.

Cyradis was weeping. All else in Garion's mind was drawn from reflection and random impressions. The one incontrovertable fact, however, was that the Seeress of Kell was crushed by her grief. At this particular time she was the most important person in the universe, and perhaps it had always been so. It might very well be, Garion thought, that the world had been created for the one express purpose of bringing this frail girl to this place at this time to make this single Choice. But could she do that now? Might it not be that the death of her guide and protector – the one person in all the world she had truly loved – had rendered her incapable of making the Choice?

Cyradis was weeping, and so long as she wept, the minutes ticked by. Garion saw now as clearly as if he were reading in that book of the heavens which guided the seers that the time of the meeting and of the Choice was not only this particular day, but would come in a specific instant of this day, and if Cyradis, bowed down by her unbearable grief, were unable to choose in that instant, all that had been all that was, and all that was yet to be would shimmer and vanish like an ephemeral dream. Her weeping must cease, or all would be forever lost.

It began with a clear-toned single voice, a voice that rose and rose in elegiac sadness that contained within it the sum of human woe. Then other voices emerging singly or in trios or in octets to join that aching song. The chorus of the group mind of the seers plumbed the depths of the grief of the Seeress of Kell and then sank in an unbearable diminuendo of blackest despair and faded off into a silence more profound than the silence of the grave.

Cyradis was weeping, but she did not weep alone. Her entire race wept with her.

That lone voice began again, and the melody was similar to the one which had just died away. To Garion's untrained ear, it seemed almost the same, but a subtle chord-change had somehow taken place, and as the other voices joined in, more chords insinuated themselves into the song, and the grief and unutterable despair were questioned in the final notes.

Yet once again the song began, not this time with a single voice but with a mighty chord that seemed to shake the very roots of heaven with its triumphant affirmation. The melody remained basically the same, but what had begun as a dirge was now an exultation.

Cyradis gently laid Toth's hand on his motionless chest, smoothed his hair, and groped across his body to touch Durnik's tear-wet face consolingly.

She rose, no longer weeping, and Garion's fears dissolved and faded as the morning fog which had obscured the reef had faded beneath the onslaught of the sun. 'Go,' she said in a resolute voice, pointing at the now-unguarded portal. 'The time approaches. Go thou, Child of Light, and thou, Child of Dark, even into the grot, for we have choices to make which, once made, may never be unmade. Come ye with me, therefore, into the Place Which Is No More, there to decide the fate of all men.' And with firm and unfaltering step, the Seeress of Kell led the way toward that portal surmounted by the stony image of the face of Torak.

Garion found himself powerless in the grip of that clear voice and he fell in beside satin-robed Zandramas to follow the slender Seeress. He felt a faint brush against his armored right shoulder as he and the Child of Dark entered the portal. It was almost with a wry amusement that he realized that the forces controlling this meeting were not so entirely sure of themselves. They had placed a barrier between him and the Sorceress of Darshiva. Zandramas' unprotected throat lay quite easily within the reach of his vengeful hands, but the barrier made her as unassailable as if she had been on the far side of the moon. Faintly, he was aware that the others were coming up behind, his friends following him, and Geran and the violently trembling Otrath trailing after Zandramas.

'This need not be so, Belgarion of Riva,' Zandramas whispered urgently. 'Will we, the two most powerful ones in all the universe, submit to the haphazard choice of this brain-sickly girl? Let us bestow our choices upon ourselves. Thus will we both become Gods. Easily will we be able to set aside UL and the others and rule all creation jointly.' The swirling lights beneath the skin of her face spun faster now, and her eyes glowed red. 'Once we have achieved divinity, thou canst put aside thine earthly wife, who is not, after all, human, and thou and I could mate. Thou couldst father a race of Gods upon me, Belgarion, and we could sate each other with unearthly delights. Thou wilt find me fair, King of Riva, as all men have, and I will consume thy days with the passion of Gods, and we will share in the meeting of Light and Dark.'

Garion was startled, even a little awed by the single-mindedness of the Spirit of the Child of Dark. The thing was as implacable and as unchangeable as adamantine rock. He perceived that it did not change because it *could* not. He began to grope his way toward something which seemed significant. Light could change. Every day was testimony to that. Dark could not. Then it was at last that he understood the *true* meaning of the eternal division which had rent the universe apart. The Dark sought immobile stasis; the Light sought progression. The Dark crouched in a perceived perfection; the Light, however, moved on, informed by the concept of perfectability. When Garion spoke, it was not in reply to the blatant inducements of Zandramas, but rather to the Spirit of Dark itself. 'It *will* change, you know,' he said. 'Nothing you can do will stop me from believing that. Torak offered to be my father, and

327

now Zandramas offers to be my wife. I rejected Torak, and I reject Zandramas. You cannot lock me into immobility. If I change only one little thing, you've lost. Go stop the tide if you can, and leave me alone to do my work.'

The gasp which came from the mouth of Zandramas was more than human. Garion's sudden understanding had actually stung the Dark, not merely its instrument. He felt a faint, almost featherlike probing, and made no effort to repel it.

Zandramas hissed, her eyes aflame with hate-filled frustration.

'Didn't you find what you wanted?' Garion asked.

The voice which came from her lips was dry, unemotional. 'You'll have to make your choice eventually, you know,' it said.

The voice which came from Garion's lips was not his own, and it was just as dry and clinical. 'There's plenty of time,' it replied. 'My instrument will choose when it is needful.'

'A clever move, but it does not yet signify the end of the game.'

'Of course not. The last move lies in the hands of the Seeress of Kell.'

'So be it, then.'

They were walking down a long, musty-smelling corridor.

'I absolutely hate this,' Garion heard Silk murmur from behind him.

'It's going to be all right, Kheldar,' Velvet told the little man comfortingly. 'I won't let anything happen to you.'

Then the corridor opened out into a submerged grotto. The walls were rough, irregular, for this was not a construction but a natural cavern. Water oozed down a far wall to trickle endlessly with silvery note into a dark pool. The grotto had a faintly reptilian smell overlaid by the odor of long dead meat, and the floor was littered with gnawed white bones. By some ironic twist, the lair of the Dragon God had become the lair of the dragon herself. No better guard had been necessary to protect this place.

On the near wall stood a massive throne carved from a single rock, and before the throne there was one of the now all-too-familiar altars. Lying on the center of that altar was an oblong stone somewhat larger than a man's head. The stone glowed red, and its ugly light illuminated the grotto. Just to one side of the altar lay a human skeleton, its bony arm extended in a gesture of longing. Garion frowned. Some sacrifice to Torak, perhaps? Some victim of the dragon? Then he knew. It was the Melcene scholar who had stolen the Sardion from the university and fled with it to this place to die here in unthinking adoration of the stone which had killed him.

Just over his shoulder, Garion heard a sudden animal-like snarl coming from the Orb, and a similar sound came from the red stone, the Sardion, which lay on the altar. There was a confused babble of sound in a multitude of languages, some drawn, for all Garion knew, from the farthest reaches of the universe. Flickering streaks of blue shot up through the milky-red Sardion, and similarly, angry red bathed the Orb in undulant waves as all the conflicts of all the ages came together in this small, confined space.

'Control it, Garion!' Belgarath said sharply. 'If you don't, they'll destroy each other – and the universe as well!'

Garion reached back over his shoulder and placed his marked palm over the Orb, speaking silently to the vengeful stone. 'Not yet,' he said. 'All in good time.' He could not have explained why he had chosen those precise words. Grumbling almost like a petulant child, the Orb fell silent, and the Sardion also grudgingly broke off its snarl. The lights, however, continued to stain the surfaces of both stones.

'*You were quite good back there,*' the voice in Garion's mind congratulated him. '*Our enemy is a bit off balance now. Don't get overconfident, though. We're at a slight*

329

disadvantage here because the Spirit of the Child of Dark is very strong in this grotto.'

'Why didn't you tell me that before?'

'Would you have paid any attention? Listen carefully, Garion. My opposite has agreed that we should leave the matter in Cyradis' hands. Zandramas, however, has made no such commitment. She's very likely to make one last attempt. Put yourself between her and the Sardion. No matter what you have to do, don't let her reach that stone.'

'All right,' Garion said bleakly. He reasoned that attempting to edge into position inch by inch would not deceive the Sorceress of Darshiva as to his intent. Instead, quite calmly and deliberately, he simply stepped in front of the altar, drew his sword, and set its point on the floor of the grotto in front of him with his crossed hands resting on the pommel.

'What art thou about?' Zandramas demanded in a harsh, suspicious tone of voice.

'You know exactly what I'm doing, Zandramas,' Garion replied. 'The two spirits have agreed to let Cyradis decide between them. I haven't heard you agree yet. Do you still think you can avoid the Choice?'

Her light-speckled face twisted with hatred. 'Thou will pay for this, Belgarion,' she answered. 'All that thou art and all that thou lovest will perish here.'

'That's for Cyradis to decide, not you. In the meantime, nobody's going to touch the Sardion until *after* Cyradis makes her Choice.'

Zandramas ground her teeth in sudden, impotent fury.

And then Poledra came closer, her tawny hair stained by the light of the Sardion. 'Very well done, young wolf,' she said to Garion.

'Thou no longer hast the power, Poledra,' the strangely abstracted words came from Zandamas' unmoving mouth.

'Point,' the familiar dry voice spoke through Poledra's lips.

'I perceive no point.'

'That's because you've always discarded your instruments when you were finished with them. Poledra was the Child of Light at Vo Mimbre. She was even able to defeat Torak there – if only temporarily. Once that power is bestowed, it can never be wholly taken away. Did not her control over the Demon Lord prove that to you?'

Garion was almost staggered by that. Poledra? The Child of Light during that dreadful battle five hundred years ago?

The voice went on. 'Do you acknowledge the point?' it asked its opposite.

'What difference can it make? The game will be played out soon.'

'I claim point. Our rules require that you acknowledge it.'

'Very well. I acknowledge the point. You've really become quite childish about this, you know.'

'A rule is a rule, and the game isn't finished yet.'

Garion went back to watching Zandramas very closely so that he might meet any sudden move she made toward the Sardion.

'When is the time, Cyradis?' Belgarath quietly asked the Seeress of Kell.

'Soon,' she replied. 'Very soon.'

'We're all here,' Silk said, nervously looking up at the ceiling. 'Why don't we get on with it?'

'This is the day, Kheldar,' she said, 'but it is not the instant. In the instant of the Choice, a great light shall appear, a light which even *I* will see.'

It was the strange detached calm which came over him that alerted Garion to the fact that the ultimate Event was about to take place. It was the same calm which had enveloped him in the ruins of Cthol Mishrak when he had met Torak.

Then, as if the thought of his name had aroused, if only briefly, the spirit of the One-Eyed God from its eternal slumber, Garion seemed to hear Torak's dreadful voice intoning that prophetic passage from the last page of the Ashabine Oracles:

'Know that we *are* brothers, Belgarion, though our hate for each other may one day sunder the heavens. We are brothers in that we share a dreadful task. That thou art reading my words means that thou hast been my destroyer. Thus must I charge *thee* with the task. What is foretold in these pages is an abomination. Do not let it come to pass. Destroy the world. Destroy the universe if need be, but do not permit this to come to pass. In thy hand is now the fate of all that was, all that is, and all that is yet to be. Hail, my hated brother, and farewell. We will meet – or have met – in the City of Endless Night, and there will our dispute be concluded. The task, however, still lieth before us in the Place Which Is No More. One of us must go there to face the ultimate horror. Should it be thou, fail us not. Failing all else, thou must reave the life from thine only son, even as thou hast reft mine from me.'

This time, however, the words of Torak did not fill Garion with weeping. They simply intensified his resolve as he finally began to understand. What Torak had seen in the vision which had come to Him at Ashaba had been so terrifying that in the moment of His awakening from His prophetic dream the maimed God had felt impelled to lay the possibility of the dreadful task upon his most hated foe. That momentary horror had surpassed even Torak's towering pride. It had only been later, after the pride had reasserted itself, that Torak had mutilated the pages of his prophecy. In that one bleak moment of sanity, the maimed God had spoken truly for perhaps the one time in his life. Garion could only imagine the agony of self-abasement that single moment of truth had cost Torak. In the silence of his mind Garion pledged his fidelity to the task his most ancient foe had lain upon him. 'I will do all that is in my power to keep this abomination from coming to pass, my brother,' he threw out his thought to the spirit of Torak. 'Return to thy rest, for here *I* take up the burden.'

The dusky red glow of the Sardion had muted the swirling lights in the flesh of Zandramas, and Garion could now see her features quite clearly. Her expression was troubled. She had quite obviously been unprepared for the sudden acquiescence of the spirit which dominated her. Her drive to win at any cost had been frustrated by the withdrawal of the support of that spirit. Her own mind – or what was left of it – still strove to evade facing the Choice. The two prophecies had agreed at the beginning of time to place the entire matter in the hands of the Seeress of Kell. The evasions, the trickery and the multitudinous atrocities that had marked the passage of the Child of Dark through the world had all come from the twisted Grolim perceptions of the Sorceress of Darshiva herself. At this moment, Zandramas was more dangerous that she had ever been.

'Well, Zandramas,' Poledra said, 'and is *this* the time thou hast chosen for our meeting? Shall we destroy each other now when we have come so close to the ultimate instant? If thou but await the Choice of Cyradis, thou wilt stand an even chance of obtaining that which thou hast so desperately sought. If thou shouldst confront *me* however, thou wilt cast the entire matter into the lap of pure chance. Wilt thou throw away thy half-chance of success in exchange for an absolute uncertainty?'

'I am stronger than thou art, Poledra,' Zandramas declared defiantly. 'I am the Child of Dark.'

'And I *was* the Child of Light. How much art thou willing to gamble on the possibility that I can still call forth the strength and power? Wilt thou gamble *all*, Zandramas? All?'

Zandramas' eyes narrowed, and Garion could clearly feel the clenching of her will. Then, with a blasting surge of energy and a vast roar, she released it. An aura of darkness suddenly surrounded her, and she seized Garion's son and lifted him. '*Thus* will I conquer, Poledra!' she hissed. She closed her hand about the struggling boy's wrist and pushed his Orb-marked hand out in front of her.

'In the instant the hand of Belgarion's son touches the Sardion, I will triumph.' Implacably, step by step, she started forward.

Garion raised his sword and leveled its point at her. 'Push her back,' he commanded the Orb. A bolt of intense blue light shot from the sword-point, but it divided as it struck that dark aura, encasing the shadow but in no way interfering with Zandramas' advance. *Do something!* Garion shouted silently.

I can't interfere, the voice told him.

'Is that really the best thou canst do, Zandramas?' Poledra asked calmly. Garion had often heard that same note in Aunt Pol's voice, but never with quite such indominable determination. Poledra raised her hand almost indifferently and released her will. The surge and the sound nearly buckled Garion's knees. The aura of dark surrounding Zandramas and Geran vanished. The Sorceress of Darshiva, however, did not falter, but continued her slow advance. 'Wilt thou kill thy son, Belgarion of Riva?' she asked, 'For thou canst not strike at me without destroying him.'

I can't do it! Garion cried out, his eyes suddenly full of tears. *I can't!*

You must. You've been warned that this might happen. If she succeeds and puts your son's hand on the Sardion, he will be worse than dead. Do what must be done, Garion.

Weeping uncontrollably, Garion raised his sword. Geran looked him steadily in the face, his eyes unafraid.

'NO!' It was Ce'Nedra. She dashed across the floor of the grotto and threw herself directly in front of Zandramas. Her face was deathly pale. 'If you intend to kill my baby, you'll have to kill me, too, Garion,' she said in a broken voice. She turned her back on Garion and bowed her head.

'So much the better,' Zandramas gloated. 'Wilt thou kill thy son and thy wife both, Belgarion of Riva? Wilt thou carry that with thee to thy grave?'

Garion's face twisted in agony as he gripped the hilt of his sword more firmly. With one stroke, he would destroy his very life.

Zandramas, still holding Geran, stared at him incredulously. 'Thou *wilt* not!' she excaimed. 'Thou *canst* not!'

Garion clenched his teeth and raised his sword even higher.

Zandramas' incredulity suddenly turned to fright. Her advance stopped, and she began to shrink back from that awful stroke.

'Now, Ce'Nedra!' Polgara's voice cracked like a whip.

The Rivan Queen, who had been coiled like a spring beneath her apparent mute submission to her fate, exploded. With a single leap, she snatched Geran from the arms of Zandramas and fled with him back to Polgara's side.

Zandramas howled and tried to follow, her face filled with rage.

'No, Zandramas,' Poledra said. 'If thou turnest away, I will kill thee – or Belgarion will. Thou hast inadvertently revealed thy decision. Thy choice hath been made, and thou art no longer the Child of Dark, but are only an ordinary Grolim priestess. There is no longer any need for thee here. Thou art free now to depart – or to die.'

Zandramas froze.

'Thus all thy subterfuge and evasion have come to naught, Zandramas. Thou hast no longer any choice. Wilt thou now submit to the decision of the Seeress of Kell?'

Zandramas stared at her, the expression on her star-touched face a mixture of fear and towering hatred.

'Well, Zandramas,' Poledra said, 'what is it to be? Wilt thou die this close to thy promised exaltation?' Poledra's golden eyes were penetrating as she looked into the face of the Grolim priestess. 'Ah, no,' she said quite calmly, 'I perceive that thou wilt not. Thou canst not. But I would hear the words from thine own mouth, Zandramas. Wilt thou *now* accept the decision of Cyradis?'

Zandramas clenched her teeth. 'I will,' she grated.

CHAPTER TWENTY-FOUR

The thunder still cracked and rumbled outside, and the wind accompanying the storm that had been brewing since the earth had been made moaned in the passageway leading into the grotto from the amphitheater outside. In an abstract sort of way as he resheathed his sword, Garion recognized precisely what his mind was doing. It had happened so often in the past that he wondered why he had not expected it. The circumstances required that he make a decision. The fact that he no longer even considered the decision, but concentrated instead on a meticulous examination of his surroundings, indicated that he had already made his choice somewhere so deep in his mind that it did not even register on the surface. There was, he conceded, a very good reason for what he was doing. Dwelling upon an impending crisis or confrontation would only rattle him, lead him into that distracting series of 'what if's' and make him begin to have those second thoughts which could quite easily lock him into an agonized indecision. Right or wrong, the choice had been made now, and to continue to worry at it would serve no purpose. The choice, he knew, was based not only upon careful reasoning but also on deep feelings. He had that serene inner peace which flowed from the knowledge that the choice, whatever it was, was right. Calmly, he turned his attention to the grotto itself.

The stones of the walls appeared, though it was hard to be sure in the pervading red light of the Sardion, to be a kind of basalt which had fractured into a myriad of flat surfaces and sharp edges. The floor was peculiarly smooth, either as a result of eons of patiently eroding water or of a single thought of Torak during His sojourn in this cave while He had contended with and ultimately rejected UL, His father. The trickle of water into the pool on the far side of the grotto was something of a mystery. This was the highest peak of the reef. Water should run *down* from here, not up to the hidden spring in the wall. Beldin could probably explain it – or Durnik. Garion knew that he needed to be alert in this strange place, and he did not want to break his concentration by pondering the ins and outs of hydraulics.

And then, since it was the only source of light in this dim grotto, Garion's almost indifferent eyes were drawn inevitably to the Sardion. It was not a pretty stone. It was streaked with pale orange and milky white in alternating stripes banded closely together, and it was now stained with the wavering blue light emanating from the Orb. It was as smooth and polished as the Orb. The Orb had been polished by the hand of Aldur, but who had polished the Sardion? Some God unknown? Some shaggy clan of the brutish precursors of man squatting in dull-eyed patience over the stone, devoting generation after generation to the single incomprehensible task of rubbing the orange and white surface smooth with calloused and broken-nailed hands that were more like paws than human appendages? Even such unthinking creatures would have felt the power of the stone, and, feeling it to be a God – or at the very least, some object descended from a God – might not their mindless polishing have been some obscure act of worship?

Then Garion let his eyes wander over the faces of his companions, the familiar faces of those who had, in response to destinies that had been written large in the stars since the beginning of days, accompanied him to this place on this particular day. The death of Toth had answered the one unanswered question, and now all was in place.

Cyradis, her face still tear-stained and marked by her grief, stepped to the altar to face them. 'The time draws nigh,' she said in a clear, unwavering voice. 'Now must

337

the choices of the Child of Light and the Child of Dark be made. All must be in readiness when the instant of *my* Choice arrives. Know ye both that your choices, once made, cannot be unmade.'

'My choice was made at the beginning of days,' Zandramas declared. 'Adown all the endless corridors of time hath the name of Belgarion's son echoed, for he hath touched Cthrag Yaska, which spurneth all other hands save the hand of Belgarion himself. In the instant that Geran touches Cthrag Sardius, will he become an omnipotent God, higher than all the rest, and he shall have lordship and dominion over all of creation. Stand forth, Child of Dark. Take thy place before the altar of Torak to await the Choice of the Seeress of Kell. In the instant that she chooses thee, reach forth thy hand and seize thy destiny.'

It was the last clue. Now Garion knew what the choice he had made in the deep silences of his mind had been, and he knew why it was so perfectly right. Reluctantly, Geran walked toward the altar, stopped and then turned, his small face grave.

'And now, Child of Light,' Cyradis said, 'the time hath come for thee to make *thy* choice. Upon which of thy companions wilt thou lay the burden?'

Garion had little sense of the melodramatic. Ce'Nedra, and even on occasion Aunt Pol, were, he knew, quite capable of extracting the last ounce of theatricality from any given situation, whereas he, a solid, practical Sendar, was more inclined toward matter-of-fact unostentation. He was quite certain, however, that Zandramas somehow knew what his choice *should* be. He also knew that, despite her reluctant agreement to leave the choice in the hands of the Seeress of Kell, the black-robed sorceress was still perfectly capable of some desperate final ploy. He had to do something to throw her off balance so that she would hesitate at the crucial moment. If he *appeared* to be on the verge of making the wrong choice, the Sorceress would exult and she would think that she had finally

338

won. Then, at the last possible instant, he could make the *correct* choice. The Child of Dark's momentary chagrin might well freeze her hand and give him time to block her. Carefully, he noted her position and that of Geran and Otrath. Geran stood perhaps ten feet in front of the altar with Zandramas no more than a few feet from him. Otrath was cowering back against the rough stone wall at the back of the grotto.

It would have to be exactly right. He would have to build up an almost unbearable suspense in the mind of Zandramas, then dash her hopes all at once. Rather artfully, he drew his face into an expression of agonized indecision. He wandered among his friends, his face filled with a purely feigned bafflement. He stopped from time to time to look deeply into their faces, even going so far as to occasionally half-raise his hand as if on the very verge of choosing the wrong person. Each time he did that, he clearly felt a wild surge of glee coming from Zandramas. She was not even attempting to hide her emotions. Better and better. His enemy by now was no longer even rational.

'What are you doing?' Polgara whispered when he stopped in front of her.

'I'll explain later,' he murmured. 'It's necessary – and important. You've got to trust me, Aunt Pol.' He moved on. When he reached Belgarath, he felt a momentary apprehension emanating from Zandramas. The Eternal Man was certainly someone to be reckoned with, and should the eminence of the Child of Light be added to that – *and* the potential for divinity as well – the old man could be a serious adversary.

'*Will* you move on with it, Garion?' his grandfather muttered.

'I'm trying to push Zandramas off-balance,' Garion whispered. 'Please watch her closely after I choose. She might try something.'

'Then you know who it's going to be?'

'Of course. I'm trying not to think about it, though. I don't want her to pick it out of my mind.'

The old man made a face. 'Do it your way, Garion. Just don't drag it out *too* long. Let's not irritate Cyradis as well as Zandramas.'

Garion nodded and moved past Sadi and Velvet, letting his mind push out toward that of Zandramas as he did. Her emotions were veering around wildly now, and it was clear that she was at a fever-pitch. To draw things out any further would serve no purpose. He stopped at last in front of Silk and Eriond. 'Keep your face straight,' he warned the rat-faced little man. 'Don't let Zandramas see any change of expression no matter what I seem to be doing.'

'Don't make any mistakes here, Garion,' Silk warned. 'I'm not looking for a sudden promotion of any kind.'

Garion nodded. It was nearly over now. He looked at Eriond, a young man who was almost his brother. 'I'm sorry about this, Eriond,' he apologized in a low murmur. 'You probably won't want to thank me for what I'm about to do.'

'It's all right, Belgarion,' Eriond smiled. 'I've known it was going to happen for quite some time now. I'm ready.'

And that clinched it. Eriond had answered the ubiquitous question, 'Are you ready?' for probably the last time. Eriond, it appeared, *was* – and probably had been since the day he was born. Everything now slipped into place to fit together so tightly that nothing could ever take it apart again.

'Choose, Belgarion,' Cyradis urged.

'I have, Cyradis,' Garion said simply. He stretched out his hand and laid it on Eriond's shoulder. 'Here is my choice. Here is the Child of Light.'

'*Perfect!*' Belgarath exclaimed.

'*Done!*' the voice in Garion's mind agreed.

Garion felt a peculiar wrench followed by a kind of regretful emptiness. He was no longer the Child of Light. It was Eriond's responsibility now, but Garion knew that he still had one last responsibility of his own. He turned slowly, trying to make it look casual. The expression on the light-speckled face of Zandramas was a mixture of rage, fear, and frustration. It confirmed that what Garion had just done had been the right thing. He had made the proper choice. He had never actually done what he tried to do next before, although he had seen and felt Aunt Pol do it many times. This was not, however, a time for random experimentation. Carefully, he sent his mind out again, looking this time not so much for overall emotional responses from Zandramas as for specifics. He had to know exactly what she was going to try to do before she could put it into motion.

The mind of the Sorceress of Darshiva was filled with a confused welter of thoughts and emotions. The wild hope Garion's subterfuge had raised in her seemed to have done its work. Zandramas floundered, unable to concentrate now on her next step. But step she must. Garion perceived that she simply *could* not leave the matter wholly in the hands of the Seeress of Kell.

'Go thou then, Child of Light, to stand beside the Child of Dark that I may choose between ye,' Cyradis said.

Eriond nodded. Then he turned and crossed the grotto to stand beside Geran.

'It's done, Cyradis,' Poledra said. 'All the choices have been made but yours. This is the appointed place and the appointed day. The moment for you to perform your task has arrived.'

'Not quite yet, Poledra,' Cyradis said, her voice trembling with anxiety. 'The signal that the instant of the Choice hath come must be delivered from from the book of the heavens.'

'But you cannot see the heavens, Cyradis,' Garion's grandmother reminded her. 'We stand beneath the earth. The book of the heavens is obscured.'

'I need not go to the book of the heavens. It will come to me.'

'Consider, Cyradis,' Zandramas urged in a wheedling tone. 'Consider my words. There is no possible choice but Belgarion's son.'

341

Garion's mind suddenly became very alert. Zandramas had made a decision. *She* knew what she was going to do, but she had somehow managed to conceal it from him. He almost began to admire his enemy. She had prepared each of her moves from the very beginning – and each of her defenses in this place as well – with an almost military precision. As each defense failed, she withdrew to the next. That was why he could not pick her thought from her mind. She already knew what she was going to do, so there was no need for her to even think about it. He could feel, however, that her next move had something to do with Cyradis herself. *That* was Zandramas' last line of defense. 'Don't do that, Zandramas,' he told the Sorceress. 'You know it's not the truth. Leave her alone.'

'Then choose, Cyradis,' the Sorceress commanded.

'I may not. The instant hath not yet arrived.' The face of Cyradis was twisted with an inhuman agony.

Then Garion felt it. Wave upon wave of indecision and doubt were emanating from Zandramas, all focusing on the blindfolded Seeress. *This* was the final desperate attempt. Failing to attack *them* successfully, Zandramas was now attacking Cyradis. '*Help her, Aunt Pol,*' Garion threw the thought out desperately. '*Zandramas is trying to keep her from making the Choice.*'

'*Yes, Garion,*' Polgara's voice came back calmly, '*I know.*'

'*Do something!*'

'*It's not time yet. It has to come at the moment of the Choice. If I try to do anything earlier, Zandramas will feel it and take steps to counteract me.*'

'Something's happening outside,' Durnik said urgently. 'There's a light of some kind coming down the corridor.'

Garion looked quickly. The light was still dim and indistinct, but it was like no other light he had ever seen.

'The time for the Choice hath come, Cyradis,' Zandramas said, her voice cruel. 'Choose!'

'I cannot!' the Seeress wailed, turning toward the growing light. 'Not yet! I'm not ready yet!' She stumbled across

342

the floor, wringing her hands. 'I'm not ready! I can't choose! Send another!'

'Choose!' Zandramas repeated implacably.

'If only I could see them!' Cyradis sobbed. 'If only I could see them!'

And then at last, Polgara moved. 'That's easily arranged, Cyradis,' she said in a calm and oddly comforting tone. 'Your vision has clouded your sight, that's all.' She reached out and gently removed the blindfold. 'Look then with human eyes and make your choice.'

'That is forbidden!' Zandramas protested shrilly as her advantage crumbled.

'No,' Polgara said. 'If it were forbidden, I would not have been able to do it.'

Cyradis had flinched back from even the faint light in the grotto. 'I cannot!' she cried, covering her eyes with her hands. 'I cannot!'

Zandramas' eyes came suddenly alight. 'I triumph!' she exulted. 'The Choice *must* be made, but now will it be made by another. It no longer lieth in the hands of Cyradis, for the decision not to choose is also a choice.'

'Is that true?' Garion quickly asked Beldin.

'There are two schools of thought on that.'

'Yes or no, Beldin.'

'I don't know. I really don't, Garion.'

There was suddenly a soundless burst of intense light from the mouth of the passageway leading to the outside. Brighter than the sun, the light swelled and grew. It was so impossibly intense that even the cracks between the stones in the grotto blazed incandescently.

'It has come at last,' Garion's inner companion said unemotionally through Eriond's lips. 'It is the instant of the Choice. Choose, Cyradis, lest all be destroyed.'

'It has come,' another equally unemotional voice spoke through the lips of Garion's son. 'It is the instant of the Choice. Choose, Cyradis, lest all be destroyed.'

Cyradis swayed, torn by indecision, her eyes darting

back and forth to the two faces before her. Again she wrung her hands.

'She cannot!' the Emperor of Mallorea exclaimed, starting forward impulsively.

'She *must*!' Garion said, catching his friend's arm. 'If she doesn't, everything will be lost!'

Again the eyes of Zandramas filled with that unholy joy. 'It is too much for her!' the priestess almost crowed. 'Thou hast made thy choice, Cyradis,' she cried. 'It cannot be unmade. Now will *I* make the Choice for thee, and I will be exalted when the Dark God comes again!'

And that may have been Zandramas' last and fatal error. Cyradis straightened and, eyes flashing, she looked full into the starry face of the sorceress. 'Not so, Zandramas,' the Seeress said in an icy voice. 'What passed before was indecision, not choice, and the moment hath not yet passed.' She lifted her beautiful face and closed her eyes. The vast chorus of the Seers of Kell swelled its organ note in the tight confines of the grotto, but it ended on a questioning note.

'Then the decision is wholly mine,' Cyradis said. 'Are all the conditions met?' She addressed the question to the two awarenesses standing unseen behind Eriond and Geran.

'They are,' the one said from Eriond's lips.

'They are,' the other said from Geran's.

'Then hear my Choice,' she said. Once again she looked full into the faces of the little boy and the young man. Then with a cry of inhuman despair, she fell into Eriond's arms. 'I choose thee!' she wept. 'For good or for ill, I choose thee!'

There was a titanic lateral lurch – not an earthquake certainly, for not one single pebble was dislodged from the walls or ceiling of the grotto. For some reason, Garion was positive that the entire world had moved – inches perhaps, or yards or even thousands of leagues – to one side. And as a corollary to that certainty, he was equally sure that the same movement had been universal. The amount of power Cyradis' agonized decision had released was beyond human comprehension.

Gradually, the blazing light diminished somewhat, and the Sardion's glow became wan and sickly. In the instant of the Choice of the Seeress of Kell, Zandramas had shrunk back, and the whirling lights beneath the skin of her face seemed to flicker. Then they began to whirl and to glow more and more brightly. 'No!' she shrieked. *'No!'*

'Perhaps these lights in thy flesh are thine exaltation, Zandramas,' Poledra said. 'Even now it may be that thou wilt shine brighter than any constellation. Well hast thou served the Prophecy of Dark, and it may yet find some way to exalt thee.' Then Garion's grandmother crossed the grotto floor to the satin-robed sorceress.

Zandramas shrank back even more. 'Don't touch me,' she said.

'It is not thee I would touch, Zandramas, but thy raiment. I would see thee receive thy reward and thine exaltation.' Poledra tore back the satin hood and ripped the black robe away. Zandramas made no attempt to conceal her nakedness, for indeed, there was no nakedness. She was now no more than a faint outline, a husk filled with swirling, sparkling light that grew brighter and brighter.

Geran ran on sturdy little legs to his mother's arms, and Ce'Nedra, weeping with joy, enfolded him and held him close to her. 'Is anything going to happen to him?' Garion demanded of Eriond. 'He's the Child of Dark, after all.'

'There *is* no Child of Dark any more, Garion,' Eriond answered the question. 'Your son is safe.'

Garion felt an enormous wave of relief. Then, something which he had felt since the moment in which Cyradis had made her choice began to intrude itself increasingly upon his awareness. It was that overwhelming sense of *presence* which he had always felt when he had come face to face with a God. He looked more closely at Eriond, and that sense grew stronger. His young friend even looked different. Before, he had appeared to be a young man of probably not much over twenty. Now he appeared to be about the same age as Garion, although his face seemed strangely ageless. His expression, which before had been sweetly innocent, had now become grave and even wise. 'We have one last thing to do here, Belgarion,' he said in a solemn tone. He motioned Zakath and then gently placed the still-weeping Cyradis into the Mallorean's arms. 'Take care of her, please,' he said.

'For all of my life, Eriond,' Zakath promised, leading the sobbing girl back to the others.

'Now, Belgarion,' Eriond continued, 'give me my brother's Orb from off the hilt of Iron-grip's sword. It's time to finish what was started here.'

'Of course,' Garion replied. He reached back over his shoulder and put his hand on the pommel of his sword. 'Come off,' he told the Orb. The stone came free in his hand, and he held it out to the young God.

Eriond took the glowing blue stone and turned to look at the Sardion and then down at the Orb in his hand. There was something inexplicable in his face as he looked at the two stones that were at the center of all division. He raised his face for a moment, his expression now serene. 'So be it then,' he said finally.

And then to Garion's horror, he gripped the Orb even more tightly and pushed his hand quite deliberately, Orb and all, into the glowing Sardion.

The reddish stone seemed to flinch. Like Ctuchik in his last moment, it first expanded, then contracted. Then it expanded one last time. And then, like Ctuchik, it exploded – and yet that explosion was tightly confined, enclosed somehow within some unimaginable globe of force that came perhaps from Eriond's will or from the power of the Orb or from some other source. Garion knew that had that force not been in place, all the world would have been torn apart by what was happening in this tightly confined place.

Even though it was partially muffled by Eriond's

immortal and indestructable body, the concussion was titanic, and they were all hurled to the floor by its force. Rocks and pebbles rained down from the ceiling, and the entire pyramidal islet which was all that was left of Korim shuddered in an earthquake even more powerful than that which had destroyed Rak Cthol. Confined within the grotto, the sound was beyond belief. Without thinking, Garion rolled across the surging floor to cover Ce'Nedra and Geran with his armored body, noting as he did so that many of his companions were also protecting loved ones in the same fashion.

The earth continued its convulsive shuddering, and what lay confined on the altar now with Eriond's hand still buried within it was no longer the Sardion but an intense ball of energy a thousand times brighter than the sun.

Then Eriond, his face still calm, removed the Orb from the center of the incandescent ball which once had been the Sardion. As if the removal of Aldur's Orb had also removed the constraint which had held the Sardion in one shape and place, the blazing fragments of Cthrag Sardius blasted upward through the roof of the grotto, ripping the top off the shuddering pyramid and sending the huge stone blocks out in all directions as if they were no more than pebbles.

The suddenly revealed sky was filled with a light brighter than the sun, a light which extended from horizon to horizon. The fragments of the Sardion streamed upward to lose themselves in that light.

Zandramas wailed, an inhuman, animal-like sound. The faint outline which was all that was left of her was writhing, twisting. 'No!' she cried, 'It cannot be! You promised!' Garion did not know, could not know, to whom she spoke. She extended her hands to Eriond in supplication. 'Help me, God of Angarak!' she cried. 'Do not let me fall into the hands of Mordja or the foul embrace of the King of Hell! Save me!'

And then her shadowy husk split apart, and the swirling

lights which had become her substance streamed inexorably upward to follow the fragments of the Sardion into that vast light in the sky.

What was left of the Sorceress of Darshiva fell to the floor like a discarded garment, shriveled and tattered like a rag no longer of any use to anyone.

The voice which came from Eriond's lips was very familiar to Garion. He had been listening to it for all his life.

'Point,' it said in a detached, emotionless tone, as if merely stating a fact. 'Point and game.'

CHAPTER TWENTY-FIVE

The sudden silence in the grotto was almost eerie. Garion rose and helped Ce'Nedra to her feet. 'Are you all right?' he asked her, his voice hushed. Ce'Nedra nodded absently. She was examining their little boy, a look of concern on her smudged face. Garion looked around. 'Is everyone all right?' he asked.

'Is that earthquake finished yet?' Silk demanded, still covering Velvet's body with his own.

'It's passed, Kheldar,' Eriond told him. The young God turned and gravely handed the Orb back to Garion.

'Aren't you supposed to keep it?' Garion asked Him. 'I thought—'

'No, Garion. You're still the Guardian of the Orb.'

For some reason, that made Garion feel better. Even in the midst of what had just happened, he had felt an empty sense of loss. Somehow he had become convinced that he would be obliged to give up the jewel now. Covetousness was not a part of Garion's nature, but over the years the Orb had become more a friend than a possession.

'May we not go forth from this place?' Cyradis asked, her voice filled with a deep sadness. 'I would not leave my dear companion alone and untended.'

Durnik touched her shoulder gently, and then they all turned and silently left the shattered grotto.

They emerged from the portal into the light which was more than the light of day. The intense brilliance which had even penetrated the dim grotto behind them had faded to the point where it was no longer blinding. Garion looked around. Though the time of day was certainly different, there was that peculiar sense that he had been through all of this before. The storm and lightning which

349

had raged over the Place Which Is No More had passed. The clouds had rolled back, and the wind which had swept the reef during the fight with the dragon and the demon Mordja had subsided to a gentle breeze. Following the death of Torak at Cthol Mishrak, Garion had felt in a strange way that he had been witnessing the dawn of the first day. Now it was noon – years later, to be sure – but somehow the noon of that self-same day. What had begun at Cthol Mishrak was only now complete. It was over, and he felt a vast sense of relief. He also felt a bit light-headed. The emotional and physical energy he had expended since the first light of this most momentous of days had crept slowly over a fog bound sea had left him weak and near to exhaustion. More than anything right now he wanted to get out of his armor, but the thought of the amount of effort that would cost made him almost quail. He settled for wearily removing his helmet. He looked around again at the faces of his friends.

Although Geran could obviously walk now, Ce'Nedra had insisted on carrying him, and she kept her cheek pressed tightly to his, pulling back only long enough to kiss him from time to time. Geran did not seem to mind.

Zakath had placed his arm about the shoulders of the Seeress of Kell, and the look on his face rather clearly indicated that he had no real intention of ever removing it. Garion remembered with a smile how, in the first moments of their openly avowed love for each other, Ce'Nedra had continually wormed her way into a very similar embrace. He walked wearily over to where Eriond stood looking out across the sun-splashed waves. 'Can I ask you something?' he asked.

'Of course, Garion.'

Garion looked pointedly at Zakath and Cyradis. 'Is that more or less a part of the way things are supposed to be?' he asked. 'What I'm getting at is that Zakath lost someone very dear to him when he was young. If he loses Cyradis now, it might destroy him. I wouldn't want that to happen.'

'Put your mind at rest, Garion,' Eriond smiled. 'Nothing will separate those two. It's one of the things that are pre-ordained.'

'Good. Do they know?'

'Cyradis does. She'll explain it to Zakath in time.'

'She's still a seeress then?'

'No. That part of her life ended when Polgara removed her blindfold. She *has* looked into the future, though, and Cyradis has a very good memory.'

Garion thought about that for a moment, and then his eyes opened very wide. 'Are you trying to say that the fate of the entire universe depended on the choice of an ordinary human being?' he asked incredulously.

'I'd hardly call Cyradis ordinary. She's been preparing for that choice since infancy. But in a way you're right. The Choice *had* to be made by a human being, and it had to be made without any help. Not even her own people could help Cyradis at that moment.'

Garion shuddered. 'That must have been terrifying for her. She had to have been desperately lonely.'

'She was, but the people who make choices always are.'

'She didn't just select at random, did she?'

'No. She wasn't really choosing between your son and me, though. She was choosing between the Light and the Dark.'

'I can't see where all the difficulty was then. Doesn't everybody prefer the light to the dark?'

'You and I might, but the Seers have always known that Light and Dark are simply opposite sides of the same thing. Don't worry too much about Zakath and Cyradis, Garion,' Eriond said, returning to the original subject. He tapped his forehead with one finger. 'Our mutual friend here has made a few arrangements about those two. Zakath's going to be very important for most of the rest of his life, and our friend has a way of encouraging people to do necessary things by rewarding them — sometimes in advance.'

'Like Relg and Taiba?'

'Or you and Ce'Nedra – or Polgara and Durnik for that matter.'

'Can you tell me what it is that Zakath's supposed to do? What could you possibly need from him?'

'He's going to complete what you started.'

'Wasn't I doing it right?'

'Of course you were, but you're not an Angarak. You'll understand in time, I think. It's not really very complicated.'

A thought came to Garion, and in the instant it emerged he was sure it was absolutely correct. 'You knew all along, didn't you? Who you really are, I mean.'

'I knew that the potential was there. It didn't really happen until Cyradis made the Choice, though.' He looked over to where the others were sadly gathering around Toth's still form. 'I think they need us now,' he said.

Toth's face was in repose, and his hands, folded across his chest, covered the wound Cthrek Goru had made when Mordja had killed him. Cyradis stood enfolded in Zakath's arms, her face wet with new tears.

'Are you sure this is the right idea?' Beldin asked Durnik.

'Yes,' the smith said simply. 'You see—'

'You don't have to explain it, Durnik,' the hunchback told him. 'I just wanted to know if you're sure. Let's build a litter for him. It has more dignity.' He made a brief gesture, and a number of smooth, straight poles and a coil of rope appeared beside Toth's body. The two of them carefully lashed the poles together to form a litter and then lifted the mute's massive body onto it. 'Belgarath,' Beldin said, 'Garion, we'll need some help here.'

Although any one of them could have translocated Toth's body into the grotto, the four sorcerers chose instead to carry it to its final resting place in a ceremony as old as mankind.

Since the upward explosion of the Sardion had unroofed the grotto, the noon sun filled the formerly dim cave with

352

light. Cyradis quailed slightly when she saw the grim altar upon which the Sardion had lain. 'It seemeth to me so dark and ugly,' she mourned in a small voice.

'It isn't really very attractive, is it? Ce'Nedra said critically. She turned to look at Eriond. 'Do You suppose—?'

'Of course,' he agreed. He glanced only briefly at the roughly squared-off altar. It blurred slightly and then became a smooth bier of snowy-white marble.

'That's much nicer,' she said. 'Thank you.'

'He was my friend, too, Ce'Nedra,' the young God responded.

It was not a formal funeral in any sense of the word. Garion and his friends simply gathered about the bier to gaze upon the face of their departed friend. There was so much concentrated power in the small grot that Garion could not be sure exactly who created the first flower. Tendrils of ivylike vines grew suddenly up the walls, but unlike ivy, the vines were covered with fragrant white flowers. Then, between one breath and another, the floor was covered with a carpet of lush green moss. Flowers in profusion covered the bier, and then Cyradis stepped forward to lay the single white rose Poledra had provided her upon the slumbering giant's chest. She kissed his cold forehead and then sighed. 'All too soon, methinks, the flowers will wither and fade.'

'No, Cyradis,' Eriond said gently, 'they won't. They'll remain fresh and forever new until the end of days.'

'I thank thee, God of Angarak,' she said gratefully.

Durnik and Beldin had retired to a corner near the pool to confer. Then they both looked up, concentrated for a moment, and roofed the grotto with gleaming quartz that refracted the sunlight into rainbows.

'It's time to leave now, Cyradis,' Polgara told the slim girl. 'We've done all we can.' Then she and her mother took the still-weeping Seeress by the arms and slowly led her back to the passage with the others following behind.

Durnik was the last to leave. He stood at the bier with his hand lying on Toth's motionless shoulder. Finally, he put out his hand and took Toth's fishing pole out of mid-air. He carefully laid it on the bier beside his friend's body and patted the huge crossed hands once. Then he turned and left.

When they were outside again, Beldin and the smith sealed the passageway with more quartz.

'There's a nice touch,' Silk observed sadly to Garion, pointing to the image above the portal. 'Which one of you thought of that?'

Garion turned to look. The face of Torak was gone, and in its place the image of Eriond's face smiled its benediction. 'I'm not really sure,' he replied, 'and I don't think it really matters.' He tapped his fingers against the breastplate of his armor. 'Do you suppose you could help me out of this?' he asked. 'I don't think I need it anymore.'

'No,' Silk agreed, 'probably not. From the look of things, I'd say you've run out of people to fight.'

'Let's hope so.'

It was much later. They had removed the Grolims from the amphitheater and cleaned up the debris which had littered the stone floor. There was very little they could do about the vast carcass of the dragon, however. Garion sat on the lowest step of the stairway leading down into the amphitheater. Ce'Nedra, still holding her sleeping child, dozed in his arms.

'Not bad at all,' the familiar voice said to him. This time, however, the voice did not echo in the vaults of his mind, but seemed instead to be right beside him.

'I thought you were gone,' Garion said, speaking quietly to avoid waking his wife and son.

'No, not really,' the voice replied.

'I seem to remember that you once said that there was going to be a new voice – awareness, I suppose would be a better term – after this was decided.'

'There is, actually, but I'm a part of it.'

'I don't quite understand.'

354

'It's not too complicated, Garion. Before the accident there was only one awareness, but then it was divided in the same way everything else was. Now it's back, but since I was part of the original, I've rejoined it. We're one again.'

'*That's* your idea of not too complicated?'

'Do you really want me to explain further?'

Garion started to say something but then he decided against it. 'You can still separate yourself, though?'

'No. That would only lead to another division.'

'Then how—' Garion decided at the last instant that he didn't really want to ask that question. 'Why don't we just let this drop?' he suggested. 'What was that light?'

'That was the accident, the thing that divided the universe. It also divided me from my opposite and the Orb from the Sardion.'

'I thought that happened a long time ago.'

'It did – a *very* long time ago.'

'But—'

'Try to listen for a change, Garion. Do you know very much about light?'

'It's just light, isn't it?'

'There's a little more. Have you ever stood a long way from somebody who's chopping wood?'

'Yes.'

'Did you notice that he'd chop and that then, a moment or so later, you heard the sound?'

'Yes, now that you mention it, I do. What causes that?'

'The interval is the amount of time the sound takes to reach you. Light moves much faster than sound, but it still takes time to go from one place to another.'

'I'll take your word for it.'

'Do you know what the accident was?'

'Something out among the stars, I understand.'

'Exactly. A star was dying, and it died in a place where that wasn't supposed to happen. The dying star was in the wrong place when it exploded, and it ignited an entire cluster of stars – a galaxy. When the galaxy exploded, it tore the fabric of the universe. She protected herself by dividing. That's what led to all of this.'

'All right. Why were we talking about light then?'

'That's what that sudden light was – the light from that exploding galaxy – the accident. It only just now reached this place.'

Garion swallowed hard. 'Just how far away *was* the accident?'

'The numbers wouldn't mean anything to you.'

'How long ago did it happen?'

'That's another number you wouldn't understand. You might ask Cyradis. She could probably tell you. She had a very special reason to have it calculated rather precisely.'

Garion slowly began to understand. 'That's it then,' he said, excited in spite of himself. 'The instant of the Choice was the instant when the light from the accident reached this world.'

'Very good, Garion.'

'Did that cluster of stars that exploded come back again after Cyradis made the Choice? I mean there has to be *something* to patch that hole in the universe, doesn't there?'

'Better and better. Garion, I'm proud of you. You remember how the Sardion and Zandramas broke up into little flecks of intense light when they blew the roof off the grotto?'

'It's not the sort of thing I'd be likely to forget.' Garion shuddered.

'There was a reason for that. Zandramas and the Sardion – or the pieces of them, at any rate, are on their way back toward that 'hole', as you put it. They're going to be the patch. They'll get bigger along the way, of course.'

'And how long—' Garion broke off. 'Another meaningless number, I suppose?'

'Very meaningless.'

'I noticed some things about Zandramas back there. She

356

had this all worked out, didn't she? Right from the very beginning?'

'My opposite was always very methodical.'

'What I'm getting at is that she made all of her arrangements in advance. She had everything in place in Nyissa before she ever went to Cherek to pick up those Bear-cultists. Then, when she went to Riva to steal Garan, everything was ready. She'd even put things in place so that we all suspected the cult instead of her.'

'She'd have probably made a very good general.'

'But she went even further. No matter how good her plans were, she always had a contingency to fall back on in case the original plan failed.' A thought come to him. 'Did Mordja get her? I mean, she blew all apart when the Sardion exploded, didn't she? Is her spirit still mixed up in those stars, or did it get pulled down into Hell? She sounded so very much afraid just before she dissolved.'

'I really wouldn't know, Garion. My opposite and I dealt with *this* universe, not with Hell – which, of course, is a universe all of its own.'

'What would have happened if Cyradis had chosen Geran instead of Eriond?'

'You and the Orb would be moving to a new address about now.'

Garion felt his skin begin to crawl. 'And you didn't warn me?' he demanded incredulously.

'Would you really have wanted to know? and what difference would it have made?'

Garion decided to let that pass. 'Was Eriond always a God?' he asked.

'Weren't you listening earlier when he explained? Eriond was intended to be the seventh God. Torak was a mistake caused by the accident.'

'He's always been around then? Eriond, I mean?'

'Always is a long time, Garion. Eriond was present – in spirit – since the accident. When you were born, he began to move around in the world.'

'We're the same age then?'

'Age is a meaningless concept to the Gods. They can be any age they choose to be. It was the theft of the Orb that started things moving toward what happened here today. Zedar wanted to steal the Orb, so Eriond found him and showed him how to do it. That's what got you moving in the first place. If Zedar hadn't stolen the Orb, you'd probably still be at Faldor's farm – married to Zubrette, I'd imagine. Try to keep your perspective about this, Garion, but in a very peculiar way this world was created just to give you something to stand on while you were fixing things.'

'Please stop joking.'

'I'm not joking, Garion. You're the most important person who's ever lived – or ever will – with the possible exception of Cyradis. You killed a bad God and replaced him with a good one. You did a lot of floundering around in the process, but you finally managed to get it all done. I'm sort of proud of you, actually. All in all, you turned out rather well.'

'I had a lot of help.'

'Granted, but you're entitled to a bit of conceit – for a moment or two, anyway. I wouldn't overdo it, though. It's not a very becoming sort of thing.'

Garion concealed a smile. 'Why me?' he asked, making it sound as plaintive and imbecilic as possible.

There was a startled silence, and then the voice actually laughed. 'Please don't go back to asking that, Garion.'

'I'm sorry. What happens now?'

'You get to go home.'

'No, I mean to the world?'

'A lot of that's going to depend on Zakath. Eriond is the God of Angarak now, and despite Urgit and Drosta and Nathel, Zakath's the real overking of Angarak. It might take a bit of doing and he may have to use up a large number of Grolims in the process, but before he's done, Zakath is going to have to ram Eriond down the throats of all the Angaraks in the world.'

358

'He'll manage,' Garion shrugged. 'Zakath's very good at ramming things down people's throats.'

'Cyradis will be able to soften that side of him, I expect.'

'All right, then. What about afterward? After all the Angaraks have accepted Eriond?'

'The movement will spread. You'll probably live long enough to see the day when Eriond is the God of the whole world. That's what was intended from the beginning.'

'"And he shall have Lordship and Dominion"?' Garion quoted with a sinking feeling, remembering certain Grolim prophecies.

'You know Eriond better than that. Can you possibly see him sitting on a throne gloating over sacrifices?'

'No, not really. What happens to the other Gods then? Aldur and the rest of them?'

'They'll move on. They've finished with what they came here to do, and there are many, many other worlds in the universe.'

'What about UL? Will he leave, too?'

'UL doesn't leave anyplace, Garion. He's everywhere. Does that more or less answer all the questions? I have some other things that need to be attended to. There are a number of people I have to make arrangements for. Oh, incidentally, congratulations on your daughters.'

'Daughters?'

'Small female children. They're devious, but they're prettier than sons, and they smell better.'

'How many?' Garion asked breathlessly.

'Quite a few, actually. I won't tell you the exact number. I wouldn't want to spoil any surprises for you, but when you get back to Riva, you'd better start expanding the royal nursery.' There was a long pause. 'Goodbye for now, Garion,' the voice said, its tone no longer dry. 'Be well.'

And then the voice was gone.

The sun was slipping down, and Garion, Ce'Nedra, and Geran had rejoined the others near the portal to the grotto. They were all subdued as they sat not far from the vast carcass of the dragon.

'We ought to do something about her,' Belgarath murmured. 'She wasn't really a bad brute. She was just stupid, and that's not really a crime. I've always felt rather sorry for her, and I'd sort of hate to just leave her out here in the open for the birds to pick over.'

'You've got a sentimental streak in you, Belgarath,' Beldin noted. 'That's very disappointing, you know.'

'We all get sentimental as we get older,' Belgarath shrugged.

'Is she all right?' Velvet asked Sadi as the eunuch returned with Zith's little bottle. 'You took quite a long time.'

'She's fine,' Sadi replied. 'One of the babies wanted to play. He thought it was funny to hide from me. It took me a while to locate him.'

'Is there any real reason for us to stay here?' Silk asked. 'We could light that beacon, and maybe Captain Kresca could pick us up before dark.'

'We're expecting company, Kheldar,' Eriond told him.

'We are? Whom are we expecting?'

'Some friends are planning to stop by.'

'Your friends or ours?'

'Some of each, actually. There's one of them now.' Eriond pointed out to sea.

They all turned to look.

Silk suddenly laughed. 'We should have known,' he said. 'Trust Barak to disobey orders.'

They all looked out at the gently rolling ocean. The *Seabird* looked a bit the worse for weather, but she wallowed through the waves ponderously on a starboard tack which was taking her on a course past the reef. 'Beldin,' Silk suggested, 'why don't we go down to the shore and light a signal for him?'

'Can't you do it yourself?'

'I'll be happy to – just as soon as you teach me how to set fire to rocks.'

'Oh, I hadn't thought of that, I guess.'

'Are you sure you're not older than Belgarath? Your memory seems to be slipping a bit, old boy.'

'Don't belabor it, Silk. Let's go see if we can signal that oversized barge in to shore.'

The two of them started down to the edge of the water.

'Was that arranged?' Garion asked Eriond. 'Barak showing up, I mean?'

'We had a hand in it, yes,' Eriond admitted. 'You're going to need transportation back to Riva, and Barak and the others are sort of entitled to find out what happened here.'

'The others, too? Is that all right? I mean, at Rheon Cyradis said—'

'There's no problem now,' Eriond smiled. 'The Choice has been made. There are quite a number of people on their way to meet us actually. Our mutual friend has a passion for tying up loose ends.'

'You've noticed that already, I see.'

The *Seabird* hove to on the lee side of the reef, and a longboat put out from her starboard side to glide across what seemed to Garion to be a molten stretch of water made golden by the setting sun. They all went down to the shore to join Silk and Beldin as the longboat ran smoothly toward the shore of the reef.

'What kept you?' Silk called across the intervening water to Barak, who stood, his beard aflame in the light of the setting sun, in the prow of the boat.

Barak was grinning broadly. 'How did things turn out?' he shouted.

'Quite well, actually,' Silk called back. Then he seemed to think of something. 'Sorry, Cyradis,' he said to the Seeress. 'That was insensitive of me, wasn't it?'

'Not entirely, Prince Kheldar. My companion's sacrifice was made willingly, and methinks his spirit doth rejoice in our success even as we do.'

They were all in the boat with Barak, Garion saw. Mandorallen's armor gleamed just behind the huge

Cherek. Hettar, lean and whiplike, was there, and Lell-dorin, and even Relg. Barak's son Unrak was chained in the stern. Unrak had grown, but the restraints upon him were puzzling.

Barak placed one huge foot on the gunwale, preparing to leap from the boat.

'Careful,' Silk told him. 'It's deep right there. There are a fair number of Grolims who found that out the hard way.'

'Did you throw them out into the water?' Barak asked.

'No. They volunteered.'

The longboat's keel grated on the wave-eroded stones of the theater, and Barak and the others clambered out. 'Did we miss very much?' the big man asked.

'Not really,' Silk replied with a shrug. 'It was just your average, run-of-the-mill saving of the universe. You know how those things are. Is your son in trouble?' Silk looked at Unrak, who seemed a bit crestfallen in his chains.

'Not exactly that,' Barak replied. 'Along about noon, he turned into a bear, that's all. We sort of thought it was significant.'

'It runs in your family, I see. But why chain him now?'

'The sailors refused to get into the longboat with him until we did.'

'I didn't follow that at all,' Zakath murmured to Garion.

'It's a hereditary sort of thing,' Garion explained. 'Barak's family members are the protectors of the Rivan King. When the situation demands it, they turn into bears. Barak did it several times when I was in danger. It appears that he passed it on to Unrak – his son.'

'Unrak's your protector now? He seems a little young, and you don't really need that much protection.'

'No. He's probably Geran's protector, and Geran was in a certain amount of danger back there in the grotto.'

'Gentlemen,' Ce'Nedra said then in a triumphant voice, 'may I introduce the Crown Prince of Riva?' She held Geran up so that they could see him.

'He's going to forget how to walk if she doesn't put him down one of these days,' Beldin muttered to Belgarath.

'Her arms should start getting tired before too much longer,' Belgarath said.

Barak and the others crowded around the little queen even as the sailors who had been rowing reluctantly removed the chains from Barak's son.

'Unrak!' Barak roared, 'Come here!'

'Yes, father.' The boy stepped out of the boat and came forward.

'This young fellow is your responsibility,' Barak told him, pointing at Geran. 'I'll be very cross if you let anything happen to him.'

Unrak bowed to Ce'Nedra. 'Your Majesty,' he greeted her, 'you're looking well.'

'Thank you, Unrak,' she smiled.

'May I?' Unrak asked, holding out his arms toward Geran. 'His Highness and I should probably get to know each other.'

'Of course,' Ce'Nedra said, giving her son to the youthful Cherek.

'We've missed you, your Highness,' Unrak grinned at the little boy he held in his arms. 'The next time you plan one of these extended trips, you should let us know. We were a little worried.'

Geran giggled. Then he reached out and tugged on Unrak's scarcely fledged red beard.

Unrak winced.

Ce'Nedra embraced each of their old friends in turn, bestowing kisses at random. Mandorallen, of course, was weeping openly, too choked up to even deliver a flowery greeting, and Lelldorin was in virtually the same condition. Relg, peculiarly, did not even shrink from the Rivan Queen's embrace. Relg, it appeared, had undergone certain philosophical modifications during the years of his marriage to Taiba.

'There seem to be a few strangers here,' Hettar noted in his quiet voice.

Silk smacked his forehead with an open palm. 'How remiss of me,' he said. 'How could I have been so forgetful? This is Lady Poledra, Belgarath's wife and Polgara's mother. The rumors about her demise appear to have been exaggerations.'

'Will you be serious?' Belgarath muttered as their friends greeted the tawny-haired woman with a certain awe.

'Not a chance,' Silk said rogueishly. 'I'm having too much fun with this, and I'm just starting to get warmed up. Please, gentlemen,' he said to their friends, 'let me get on with this. Otherwise the introductions are likely to last until midnight. This is Sadi. You should remember him — Chief Eunuch in the palace of Queen Salmissra.'

'*Formerly* Chief Eunuch, Kheldar,' Sadi corrected. 'My Lords,' he bowed.

'Your Excellency,' Hettar replied. 'I'm sure there'll be all sorts of explanations later.'

'You all remember Cyradis, of course,' Silk went on, 'the Holy Seeress of Kell. She's a little tired just now. She had to make a fairly important decision about noon today.'

'Where's that big fellow who was with you at Rheon, Cyradis?' Barak asked her.

'Alas, my Lord of Trellheim,' she said. 'My guide and protector gave up his life to insure our success.'

'I'm deeply sorry,' Barak said simply.

'And this, of course,' Silk said in an off-hand voice, 'is his Imperial Majesty, Kal Zakath of Mallorea. He's been rather helpful from time to time.'

Garion's friends looked at Zakath warily, their eyes filled with surprise.

'I'd assume that we can set aside certain unpleasantnesses from the past,' Zakath said urbanely. 'Garion and I have more or less resolved our differences.'

'It pleaseth me, your Imperial Majesty,' Mandorallen said with a creaking bow, 'to have lived to see near-universal peace restored to all the world.'

'Thy reputation, the marvel of the known world, hath preceeded thee, My Lord of Mandor,' Zakath replied in an almost perfect Mimbrate dialect. 'I do perceive now, however, that reputation is but a poor shade of the stupendous reality.'

Mandorallen beamed.

'You'll do just fine,' Hettar murmured to Zakath.

Zakath grinned at him. Then he looked at Barak. 'The next time you see Anheg, my Lord of Trellheim, tell him that I'm still going to send him a bill for all those ships of mine he sank in the Sea of the East after Thull Mardu. I think some reparations might be in order.'

'I wish you all the luck in the world, your Majesty,' Barak grinned, 'but I think you'll find that Anheg's *very* reluctant to open the doors of his treasury.'

'Never mind,' Garion said quietly to Lelldorin, who had drawn himself up, pale-face and furious at the mention of Zakath's name.

'But—'

'It wasn't his fault,' Garion said. 'Your cousin was killed in a battle. Those things happen, and there's no point in holding grudges. That's what's kept things stirred up in Arendia for the last twenty-five hundred years.'

'And I'm sure you all recognize Eriond – formerly Errand,' Silk said once again in a deliberately off-hand manner, 'the new God of Angarak.'

'The *what*?' Barak exclaimed.

'You really should try to keep abreast of things, my dear Barak,' Silk said, buffing his nails on the front of his tunic.

'Silk,' Eriond said reprovingly.

'I'm sorry,' Silk grinned. 'I couldn't resist. Can you find it in Your heart to forgive me, your Divinityship?' He frowned. 'That's really very cumbersome, you know. What *is* the correct form of address?'

'How about just Eriond?'

Relg had gone deathly pale and he almost instinctively fell to his knees.

'Please don't do that, Relg,' Eriond told him. 'After all, you've known me since I was just a little boy, haven't you?'

'But—'

'Stand up, Relg,' Eriond said, helping the Ulgo to his feet. 'Oh, my Father sends his best, by the way.'

Relg looked awed.

'Oh well,' Silk said wryly, 'we might as well get it out into the open, I suppose. Gentlemen,' he said, 'I'm sure you all remember the Margravine Liselle, my fiancée.'

'Your *fiancée*?' Barak exclaimed in amazement.

'We all have to settle down sometime,' Silk shrugged.

They gathered around to congratulate him. Velvet, however, did not look pleased.

'Was something the matter, dear?' Silk asked her, all innocence.

'Don't you think you've forgotten something, Kheldar?' she asked acidly.

'Not that I recall.'

'You neglected to ask me about this first.'

'Really? Did I actually forget that? You weren't planning to refuse, were you?'

'Of course not.'

'Well, then—'

'You haven't heard the last of this, Kheldar,' she said ominously.

'I seem to be getting off to a bad start here,' he observed.

'Very bad,' she agreed.

They built a large bonfire in the amphitheater not too far from the huge carcass of the dragon. Durnik had rather shamefacedly translocated a sizable stack of driftwood in from various beaches here and there on the reef. Garion looked critically at the stack. 'I seem to remember a number of very wet evenings when Eriond and I spent hours looking for dry firewood,' he said to his old friend.

'This is sort of a special occasion, Garion,' Durnik

explained apologetically. 'Besides, if you'd have wanted it done this way, you could have done it yourself, couldn't you?'

Garion stared at him, then he suddenly laughed. 'Yes, Durnik,' he admitted, 'I suppose I could have at that. I don't know that we have to tell Eriond, though.'

'Do you really think he doesn't know?'

They talked until quite late. A great deal had happened since they had last seen each other, and they all had a lot of catching up to do. Finally, one by one, they drifted off to sleep.

It was still a few hours before dawn when Garion came suddenly awake.

It was not a sound had awakened him, but a light. It was a single beam of intense blue that bathed the amphitheater in its radiance, and it was soon joined by others that streamed down from the night sky in great glowing columns, red and yellow and green and shades for which there were no names. The columns stood in a semi-circle not far from the edge of the water, and there in the center of their rainbow-hued light, the pristine white albatross hovered on seraphlike wings. The incandescent forms Garion had seen before at Cthol Mishrak began to appear in the columns of pure light. Aldur and Mara, Issa and Nedra, Chaldan and Belar, the Gods stood, their faces filled with the joy of welcome.

'It's time,' Poledra sighed from where she sat enfolded in Belgarath's arms. She firmly took his arms from about her shoulders and rose to her feet.

'No,' Belgarath protested in an anguished tone, his eyes filled with tears. 'There's time yet.'

'You knew this was going to happen, Old Wolf,' she said gently. 'It has to be this way, you know.'

'I'm not going to lose you twice,' he declared. He also rose. 'There's no longer any meaning to any of this.' He looked at his daughter. 'Pol,' he said.

'Yes, father,' she replied, rising to her feet with Durnik at her side.

'You'll have to look after things now. Beldin and Durnik and the twins will help you.'

'Will you orphan me in one single stroke, father?' Her voice was throbbing with unshed tears.

'You're strong enough to bear it, Pol. Your mother and I are not displeased with you. Be well.'

'Don't be foolish, Belgarath,' Poledra said firmly.

'I'm not. I won't live without you again.'

'It's not permitted.'

'It can't be prevented. Not even our Master can prevent me now. You won't leave alone, Poledra. I'm going with you.' He put his arms about his wife's shoulders and looked deeply into her golden eyes. 'It's better this way.'

'As you decide, my husband,' she said finally. 'We must act now, however, before UL arrives. *He* can prevent it, no matter how much you bend your will to its accomplishment.'

Then Eriond was there. 'Have you really considered this, Belgarath?' He said.

'Many times in the last three thousand years, yes. I had to wait for Garion, though. Now he's here, and there's nothing to hold me any longer.'

'What would make you change your mind?'

'Nothing. I *won't* be separated from her again.'

'Then I'll have to see to that, I suppose.'

'That's forbidden, Eriond,' Poledra objected. 'I agreed to this when my task was laid upon me.'

'Agreements are always subject to renegotiation, Poledra,' he said. 'Besides, my Father and my brothers neglected to advise me of Their decision, so I'll have to deal with the situation without Their advice.'

'You *can't* defy your father's will,' she objected.

'But I don't *know* my father's will as yet. I'll apologize, of course. I'm sure he won't be *too* angry with me, and no one stays angry forever – not even my father – and no decision is irrevocable. If necessary, I'll remind him of the change of heart he had at Prolgu when Gorim persuaded him to relent.'

'That sounds awfully familiar,' Barak murmured to Hettar. 'It looks as if the new God of Angarak has spent a little too much time with our Prince Kheldar.'

'It might be contagious,' Hettar agreed.

An impossible hope had sprung up in Garion's heart.

'May I borrow the Orb again, Garion' Eriond asked politely.

'Of course.' Garion almost snatched the Orb from the pommel of the sword and offered it to the youthful God.

Eriond took the glowing jewel and approached Belgarath and his wife. Then He reached out with it and gently touched it to each of their foreheads. Garion, knowing that the touch of the jewel meant death, leaped forward with a strangled cry, but it was too late.

Belgarath and Poledra began to glow with a blue nimbus as they looked deeply into each others' eyes. Then Eriond handed the Orb back to the Rivan King.

'Won't you get into trouble about this?' Garion asked.

'It's all right, Garion,' Eriond assured him. 'I'm probably going to have to break all kinds of rules in the next several years, so I might as well get into practice.'

A deep organ note came from the incandescent columns of light at the edge of the water. Garion looked quickly at the assembled Gods and saw that the albatross had become so intensely bright that he could not bear to look at it.

And then the albatross was gone, and the Father of the Gods stood where it had hovered, and he was surrounded by His sons. 'Very well done, my Son,' UL said.

'It took me a little while to perceive what thou hadst in thy mind, Father,' Eriond apologized. 'I'm sorry to have been so dense.'

'Thou art unaccustomed to such things, my Son,' UL forgave him. 'Thy use of thy Brother's Orb in this was unanticipated, however, and most ingenious.' A faint smile touched the Eternal Face. 'Even had I been inclined not to relent, that alone would have forestalled me.'

'I thought such might be the case, Father.'

'I pray thee, Poledra,' UL said then, 'forgive me my cruel-seeming subterfuge. Know that the deception was not meant for thee, but for my son. He hath ever been of a retiring nature, reluctant to exercise his will, but his will shall prevail upon this world, and He must learn now to unleash it or to restrain it as seemeth him best.'

'It was a test, then, Most Holy?' Belgarath's voice had a slight edge to it.

'All things which happen are tests, Belgarath,' UL explained calmly. 'Thou mayest take some satisfaction in the knowledge that thou and thine espoused wife did very well in this. It was the decisions of you two which compelled my Son to make his. Still do you both serve even now, when all seems complete. And now, Eriond, join with me and thy brothers. Let us go apart a ways that we may welcome Thee unto this world which we now deliver into thy hands.'

CHAPTER TWENTY-SIX

The sun had risen, a golden disc hanging low on the eastern horizon. The sky was intensely blue and the light breeze blowing steadily in from the west touched the tops of the waves with white. There was still the faint, damp smell of the previous day's fog lingering on the stones of the strangely shaped pyramid which jutted up out of the sea to form the center of the reef.

Garion was light-headed with exhaustion. His body screamed for rest, but his mind skittered from impression to thought to image and back again, keeping him awake but all bemused on the very edge of sleep. There would be time later to sort out everything which had happened here in the Place Which Is No More. And then he rearranged his thinking about that. If ever there was a place that *was*, it was Korim. Korim was more eternally real than Tol Honeth, Mal Zeth, or Val Alorn. He gathered his sleeping wife and his son closer in his arms. They smelled good. Ce'Nedra's hair had its usual, flowerlike fragrance, and Geran smelled like every little boy who had ever lived — a small creature probably at least marginally in need of a bath. Garion's own need for bathing was, he concluded, somewhat more than marginal. Yesterday had been very strenuous.

His friends were gathered in strange little groupings here and there around the amphitheater. Barak, Hettar, and Mandorallen were talking with Zakath. Liselle sat with a look of abstract concentration on her face, combing Cyradis' hair. The ladies all seemed quite determined to take the Seeress of Kell in hand. Sadi and Beldin sprawled on the stones near the carcass of the dragon, drinking ale. Sadi's expression was polite, but it nonetheless revealed that he was consuming the bitter brew more out of politeness than from any sense of gusto. Unrak was exploring, and close on his heels was Nathel, the slack-faced young King of the Thulls. The Archduke Otrath stood alone near the now-sealed portal to the grotto, his face filled with apprehensive dread. Kal Zakath had not yet seen fit to discuss certain matters with his kinsman, and Otrath was obviously not looking forward to their conversation. Eriond was talking quietly with Aunt Pol, Durnik, Belgarath, and Poledra. The young God had a strange nimbus of pale light about Him. Silk was nowhere in sight.

And then the little man came around the shoulder of the pyramid. Behind him, on the far side of the peak, rose a column of dark smoke. He came down the stairway to the floor of the amphitheater and crossed to where Garion was sitting.

'What were you doing?' Garion asked him.

'I set out a signal for Captain Kresca,' Silk replied. 'He knows the way back to Perivor, and I've seen Barak navigate in confined waters before. Seabird's meant for the open sea, not for close quarters.'

'You'll hurt his feelings if you tell him that, you know.'

'I wasn't planning to tell him.' The rat-faced little man sprawled on the stones beside Garion and his family.

'Did Liselle have that little chat with you as yet?' Garion asked.

'I think she's saving it up. She wants to have plenty of uninterrupted time for it. Is marriage always like this? I mean, do you always live in perpetual apprehension, waiting for these conversations?'

'It's not uncommon. You're not married yet, though.'

'I'm closer to it than I ever thought I'd be.'

'Are you sorry?'

'No, not really. Liselle and I are suited for each other. We have a great deal in common. I just wish she wouldn't keep things hanging over my head is all.' Silk looked sourly around the amphitheater. 'Does he *have* to glow like that?' he asked, pointing at Eriond.

'He probably doesn't even know He's doing it. He's new at this. He'll get better at it as he goes along.'

'Do you realize that we're sitting around criticizing a God?'

'He was a friend first, Silk. Friends can criticize us without giving offense.'

'My, aren't *we* philosophical this morning? My heart almost stopped when He touched Belgarath and Poledra with the Orb, though.'

'Mine, too,' Garion admitted, 'but it appears he knew what he was doing.' He sighed.

'What's the problem?'

'It's all over now. I think I'm going to miss it – at least I will just as soon as I get caught up on my sleep.'

'It *has* been a little hectic for the past few days, hasn't it? I suppose that if we put our heads together, we can come up with something exciting to do.'

'I know what *I'm* going to be doing,' Garion told him.

'Oh? What's that?'

'I'm going to be very busy being a father.'

'Your son won't stay young forever, Garion.'

'Geran isn't going to be an only child. My friend up here in my head warned me to expect large numbers of daughters.'

'Good. It might help to settle you down a bit. I don't want to seem critical, Garion, but sometimes you're awfully flighty. Hardly a year goes by when you're not running off to some corner of the world with that burning sword in your hand.'

'Are you trying to be funny?'

'Me?' Silk leaned back comfortably. 'You're not going to have all *that* many daughters, are you? What I'm getting at is that women are only of child-bearing age for just so long.'

'Silk,' Garion said pointedly, 'Do you remember Xbell,

that Dryad we met down near the River of the Woods in southern Tolnedra?'

'The one who was so fond of men – all men?'

'That's the one. Would you say that she's still of child-bearing age?'

'Oh, my yes.'

'Xbell is over three hundred years old. Ce'Nedra's a Dryad, too, you know.'

'Well, maybe *you'll* get too old to—' Silk broke off and looked at Belgarath. 'Oh, dear,' he said. 'You *have* got a bit of a problem, haven't you?'

It was almost noon when they boarded the *Seabird*. Barak had agreed, although somewhat reluctantly, to follow Captain Kresca to Perivor. After the two men had met and inspected each others' ships, however, things went more smoothly. Kresca had been lavish in his praise of *Seabird*, and that was always a way to get on the good side of Barak.

As they weighed anchor, Garion leaned on the starboard rail gazing at the strange-looking pyramid sticking out of the sea with a pillar of greasy smoke rising from the amphitheater on its north side.

'I'd have given a great deal to have been here,' Hettar said quietly, leaning his elbows on the rail beside Garion. 'How was it?'

'Noisy,' Garion told him.

'Why did Belgarath insist on burning that dragon?'

'He felt sorry for her.'

'Belgarath's funny sometimes.'

'He is indeed, my friend. How are Adara and the children?'

'Fine. She's with child again, you know.'

'*Again?* Hettar, you two are almost as bad as Relg and Taiba.'

'Not quite,' Hettar said modestly. 'They're still a few ahead of us.' He frowned critically, his hawklike face outlined against the sun. 'I think somebody's cheating, though. Taiba keeps having babies in twos and

374

threes. That makes it very hard for Adara to keep up.'

'I wouldn't want to point any fingers, but I'd suspect that Mara's been interfering there. It's going to take awhile to repopulate Maragor.' He looked over to where Unrak stood in the bow with his shadow, Nathel, just behind him. 'What's that all about?' he asked.

'I'm not sure,' Hettar said. 'Nathel's a pathetic sort of boy, and I think Unrak feels sorry for him. I gather there hasn't been too much kindness in Nathel's life, so he'll even accept pity. He's been following Unrak around like a puppy ever since we picked him up.' The tall Algar looked at Garion. 'You look tired,' he said. 'You should get some sleep.'

'I'm exhausted,' Garion admitted, 'but I don't want to get my days and nights turned around. Let's go talk with Barak. He seemed just a bit surly when he came ashore.'

'You know how Barak is. Missing a fight always makes him discontent. Tell him some stories. He likes a good story almost as much as he likes a good fight.'

It was good to be back among his old friends again. There had been a sort of emptiness in Garion since he had left them behind at Rheon. The absence of their burly self-confidence had been part of it, of course, but even more than that, perhaps, had been the camaraderie, that sense of good-natured friendship that lay under all the apparent bickering. As they started aft to where Barak stood with one beefy hand on the tiller, Garion saw Zakath and Cyradis standing on the lee side of a longboat. He motioned to Hettar to stop and laid one finger to his lips.

'Eavesdropping isn't very nice, Garion,' the tall Algar whispered.

'It's not exactly eavesdropping,' Garion whispered back. 'I just need to be sure that I won't have to take steps.'

'Steps?'

'I'll explain later.'

'And what will you do now, Holy Seeress?' Zakath was asking the slim girl, his heart in his voice.

'The world lies open before me, Kal Zakath,' she replied a little sadly. 'The burden of my task hath been lifted, and thou needst no longer address me as "Seeress," for, indeed, that burden hath also been lifted. Mine eyes are now fixed on the plain, ordinary light of day, and I am no more than a plain, ordinary woman.'

'Hardly plain, Cyradis, and far from ordinary.'

'Thou art kind to say so, Kal Zakath.'

'Let's drop that "Kal", shall we, Cyradis? It's an affectation. It means King and God. Now that I've seen *real* Gods, I know just how presumptuous it was of me to encourage its use. But let's return to the point. Your eyes have been bound for years, haven't they?'

'Yes.'

'Then you haven't had occasion to look into a mirror lately, have you?'

'Neither occasion nor inclination.'

Zakath was a very shrewd man and he fully realized when the time had come for extravagance. 'Then let mine eyes be thy mirror, Cyradis,' he said. 'Look into them and see how fair thou art.'

Cyradis blushed. 'Thy flattery doth quite catch my breath away, Zakath.'

'It's not exactly flattery, Cyradis,' he said clinically, lapsing back into his usual speech. 'You're by far the most beautiful woman I've ever met, and the thought of having you go back to Kell – or anywhere else, for that matter – leaves a vast emptiness in my heart. You've lost your guide and your friend. Let me become both for you. Return with me to Mal Zeth. We've got much to discuss, and it may take us the rest of our lives.'

Cyradis turned her pale face away slightly, and the faintly triumphant smile which touched her lips said quite clearly that she saw a great deal more than she was willing to reveal. She turned back to the Mallorean

Emperor, her eyes innocently wide. 'Wouldst thou indeed take some small pleasure in my company?' she asked.

'Thy company would fill my days, Cyradis,' he said.

'Then gladly will I accompany thee to Mal Zeth,' she said, 'for thou art now my truest friend and dearest companion.'

Garion motioned with his head, and he and Hettar went on aft.

'What were we doing?' Hettar asked. 'That seemed like a fairly private conversation.'

'It was,' Garion told him. 'I just needed to be sure that it took place, that's all. I was told that it was going to happen, but I like a little verification now and then.'

Hettar looked puzzled.

'Zakath's been the loneliest man in the world,' Garion told him. 'That's what made him so empty and soulless – and so dangerous. That's changed now. He isn't going to be lonely any more, and that should help him with something he has to do.'

'Garion, you're being awfully cryptic. All I saw was a young lady rather skillfully wrapping a man around her finger.'

'It did sort of look that way, didn't it?'

Early the next morning, Ce'Nedra bolted from her bed and ran up the stairs to the deck. Alarmed, Garion followed her. 'Excuse me,' she said to Polgara, who was leaning out over the rail. Then she took her place beside the ageless woman, and the two of them stood for some time retching over the side.

'You, too?' Ce'Nedra said with a wan smile.

Polgara wiped her lips with a kerchief and nodded.

Then the two of them embraced each other and began to laugh.

'Are they all right?' Garion asked Poledra, who had just come up on deck with the ubiquitous wolfpup again at her side. 'Neither one of them *ever* gets sea-sick.'

'They aren't sea-sick, Garion,' Poledra said with a mysterious smile.

'But why are they—'

'They're just fine, Garion. More than fine. Go on back down to your cabin. I'll take care of this.'

Garion had just awakened, and his mind was a little foggy. So it was that it was not until he was halfway down the stairs before it slowly dawned on him. He stopped, his eyes very wide. *'Ce'Nedra?'* he exclaimed. 'And *Aunt Pol?'* Then he, too, began to laugh.

The appearance of Sir Mandorallen, the invincible Baron of Vo Mandor, in the court of King Oldorin caused an awed silence. Because of Perivor's remote location, Mandorallen's towering reputation had not reached the island, but his very presence – that overpowering sense of his nobility and perfection – stunned the king's court. Mandorallen was the ultimate Mimbrate, and it showed.

Garion and Zakath, once again in full armor, approached the throne with the stupendous knight between them. 'Your Majesty,' Garion said with a bow, 'it pleaseth me beyond measure to announce that our quest hath come to a happy and successful conclusion. The beast which plagued thy shores is no more, and the evil which beset the world is quelled for good and all. Fortune, which sometimes doth bestow blessings with open-handed generosity, hath also seen fit to reunite my companions and me with old and well-loved friends – most of whom I shall present to thee anon. A keen awareness, however, of a fact which, methinks, will be of supreme importance to thee and to thy court, doth impel me to present at once a puissant knight from far-off Arendia, who doth ever stand at the right hand of his Majesty, King Korodullin, and who, doubtless, will greet thee in kinship and love. Your Majesty, I have the honor to present Sir Mandorallen, Baron of Vo Mandor and the paramount knight in all the world.'

'You're getting better at that,' Zakath said quietly.

'Practice,' Garion said deprecatingly.

'Lord King,' Mandorallen said in his resonant voice, bowing to the throne, 'gladly do I greet thee and the

378

members of thy court, and dare to call ye all kinsmen. I presume to bear thee warmest greetings from their Majesties, King Korodullin and Queen Mayaserana, monarchs of well-loved Arendia, for, doubtless, as soon as I return to Vo Mimbre and reveal that those who were once lost are now joyfully found again, their Majesties' eyes will fill to overflowing with tears of thanksgiving, and they shall embrace thee from afar, if needs be, as a brother, and, as great Chaldan gives me strength, shall I presently return to thy magnificent city with missives top-filled with their regard and affection which shall, methinks, pressage a soon-to-be accomplished reunion – may I dare even hope, a reunification – of the dissevered branches of the holy blood of sacred Arendia.'

'He managed to say all that in one sentence?' Zakath murmured to Garion with some awe.

'Two, I think,' Garion murmured back. 'Mandorallen's in his element here. This is liable to take awhile – two or three days, I'd imagine.'

It did not take quite *that* long, but almost. The speeches of the nobles of Perivor were at first somewhat rudimentary, since the members of King Oldorin's court had been taken by surprise by Mandorallen's sudden appearance and had been rendered almost tongue-tied by his eloquence. A sleepless night spent in fevered composition, however, remedied that. The following day was given over to flowery speeches, to an extended banquet, and assorted entertainments. Belgarath was prevailed upon to present an only slightly embellished account of the events which had transpired on the reef. The old man rather judiciously avoided references to some of the more incredible incidents. The sudden appearance of divinities in the middle of an adventure story sometimes stirs scepticism in even the most credulous audience.

Garion leaned forward to quietly speak to Eriond, who sat across the banquet table from him. 'At least he protected your anonymity,' he said quietly.

379

'Yes,' Eriond agreed. 'I'll have to think of some way to thank him for that.'

'Restoring Poledra to him is probably all the thanks he can handle right now. It's going to come out eventually though, you know – your identity, I mean.'

'I think it's going to need a bit of preparation, though. I'll need to have a long talk with Ce'Nedra, I think.'

'Ce'Nedra?'

'I want some details on how she got started when she raised the army she took to Thull Mardu. It seems to me she began on a small scale and then worked her way up. That might be the best way to go at it.'

'Your Sendarian background is starting to show, Eriond,' Garion laughed. 'Durnik left his mark on both of us, didn't he?' Then he cleared his throat a little uncomfortably. 'You're doing it again,' he cautioned.

'Doing what?'

'Glowing.'

'Does it show?'

Garion nodded. 'I'm afraid so.'

'I'll have to work on that.'

The banquets and entertainments lasted well into the night for several days, but since nobles are not customarily early risers, this left the mornings free for Garion and his friends to discuss all that had happened since they had separated at Rheon. The accounts of those who had remained at home were filled with domesticity – children, weddings and affairs of state. Garion was quite pleased to hear that Brand's son Kail was managing the Kingdom of Riva probably as least as well as he might have himself. Moreover, since the Murgos were preoccupied with the Mallorean presence in southeastern Cthol Murgos, peace by and large prevailed among the western kingdoms, and trade flourished there. Silk's nose began to twitch at that information.

'This is all well and good,' Barak rumbled. 'But could we possibly skip over what's happening back home and get down to the real story? I'm dying of curiosity.'

380

And so they began. No attempt to gloss things over was permitted. Every detail was savored.

'Did you really do that?' Lelldorin asked Garion at one point after Silk had luridly described their first encounter with Zandramas, who had assumed the form of the dragon in the hills above the Arendish plain.

'Well,' Garion replied modestly, 'not her *whole* tail, only about four feet of it. It seemed to get her attention, though.'

'When he gets home, our splendid hero here is going to look into the career opportunities available in the field of dragon-molesting.' Silk laughed.

'But there aren't any more dragons, Kheldar,' Velvet pointed out.

'Oh, that's all right, Liselle,' he grinned. 'Maybe Eriond can make a few for him.'

'Never mind,' Garion told him.

Then, at a certain point in the narrative, they all had to see Zith, and Sadi rather proudly displayed his little green snake and her wriggling brood.

'She doesn't look all that dangerous to me,' Barak grunted.

'Go tell that to Harakan,' Silk grinned. 'Liselle threw the little dear into his face at Ashaba. Zith nipped him a few times and absolutely petrified him.'

'Was he dead?' the big man asked.

'I've never seen anybody any deader.'

'You're getting ahead of the story,' Hettar chided.

'There's no way we're going to be able to tell you about everything that happened in one morning, Hettar,' Durnik said.

'That's all right, Durnik,' Barak said. 'It's a long way back home. We'll have plenty of time at sea.'

That afternoon, by more or less popular demand, Beldin was obliged to repeat the performance he had given prior to their departure for the reef. Then, simply to demonstrate some of the gifts of his companions, Garion suggested that they adjourn to the tournament grounds to give them more room. Lelldorin showed the king and his court some of the finer points of archery, culminating the demonstration by showing them an entirely new way to pick plums from a distant tree. Barak bent an iron bar into something resembling a pretzel, and Hettar put them into a state verging on stunned amazement by a dazzling display of horsemanship. The culmination of the affair did not come off too well, however. When Relg walked through a solid stone wall, many ladies fainted, and some of the younger members of the audience fled screaming.

'They don't seem to be ready for that yet,' Silk said. Silk had resolutely turned his back when Relg had approached the wall. 'I know *I'm* not,' he added.

About noon a few days later, two ships entered the harbor from different directions. One of the ships was a familiar Cherek war boat, and General Atesca and Bureau Chief Brador disembarked from the other. Greldik led King Anheg and Emperor Varana down the gangway of the war boat.

'Barak!' Anheg roared as he came down the gangway, 'can you think of any reason I shouldn't take you back to Val Alorn in chains?'

'Testy, isn't he?' Hettar observed to the red-bearded man.

'He'll calm down after I get him drunk.' Barak shrugged.

'I'm sorry, Garion,' Anheg said in a booming voice. 'Varana and I tried to catch him, but that big scow of his moves faster than we thought.'

'Scow?' Barak protested mildly.

'It's all right, Anheg,' Garion replied. 'They didn't arrive until after everything was finished.'

'You got your son back, then?'

'Yes.'

'Well, trot him out, boy. We all invested a lot of effort in trying to find him for you.'

Ce'Nedra came forward carrying Geran, and Anheg enfolded them both in a bear-hug. 'Your Majesty,' he greeted the Rivan Queen, 'and you, Your Highness.' He grinned and tickled the little boy. Geran giggled.

Ce'Nedra tried a curtsy.

'Don't do that, Ce'Nedra,' Anheg told her. 'You'll drop the baby.'

Ce'Nedra laughed and then smiled at Emperor Varana. 'Uncle,' she said.

'Ce'Nedra,' the silvery-haired emperor replied. 'You're looking well.' He squinted at her. 'Is it my imagination, or are you putting on a little weight?'

'It's just temporary, uncle,' she replied. 'I'll explain later.'

Brador and Atesca approached Zakath. 'Why, your Imperial Majesty,' Atesca said to his emperor in feigned surprise. 'Imagine meeting you here – of all places.'

'General Atesca,' Zakath said to him, 'don't we know each other well enough to ignore these subterfuges?'

'We were worried about you, your Majesty,' Brador said. 'Since we were in the vicinity anyway . . .' The bald man spread his hands.

'And just what were you two doing in this vicinity? Didn't I leave you back on the banks of the Magan?'

'Something came up, your Majesty,' Atesca put in. 'Urvon's army fell all apart, and the Darshivans seemed to be distracted. Brador and I seized the opportunity to bring Peldane and Darshiva back into the empire, and we've been pursuing the remnants of the Darshivan army all over eastern Dalasia.'

'Very good, gentlemen,' Zakath approved. 'Very, very good. I should take a vacation more often.'

'*This* was his idea of a vacation?' Sadi murmured.

'Of course,' Silk replied. 'Fighting dragons can be very invigorating.'

Zakath and Varana had been eyeing each other speculatively.

'Your Imperial Majesties,' Garion said politely, 'I should probably introduce you. Emperor Varana, this is his Imperial Majesty, Kal Zakath of Mallorea. Emperor

Zakath, this is his Imperial Majesty, Ran Borune XXIV of the Tolnedran Empire.'

'Just Varana will do, Garion,' the Tolnedran said. 'We've all heard a lot about you, Kal Zakath,' he said, extending his hand.

'None of it good, I'm sure, Varana,' Zakath smiled, shaking the other emperor's hand warmly.

'Rumors are seldom accurate, Zakath.'

'We have much to discuss, your Imperial Majesty,' Zakath said.

'Indeed we do, your Imperial Majesty.'

King Oldorin of Perivor appeared to be in a state verging on nervous prostration. His island kingdom, it seemed, was quite suddenly awash with royalty. Garion made the introductions as gently and, he hoped, as painlessly as possible. King Oldorin mumbled a few greetings, almost forgetting his thee's and thou's. Garion drew him to one side. 'This is a momentous occasion, your Majesty,' he said. 'The presence in one place of Zakath of Mallorea, Varana of Tolnedra, and Anheg of Cherek doth presage the possibility of tremendous steps toward that universal peace for which the world hath longed for eons.'

'Thine own presence doth not diminish the occasion, Belgarion of Riva.'

Garion bowed his acknowledgement. 'Though the courtesy and hospitality of thy court are the marvel of the known world, your Majesty,' he said, 'it were foolish of us not to seize this opportunity in so noble a cause. Thus I implore thee that my friends and I may closet separately for some time to explore the possibilities of this chance meeting, although it seemeth me that chance hath had but small part in its coming to pass. Surely the Gods themselves have had a hand in it.'

'I am certain of it, your Majesty,' Oldorin agreed. 'There are council chambers on the top-most floor of my palace, King Belgarion. They are at the immediate disposal of thyself and thy royal friends. I have no doubt that momentous things may emerge from this meeting, and the honor I shall accrue that it is to take place beneath my roof doth overwhelm me quite.'

It was an impromptu meeting that was held in the upper chambers of the palace. Belgarath, by common consent, presided. Garion agreed to look after the interests of Queen Porenn, and Durnik to those of King Fulrach. Relg spoke for Ulgo – and Maragor. Mandorallen represented Arendia, and Hettar spoke for his father. Silk stood in for his brother, Urgit. Sadi spoke for Salmissra, and Nathel spoke for the Thulls, although very seldom. No one was particularly interested in taking the part of Drosta lek Thun of Gar og Nadrak.

Right at the outset there was, to Varana's obvious disappointment, an agreement that matters of trade be excluded from the discussion, and then they got down to business.

About midway through the second day, Garion leaned back in his chair, only half-listening as Silk and Zakath haggled incessantly over a peace treaty between Mallorea and Cthol Murgos. Garion sighed pensively. Only a few days ago, he and his friends had witnessed – and participated in – the most momentous Event in the history of the universe, and now they sat around a table deeply involved in the mundane matters of international politics. It seemed so anti-climactic somehow, and yet, Garion knew that most of the people in the world would be far more concerned about what happened around this table than what had happened at Korim – for a while, anyway.

Finally, the Accords of Dal Perivor were reached. They were tentative, to be sure, and couched in broad generalities. They were subject, of course, to ratification by those monarchs not actually present. They were tenuous and based more on goodwill than on the rough give and take of true political negotiation. They were nonetheless, Garion felt, the last, best hope of mankind. Scribes were summoned to copy from Beldin's copious notes, and it was decided that the document should be issued over the seal of King Oldorin of Perivor as host monarch.

The ceremony of the signing was stupendous. Mimbrates are very good at stupendous ceremonies.

Then, on the following day came the goodbyes. Zakath, Cyradis, Eriond, Atesca, and Brador were to depart for Mal Zeth while the rest of them were to board the *Seabird* for the long voyage home. Garion spoke at some length with Zakath. They both promised to correspond and, when affairs of state permitted it, to visit. The correspondence would be easy, they both knew. The visits, however, were far more problematical.

Then Garion joined his family while they took their leave of Eriond. Garion then walked the young and as yet unknown God of Angarak down to the quay where Atesca's ship waited. 'We've come a long way together, Eriond,' he said.

'Yes,' Eriond agreed.

'You've got a lot ahead of You, You know.'

'Probably more than you can even imagine, Garion.'

'Are you ready?'

'Yes, Garion, I am.'

'Good. If You ever need me, call on me. I'll come to wherever You are as quickly as I can.'

'I'll remember that.'

'And don't get so busy that You let Horse get fat.'

Eriond smiled. 'No danger of that,' He said. 'Horse and I still have a long way to go.'

'Be well, Eriond.'

'You, too, Garion.'

They clasped hands and then Eriond went up the gangway to his waiting ship. Garion sighed and made his way to where *Seabird* was moored. He went up the gangway to join the others as they watched Atesca's ship sail slowly out of the harbor, veering slightly around

Greldik's ship, which waited with the impatience of a leashed hound.

Then Barak's sailors cast off all lines and rowed out into the harbor. The sails were raised, and *Seabird* turned her prow toward home.

CHAPTER TWENTY-SEVEN

The weather held clear and sunny, and a steady breeze filled *Seabird*'s sails to drive her northwesterly in the wake of Greldik's patched and weatherbeaten warboat. At Unrak's insistence, the two vessels were making a side-trip to Mishrak ac Thull to deposit Nathel in his own kingdom.

The days were long and filled with sunshine and the sharp smell of brine. Garion and all his friends spent most of those days in the sunny main cabin. The story of the quest to Korim was long and involved, but those who had not been with Garion and the others wanted as much in the way of detail as they could possibly get. Their frequent interruptions and questions led to extended digressions, and the story jumped back and forth in time, but it proceeded, albeit at a frequently limping pace. There was much in the story that an average listener might have found incredible. Barak and the others, however, accepted it. They had spent enough time with Belgarath, Polgara, and Garion to know that almost nothing was impossible. The only exception to this rule was Emperor Varana, who remained adamantly sceptical – more on philosophical grounds, Garion suspected, than from any real disbelief.

Unrak gave Nathel some very extended advice before the King of the Thulls was deposited in a seaport town in his own kingdom. The advice had to do with the need for Nathel to assert himself and to break free of the domination of his mother. Unrak didn't look all that optimistic after the young Thull departed.

The *Seabird* turned her course southward then, still following Greldik's wake as they ran along the baren, rocky coast of Goska in northeastern Cthol Murgos. 'That's disgraceful, you know that?' Barak said to Garion one day, pointing at Greldik's vessel. 'It looks like a floating shipwreck.'

'Greldik uses his ship rather hard,' Garion agreed. 'I've sailed with him a few times.'

'The man has no respect for the sea,' Barak grumbled, 'and he drinks too much.'

Garion blinked. 'I beg your pardon?' he said.

'Oh, I'll be the first to admit that I take a tankard of ale now and then, but Greldik drinks at sea. That's revolting, Garion. I think it might even be irreligious.'

'You know more about the sea than I do,' Garion admitted.

Greldik's ship and *Seabird* sailed through the narrow strait between the Isle of Verkat and the southern coasts of Hagga and Gorut. Since it was summer in the southern latitudes, the weather continued fair and they made good time. After they had passed through the dangerous cluster of rocky islets strung down from the tip of the Urga peninsula, Silk came up on deck. 'You two have taken to living up here,' he observed to Garion and Barak.

'I like to be on deck when we're in sight of land,' Garion said. 'When you can see the shoreline slipping by, it gives you the sense that you're getting somewhere. What's Aunt Pol doing?'

'Knitting,' Silk shrugged. 'She's teaching Ce'Nedra and Liselle how it's done. They're creating whole heaps of little garments.'

'I wonder why,' Garion said with a perfectly straight face.

'I've got a favor to ask, Barak,' Silk said.

'What do you need?'

'I'd like to stop at Rak Urga. I want to give Urgit a copy of those accords, and Zakath made a couple of proposals at Dal Perivor that my brother really ought to know about.'

'Will you help chain Hettar to the mast while we're in port?' Barak asked him.

Silk frowned slightly, then he seemed to suddenly understand. 'Oh,' he said. 'I'd sort of forgotten that. It wouldn't be a very good idea to take Hettar into a city full of Murgos, would it?'

'A bad idea, Silk. Disastrous might come even closer.'

'Let me talk with him,' Garion suggested. 'Possibly I can calm him down a bit.'

'If you can manage that, I'll have you come up on deck and talk to the next gale we run into,' Barak said. 'Hettar's *almost* as reasonable as the weather where Murgos are concerned.'

The tall Algar, however, did not, in fact go stony-faced and reach for his saber at the mention of the word 'Murgo.' They had told him about Urgit's real background during the voyage, and his hawklike face became alive with curiosity when Garion rather hesitantly told him of the plan to stop at Rak Urga. 'I'll control my instincts, Garion,' he promised. 'I think I'd really like to meet this Drasnian who's managed to become the King of the Murgos.'

Because of the hereditary and by now almost instinctive animosity between Murgos and Alorns, Belgarath advised caution in Rak Urga. 'Things are quiet now,' he said. 'Let's not stir them up. Barak, run up a flag of truce, and when we get to within hailing distance of the wharves, I'll send for Oskatat, Urgit's Seneschal.'

'Can he be trusted?' Barak asked dubiously.

'I think so, yes. We won't all trek up to the Drojim, though. Have *Seabird* and Greldik's ship pull back out into the harbor after we go ashore. Not even the most rabid Murgo sea-captain would attack a pair of Cherek warboats in open water. I'll keep in touch with Pol, and we'll send for help if the occasion arises.'

It took some fairly extensive shouting between ship and shore to persuade a Murgo colonel to send to the Drojim Palace for Oskatat. The colonel's decision may have been tipped in that direction when Barak ordered his catapults loaded. Rak Urga was not a very attractive town, but

390

the colonel quite obviously didn't want it burned to the ground.

'Are you back already?' Oskatat bellowed across the intervening water when at last he arrived on the wharf.

'We were in the vicinity and we thought we'd pay a call,' Silk said lightly. 'We'd like to speak with his Majesty if possible. We'll control these Alorns if you can keep your Murgos leashed.'

Oskatat gave a number of very abrupt commands that were accompanied by some fairly grisly threats, and Garion, Belgarath, and Silk took to *Seabird*'s long-boat. They were accompanied by Barak, who had left Unrak in charge, and by Hettar and Mandorallen.

'How did it go?' Oskatat asked Silk as the party, accompanied by a contingent of King Urgit's black-robed household guard, rode up from the harbor to the Drojim.

'Things turned out rather well,' Silk smirked.

'His Majesty should be pleased to hear that.'

They entered the garish Drojim Palace, and Oskatat led them down a smoky, torch-lit hall toward the throne room. 'His Majesty has been expecting these people,' Oskatat said harshly to the guards. 'He will see them now. Open the door.'

One of the guards seemed to be new. 'But they're Alorns, Lord Oskatat,' he objected.

'So? Open the door.'

'But—'

Oskatat coolly drew his heavy sword. 'Yes?' he said in a deceptively mild tone.

'Ah – nothing, my Lord Oskatat,' the guard repeated. 'Nothing at all.'

'Why is the door still closed then?'

The door was quickly snatched open.

'Kheldar!' It was a ringing shout, and it came from the far end of the throne room. King Urgit bolted down the steps of the dais, flinging his crown over one shoulder as he ran. He caught Silk in a rough embrace, laughing uncontrollably. 'I thought you were dead,' he crowed.

391

'You're looking well, Urgit,' Silk said to him.

Urgit made a slight face. 'I'm married now, you know,' he said.

'I was afraid Prala might get you eventually. I'm getting married myself shortly.'

'The blond girl? Prala told me about how she felt about you. Imagine that, the invincible Prince Kheldar, married at last.'

'Don't make any large wagers on it just yet, Urgit,' Silk told his brother. 'I may still decide to fall on my sword instead. Are we sort of alone here? We've got some things to tell you, and our time's a bit short.'

'Mother and Prala are here,' Urgit told him, 'and my stepfather here, of course.'

'*Stepfather?*' Silk exclaimed, looking at Oskatat in surprise.

'Mother was getting lonely. She missed all the playful abuse Taur Urgas used to bestow on her. I used my influence to marry her off to Oskatat. I'm afraid he's been a terrible disappointment to her, though. So far as I know, he hasn't knocked her down a single flight of stairs or kicked her in the head even once.'

'He's impossible when he's like this,' Oskatat apologized for his king.

'Just brimming over with good spirits, Oskatat,' Urgit laughed. 'By Torak's boiling eye, I've missed you, Kheldar.' Then he greeted Garion and Belgarath and looked inquiringly at Barak, Mandorallen, and Hettar.

'Barak, Earl of Trellheim,' Silk introduced the red-bearded giant.

'He's even bigger than they say he is,' Urgit noted.

'Sir Mandorallen, Baron of Vo Mandor,' Silk went on.

'The Gods' own definition of the word gentleman,' Urgit said.

'And Hettar, son of King Cho Hag of Algaria.'

Urgit shrank away, his eyes suddenly fearful. Even Oskatat took a step backward.

'Not to worry, Urgit,' Silk said grandly. 'Hettar came all

the way through the streets of your capital, and he didn't kill even one of your subjects.'

'Remarkable,' Urgit murmured nervously. 'You've changed, Lord Hettar,' he said. 'You're reputed to be a thousand feet tall and to wear a necklace of Murgo skulls.'

'I'm on vacation,' Hettar said drily.

Urgit grinned. 'We aren't going to be unpleasant to each other, are we?' he asked, still slightly apprehensive.

'No, your Majesty,' Hettar told him, 'I don't think we are. For some reason, you intrigue me.'

'That's a relief,' Urgit said. 'If you find yourself getting edgy, though, be sure to let me know. There are still a dozen of so of my father's generals lurking about the Drojim. Oskatat hasn't found a reason to have them beheaded yet. I'll send for them, and you can settle your nerves. They're just a bother to me anyway.' He frowned. 'I wish I'd known you were coming,' he said. 'I've wanted to send your father a present for years now.'

Hettar looked at him, one eyebrow raised.

'He did me the greatest service any man can ever do for another. He ran his saber through Taur Urgas' guts. You might tell him that I tidied up for him afterward.'

'Oh? My father doesn't usually need to be tidied up after.'

'Oh, Taur Urgas was dead enough all right,' Urgit assured him, 'but I didn't want some Grolim to come along and accidentally resurrect him, so I cut his throat before we buried him.'

'Cut his throat?' Even Hettar seemed startled by that.

'From ear to ear,' Urgit said happily. 'I stole a little knife when I was about ten, and I spent the next several years sharpening it. After I slit his weasand, I drove a stake through his heart and buried him seventeen feet deep — head down. He looked better than he had in years with just his feet sticking up out of the dirt. I paused to enjoy that sight while I was resting from all the shoveling.'

'You buried him yourself?' Barak asked.

'I certainly wasn't going to let anybody else do it. I wanted to be sure of him. After I had him well planted, I stampeded horses across his grave several times to conceal the spot. As you may have guessed, my father and I were not on the best of terms. I take some pleasure in knowing that not a single living Murgo knows exactly where he's buried. Why don't we go join my queen and my mother? Then you can tell me your splendid news – whatever it is. Dare I hope that Kal Zakath rests in the arms of Torak?'

'I wouldn't think so.'

'Pity,' Urgit said.

As soon as they found out that Polgara, Ce'Nedra, and Velvet were still on board *Seabird*, Queen Prala and Queen Mother Tamazin excused themselves and left the throne room to renew old acquaintances.

'Find seats, gentlemen,' Urgit said after they had left. He sprawled on his throne with one leg cocked up over the arm. 'What are these things you wanted to tell me, Kheldar?'

Silk sat down on the edge of the dais and reached inside his tunic.

'Please don't do that, Kheldar,' Urgit told him, shying away. 'I know how many daggers you carry.'

'Not a dagger this time, Urgit,' Silk assured him. 'Only this.' He handed over a folded parchment packet.

Urgit opened it and scanned it quickly. 'Who's Oldorin of Perivor?' he asked.

'He's the king of an island off the south coast of Mallorea,' Garion told him. 'A group of us met in his palace.'

'*Quite* a group, I see,' Urgit said, looking over the signatures. He frowned. 'I *also* see that you spoke for me,' he said to Silk.

'He protected your interests rather well, Urgit,' Belgarath assured him. 'The details we hammered out are mostly generalities, you'll notice, but it's a start.'

'It is indeed, Belgarath,' Urgit agreed. 'I notice that no one spoke for Drosta.'

394

'The king of Gar og Nadrak was unrepresented, your Majesty,' Mandorallen told him.

'Poor old Drosta,' Urgit chuckled. 'He always seems to get left out. This is all very nice, gentlemen, and it might even insure a decade or so of peace – provided you promised to let Zakath have my head on a plate to decorate some unimportant room in his palace at Mal Zeth with.'

'That's the main thing we came to discuss with you,' Silk told him. 'Zakath returned to Mal Zeth when we all left Perivor, but I talked with him for quite a while before we separated, and he finally agreed to accept peace overtures.'

'Peace?' Urgit scoffed. 'The only peace Zakath wants is eternal peace – for every living Murgo, and I'm at the top of his list.'

'He's changed a bit,' Garion told him. 'He has something more important on his mind right now than exterminating Murgos.'

'Nonsense, Garion. *Everybody* wants to exterminate the Murgos. Even *I* want to exterminate them, and I'm their king.'

'Send some ambassadors to Mal Zeth,' Silk advised him. 'Give them enough power to negotiate in good faith.'

'Give a Murgo power? Kheldar, are you out of your mind?'

'I can find some trustworthy men, Urgit,' Oskatat assured him.

'In Cthol Murgos? Where? Under some damp rock?'

'You're going to have to start trusting people, Urgit,' Belgarath told him.

'Oh, of course, Belgarath,' Urgit said with heavy sarcasm. 'I sort of *have* to trust you, but that's because you'll turn me into a frog if I don't.'

'Just send your ambassadors to Mal Zeth, Urgit,' Silk said patiently. 'You may be pleasantly surprised at the outcome.'

'Any outcome that doesn't leave me without my head would be pleasant.' Urgit squinted shrewdly at his brother. 'You've got something else on your mind, Kheldar,' he said. 'Go ahead and spit it out.'

'The world's right on the verge of breaking out in a bad case of peace,' Silk told him. 'My partner and I have been on a wartime footing for years now. Our enterprises are very likely to collapse if we don't find new markets – and markets for peacetime goods. Cthol Murgos has been at war for a generation now.'

'Longer than that, actually. Technically, we've been at war since the ascension of the Urga Dynasty – which I have the distinct displeasure of representing.'

'There must be quite a hunger for peace-time amenities in your kingdom then – little things, like roofs for the houses, pots to cook in, something to cook in them – things like that.'

'I'd imagine so, yes.'

'Good. Yarblek and I can ship goods to Cthol Murgos by sea and turn Rak Urga into the largest commercial center on the southern half of the continent.'

'Why would you want to? Cthol Murgos is bankrupt.'

'The bottomless mines are still there, aren't they?'

'Of course, but they're all in territories controlled by the Malloreans.'

'But if you conclude a peace treaty with Zakath, the Malloreans will be leaving, won't they? We'll have to move fast on this, Urgit. As soon as the Malloreans withdraw, you'll have to move in, not only with troops, but also with miners.'

'What do I get out of it?'

'Taxes, brother mine, taxes. You can tax the gold miners, you can tax me, and you can tax my customers. You'll be rolling in money in just a few years.'

'And the Tolnedrans will swindle me out of all of it in just a few weeks.'

'Not too likely,' Silk smirked. 'Varana's the only Tolnedran in the world who knows about this, and he's

396

on Barak's ship out in the harbor right now. He won't get back to Tol Honeth for several weeks.'

'What difference does that make? Nobody can make a move of any kind until I conclude a peace treaty with Zakath, can they?'

'That's not entirely true, Urgit. You and I can draw up an agreement guaranteeing me exclusive access to the Murgo market. I'll pay you handsomely for it, of course, and the agreement will be perfectly legal – and iron-clad. I've drawn up enough trade agreements to be able to see to that. We can hammer out the details later, but the important thing right now is to get something down in writing with both our names on it. And then, when peace breaks out, the Tolnedrans will swarm down here. You can show them the document and send them all home again. If I've got exclusive access, we'll make millions. Millions, Urgit, millions!'

Both of their noses were twitching violently now.

'What sort of provisions would we want to put in this agreement of exclusivity?' Urgit asked cautiously.

Silk grinned broadly at him and reached inside his doublet again. 'I've taken the liberty of drawing up an interim document,' he said, pulling out another parchment, 'just to save time, of course.'

Sthiss Tor was still a very unattractive city, Garion noticed as Barak's sailors moored *Seabird* to the familiar wharf in the Drasnian trade enclave. The hawsers were no sooner tied off when Silk leaped across to the wharf and hurried up the street. 'Is he likely to have any trouble?' Garion asked Sadi.

'Not too likely,' Sadi, who was crouched down behind a longboat, replied. 'Salmissra knows who he is, and I know my queen. Her face doesn't show any emotion, but her curiosity is very strong. I've spent the last three days composing that letter. She'll see me. I can practically guarantee that. Could we go below, Garion? I'd really rather not have anybody see me.'

It was perhaps two hours later when Silk returned accompanied by a platoon of Nyissan soldiers. The platoon leader was familiar.

'Is that you, Issus?' Sadi called out through the porthole of the cabin in which he was hiding. 'I thought you'd be dead by now.'

'Hardly,' the one-eyed assassin said.

'You're working at the palace now?'

'Yes.'

'For the queen?'

'Among others. I take on a few odd jobs for Javelin now and then.'

'Does the queen know about that?'

'Of course. All right, Sadi. The queen's agreed to a two-hour amnesty for you. We'd better hurry. I'm sure you'll want to be gone from here before those two hours run out. The queen's fangs start to itch every time she hears your name, so let's go – unless you'd like to reconsider and start running right now.'

'No,' Sadi said. 'I'll be right up. I'm bringing Polgara and Belgarion with me, if that's all right.'

'That's up to you,' Issus said with an indifferent shrug.

The palace was still infested with snakes and with dreamy-eyed eunuchs. A pimply-faced official with broad hips and a grotesqely made-up face met them at the palace door. 'Well, Sadi,' he said in a piping soprano voice, 'I see you've returned.'

'And I see you've managed to stay alive, Y'sth,' Sadi replied coldly. 'That's a shame, really.'

Y'sth's eyes narrowed with undisguised hatred. 'I'd be a little careful about what I say, Sadi,' he squeaked. 'You're not Chief Eunuch anymore. As a matter of fact, I may soon hold that position myself.'

'May the heavens defend poor Nyissa then,' Sadi murmured.

'You've heard of the queen's command that Sadi be given safe-conduct?' Issus asked the eunuch.

'Not from her own lips.'

'Salmissra doesn't have lips, Y'sth, and you've just heard about it – from me. Now, are you going to get out of our way? Or am I going to have to slit you up the middle?'

Y'sth backed away. 'You can't threaten me, Issus.'

'I wasn't threatening you. I was just asking a question.' Then the assassin led the way up the polished stone corridor leading to the throne room.

The room they entered was unchanged and probably unchangeable. Thousands of years of tradition had seen to that. Salmissra, her coils stirring restlessly and her blunt, crowned head weaving sinuously in front of her mirror, occupied the throne.

'Sadi the eunuch, My Queen,' Issus announced with a bow. Issus, Garion noted, did not prostrate himself before the throne as did other Nyissans.

'Ah,' Salmissra hissed, 'and the beautiful Polgara and King Belgarion. You've fallen in with important people since you left my service, Sadi.'

'Pure chance, my Queen,' Sadi lied glibly.

'What is this vital matter that impelled you to risk your life by coming into my presence again?'

'Only this, Eternal Salmissra,' Sadi replied. He set his red leather case on the floor, opened it, and removed a folded parchment. He casually kicked a groveling eunuch in the ribs. 'Take this to the queen,' he commanded.

'You're not enhancing your popularity here, Sadi,' Garion cautioned quietly.

'I'm not running for public office, Garion. I can be as disagreeable as I choose to be.'

Salmissra quickly perused the Accords of Dal Perivor. 'Interesting,' she hissed.

'I'm sure your Majesty can see the opportunities implicit in those accords,' Sadi said. 'I felt it was my responsibility to make you aware of them.'

'Of course I can see what's involved, Sadi,' she said. 'I'm a snake, not a cretin.'

'Then I'll bid you goodbye, my Queen. I've performed my last duty to you.'

Salmissra's eyes had gone flat with concentration. 'Not just yet, my Sadi,' she said in a whisper that was almost a purr. 'Come a little closer.'

'You gave your word, Salmissra,' he said apprehensively.

'Oh, *do* be sensible, Sadi,' she said. 'I'm not going to bite you. It was all a ploy, wasn't it? You had discovered the possibility that these accords might be in the making and you deliberately set out to have yourself disgraced so that you could pursue them. Your negotiations on my behalf were brilliant, I must say. You have done very well, Sadi – even if your actions involved deceiving me. I am well-pleased with you. Would you consent to resume your former position here in the palace?'

'Consent, my Queen?' he blurted almost boyishly. 'I'd be overjoyed. I live but to serve you.'

Salmissra swiveled her head around to regard the prostrated eunuchs. 'You will all leave me now,' she commanded them. 'I want you to go throughout the palace and spread the word that Sadi has been rehabilitated and that I've reinstated him. If anyone cares to dispute my decision, send him to me, and I'll explain it to him.'

They stared at her, and Garion noticed that not a few faces were filled with chagrin.

'How tiresome,' Salmissra sighed. 'They're too delighted to move. Please drive them out, Issus.'

'As my Queen desires,' Issus said, drawing his sword. 'Did you want them all to survive?'

'A few of them, Issus – the more nimble ones.'

The throne room was vacated almost immediately.

'I cannot sufficiently thank your Majesty,' Sadi said.

'I'll think of a way, my Sadi. First of all, we'll both pretend that the motives I suggested a moment ago were genuine, won't we?'

'I understand perfectly, Divine Salmissra.'

'After all,' she added, 'we must protect the dignity of

the throne. You will assume your former duties and your former quarters. We'll think of suitable honors and rewards later.' She paused. 'I've missed you, my Sadi. I don't think anyone can ever know how much.' Her head moved slowly around, and she regarded Polgara. 'And how did your encounter with Zandramas go, Polgara?' she asked.

'Zandramas is no longer with us, Salmissra.'

'Splendid. I never really liked her. And is the universe restored again?'

'It is, Salmissra.'

'I think I'm glad of that. Chaos and disruption are irritating to a snake, you know. We're partial to calm and to order.'

Garion noticed that a small green snake had slithered out from under Salmissra's throne to approach Sadi's red leather case, which lay open and forgotten on the marble floor. The little snake reared up to regard the earthenware bottle. He was purring seductively.

'And did you recover your son, your Majesty?' Salmissra asked Garion.

'We did, your Majesty.'

'Congratulations. Give my regards to your wife.'

'I will, Salmissra.'

'We must leave now,' Polgara said. 'Goodbye, Sadi.'

'Goodbye, Lady Polgara.' Sadi looked at Garion. 'Goodbye, Garion,' he said. 'It's been a lot of fun, hasn't it?'

'Yes, it has,' Garion agreed, shaking the eunuch's hand.

'Say goodbye to the others for me. I rather imagine we'll all see each other from time to time on state business, but it won't be exactly the same, will it?'

'No, probably not.' Garion turned to follow Aunt Pol and Issus from the throne room.

'A moment, Polgara,' Salmissra said.

'Yes?'

'You've changed many things here. At first, I was very angry with you, but now I've had time to reconsider.

Everything's turned out for the best after all. You have my thanks.'

Polgara inclined her head.

'Congratulations on your forthcoming blessing,' Salmissra added.

Polgara's face gave no hint of surprise at the Serpent Queen's perception of her condition. 'Thank you, Salmissra,' she said.

They stopped off in Tol Honeth to deliver Emperor Varana to the palace. The heavy-shouldered professional soldier seemed a bit abstracted, Garion noticed. He spoke briefly with a palace functionary as the group moved toward his quarters, and the official scurried away.

Their farewells were brief, almost abrupt. Varana was, as always, the soul of courtesy, but he obviously had other things on his mind.

Ce'Nedra was fuming as they left the palace. She was, as she almost always was now, carrying her young son, and was absently running her fingers through his blond curls. 'He was almost rude,' she said indignantly.

Silk looked down the broad marble drive leading up to the palace. Spring was approaching in these northern latitudes, and the leaves were beginning to appear on the huge old trees lining the drive. A number of richly dressed Tolnedrans were almost running up the drive toward the palace. 'Your uncle, – or brother, whichever you want to call him – has something very important to attend to just now,' the little man told Ce'Nedra.

'What could possibly be more important than common courtesy?'

'Cthol Murgos, at the moment.'

'I don't understand.'

'If Zakath and Urgit work out a peace treaty, there'll be all sorts of commercial opportunities in Cthol Murgos.'

'I understand that,' she said tartly.

'Of course you do. You're a Tolnedran, after all.'

'Why aren't *you* doing something about it?'

'I already have, Ce'Nedra,' he smiled, polishing a large ring on the front of his pearl gray doublet. 'Varana may be very cross with me when he finally finds out what I've done to him.'

'What exactly *did* you do?'

'I'll tell you once we're back out to sea. You're still a Borune and you might have some residual family loyalties. I wouldn't want you to spoil the surprise for your uncle.'

They sailed north along the west coast, and then up the River Arend to the shallows a few leagues west of Vo Mimbre. Then they took to horse and rode through spring sunshine to the fabled city of the Mimbrate Arends.

The court of King Korodullin was thunderstruck by Mandorallen's announcement that Mimbrate Arends had been discovered on the far side of the world. Courtiers and functionaries were sent scurrying off to various libraries to compose suitable replies to the greetings sent from King Oldorin.

The copy of the Accords of Dal Perivor delivered to the throne by Lelldorin, however, evoked troubled expressions on the faces of several of the more seasoned members of the court. 'I do fear me, your Majesties,' one elderly courtier observed to Korodullin and Mayaseran, 'that our poor Arendia hath once more fallen behind the rest of the civilized world. Always in the past have we taken some comfort in the well-nigh eternal strife between Alorn and Angarak and the more recent conflict between Mallorean and Murgo, thinking perhaps that *their* discord in some measure excused ours. This scant comfort, methinks, will not long be available to us. Shall we let it be said that only in this most tragic of kingdoms doth rancor and rude war still prevail? How may we hold up our heads in a peaceful world so long as childish bickering and idiotic intestine war do mar our relationships with each other?'

'I find thy words highly offensive, my Lord,' a stiff-necked young baron denounced the old man. 'No true Mimbrate could ever refuse to heed the stern urgings of honor.'

'I speak not of Mimbrates only, my Lord,' the old man replied mildly. 'I speak of all Arends, Asturians as well as Mimbrates.'

'Asturians *have* no honor,' the baron sneered.

Lelldorin immediately went for his sword.

'Nay, my young friend,' Mandorallen said, restraining the impetuous youth. 'the insult hath been delivered here – on Mimbrate soil. Thus it is *my* responsibility – and pleasure – to answer it.' He stepped forward. 'Thy words were perhaps hasty, my Lord,' he said politely to the arrogant baron. 'I pray thee, reconsider them.'

'I have said what I have said, Sir Knight,' the young hothead declared.

'Thou hast spoken discourteously to a revered counsellor of the king,' Mandorallen said firmly, 'and thou hast delivered a mortal insult unto our brethren of the north.'

'I *have* no Asturian brethren,' the knight declared. 'I do not deign to acknowledge kinship with miscreants and traitors.'

Mandorallen sighed. 'I pray thee, forgive me, your Majesty,' he apologized to the king. 'Mayhap thou wouldst have the ladies withdraw, for I propose to speak bluntly.'

No force on earth, however, could have dragged the ladies of the court from the throne room at that time.

Mandorallen turned back toward the insolently sneering baron. 'My Lord,' the great knight said distantly, 'I find thy face apelike and thy form misshapen. Thy beard, moreover, is an offense against decency, resembling more closely the scabrous fur which doth decorate the hinder portion of a mongrel dog than a proper adornment for a human face. Is it possible that thy mother, seized by some wild lechery, did dally at some time past with a randy goat?'

The baron went livid and he spluttered, unable to speak.

'Thou seemeth wroth, my Lord,' Mandorallen said to him in that same deceptively mild tone, 'or mayhap thine unseemly breeding hath robbed thy tongue of human speech.' He looked critically at the baron. 'I do perceive, my Lord, that thou art afflicted with cowardice as well as lack of breeding, for, in truth, no man of honor would endure such deadly insult as those which I have delivered unto thee without some response. Therefore, I fear I must goad thee further.' He removed his gauntlet.

As all the world knew, it was customary to hurl one's gauntlet to the floor when issuing a challenge. Mandorallen somehow missed the floor. The young baron staggered backward, spitting teeth and blood. 'Thou art no longer a youth, Sir Mandorallen,' he raged. 'Long hast thou used thy questionable reputation to avoid combat. Methinks it is time for thee to be truly tried.'

'It speaks,' Mandorallen said with feigned astonishment. 'Behold this wonder, My Lords and Ladies – a talking dog.'

The court laughed at that.

'Let us proceed to the lower court, My Lord of Fleas,' Mandorallen continued. 'Mayhap a pass at arms with so elderly and feeble a knight shall give thee entertainment.'

The next ten minutes were very long for the insolent young baron. Mandorallen, who could undoubtedly have split him down the middle with one stroke, toyed with him instead, inflicting numerous painful and humiliating injuries. None of the bones the great knight broke were absolutely essential, however, and none of the cuts and contusions were incapacitating. The baron reeled about, trying desperately to protect himself as Mandorallen skillfully peeled his armor off him in chunks and pieces. Finally, apparently growing bored with the whole business, the champion of Arendia broke both of the young man's shinbones with a single stroke. The baron howled with pain as he fell.

'Prithee, my Lord,' Mandorallen chided, 'modulate thy shrieks of anguish, lest thou alarm the ladies. Groan quietly, an it please thee, and keep this unseemly writhing to a minimum.' He turned sternly to a hushed and even frightened crowd. 'And, he added, 'should any other here share this rash youth's prejudices, let him speak now, 'ere I sheath my sword, for truly, it is fatigueing to draw the weapon again and again.' He looked around. 'Let us proceed then, my Lords, for this foolishness doth weary me, and presently I shall grow irritable.'

Whatever their views were, the knights of the royal court chose at that point to keep them to themselves.

Ce'Nedra gravely stepped out into the courtyard. 'My knight,' she said proudly to Mandorallen. Then her eyes sparkled with mischief. 'I do perceive that thy prowess doth remain undiminished even though cruel eld doth palsy thy limbs and snow down silvery hair upon thy raven locks.'

'Eld?' Mandorallen protested.

'I'm only teasing, Mandorallen,' she laughed. 'Put away your sword. No one else wants to play with you today.'

They bade farewell to Mandorallen, Lelldorin, and Relg, who intended to return to Taiba and their children in Maragor from Vo Mimbre.

'Mandorallen!' King Anheg bellowed as they rode away from the city, 'when winter gets here, come up to Val Alorn, and we'll take Barak and go boar-hunting.'

'I surely will, your Majesty,' Mandorallen promised from the battlements.

'I *like* that man,' Anheg said expansively.

They took ship again and sailed north to the city of Sendar to advise King Fulrach of the Accords of Dal Perivor. Silk and Velvet were to sail north on *Seabird* with Barak and Anheg, and the rest of them planned a leisurely ride across the mountains to Algaria and from thence down into the Vale.

The farewells at wharfside were brief, in part because they would all see each other again shortly, and in part because none of them wanted to appear over-emotional. Garion took his leave of Silk and Barak in particular with a great deal of reluctance. The two oddly matched men had been his companions for more than half his life, and the prospect of being separated from them caused him an obscure kind of pain. The earth-shaking adventures were over now, and things would not ever really be the same.

'Do you think you can stay out of trouble now?' Barak asked him gruffly, obviously feeling the same way. 'It upsets Merel when she wakes up in the morning to find that she's been sharing her bed with a bear.'

'I'll do my best,' Garion promised.

'Do you remember what I told you that time just outside Winold – when it was so frosty that morning?' Silk asked.

Garion frowned, trying to remember.

'I said that we were living in momentous times, and that now was the time to be alive to share in those events.'

'Oh yes, now I remember.'

'I've had some time to think about it, and I believe I'd like to reconsider.' Silk grinned suddenly, and Garion knew that the little man did not mean one word he said.

'We'll see you at the Alorn council later this summer, Garion,' Anheg shouted across the rail as *Seabird* prepared to depart. 'It's at your place this year. Maybe if we work on it, we can teach you to sing properly.'

They left the city of Sendar early the next morning and took the high road to Muros. Although it was not, strictly speaking, necessary, Garion had decided to see his friends all home. The gradual eroding of their company as they had sailed north had been depressing, and Garion was not quite ready yet to be separated from *all* of them.

They rode across Sendaria in late spring sunshine, crossed the mountains into Algaria, and reached the Stronghold a week or so later. King Cho-Hag was over-joyed at the outcome of the meeting at Korim, and startled at the results of the impromptu conference at Dal Perivor. Because Cho-Hag was far more stable than the brilliant but sometimes erratic Anheg, Belgarath and Garion went into somewhat greater detail about the astonishing elevation of Eriond.

'He always was a strange boy,' Cho-Hag mused in his deep, quiet voice when they had finished, 'but then, this entire series of events has been strange. We've been privileged to live in important times, my friends.'

'We have indeed,' Belgarath agreed. 'Let's hope that things quiet down now – for a while, at least.'

'Father,' Hettar said then, 'King Urgit of the Murgos asked me to convey his appreciation to you.'

'You met the Murgo King? And we're not at war?' Cho-Hag was amazed.

'Urgit's not like any other Murgo you've ever met, Father,' Hettar told him. 'He wanted to thank you for killing Taur Urgas.'

'That's a novel sentiment coming from a son.'

Garion explained Urgit's peculiar background, and the normally reserved King of Algaria burst out in peal after peal of laughter. 'I knew Prince Kheldar's father,' he said. 'That's exactly the kind of thing he *would* have done.'

The ladies were gathered about Geran and about Adara's growing brood of children. Garion's cousin was at the ungainly stage of her pregnancy, and she sat most of the time now with a dreamy smile on her face as she listened to the inexorable changes nature was imposing on her body. The revelation of the dual pregnancies of Ce'Nedra and Polgara filled Adara and Queen Silar with wonder, and Poledra sat among them, smiling mysteriously. Poledra, Garion was sure, knew far more than she was revealing.

After about ten days, Durnik grew restless. 'We've been away for a long while, Pol,' he said one morning. 'There's still time to put in a crop, and I'm sure we'll need to tidy up a bit – mend fences, check the roof, that sort of thing.'

'Anything you say, dear,' she agreed placidly. Pregnancy had notably altered Polgara. Nothing seemed to upset her now.

On the day of their departure, Garion went down to the courtyard to saddle Chretienne. Although there were plenty of Algar clansmen here in the Stronghold who would have been more than willing to have performed the task for him, he feigned a desire to attend to it himself. The others were engaged in extended farewells, and Garion knew that about one more goodbye right now would probably reduce him to tears.

'That's a very good horse, Garion.'

It was his cousin Adara. Her face had the serenity that pregnancy bestowed upon women, and looking at her convinced Garion once again just how lucky Hettar really was. Since he had first met her, there had always been a special bond and a special kind of love between Garion and Adara. 'Zakath gave him to me,' he replied. If they confined their conversation to the subject of horses, he was fairly certain that he'd be able to keep his emotions under control.

Adara, however, was not there to talk about horses. She put one hand gently to the back of his neck and kissed him. 'Farewell, my kinsman,' she said softly.

'Goodbye, Adara,' he said, his voice growing thick. 'Goodbye.'

CHAPTER TWENTY-EIGHT

King Belgarion of Riva, Overlord of the West, Lord of the Western Sea, Godslayer, and general all-round hero had an extended arguement with his co-ruler, Queen Ce'Nedra of Riva, Imperial Princess of the Tolnedran Empire and Jewel of the House of Borune. The subject of their discussion hinged on the question of just who should have the privilege of carrying Crown Prince Geran, Heir to the Throne of Riva, hereditary Keeper of the Orb and, until recently, The Child of Dark. The conversation lasted for quite some time as the royal pair rode with their family from the Stronghold of the Algars to the Vale of Aldur.

Ultimately, albeit somewhat reluctantly, Queen Ce' Nedra relented. As Belgarath the Sorcerer had predicted, Queen Ce'Nedra's arms had at last grown tired of continually carrying her young son, and she relinquished him with some relief.

'Make sure he doesn't fall off,' she warned her husband.

'Yes, dear,' Garion replied, settling his son on Chretienne's neck just in front of the saddle.

'And don't let him get sunburned.'

Now that he had been rescued from Zandramas, Geran was a good-natured little boy. He spoke in half-phrases, his small face very serious as he tried to explain things to his father. Very importantly, he pointed out deer and rabbits as they rode south, and he dozed from time to time, resting his blond, curly head against his father's chest in absolute contentment. He was restive one morning, however, and Garion, without really thinking about it, removed the Orb from the pommel of his sword and gave it to his son to play with. Geran was delighted, and with a kind of bemused wonder he held the glowing jewel between his hands to stare with fascination into its depths. Often, he would hold it to his ear to listen by the hour to its song. The Orb, it appeared, was even more delighted than the little boy.

'That's really very disturbing, Garion,' Beldin chided. 'You've turned the most powerful object in the universe into a child's plaything.'

'It's his, after all – or it will be. They ought to get to know each other, wouldn't you say?'

'What if he loses it?'

'Beldin, do you really think the Orb *can* be lost?'

The game, however, came rather abruptly to an end when Poledra reined in her horse beside the Overlord of the West. 'He's too young to be doing this sort of thing, Garion,' she said reprovingly. She reached out her arm and a curiously twisted and knotted stick appeared in her hand. 'Put the Orb away, Garion,' she said. 'Give him this to play with instead.'

'That's the stick with only one end, isn't it?' he said suspiciously, remembering the toy Belgarath had once shown him in the cluttered tower – the toy which had occupied Aunt Pol's mind during her babyhood.

Poledra nodded. 'It should keep him busy,' she said.

Geran willingly gave up the Orb for the new toy. The Orb, however, muttered complaints in Garion's ear for the next several hours.

They reached the cottage a day or so later. Poledra looked rather critically down from the hill-top above it. 'You've made some changes, I see,' she said to her daughter.

'Do you mind, mother?' Aunt Pol asked.

'Of course not, Polgara. A house should reflect the character of its owner.'

'I'm sure there are a million things to do,' Durnik said. 'Those fences really need attention. We'll have hundreds of Algar cows in the dooryard if I don't mend them.'

'And I'm sure the cottage needs a thorough cleaning,' his wife added.

411

They rode down the hill, dismounted, and went inside. 'Impossible,' Polgara exclaimed, looking about in dismay at the negligibly thin film of dust lying over everything. 'We'll need some brooms, Durnik,' she said.

'Of course, dear,' he agreed.

Belgarath was rummaging through the pantry.

'None of that now, father,' Polgara told him crisply. 'I want you and Uncle Beldin and Garion to go out there and clear the weeds out of my kitchen garden.'

'*What?*' he demanded incredulously.

'I'll want to plant tomorrow,' she told him. 'Open the ground for me, Father.'

Garion, Beldin, and Belgarath rather disconsolately went out to the leanto where Durnik kept his tools.

Garion looked with a sense of defeat at Aunt Pol's kitchen garden, which seemed quite large enough to provide food for a small army.

Beldin gave the ground a few desultory chops with his hoe. 'This is ridiculous!' he burst out. He threw down his hoe and pointed one finger at the ground. As he moved the finger, a neat furrow of freshly plowed earth moved resolutely across the garden.

'Aunt Pol will be angry,' Garion warned the hunchback.

'Not if she doesn't catch us,' Beldin growled, looking at the cottage where Polgara, Poledra, and the Rivan Queen were busy with brooms and dust-cloths. 'Your turn, Belgarath,' he said. 'Try to keep the furrows straight.'

'Let's see if we can coax some ale from Pol before we rake it,' Beldin suggested when they had finished. 'This is hot work – even doing it this way.'

As it happened, Durnik had also returned to the house briefly to refresh himself before returning to the fence-line. The ladies were busily wielding their brooms, stirring up the dust, which, Garion observed, stubbornly settled back on places already swept. Dust was like that sometimes.

'Where's Geran?' Ce'Nedra suddenly exclaimed, dropping her broom and looking around in dismay.

Polgara's eyes went distant. 'Oh, dear,' she sighed.

'Durnik,' she said quite calmly, 'go fish him out of the creek, please.'

'*What?*' Ce'Nedra almost screamed as Durnik, moving rapidly, went outside.

'He's all right, Ce'Nedra,' Polgara assured her. 'He just fell into the creek, that's all.'

'That's *all?*' Ce'Nedra's voice went up another octave.

'It's a common pastime for little boys,' Polgara told her. 'Garion did it, Eriond did it, and now Geran's doing it. Don't worry. He swims rather well, actually.'

'How did he learn to swim?'

'I haven't the faintest idea. Maybe little boys are born with the ability – some of them, anyway. Garion was the only one who tried drowning.'

'I was starting to get the hang of swimming, Aunt Pol,' he objected, 'before I came up under that log and hit my head.'

Ce'Nedra stared at him in horror, and then she quite suddenly broke down and began to cry.

Durnik was carrying Geran by the back of his tunic when he returned. The little boy was dripping wet, but seemed quite happy, nonetheless. 'He's really very muddy, Pol,' the smith noted. 'Eriond used to get wet, but I don't think he ever got this muddy.'

'Take him outside, Ce'Nedra,' Polgara instructed. 'He's dripping mud on our clean floor. Garion, there's a washtub in the leanto. Put it in the dooryard and fill it.' She smiled at Geran's mother. 'It's about time for him to have a bath anyway. For some reason, little boys always seem to need bathing. Garion used to get dirty even while he was asleep.'

On one perfect evening, Garion joined Belgarath just outside the cottage door. 'You seem a bit pensive, Grandfather. What's the problem?'

'I've been thinking about living arrangements. Poledra's going to be moving back into my tower with me.'

'So?'

'We're probably going to become involved in a decade

413

or so of cleaning – and hanging window curtains. How can a man look out at the world with window curtains in his way?'

'Maybe she won't make such an issue of it. Back on Perivor, she said that wolves aren't as compulsively tidy as birds are.'

'She lied, Garion. Believe me, she lied.'

Two guests rode up a few days later. Despite the fact that it was almost summer now, Yarblek still wore his shabby felt overcoat, his shaggy fur hat, and a disconsolate expression. Vella, the overwhelmingly sensual Nadrak dancer, wore her usual tight-fitting black leather.

'What are you up to, Yarblek?' Belgarath asked Silk's partner.

'This wasn't my idea, Belgarath. Vella insisted.'

'All right,' Vella said in a commanding voice, 'I haven't got all day. Let's get on with this. Get everybody out of the house. I want witnesses to this.'

'What exactly are we witnessing, Vella?' Ce'Nedra asked the dark-haired girl.

'Yarblek's going to sell me.'

'*Vella!*' Ce'Nedra exclaimed, outraged, *'that's revolting!'*

'Oh, bother that,' Vella snapped. Bother was not precisely the word Vella used. She looked around. 'Are we all here?'

'That's everybody,' Belgarath told her.

'Good.' She slid down from her saddle and sat cross-legged on the grass. 'Let's get down to business. You – Beldin, or Feldegast, or whatever you want to call yourself – one time back in Mallorea, you said you wanted to buy me. Were you serious?'

Beldin blinked. 'Well—' he floundered, 'I suppose I was, sort of.'

'I want a yes or a no, Beldin,' she said crisply.

'All right then, yes. You're not a bad-looking wench, and you curse and swear rather prettily.'

'Good. What are you prepared to offer for me?'

Beldin choked, his face going suddenly red.

'Don't dawdle, Beldin,' she told him. 'We haven't got all day for this. Make Yarblek an offer.'

'Are you serious?' Yarblek exclaimed.

'I've never been more serious in my life. How much are you willing to pay for me, Beldin?'

'Vella,' Yarblek protested, 'this is absolute nonsense.'

'Shut up, Yarblek. Well, Beldin? How much?'

'Everything I own,' he replied, his eyes filled with a kind of wonder.

'That's a little unspecific. Give me a number. We can't haggle without a number.'

Beldin scratched at his matted beard. 'Belgarath,' he said, 'have you still got that diamond you found in Maragor that time before the Tolnedran invasion?'

'I think so. It's somewhere in my tower, I believe.'

'So's half the clutter in the world.'

'It's in the bookcase on the south wall,' Poledra supplied, 'behind that rat-chewed copy of the Darine Codex.'

'Really?' Belgarath said. 'How did you know about that?'

'Remember what Cyradis called me at Rheon?'

'The woman who watches?'

'Does that answer your question?'

'Would you lend it to me?' Beldin asked his brother. 'I suppose "give" would be a better word. I doubt that I'll ever be in a position to repay you.'

'Certainly, Beldin,' Belgarath said. 'I wasn't really using it anyway.'

'Could you get it for me?'

Belgarath nodded, and then he concentrated, holding out his hand.

The diamond that suddenly appeared in his hand was almost like a chunk of ice, except that it had a definite pinkish cast to it.

It was also somewhat larger than an apple.

'Torak's teeth and toenails!' Yarblek exclaimed.

'An' would th' two of ye, consumed with greed though

415

ye may be, consider this triflin' thing a suitable price fer this beguilin' wench yer both so set on sellin'?' Beldin said, lapsing into Feldegast's brogue and pointing at the stone resting on Belgarath's hand.

'That's worth a hundred times more than has ever been paid for any woman since time began,' Yarblek said in an awed tone.

'Then that ought to be about the right price,' Vella said triumphantly. 'Yarblek, when you get back to Gar og Nadrak, I want you to spread that word around. I want every woman in the kingdom for the next hundred years to cry herself to sleep every night just thinking about the price I brought.'

'You're a cruel woman, Vella,' Yarblek grinned.

'It's a question of pride,' she said, tossing her blue-black hair. 'There, now, that didn't take too long at all, did it?' She rose to her feet and dusted off her hands. 'Yarblek,' she said, 'have you got my ownership papers?'

'Yes.'

'Get them and sign me over to my new owner.'

'We have to divide up the price first, Vella.' He looked mournfully at the pink stone. 'It's really going to be a shame to split that beauty,' he said.

'Keep it,' she said indifferently. 'I don't need it.'

'Are you sure?'

'It's yours. Get those papers, Yarblek.'

'Are you *really* sure about all this, Vella?' he asked her again.

'I've never been more sure of anything in my life.'

'But he's so *ugly* – sorry, Beldin, but it's the truth. Vella, what could possibly have made you choose *him*?'

'Only one thing,' she said.

'What's that?'

'He can fly.' Her tone was filled with a kind of wonder.

Yarblek shook his head and went to his saddlebag. He brought back the ownership papers and signed them over to Beldin.

'An' what would I be wantin' with these?' Beldin

416

asked. The brogue, Garion realized, was a way to hide emotions so deep that the hunchback was almost afraid of them.

'Keep them or throw them away,' Vella shrugged. 'They don't have any meaning for me any more.'

'Very well then, me darlin',' he said. He crumpled the papers up into a ball and held the ball out on the palm of his hand. The wad of paper burst into flame and burned down to ashes. 'There,' he said, blowing the ashes away. 'Now they won't be troublin' us any more. Is that it? Is that all there is to it?'

'Not quite,' she said. She bent and removed the two daggers from her boot-tops. Then she took the other from her belt. 'Here,' she said, her eyes now very soft, 'I won't be needing these anymore.' She handed the daggers to her new owner.

'Oh,' Polgara said, her eyes filling with tears.

'What is it, Pol?' Durnik asked, his face filled with concern.

'That's the most sacred thing a Nadrak woman can do,' Polgara answered, touching at her eyes with the hem of her apron. 'She just totally surrendered herself to Beldin. That's just beautiful.'

'An' what would I be needin' knives fer?' Beldin asked with a gentle smile. One by one he tossed the daggers into the air, where they vanished in little puffs of smoke. He turned. 'Goodbye, Belgarath,' he said to the old sorcerer. 'We've had some fun, haven't we?'

'I've enjoyed it.' Belgarath had tears in his eyes.

'And Durnik,' Beldin said, 'it looks as if you're here to replace me.'

'You talk like a man about to die,' Durnik said.

'Oh, no, Durnik, I'm not going to die. I'm just going to change a bit. You two say goodbye to the twins for me. Explain things to them. Enjoy your good fortune, Yarblek, but I still think I got the better of that bargain. Garion, try to keep the world running.'

'Eriond's supposed to take care of that.'

'I know, but keep an eye on him. Don't let Him get into trouble.'

Beldin didn't say anything to Ce'Nedra. He simply kissed her rather noisily. Then he also kissed Poledra. She regarded him fondly, her golden eyes filled with love.

'Goodbye, old cow,' he said at last to Polgara, slapping her familiarly on the bottom. He looked meaningfully at her waist. 'I told you that you were going to get fat if you kept eating all those sweets.'

She kissed him then with tears in her eyes.

'An' now, me darlin',' he said to Vella, 'let's be walkin' a bit apart. There's much t' be said before we leave.' Then the two of them walked hand in hand up toward the top of the hill. When they reached it, they stopped and spoke together for a while. Then they embraced and exchanged a long, fervent kiss, and then, while they were still locked in each others' arms, they shimmered and seemed almost to dissolve.

The one hawk was very familiar. The bands on his wings were electric blue. The other hawk, however, had lavender bands on *her* wings. Together, they thrust themselves into the air and rose in an effortless spiral up and up through the glowing air. Higher and higher they spun in that formal wedding dance until they were no more than a pair of specks winging up and out over the Vale.

And then they were gone, never again to return.

Garion and the others remained at the cottage for another two weeks. Then, noting that Polgara and Durnik were beginning to show signs of wanting to be alone, Poledra suggested that the rest of them go on to the Vale. Promising to return that evening, Garion and Ce'Nedra took their son and the nearly grown wolf pup and accompanied Belgarath and Poledra down into the heart of the Vale.

They reached Belgarath's familiar squat tower about noon and started up the stairway to the circular room at the top. 'Watch that step,' the old man said absently as they climbed. This time, however, Garion stopped, letting the rest go on ahead. He reached down, heaved up the stone slab that was the step, and looked under it. A round stone about the size of a hazel-nut lay under the slab. Garion removed the stone, put it in his pocket, and replaced the slab. He noticed that the other steps were worn in the center, but this one was not, and he wondered just how many centuries – or eons – the old man had been stepping over it. He went on up, feeling rather pleased with himself.

'What were you doing?' Belgarath asked him.

'Fixing that step,' Garion replied. He handed the old man the round pebble. 'It was rocking because this was under it. It's steady now.'

'I'm going to miss that step, Garion,' his grandfather complained. He stared at the pebble, frowning. 'Oh,' he said, 'now I remember. I put this under the step on purpose.'

'Whatever for?' Ce'Nedra asked him.

'It's a diamond, Ce'Nedra,' Belgarath shrugged. 'I wanted to find out how long it would take to grind it down to a powder.'

'A diamond?' she gasped, her eyes widening.

'You can have it, if you'd like,' he said, tossing it to her.

Then, taking into account her Tolnedran heritage, Ce'Nedra performed an act of sheer unselfishness. 'No thanks, Belgarath,' she said. 'I wouldn't want to separate you from an old friend. Garion and I can put it back where it was when we leave.'

Belgarath laughed.

Geran and the young wolf were playing together near one of the windows. There was a fair amount of mauling involved in their play, and the wolf was cheating outrageously, seizing every chance to lick Geran's neck and face, which always sent the little boy into uncontrolled giggling.

Poledra was looking around at the cluttered circular room. 'It's good to be home,' she said. She was fondly caressing the back of the owl-clawed chair. 'I spent almost a thousand years perched on this chair,' she told Garion.

'What were you doing, Grandmother,' Ce'Nedra asked her. Ce'Nedra had begun, perhaps without realizing it, to mimic Garion's customary forms of address.

'Watching *him*,' the tawny-haired woman replied. 'I knew that eventually he'd get around to noticing me. I didn't really think it would take him all that long, though. I really had to do something out of the ordinary to get his attention.'

'Oh?'

'I chose *this* form,' Poledra said, touching one hand to her breasts. 'He seemed more interested in me as a woman than he did when I was an owl – or a wolf.'

'There was something I always meant to ask you,' Belgarath said. 'There weren't any other wolves around when we met. What were you doing out there?'

'Waiting for you.'

He blinked. 'You knew I was coming?'

'Of course.'

'When was that?' Ce'Nedra asked.

'Just after Torak stole the Orb from Aldur,' Belgarath replied, his mind obviously on something else. 'My Master had sent me north to advise Belar of what had happened. I took the form of the wolf to make better time. Poledra and I met somewhere in what's now northern Algaria.' He looked at his wife. 'Who told you I was coming?' he asked her.

'No one had to tell me, Belgarath,' she replied. 'I was born knowing you'd come – someday. You certainly took your time about it, though.' She looked around critically. 'I think we should tidy up a bit here,' she suggested, 'and those windows definitely need some curtains.'

'See?' Belgarath said to Garion.

There were kisses and embraces and handshakes and a few tears – although not really very many of those. Then Ce'Nedra picked up Geran, and Garion the wolf, and they started down the stairs.

'Oh,' Garion said when they were halfway down, 'give me the diamond. I'll put it back where it belongs.'

'Wouldn't an ordinary pebble work just as well, Garion?' Her eyes were suddenly calculating.

'Ce'Nedra, if you want a diamond so badly, I'll buy you one.'

'I know, Garion, but if I keep this one I'll have two.'

He laughed, firmly took the diamond from her tightly clenched little fist, and returned it to its place under the step.

They mounted their horses and rode slowly away from the tower in the bright sunshine of a spring noon. Ce'Nedra held Geran, and the wolf scampered alongside, dashing out from time to time to chase rabbits.

After they had gone a little way, Garion heard a familiar whisper of sound. He reined Chretienne in. 'Ce'Nedra,' he said, pointing back at the tower, 'look.'

She looked back. 'I don't see anything.'

'Wait. They'll be out in a moment.'

'They?'

'Grandmother and Grandfather. There they come now.'

Two wolves bounded out through the open door of the tower and ran across the grassy plain, matching stride for stride as they ran. There was a kind of unbridled freedom and an intense joy in the way they ran.

'I thought they were going to get started with the cleaning,' Ce'Nedra said.

'This is more important, Ce'Nedra. Much, much more important.'

They reached the cottage just as the sun was going down. Durnik was still busy in the fields, and they could hear Polgara singing softly in the kitchen. Ce'Nedra went inside, and Garion and the wolf crossed the field to join Durnik.

The meal that evening consisted of a roast goose and everything that went with it: gravy, dressing, three kinds of vegetables, and freshly baked bread, still hot from the oven and dripping with butter.

'Where did you get the goose, Pol?' Durnik asked.

'I cheated,' she admitted calmly.

'Pol!'

'I'll explain it some other time, dear. Let's eat it before it all gets cold.'

After supper they sat near the fire. They didn't really need a fire – indeed, the doors and windows were even open – but fire and hearth were a part of home, sometimes necessary even when not, strictly speaking, needed.

Polgara held Geran, her cheek against his curls and a dreamy look of contentment on her face. 'Just practicing,' she said quietly to Ce'Nedra.

'There's no way you could ever forget that, Aunt Pol,' the Rivan Queen said. 'You've raised hundreds of little boys.'

'Well, not quite *that* many, dear, but it never hurts to keep one's hand in.'

The wolf lay sound asleep on the hearth before the fire. He was making small yipping noises, however, and his feet were twitching.

'He's dreaming,' Durnik smiled.

'I wouldn't be surprised,' Garion said. 'He spent the whole time while we were coming back from Grandfather's tower chasing rabbits. He didn't catch any, though. I don't think he was really trying.'

'Speaking of dreaming,' Aunt Pol said, rising to her feet. 'You two and your son and your puppy will want an early start in the morning. Why don't we all go to bed.'

They arose at first light the next morning, ate a hearty breakfast, and then Durnik and Garion went out to saddle the horses.

The farewells were not prolonged. There was no real need for extended farewells among these four, because they would never really be apart. There were a few brief words, a few kisses and a gruff handshake between Durnik and Garion, and then the Rivan King and his family rode up the hill.

Halfway to the top, Ce'Nedra turned in her saddle. 'Aunt Pol,' she called, 'I love you.'

'Yes dear,' Polgara called back, 'I know. I love you too.'

And then Garion led the way on up the hill and toward home.

EPILOGUE

It was mid autumn. The Alorn council had taken place at Riva late that summer, and it had been boisterous, even rowdy. It had been attended by many who would not normally have been present. Non-Alorn rulers – and their queens – had virtually outnumbered the Alorn monarchs. Ladies from all over the west had descended upon Ce'Nedra and Polgara, showering them with congratulations, and young children had gathered about Geran, attracted by his sunny disposition – and by the fact that the little boy had somehow discovered a long-unused route to the pastry kitchen and all the treasures contained therein. If the truth were to be known, there was very little in the way of business conducted that year. And then, as always, a series of late summer storms announced that the meetings were at an end and it was time for the visitors to begin thinking seriously about going home. This had always been the advantage of holding the council in Riva. Although guests might prefer to linger, the steady march of the seasons persuaded them that it was time to depart.

Affairs had settled down in Riva. There had been a wild celebration when the king and his wife had at last returned with Crown Prince Geran, but no people, no matter how emotional, could celebrate forever, and after a few weeks things had returned to normal.

Garion spent most days closeted with Kail now. Many decisions had been made in his absence. Although, almost without exception, he approved of Kail's handling of those matters, he still needed to be briefed on them and some of those decisions needed to be ratified by the royal signature.

Ce'Nedra's pregnancy was proceeding along expected

lines. The little queen bloomed and swelled and became increasingly short-tempered. The peculiar hungers for exotic foods which sometimes beset ladies in that delicate condition were not nearly as much fun for the Rivan Queen as they were for most other ladies. There has long been a suspicion in the male half of the population that these gastronomical yearnings are nothing more than a peculiar form of entertainment for their wives. The more exotic and unobtainable a given food might be and the more extreme the lengths to which a doting husband must go to put his hands on it, the more the ladies would insist that they would absolutely *die* if it were not provided in abundance. Garion privately suspected that the whole business involved little more than a desire for reassurance. If a husband proved willing to disassemble the known world to obtain strawberries out of season or strange seafoods normally found only in waters half a world away, it was a sure sign that he still loved his wife, despite her disappearing waistline. It was not nearly as much fun for Ce'Nedra, because each time she made a seemingly impossible request, Garion simply stepped into the next room, created the foodstuff in question on the spot, and presented it to her – usually on a silver platter. Ce'Nedra grew increasingly sulky about the whole business and finally gave up on it entirely.

And then late on a very frosty autumn evening, an ice-coated Mallorean ship entered the harbor, and her captain delivered a packet of neatly folded parchment bearing the seal of Zakath of Mallorea. Garion thanked the seaman profusely, offered him and his crew the hospitality of the Citadel and then immediately carried Zakath's letter to the royal apartment. Ce'Nedra was sitting by the fire, knitting. Geran and the young wolf were lying together on the hearth, both of them dozing and twitching slightly as they dreamed. The two always slept together. Ce'Nedra had finally given up the idea of trying to keep them separate at night, since no door in the world could be effectively locked from both sides.

'What is it, dear?' she asked as Garion entered.

'We just received a letter from Zakath,' he replied.

'Oh? What does he say?'

'I haven't read it yet.'

'Open it, Garion. I'm dying to find out what's happening in Mal Zeth.'

Garion broke the seal and unfolded the parchment. 'For his Majesty, King Belgarion of Riva,' he read aloud, 'Overlord of the West, Godslayer, Lord of the Western Sea, and for his revered Queen, Ce'Nedra, co-ruler of the Isle of the Winds, Princess of the Tolnedran Empire, and Jewel of the House of Borune from Zakath, Emperor of all of Angarak.' . . .

'I hope this finds you both in good health and I send greetings to your daughter, whether she has already arrived or if her birth be still impending. (I have not, I hasten to assure you, become suddenly clairvoyant. Cyradis said once that she was no longer blessed with her vision. I have come to suspect that she was not entirely truthful on that score.)

A great deal has happened here since we parted. The imperial court, I suspect, was more than a little pleased by the alteration in my personality which was the direct result of our journey to Korim and by what happened there. I must have been an impossible ruler to deal with. This is not to suggest that all here in Mal Zeth has become a fairy tale of good feeling and felicity. The general staff was mightily upset when I declared my intention to conclude a peace treaty with King Urgit. You know how generals are. If you take their favorite war away from them, they snivel and complain and pout like spoiled children. I had to step on a few necks quite firmly. Incidentally, I recently promoted Atesca to the position of Commander-in-Chief of the armies of Mallorea. This also enraged the other members of the general staff, but no one can please everybody. Urgit and I have been in communication with each other, and I find him to be a rare fellow – quite nearly as droll as his brother. I think we'll get on well together. The bureaucracy very nearly went into collective apoplexy when I announced the autonomy of the Dalasian Protectorates. It's my feeling that the Dals must be permitted to go their own way, but many members of the bureaucracy have vested interests there, and they sniveled and complained and pouted almost as much as the generals did. That came to an abrupt halt however, when I announced my intention to have Brador conduct a thorough audit of the affairs of every Bureau Chief in the government. The sound of a massive divestiture of all holdings in the protectorates was well-nigh deafening.

Rather surprisingly, an ancient Grolim arrived at the palace shortly after we returned from Dal Perivor. I was about to send him away, but Eriond insisted rather firmly that he remain. The old fellow had some unpronounceable Grolim name, but Eriond changed it to Pelath for some reason. The old boy has a sweet disposition, but he sometimes speaks very strangely. The language he uses sounds very much like that of the Ashabine Oracles or the Mallorean Gospels of the Dals. Very peculiar.'

'I'd almost forgotten that,' Garion interrupted his reading.

'What's that, dear?' Ce'Nedra asked him, looking up from her knitting.

'Do you remember that old Grolim we met in Peldane? That night when the chicken bit you?'

'Yes. He seemed like a very nice old man.'

'He was more than that, Ce'Nedra. He was also a prophet, and the Voice told me that he was going to become Eriond's first disciple.'

'Eriond has a very long arm, hasn't he? Keep reading, Garion.'

'Cyradis, Pelath and I have conferred extensively with Eriond and we've all agreed that His status should remain concealed for the time being at least. He is such an innocent that I don't want to expose Him to the depths of human depravity and chicanery just yet. Let's not discourage Him so early in His career. We all remembered Torak and His overpowering hunger for worship, but when we offered to worship Eriond, He just laughed at us. Did Polgara perhaps leave something out when she was raising him?

We did make one exception, however. A group of us, accompanied by the third, seventh, and ninth armies, visited Mal Yaska. The Temple Guardmen and Chandim attempted to flee, but Atesca rather effectively rounded them up. I waited until Eriond was off for His morning ride on that unnamed horse of His and spoke quite firmly with the assembled Grolims. I didn't want to cause Eriond any distress, but I indicated to the Grolims that I would be *most* unhappy if they did not change their religious affiliation forthwith. Atesca stood at my side, playing with his sword, so they immediately got my drift. Then, with no warning at all, Eriond appeared in the Temple. (How *does* that horse of His move so fast? The last time he had been observed that morning, He had been more than three leagues from the city.) He told them that black robes were not really all that attractive and that white ones would become them much more. Then, with no more than a faint smile, He actually changed the color of every Grolim robe in the temple. So much for His anonymity in that part of Mallorea, I'm afraid. Next, He told them that they'd no longer need their knives, and every dagger in the place disappeared. Then He extinguished the fires in the sanctum and decorated the altar with flowers. I have since been advised that these trifling modifications are universal here in Mallorea. Urgit is presently investigating to determine if similar conditions prevail in Cthol

Murgos. Our new God, I think, will take a bit of getting used to.

To make it short, the Grolims all fell down on their faces. I still suspect that at least *some* of those conversions may have been fraudulent, so I'm not contemplating a demobilization of the army just yet. Eriond told them to get back on their feet and go out and care for the sick, the poor, the orphaned, and the homeless.

On our way back to Mal Zeth, Pelath pulled his horse in beside mine, smiled that sickeningly sweet smile of his at me, and said, "My Master believes that it's time for you to change your status, Emperor of Mallorea." That gave me a bit of a turn. I was about half afraid that Eriond might suggest that I abdicate and take up sheepherding or something. Then Pelath went on. "My Master believes that you've delayed something for quite long enough."

"Oh?" I said cautiously.

"The delay is causing the Seeress of Kell a certain distress. My Master strongly suggests that you ask her to marry you. He wants that settled before anything comes along to interfere."

So, when we got to Mal Zeth, I made what I thought was a very sensible proposal and Cyradis turned me down flat! I thought my heart would stop. Then our mystic little Seeress waxed eloquent. She told me – at great length – what she thought of sensible. I've never seen her behave that way before. She was actually passionate, and some of the words she used, though archaic, were hardly flattering. I had to look some of them up, they were so obscure.'

'Good for her,' Ce'Nedra said fiercely.

'Just to make peace,' the letter went on, 'I fell to my knees and made a fatuous and embarrassingly gushy

429

proposal, and she was moved by my eloquence to relent and accept me.'

'*Men!*' Ce'Nedra snorted.

'The cost of the wedding very nearly bankrupt me. I even had to borrow money from one of Kheldar's business associates – at an outrageous rate of interest. Eriond officiated, of course, and having a God perform the ceremony really nailed down the lid on my coffin. At any rate, Cyradis and I were married last month, and I can truly say that I've never been happier in my life.'

'Oh,' Ce'Nedra said with that familiar catch in her voice, 'that's just lovely.' She went to the handkerchief.
'There's more,' Garion told her.
'Keep going,' she said, dabbing at her eyes.

'The Angarak Malloreans were not really pleased that I had chosen to marry a Dal, but they're wisely keeping their displeasure to themselves. I've changed a great deal, but not *that* much. Cyradis is having some difficulty adapting to her new status, and I simply cannot convince her that jewels are a necessary adornment for an empress. She wears flowers instead, and the slavish imitation of the ladies of the court has caused universal despair in the hearts of the jewelers here in Mal Zeth.

I was going to have my distant cousin, the Archduke Otrath, shortened by the length of his head, but he's such a pathetic fool that I discarded the idea and sent him home instead. Following a suggestion your friend Beldin made in Dal Perivor, I ordered the cretin to set his wife up in a palace in the City of Melcene and never to go near her again for the rest of his life. I understand that the lady is something of a scandal in Melcene, but she probably deserves *some* recompense for putting up with that silly ass for all those years.

That's about all from here, Garion. We're really hungry for news of all our friends and we send them our warmest greetings and affection.

Sincerely,
K̶ä̶lZakath and Empress Cyradis
Note that I'm deleting that ostentatious prefix. Oh, by the way, my cat was unfaithful to me again a few months ago. Would Ce'Nedra like a kitten? – or maybe one for your new daughter? I can send two, if you'd like.'

Z

In the early winter of that year, the Rivan Queen grew increasingly discontent, a discontentment and a waspish temper almost in direct proportion to her increasing girth. Some ladies might be uniquely suited for pregnancy; the Rivan Queen was uniquely not. She was snippy with her husband; she was short with her son; and on one occasion she even made an awkward attempt to kick the inoffending young wolf. The wolf nimbly dodged the kick, then looked with some puzzlement at Garion. 'Has one somehow given offense?' he asked.

'No,' Garion told him. 'It is only that one's mate is in some distress. The time of her whelping is approaching, and this always makes the she's of the man-things uncomfortable and short-tempered.'

'Ah,' the wolf said. 'The man-things are very strange.'

'Truly,' Garion agreed.

It was Greldik, naturally, who delivered Poledra to the Isle of the Winds in the middle of a howling blizzard.

'How did you find your way?' Garion asked the fur-clad seaman as the two of them sat before the fire in the low-beamed dining hall with tankards of ale in their hands.

'Belgarath's wife pointed the way.' Greldik shrugged. 'That's a remarkable woman, do you know that?'

'Oh, yes.'

'Do you know that not one man in my whole crew took

431

a single drink while we were at sea? Not even me. For some reason, we just didn't want any.'

'My Grandmother has strong prejudices. Will you be all right here? I want to go up and have a chat with her.'

'That's all right, Garion,' Greldik grinned, patting the nearly full ale keg affectionately. 'I'll be just fine.'

Garion went upstairs to the royal apartments.

The tawny-haired woman sat by the fire, idly stroking the young wolf's ears. Ce'Nedra was sprawled rather awkwardly on a divan.

'Ah, there you are, Garion,' Poledra said. She sniffed the air rather delicately. 'I notice you've been drinking.' Her tone was disapproving.

'I had one tankard with Greldik.'

'Would you please sit over there on the other side of the room then? One's sense of smell is quite acute, and the odor of ale turns one's stomach.'

'Is that why you disapprove of drinking?'

'Of course. What other reason could there be?'

'I think Aunt Pol disapproves on some sort of moral grounds.'

'Polgara has some obscure prejudices. Now then,' she went on seriously. 'My daughter is in no condition to travel just now, so I'm here to deliver Ce'Nedra's baby. Pol gave me all sorts of instructions, most of which I intend to ignore. Giving birth is a natural process, and the less interference the better. When it starts, I want you to take Geran and this young wolf here and go to the extreme far end of the Citadel. I'll send for you when it's all over.'

'Yes, Grandmother.'

'He's a nice boy,' Poledra said to the Rivan Queen.

'I rather like him.'

'I certainly hope so. All right, then, Garion, just as soon as the baby's born and we're sure everything's all right, you and I are going to return to the Vale. Polgara's a few weeks behind Ce'Nedra, but we really don't have too much time to waste. Pol wants you to be there when she gives birth.'

432

'You *have* to go, Garion,' Ce'Nedra said. 'I only wish *I* could.'

Garion was a bit dubious about leaving his wife so soon after she was delivered, but he definitely *did* want to be in the Vale when Aunt Pol had her baby.

It was three nights later. Garion was having a splendid dream that involved riding down a long, grassy hill with Eriond.

'Garion,' Ce'Nedra said, nudging him in the ribs.

'Yes, dear?' He was still about half asleep.

'I think you'd better go get your grandmother.'

He was fully awake immediately. 'Are you sure?'

'I've been through this before, dear,' she told him.

He rolled quickly out of bed.

'Kiss me before you go,' she told him.

He did that.

'And don't forget to take Geran and the puppy when you go off to the other end of the building. Put Geran back to bed when you get there.'

'Of course.'

A strange expression came over her face. 'I think you'd better hurry, Garion,' she suggested.

Garion bolted.

It was nearly dawn when the Queen of Riva was delivered of a baby girl. The infant had a short crop of deep red hair and green eyes. As it had for so many centuries, the Dryad strain bred true. Poledra carried the blanket-wrapped baby through the silent halls of the Citadel to the rooms where Garion sat before a fire and Geran and the wolf slept in a tangle of arms, legs, and paws on a divan.

'Is Ce'Nedra all right?' Garion asked, coming to his feet.

'She's fine,' his grandmother assured him, 'a little tired is all. It was a fairly easy delivery.'

Garion heaved a sigh of relief, then turned back the corner of the blanket to look at the small face of his daughter. 'She looks like her mother,' he said. People the world over always made that first observation, pointing out the similarities of a new-born to this parent or that as if such resemblances were somehow remarkable. Garion gently took the baby in his arms and looked into that tiny red face. The baby looked back at him, her green-eyed gaze unwavering. It was a familiar gaze. 'Good morning, Beldaran,' Garion said softly. He had made that decision quite some time ago. There would be other daughters, and they would be named after a fair number of female relatives on both sides of the family, but it somehow seemed important that his first daughter should be named for Aunt Pol's blond twin sister, a woman who, though Garion had seen only her image and then only once, was still somehow central to all their lives.

'Thank you, Garion,' Poledra said simply.

'It seems appropriate somehow,' Garion told her.

Prince Geran was not too impressed with his baby sister, but boys seldom are. 'Isn't she awfully little?' he asked when his father woke him to introduce them.

'It's the nature of babies to be little. She'll grow.'

'Good.' Geran looked at her gravely. Then, apparently feeling that he should say *something* nice about her, he added, 'She has nice hair. It's the same color as mother's, isn't it?'

'I noticed that myself.'

The bells of Riva pealed out that morning in celebration, and the Rivan people rejoiced, although there were some, many perhaps, who secretly wished that the royal infant might have been another boy, just for the sake of dynastic security. The Rivans, kingless for so many centuries, were nervous about that sort of thing.

Ce'Nedra, of course, was radiant. She expressed only minimal dissatisfaction with Garion's choice of a name for their daughter. Her Dryad heritage felt rather strongly the need for a name beginning with the traditional 'X'. She worked with it a bit, however, and came up with a satisfactory solution to the problem. Garion was fairly certain that in her own mind she had inserted an 'X' somewhere in Beldaran's name. He decided that he didn't really want to know about it.

The Rivan Queen was young and healthy, and she recovered from her confinement quickly. She remained in bed for a few days – largely for the dramatic effect on the stream of Rivan nobility and foreign dignitaries who filed through the royal bedchamber to view the tiny queen and the even tinier princess.

After a few days, Poledra spoke with Garion. 'That more or less takes care of business here,' she said, 'and we really should get started back to the Vale. Polgara's time is coming closer, you know.'

Garion nodded. 'I asked Greldik to stay,' he told her. 'He'll get us back to Sendaria faster than anybody else can.'

'He's a very undependable man, you know.'

'Aunt Pol said exactly the same thing. He's still the finest sailor in the world. I'll make arrangements to have horses put on board his ship.'

'No,' she said shortly. 'We're in a hurry, Garion. Horses would only slow us down.'

'You want to run all the way from the coast of Sendaria to the Vale?' he asked her, a little startled.

'It's not really all that far, Garion,' she smiled.

'What about supplies?'

She gave him an amused look, and he suddenly felt very foolish.

Garion's goodbyes to his family were emotional, though brief. 'Be sure to dress warmly,' Ce'Nedra instructed. 'It's winter, you know.'

He decided not to tell her exactly how he and his grandmother intended to travel.

'Oh,' she said, handing him a parchment sheet, 'give this to Aunt Pol.'

Garion looked at the sheet. It was a rather fair artist's sketch, in color, of his wife and daughter.

'It's quite good, isn't it?' Ce'Nedra said.

'Very good,' he agreed.

'You'd better run along now,' she said. 'If you stay much longer, I won't let you go at all.'

'Keep warm, Ce'Nedra,' he said, 'and look after the children.'

'Naturally. I love you, your Majesty.'

'I love you, too, your Majesty.' He kissed her and his son and daughter and quietly left the room.

The weather at sea was blustery, but the militantly impetuous Greldik paid almost no attention to weather, no matter how foul. His patched and decidedly scruffy-looking ship ran before the wind across a storm sea under far more sail than even a marginally prudent sea-captain would have crowded onto his masts, and two days later, they reached the coast of Sendaria.

'Any empty beach will do, Greldik,' Garion told him. 'We're in sort of a hurry, and if we stop at Sendar, Fulrach and Layla will tie us up with congratulations and banquets.'

'How do you propose to get off a beach without horses?' Greldik asked bluntly.

'There are ways,' Garion told him.

'More of *that* sort of thing?' Greldik said with a certain distaste.

Garion nodded.

'That's unnatural, you know.'

'I come from an unnatural sort of family.'

Greldik grunted disapprovingly and ran his ship in close to a wind-swept beach bordered on its upper edge with the rank grass of a salt-flat. 'Does this one suit you?' he asked.

'It's just fine,' Garion said.

Garion and his grandmother waited on the windy beach with their cloaks whipping around them until Greldik was well out to sea. 'I suppose we can get started now,' Garion said, shifting his sword into a more comfortable position.

'I don't know why you brought that,' Poledra said.

'The Orb wants to see Aunt Pol's baby,' he shrugged.

436

'That may just be the most irrational thing I've ever heard anyone say, Garion. Shall we go?'

They shimmered and blurred, and then two wolves loped up the beach to the bordering grass and ran smoothly inland.

It took the two of them a little more than a week to reach the Vale. They stopped only rarely to hunt and even more infrequently to rest. Garion learned a great deal about being a wolf during that week. Belgarath had given him a certain amount of instruction in the past, but Belgarath had come into wolfhood when he had been full-grown. Poledra, on the other hand, was the genuine article.

They crested the hill overlooking the cottage one snowy evening and looked down at the tidy farmstead with its fence-lines half buried in snow and the windows of the cottage glowing a warm, welcoming yellow.

'Are we in time?' Garion asked the golden-eyed wolf beside him.

'Yes,' Poledra replied. 'One suspects, however, that the decision not to burden ourselves with the beasts of the man-things was wise. The time is very close. Let us go down and find out what is happening.'

They loped on down the hill through swirling snow-flakes and changed back into their own forms in the dooryard.

The interior of the cottage was warm and bright. Polgara more than a little ungainly, was setting places for Garion and her mother at the table. Belgarath sat near the fire, and Durnik was patiently mending harness.

'I saved some supper for you,' Pol told Garion and Poledra. 'We've already eaten.'

'You knew we'd get here this evening?' Garion asked.

'Of course, dear. Mother and I always stay more or less in constant contact. How's Ce'Nedra?'

'She and Beldaran are just fine.' He said it in an offhand sort of way. Aunt Pol had surprised *him* often enough in the past. Now it was his turn.

437

She almost dropped a plate, and her glorious eyes grew wide. 'Oh, Garion,' she said, embracing him suddenly.

'Does the name please you? Just a little?'

'More than you could ever know, Garion.'

'How are you feeling, Polgara?' Poledra asked, removing her cloak.

'Fine – I think.' Aunt Pol smiled. 'I know about the procedure, of course, but this is the first time I've experienced it personally. Babies spend a great deal of time kicking at this stage, don't they? A few minutes or so ago, I think mine kicked me in three separate places at once.'

'Maybe he's punching, too,' Durnik suggested.

'He?' she smiled.

'Well – the word's just for the sake of convenience, Pol.'

'If you'd like, I could have a look and tell you if it's a he or a she,' Belgarath offered.

'Don't you dare!' Polgara told him. 'I want to find out for myself.'

The snow let up shortly before daybreak, and the clouds blew off by midmorning. The sun came out, and it glittered brightly on the new-fallen blanket of white around the cottage. The sky was intensely blue, and, though it was cold that day, the bitter chill of mid-winter had not yet set in.

Garion, Durnik, and Belgarath had been banished from the house at dawn, and they wandered about with that odd sort of uselessness men usually feel in such circumstances. At one point they stopped on the bank of the small stream that threaded its way through the farmstead. Belgarath looked down into the clear water, noting a number of dark, slim shapes just below the surface. 'Have you had time to do any fishing?' he asked Durnik.

'No,' Durnik said a bit sadly, 'and I don't seem to have the enthusiasm for it I used to.'

They all knew why, but none of them mentioned it.

Poledra brought their meals to them, but firmly insisted that they remain outside. Late in the afternoon, she put them to work boiling water over Durnik's forge, which sat in the tool shed.

'I've never seen any reason for this,' Durnik confessed, lifting another steaming kettle from his forge. 'Why do they always need boiling water?'

'They don't,' Belgarath told him. Belgarath was comfortably sprawled on a woodpile and was examining the intricately carved cradle Durnik had built. 'It's just a way to keep the men folk out from underfoot. Some female genius came up with the idea thousands of years ago, and women have been honoring the custom ever since. Just boil water, Durnik. It makes the women happy, and it's not that big a chore.'

The moon had been rising late, but the stars touched the snow with a fairy light, and all the world seemed somehow bathed in a gentle blue-white glow. It was, of all nights, among the closest to perfect Garion had ever seen, and all of nature seemed to be holding its breath.

Garion and Belgarath, noting Durnik's increasing edginess, suggested that they walk to the top of the hill to settle their suppers. They had both observed in the past that Durnik usually banished uncomfortable emotions by keeping busy.

The smith looked up at the night sky as they trudged through the snow toward the top of the hill. 'It's really a special sort of night, isn't it.' He laughed a little sheepishly. 'I suppose I'd feel that way even if it were raining,' he said.

'I know I always do,' Garion said. Then he too laughed, his breath steaming in the chill night air. 'I don't know that twice qualifies as much of an always, though,' he conceded, 'but I know what you mean. I was feeling sort of the same way myself earlier.' He looked beyond the cottage across the snowy plain lying white and still beneath the icy stars. 'Does it seem very, very quiet to you two as well?'

'There's not a hint of a breeze,' Durnik agreed, 'and the snow muffles all the sound.' He cocked his head. 'Now that you mention it, though, it does seem awfully quiet, and the stars are really bright tonight. There's a logical explanation for it, I suppose.'

Belgarath smiled at them. 'There's not a single ounce of romance in either one of you, is there? Didn't it ever occur to you that this might just *be* a very special night?'

They looked at him oddly.

'Stop and think about it,' he said. 'Pol's devoted most of her life to raising children that weren't hers. I've watched her do it, and I could feel an obscure kind of pain in her each time she took a new baby in her arms. That's going to change tonight, so in a very real sense this *is* a special night. Tonight, Polgara's going to get a baby of her very own. It may not mean all that much to the rest of the world, but I think it does to us.'

'It does indeed,' Durnik said fervently. Then a thoughtful expression came into the good man's eyes. 'I've been sort of working on something lately, Belgarath.'

'Yes. I've heard you.'

'Doesn't it seem to you that we're all sort of coming back to the places where we started? It's not exactly the same, of course, but things sort of feel familiar.'

'I've been thinking sort of the same thing,' Garion admitted. 'I keep getting this strange feeling about it.'

'It's only natural for people to go home after they've been on a long journey, isn't it?' Belgarath said, kicking at a lump of snow with one foot.

'I don't think it's that simple, Grandfather.'

'Neither do I,' Durnik agreed. 'This seems more important for some reason.'

Belgarath frowned. 'I think it does to me as well,' he admitted. 'I wish Beldin were here. He could explain it in a minute. Of course none of us would understand the explanation, but he'd explain it all the same.' He scratched at his beard. 'I've found something that *might* explain it,' he said a bit dubiously.

'What's that?' Durnik asked him.

'Garion and I have had an extended conversation

over the last year or so. He'd noticed that things kept happening over and over again. You probably heard us talking about it.'

Durnik nodded.

'Between us, we came up with the notion that things kept repeating themselves because the accident made it impossible for the future to happen.'

'That makes sense, I guess.'

'Anyhow, that's changed now. Cyradis made her Choice, and the effects of the accident have been erased. The future *can* happen now.'

'Then why is everybody going back to the place where he started?' Garion asked.

'It's only logical, Garion,' Durnik told him quite seriously. 'When you're starting something – even the future – you almost have to go back to the beginning, don't you?'

'Why don't we just assume that's the explanation,' Belgarath said. 'Things got stopped. Now they're moving again, and everybody got what he deserved. We got the good things, and the other side got the bad ones. It sort of proves that we picked the right side, doesn't it?'

Garion suddenly laughed.

'What's so funny?' Durnik asked him.

'Just before our baby was born, Ce'Nedra got a letter from Velvet – Liselle. She's managed to push Silk into naming a day. It's probably what he deserves, all right, but I imagine his eyes get a little wild every time he thinks about it.'

'When's the wedding?' Durnik asked.

'Next summer sometime. Liselle wants to be sure that everybody can be in Boktor to witness her triumph over our friend.'

'That's a spiteful thing to say, Garion,' Durnik reproved.

'It's probably the truth, though,' Belgarath grinned. He reached inside his tunic and drew out an earthenware flagon. 'A touch of something to ward off the chill?' he offered. 'It's some of that potent Ulgo brew.'

'Grandmother won't like that,' Garion warned.

'Your grandmother isn't here right now, Garion. She's a little busy at the moment.'

The three of them stood atop the snowy hill looking down at the farmstead. The thatched roof was thick with snow, and icicles hung like glittering jewels from the eaves. The small panes of the windows glowed with golden lamplight that fell softly out over the gently mounded snow in the dooryard, and the ruddy glow from the forge where the menfolk had spent the afternoon boiling unneeded water came softly from the shed. A column of blue wood smoke rose straight and unwavering from the chimney, reaching so high that it seemed to almost be lost among the stars.

A peculiar sound filled Garion's ears, and it took him a while to identify it. It was the Orb, and it was singing a song of unutterable longing.

The silence seemed almost palpable now, and the glittering stars seemed to draw even closer to the snowy earth.

And then from the cottage there came a single cry. It was an infant voice, and it was not filled with that indignation and discomfort so common in the cries of most newborns but rather with a kind of wonder and ineffable joy.

A gentle blue light suddenly came from the Orb, and the longing in its note turned to joy.

As the song of the Orb faded, Durnik drew in a deep breath. 'Why don't we go down?' he said.

'We'd better wait a bit,' Belgarath suggested. 'There's always some cleaning up to do at this point, and we should give Pol a chance to brush her hair.'

'I don't care if her hair's a little mussed,' Durnik said.

'*She* does. Let's wait.'

Strangely, the Orb had renewed its yearning melody. The silence remained as palpable as before, broken now only by the thin, joyous wail of Polgara's baby.

The three friends stood on the hilltop, their breath steaming in the cold night air as they listened to that distant, piping song.

'Good healthy lungs,' Garion complimented the new father.

Durnik grinned briefly at him, still listening to the cry of his child.

And then that single cry was not alone. Another voice joined in.

This time the light which burst from the Orb was a sudden blaze of blue that illuminated the snow around them, and its joyous song was a triumphant organ note.

'I *knew* it!' Belgarath exclaimed with delight.

'*Two?*' Durnik gasped. '*Twins?*'

'It's a family trait, Durnik,' Belgarath laughed, catching the smith in a rough embrace.

'Are they boys or girls?' Durnik demanded.

'What difference does it make right now? But we might as well go on down there and find out, I suppose.'

But as they turned, they saw that something seemed to be happening in the vicinity of the cottage. They stared at the single shaft of intensely blue light descending from the starry sky, a shaft which was soon joined by one of a paler blue. The cottage was bathed in their azure light as the two lights from the heavens touched the snow. Then those lights were joined by other lights, red and yellow and green and lavender and a shade Garion could not even put a name to. Lastly, the lights from the sky were joined by a single shaft of blinding white. Like the colors of the rainbow, the lights stood in a semi-circle in the dooryard, and the brilliant columns from which they had descended rose above them to fill the night sky with a pulsing curtain of many-hued, shifting light.

And then the Gods were there, standing in the dooryard with their song joining with that of the Orb in a mighty benediction.

Eriond turned to look up the hill at them. His gentle face glowed with a smile of purest joy. He beckoned to them. 'Join us,' he said.

'Now it is complete.' UL's voice was also joyous. '*All is well now.*'

Then, with the God-light bathing their faces, the three friends started down from the snowy hilltop to view that miracle, which, though it was most commonplace, was a miracle nonetheless.

And so, my children, the time has come to
close the book. There will be other days and
other stories, but this tale is finished.

THE END

THE MALLOREON
DAVID EDDINGS

It had all begun with the theft of the Orb that had so long protected the West from the evil God Torak. Now, warned by the prophecy that a new and greater danger threatens the west, Garion, Belgarath and Polgara must begin another quest to save the lands from great evil.

A magnificent epic of immense scope, *The Malloreon* is an outstanding piece of imaginative storytelling.

Read on to discover how the prophecy unfolds, and how Garion comes to discover his true heritage . . .

If you enjoyed *The Malloreon*, read the earlier
adventures of Garion, Polgara, Belgarath and others in

THE BELGARIAD
DAVID EDDINGS

A magnificent fantasy epic set against a
history of seven thousand years of struggles
between Gods and Kings and men.

Read on to discover how the prophecy unfolds, and
how Garion comes to discover his true heritage . . .